I0818190

Fate's Keep

BOOK 2 OF HER DARK DESTINY

T. RAE MITCHELL

ORIGINAL MIX MEDIA

PRAISE FOR FATE'S KEEP

"MITCHELL'S USE OF MYTHS, LEGENDS AND FANTASY FEEL MORE REAL THAN IMAGINED."

"This fantasy hits all the right spots as you're whisked along a new compelling adventure with Fate at the reins. There's plenty of action, romance and her great character development flexes its muscle with new characters to add to her ever growing vibrantly created world."

~ Artistic Bent ★★★★★

"T. RAE MITCHELL DID IT AGAIN!"

"The dialogue is brilliant, witty and funny, a joy to read. The introduction of new characters was exciting and it's nice how they all have their roles in the story, there are no loose ends, everyone fits into the plot perfectly."

~ Book Traveller ★★★★★

"A HIGHLY ADDICTING SERIES... BE PREPARED TO LET THE REST OF THE WORLD GO BY."

"T. Rae Mitchell writes a fantastical transition between Fate's Fables and this new book: Fate's Keep. The story between Fate and Finn during an ever-changing conflict, is what hooks readers and grasps the imagination in this action-packed adventure. If you're a fan of fairy tales and action, this is the series for you."

~ Amazon Reviewer ★★★★★

"MITCHELL'S WILD IMAGINATION AND INCREDIBLE WORLD BUILDING FLOORS ME WITH EVERY BOOK!"

"Her skilled use of myth and pop culture are especially evident in this second book but she still grounds the story with fully rounded and believable characters."

~ Best selling author, Nora Snowdon ★★★★★

"FAROUK TAKES THE ROLE IN THIS STORY."

It takes cleverness on the author's part to create Faurok's dialogue because he mixes words up to make new ones. I was so happy when Sithias made an appearance in this story because I missed him and his fun personality and his extra s's on his words!"

~ Hugs And Kisses For Books ★★★★★

"ANOTHER FANTASTIC BOOK FROM T. RAE MITCHELL."

"I totally recommend this if you like sci-fi or fantasy. An excellent followup to Fate's Fables.."

~ Amazon Reviewer ★★★★★

"DELIGHTFULLY ENTERTAINING AS WELL AS INVENTIVE."

"T. Rae Mitchell's second novel in the series is a wonderfully satisfying sequel to Fate's Fables. Mitchell's imagination and unique storytelling style totally blew my mind."

~ Award winning author, Kay Gregory ★★★★★

Original Mix Media Inc.
1685 H Street #1046
Blaine, WA 98230
www.originalmixmedia.com

Ordering Information:
Quantity sales. Special discounts are available on quantity purchases by corporations, associations, and others. For details, contact the publisher at the address above.
Orders by U.S. trade bookstores and wholesalers. Please contact Big Distribution:
Tel: (604) 725-4284 or visit www.originalmixmedia.com.

Printed in the United States of America

Library of Congress Cataloging-in-Publication data
Mitchell, T. Rae.
Fate's Keep / T. Rae Mitchell.
p. cm.—(bk. 1)

Summary: Seventeen year old Fate Floyd travels across the universe, where she confronts the mysterious Keep and unimaginable creatures of myth and legend that threaten to destroy the arcane storehouse of magical objects. Her only chance to survive is through a series of desperate quests and battles, any one of which may mark the end of everything she holds dear.

ISBN 978-1-7771472-0-4 (hardcover)
ISBN 978-1-9990241-2-3 (paperback)
ISBN 978-0-9917987-5-9 (ebook)

[1. Supernatural–Fiction. 2. Myths–Fiction. 3. Legends–Fiction. 4. Secret Portal–Fiction. 5. Fairies–Fiction. 6. Druids–Fiction. 7. Magic–Fiction. 8. Sorcery–Fiction. 9. Romance–Fiction] 1. Title.

10 9 8 7 6 5 4 3 2 1

To the wise and wonderful Margarets
who came before me.

Fables
BOOKSTORE

I
BACK TO THE BEGINNING

FATE FLOYD TUMBLED THROUGH space toward a world in which she no longer belonged. A dull, ordinary place, where most everyone craved make-believe and magic, because without it, reality was too dreary to face. She used to be one of those addicted daydreamers.

Not anymore.

She'd since found out magic was real, and there was nothing pink and sparkly about it. Magic was scary and far deadlier than she could've ever imagined.

Yet she would've stayed in that dangerous realm, risking her life, over and over, if she thought it would help Finn. She closed her eyes against the sudden tears and sharp pang in her chest. Leaving him behind inside the *Book of Fables* had left a hole where her heart used to be.

The second she opened her eyes, the hardwood floor of the bookstore filled her vision and slammed into her shoulder. Pain drilled down her arm as she rolled with the momentum of the fall and slid to a stop. She was almost grateful for the pain, because all thoughts of Finn vanished…at least for a moment.

Rising on an elbow, she searched the dim interior for Gerdie. They'd been holding hands only seconds ago. Instead, her gaze landed on the *Book of Fables*. The ten-foot-tall book, which had just spit her out like some giant who didn't care for how she tasted.

She could hardly believe she was back. The massive tome was closed and leaning against the brick wall of the deserted bookstore where she'd originally found it, in what seemed like eons ago. She'd been so clueless then, thinking the book was just a big sign that once hung on the outside of Fables Bookstore. Nothing could have been further from the truth. Giant chroniclers had created the *Book of Fables* to preserve a record of ancient magic within its yellowed pages in the form of eight horribly unfortunate fairy tales, each of which she'd had the great displeasure of experiencing up close and personal.

Fate started to stand, when a blow from behind flattened her to the floor, knocking the air from her lungs.

"Sorry," Gerdie muttered from where she'd landed on Fate's back. "But thanks for the soft landin' all the same."

"Glad I could be of service," Fate groaned, though relieved to have her small companion back.

Gerdie jumped off. She blew a frizzy, fawn-colored strand of hair out of her brown eyes. A serious expression hardened her elfin features as she took in her surroundings.

As Fate sucked in a lungful of air, a horrendous stench caught in her throat. Gagging, she covered her nose while searching for the offending odor. She was surprised to find her grandmother's old bookstore exactly as she'd left it. Dark, decrepit and lit with a feeble fire burning in a metal wastebasket.

She'd been gone such a long time, yet she was certain this was the same fire Finn had lit the night they first met. She could almost see him kneeling there, the flames lighting the dark gold of his hair, the sweet curve of his mouth and smiling, leaf-green eyes. Tears welled up again as she reached out to the flickering light. Was it possible she'd somehow gone back in time to when he was there?

She was about to call his name when the next inhale assaulted her nose, pushing her to face the awful truth. She'd been forced to leave Finn behind in the last fable and no amount of wishing for some time-twisting miracle was going to change the dismal reality that he'd traded his own freedom to save her from being imprisoned inside a giant oak.

The cloying, sickly smell was thick now. Bile burned at the back of Fate's throat as she peered at her shadowy surroundings. The hair on the back of her neck rose. Someone was sitting in one of the wing-backed chairs of the reading corner. The person sat still. Unnaturally so. Fate's skin crawled as she stared at the figure. The moment she registered what she was looking at, she scrabbled back on all fours until she banged into the giant book. "Is that what I think it is?"

Gerdie hadn't moved. "Yup. Looks like a pruned-up carcass to me." Stepping closer to the seated corpse, she poked its arm. "I take that back. It's still juicy."

Fate jumped to her feet. "What are you doing? Hasn't anyone told you not to play with dead things?"

"I'm no stranger to dealin' with the dead. Pretty much comes with the territory, when you've been livin' near an evil old hag who's eatin' babies for breakfast, lunch and supper."

There wasn't much Fate could say to that. Gerdie had managed to stay out of Old Mother Grim's clutches all by herself, for what may have been centuries before they'd met. It was still easy to forget Gerdie wasn't a child. The six-year-old had been suspended in time the moment her black-hearted sister, Brune, had abandoned her inside the *Book of Fables*.

Brune was responsible for throwing Fate into the cursed book as well. Worse yet, she and Brune were related. Fate's grandmother, Gerdie and Brune were all sisters. Fate was happy to have Gerdie as her great-aunt, but she hated sharing Brune's bad blood.

Covering her nose with her sleeve, Gerdie leaned closer to the dead body, staring at the necklace hanging around the shriveled gray neck. "Just like I thought," she muttered. "It's Brune."

"Really? How can you be sure?"

"She's wearin' the Orb of Aeternitis."

Unwilling to move any closer, Fate strained to see through the gloom to get a better look at the Orb. The whole reason Brune had forced Fate into the *Book of Fables* had been to find and retrieve the Orb's counterpart, the Rod of Aeternitis. From what little she understood, combining the two powerful pieces grants the owner godlike powers. With that kind of power she could free Finn with a mere thought and save him from an eternity of suffering.

Fate reached for the slim gold bar resting against her breastbone. The chain holding the pendant was cold, but the Rod was warm and vibrating, calling out to the Orb. She took an uneasy step forward. She'd paid a terrible price to get the Rod and her hands would be stained with blood forever because of it

Gerdie glanced back at Fate. "How lucky are we? And here I thought I'd have to duke it out with Brune to get the Orb."

"Yeah, dandy. How about I leave you to the grave robbing?" Fate had seen her fill of rotting corpses one too many times inside the *Book of Fables*.

Gerdie tugged on the Orb, tipping Brune's corpse forward. She shoved it back and gave the necklace a harder tug. Fate shuddered as the head lolled to one side with a bone-cracking sound and dangled at a disturbing angle. Undaunted by the grisly interaction, Gerdie gave the necklace another solid yank to break the chain, when a bony hand shot out and grabbed the girl's wrist.

Gerdie and Fate both screamed.

Brune pulled Gerdie close to her mummified face. They were practically nose to nose. "You really think it'll be that easy to take what's mine?" Brune's voice was a wet rattle. The smell had to be atrocious, because Gerdie convulsed with nausea.

Gerdie wrestled free and ran over to Fate. "She's alive!"

"It's not a she," Fate argued. "That's what you call a zombie.

And FYI, they eat brains."

Fate reached instinctively for one of the daggers she was used to having strapped on her thigh. There was nothing there. "Damn, I forgot to get my gear back," she grumbled. She'd been relieved of her sword, dagger and crossbow when an army of soldier hawks had captured her and Gerdie. They'd been allowed to leave in the end, so why hadn't she asked for her weapons back?

Stupid.

Brune remained seated while she swung the Orb on its long chain in wide circles. Golden tracers began to build into a solid band of light with every swing.

Gerdie dug her hand in the pocket of her dress, pulled out a little ball of dark red wax and aimed her clenched fist at Brune. "*Avra Kedavra*, Brune!"

"Whoa, whoa, whoa," Fate interjected, worriedly. "That sounds an awful lot like the Killing Curse. But just so you know, that's fiction. Fantastic fiction, but fiction nonetheless."

Gerdie frowned at her. "Don't know what you're goin' on about, but you need to stop interruptin' and make yourself useful." She shoved a cloth bag full of dried, ground herbs into Fate's hand. "Pour this all the way around her. And do it fast!"

Holding her breath, Fate raced over with the pouch, hastily sprinkling the herbs.

"I cast this circle and bind you, Brune!" Gerdie commanded, though her voice quavered. "*Avra Kedavra. Avra Kedavra. Avra Kedavra.*"

Fate finished laying down the circle and ran back to Gerdie, encouraged by the dying gasps and croaks coming from Brune. Fate undid the clasp of her own necklace and swung the Rod in plain sight. She'd been looking forward to this moment for a long time. "I've got the Rod, Brune. But guess what? I'm keeping it! How do you like them apples? Look who's in control now."

Brune's body shuddered as she continued to swing the Orb round and round, its light now sweeping out in concentric circles, rippling further and further out, expanding toward Fate and Gerdie. Fate's blood ran cold with the realization that Brune was shaking with fits of laughter. And they weren't dying gasps. They were raspy cackles.

Before Fate could ask Gerdie why the counter spell wasn't working, her mouth filled with a coppery taste. The air turned hot, stinging her skin, scorching her lungs. An explosion of molten sparks penetrated deep inside, searing tissue and cells, pulling her muscles so tight she couldn't move.

Fate knew this fiery pain. She'd experienced it before. The constricting pain, combined with the stench of Brune's rotting flesh, had been her last memories before waking inside the *Book of Fables*.

"Bring me the Rod," Brune croaked.

An invisible force seized Fate. Spasms of pain shot through her muscles, forcing her limbs into action. Tears blurred her vision as her body marched of its own accord across the room. Fate fought and resisted from within, but no amount of will power could stop her legs from carrying her forward with the Rod held out to Brune like a gift. All that was missing was a silver platter.

2
THE OATH

FATE JOLTED TO A sudden halt just outside the circle of herbs spread around Brune's chair.

"Closer, give me the Rod." Brune's decayed, skeletal frame strained to lean forward.

Struggling to obey Brune's command, Fate's body fought against an unseen force preventing her from taking another step. Her muscles seized into excruciating bands of resistance, while the sickening odor of rotting flesh suffocated her. Vomit churned in her stomach and her eyes watered.

Gerdie continued with her incantations as she stepped in beside Fate.

Brune craned her lopsided head in the little girl's direction. "You can't kill what's already dead."

"True. I was expectin' you to be alive. You might be dead, but you're still stubborn as ever." Gerdie held the ball of red wax out in front of her. "But I can keep you from takin' that Rod from Fate 'til the cows come home. I made one of Oma's *Imperio Evocati* charms."

A ghastly smile spread over Brune's withered face. "You don't have my handwriting. Or my blood to be able to do that.

Reaching into her dress pocket, Gerdie pulled out a tattered notebook and held it high. "Remember Oma's spell book?"

The Orb's circular swinging lost velocity as Brune's fogged eyes fixed on the book in Gerdie's hand.

"It's been a long time since you left me in that fairy tale nightmare, so you've probably forgotten you wrote down a few spells of your own in here." Gerdie tucked the notebook back in her pocket. "So yeah, I've got your handwritin' balled up inside the wax all good and proper."

The more Brune became distracted, the less attention she put on the Orb. As the pendant's rotation slowed, the pain and tension in Fate's body eased a few degrees.

"But the blood," Brune rasped.

Gerdie snickered. "Boy, you're real rusty with the magics. I didn't need to stick a pin in you, Brune. For the first time in my life bein' your sister worked in my favor. We come from the same blood, you and me, so I just used mine. Then all I had to do was tweak the recipe with a strand of your hair. And before you go askin' where I got it, I'll just remind you of Oma's locket. Remember how she kept snips from all us grandkids?"

Grief and anger replaced Gerdie's smug expression. "Guess you thought the locket burned with Oma, but she ripped it off and dropped it on the ground before they tied her to that stake. I saw it all. I stayed hidden, coverin' my ears to her screams, closin' my eyes to the flames that turned her into a twisted lump of coal."

Fate was familiar with how Gerdie, Brune and their grandmother, had been trapped inside the *Book of Fables* long before Fate had entered the book. After making it through five of the eight fables, Brune had betrayed her own grandmother in the sixth fable by telling the villagers she was to blame for their missing children, when in fact, Old Mother Grim had stolen them. Until now, Gerdie had always left out the heartbreaking details.

Gerdie's voice hit a sharp pitch. "I hid behind that thicket all night, not wantin' to leave her there like that. But what could a little kid do? Nothin'. That's what. I was too puny to dig a hole and bury her in the ground."

Brune held very still. Then she dropped the chain, letting the Orb hang motionless from her neck.

Free of the Orb's control, Fate muscles loosened like a rope unraveling and she crumpled to the floor before scrambling backwards to escape the foul air she'd been forced to share. "Finish her off, Gerdie."

Gerdie walked over to Fate. "I can't," she whispered.

Fate rose shakily to her feet. "You have to, for your own good. She can't be trusted."

"It's not for lack of wantin' to. But as long as she's got the Orb, she can control you."

"But you've got that wax thingy. Use it to make her give it to us."

"*Imperio Evocati* charms are only made to work with the destruction curse. But since you can't make dead any deader, at this point, it's only good for protection. If she tries anything on me, it'll be like hurtin' herself."

"What about the Rod? Can't I do some swinging of my own? You know, like make her dance to Thriller out on the interstate until she becomes road kill?"

"No, the Rod's not like the Orb. It pretty much just unlocks the full power of the Orb and makes it work a whole lot better."

"Great. How'd I end up with the short end of the stick?"

Gerdie shrugged. "Let's just be glad you've got the Rod and not her."

"Yeah. Now if I can just get my hands on the Orb." Fate glanced at Brune. "So now what? We're pretty much at a stalemate."

"We've gotta work out some sort of deal with her."

Fate paused to think, but only for a second. "I hate it."

"Hate it all you want, but that's the facts. Stay here, I'll handle this."

Fate stared at her in surprise. Gerdie had always been tough and independent, but now that the little girl was finally facing the sister who'd betrayed her, the furious old soul dwelling inside the six-year-old was all she could see.

Happy to leave Gerdie to nailing down the terms, Fate grabbed a few books off a nearby shelf to add to the dying fire. As paper dust spilled from between the books' moldering covers, she remembered questioning why all the books were falling apart. She dropped them into the wastebasket, realizing she was no closer to figuring out the reason than she was before her unwelcome departure.

There was no logical explanation for such rapid decay. It was not like the doors of Fables Bookstore had been closed a thousand years. Yes, they'd been shut since the day of her grandmother's death, but that was only seven years ago. The contents remained exactly as Gran had left them, waiting for the day when Fate was old enough to carry on the tradition of the historic bookstore. A legacy she'd promised her Gran she'd continue.

She wished she'd never made such a promise. Too much had changed since then and she had only one goal in mind at the moment. Finding a way back to Finn. She had no idea what that way was, only that she would never ever find it by going back into the *Book of Fables*.

Fate prayed Gerdie was right about returning to the bookstore to face Brune and gain access into the Keep. She'd described it as some sort of giant storehouse filled with portals and vaults holding powerful objects of magic, and Gerdie was certain there'd be a portal leading back into Oldwilde, the hidden realm inside the *Book of Fables*.

There was a time when Fate would've given anything to explore such a place. She'd spent her whole life reading fantastical stories and writing her own wishful tales. Before her nightmarish trek through the *Book of Fables*, she'd even spent a month on a major book signing tour for her first published novel, *Magic Brew*, which had been gathering a rapidly growing fan base of fellow fantasy geeks. Some of whom were overly zealous cosplayers. Not that she minded much. Back then she'd lived by her motto: Reality sucks. Make-believe rocks. But she'd since embraced a new motto: Make-believe sucks. Reality rocks, even if it's boring.

As the fire in the wastebasket blazed brighter, Fate caught sight of her purse lying on the floor. She scooped it up and dug inside for her phone. There was still no cell service, but she was shocked the date hadn't changed and only four hours had passed from the time she'd left the book signing in Seattle.

She sucked in a tense breath. "Eustace," she whispered. Her father would be upset by how she'd taken off to the family bookstore sixty miles north of Seattle instead of going to meet her best friend Jessie. Unless he didn't know yet.

Gerdie appeared next to her. "The deal's done."

Fate jumped, so deep in thought, she hadn't been paying attention to the negotiations. "I hope you didn't have to spit and shake on it." She glanced back at Brune with a grimace.

"Worse. One of us, meaning you, has to become the new Keep Guardian. I'd do it, but the Key won't respond to me cuz I'm not big enough to even lift it. And it's not workin' for Brune, for obvious reasons."

"Sorry, you've lost me."

Gerdie pointed at the huge bronze key lying near the *Book of Fables*. "That's the Key to the Keep."

"No it's not. That key opens the *Book of Fables*." Fate's throat constricted. Finn had been the one who'd tested the key to see if it unlocked the book. She could almost see him lifting the huge key to the intricate wrought iron lock secured on the front of the enormous carved wooden book.

"It does that too. But the Lock to the Keep is hidden inside the lock on the book. Don't ask me why but the two are connected to each other," Gerdie explained. "Once the new guardian locks the *Book of Fables*–hopefully forever this time–the hiding place'll open and we'll be able to get at the Keep Lock. After that's done, the Key'll shrink down to a more normal size and fit into the Lock."

"Oh that doesn't sound complicated at all." Fate bent to pick up the Key. The weight of it pulled her off balance and required a huge effort to lift. She was glad for the muscle she'd gained during her three-month stint in the seventh fable, where she'd undergone intensive training in hand-to-hand combat, archery and sword fighting. Unfortunately, the supernatural strength she'd enjoyed after being knighted by the war goddess was gone.

She was an ordinary person again.

Fate hoisted the Key to the book's lock, which was level with her head, and shoved it into the keyhole. She started to turn the Key, when Gerdie yanked on her arm.

"Wait. You have to say the oath first."

"Like what? I, Fate Floyd, do solemnly swear that I will be a good guardian and remember to lock up before I leave?"

"No." Gerdie handed her a large, aged envelope. Her apologetic expression filled Fate with apprehension. "I'm real sorry. I wish it was me instead of you havin' to read this."

Fate pulled out a letter-sized piece of thin parchment with a few lines of script that looked as if they'd been penned with a quill. "Where'd this come from?"

"Brune. She came prepared."

As Fate glanced over the words, all the blood in her head rushed to her feet. She swayed with dizziness. "No way, I'm not saying this. Reading ancient writing out loud is what got me into all this trouble in the first place!"

"If you don't, none of us are gettin' into the Keep."

"But I don't want to sacrifice all my worldly ties and dedicate the remaining years of my life protecting the Keep until the day of my death or 90th birthday, whichever comes first. I have places to be, people to see. And oh yeah, I have to save Finn from the hell I left him in!"

Gerdie threw an anxious look at Brune before turning back to Fate. "Brune said she'll show you how to break the oath, but only if we promise to get her into the Keep and restore her back to life."

"Really? Well in that case I feel so much better knowing Brune says she'll get me out of this magically iron-clad oath." Fate stared at Gerdie. "Are you nuts? She's been playing us for suckers from day one."

"I want what you don't," Brune croaked weakly from the other side of the room. "And you want what I don't. If we wanted the same thing, we'd have a problem."

"She's got a point," Gerdie agreed. "She wants to be Keep Guardian again more than anything else. You know what she did to take it from Oma, so there's no need to go worryin' about bein' stuck with the job. You want out and she wants in. If you're determined to keep going so we can save Finn, then I say we go for it."

Fate leaned down, whispering to make sure Brune couldn't overhear. "I'd never give up on Finn, but Brune's always going to see you and me as a threat. And she's wrong about her and I not wanting the same thing. She wants the Rod and I want the Orb."

"Tell me somethin' I don't know." Gerdie's brow furrowed. "I saw what you did with the Words of Makin', and we all know how that turned out. So I don't think you can be trusted with that much power any more than Brune can."

Fate's stomach twisted with guilt. "Ouch. You really know how to hurt a girl." But she couldn't exactly disagree either. She hadn't known how to wield that kind of power. What made her think she'd be any better at it now?

Gerdie patted her arm. "You really don't have to do any of this, you know. You could go back to your old life. It's not too late, like it is for me. There's people waitin' for you."

"That's just it, Gerdie. It is too late. As much as I miss my dad, I can't go back to a normal life. I'd never be able to live with myself knowing I could've helped Finn and didn't."

A flicker of disappointment sparked in Gerdie's brown eyes "Then you have to take the oath."

"You don't think I should, do you?"

Gerdie's impish features, always so soft and playful, became stern. "Family's somethin' you should never take for granted. Ever."

"I'm not." Fate pushed away the indecision suddenly rising to the surface. "I love my dad as much as I love Finn. But my dad's safe and happy. Other than worrying about where I disappeared to."

"Which is torture for any parent."

"I know but at least my dad's got a life. Finn doesn't. He's trapped inside that tree, unable to move, tortured by his thoughts and all alone. I can't leave him there to suffer like that."

"It's just two kinds of sufferin', but it's still sufferin' all the same."

Compounded guilt knifed into Fate. Frustrated, she punched a nearby bookcase. Pain stabbed her knuckles. Muffling a scream, she cradled her aching hand, once again reminded of her lost super powers. Less than an hour ago she would've splintered the wood without feeling it.

She loathed being weak and vulnerable. Especially when she knew what real strength felt like. She was finding it impossible to accept she'd gone from being a warrior of the most formidable army in Oldwilde to being her old, unexceptional self in one fell swoop. It was infuriating.

Her thoughts returned to her father. "As it stands, I've only been gone a few hours. Which means I'll just have to make sure I find a way to turn back time so Eustace won't have to worry about me any longer than he already has."

Gerdie nodded sadly.

Unable to face Gerdie's warning stare any longer, Fate turned her attention to the parchment in her hand. Fearing she'd lose courage if she delayed any further, Fate read the words of the oath out loud. With each word spoken, she felt a shift of energy, ties falling away, guilt dissipating and a feeling of detachment settling in. A sense of purpose slotted itself into the forefront of her mind, igniting a desire to get on with her new mission.

The moment she turned the Key, light blasted from inside the huge lock on the book and fire scorched the ornate wrought iron. She ducked as blue flames shot from the center of the oak tree carved into the book's scarred, wooden cover. The lock's inner workings glowed red-hot as tumblers inside the large mechanism clinked like well-oiled steel.

Fate pulled the cumbersome Key out. The metal was surprisingly cool and tingled against her skin as the Key vibrated. For a few brief seconds it seemed as if the whole world was being pulled inward, like the air was being sucked out of the room, but it was actually the Key compressing, shrinking before her very eyes. Within seconds, the Key was small enough to lie in the palm of her hand.

Then the round lock rotated counterclockwise. Upon a full rotation, the starburst design surrounding the keyhole flapped open like flower petals, revealing another keyhole against a background of clockwork pieces. It matched the size of the newly shrunken Key.

With a growing sense of urgency, Fate slid the Key in, activating another series of clicks. Slidebars pushed aside, gears turned and flaps opened, before a much smaller lock pushed up and out of a fitted slot. As soon as Fate pulled it free, the starburst pieces snapped shut.

Fate turned the plain pewter lock over in her hand. "I've seen this before."

Gerdie nodded. "On the janitor door."

Fate looked at Gerdie in surprise. "Yeah. So this unimpressive old thing is the all-important Lock to the Keep?" She shook her head in disbelief.

"Mount it on the door," Brune rasped. "We're running out of time."

Fate nodded in agreement. She didn't know why, but she knew Brune was speaking the truth. Something was wrong. It was as if part of her soul had stretched across space to a place she needed to protect because serious trouble was brewing there

The Lock jolted in her hand. Fate ran through the maze of bookcases to the back of the store, pushed through the green velvet curtains hiding the storage room and stopped in front of the door marked *Janitor*. The Lock flew from her grasp, banging against the door just above the door handle with a loud thud. The Lock's starburst screws rotated swiftly, anchoring itself firmly in place.

Fate turned to Gerdie as she entered the storeroom. "That was easy enough."

"Glad you enjoyed it, cuz it's time for the hard part."

"You mean the Keep?"

"No, a car just pulled in outside and a man got out. From the way you described him, I think it might be your dad."

3
A LITTLE GAME OF HIDE AND SEEK

THE DELIVERY DOOR OPENED to the sound of heavy rain and her father's voice. "Hello? Fate? Are you in here?"

All the guilt, stress and tension she'd been holding at arm's length for the last six months unraveled into a big sloppy mess. "Dad?" Fate called out from within the shadows of the dark room.

The door burst open and moonlight revealed Eustace's tall silhouette filling the doorframe. His thick, silver-dusted hair dripped with rain and the shoulders of his cream-colored blazer were soaked through. "Fate," he said, his voice cracking with relief.

She ran over to him, flinging her arms around his waist. Fate buried her face in the softness of his sweater, breathing in the comforting scent of the cigars he carried in the breast pocket of his blazer. She was suddenly ten-years-old again. Tears spilled down her face as his arms folded around her, safe and warm. *Home.* Pain and joy mixed together in a confusing jumble, until she shook with uncontrollable sobs.

Eustace remained quiet, holding her tight as she slowly calmed down.

"I'm so sorry I left. I'm so sorry," she cried.

He gave her a squeeze. "It's okay." Stepping back to have a look at her, he brushed aside the strands of hair sticking to her wet face. "There was no real harm done. I just wish you would've told me where you were going."

"I know I should've told you."

"When Jessie called wanting to see you, I knew something

was wrong."

The ceiling light suddenly came on, startling them both.

Eustace frowned. "That's odd. Did you call to have the electricity turned on?"

Gulping, Fate glanced around for Gerdie but didn't see her. "No."

He stared at her through his rain-spotted glasses. His troubled gaze landed on the leather armor she was wearing. "Why are you dressed like this?"

"I, uh…"

"She's ready for her first *Magic Brew* convention of course," someone interjected.

Fate leaned around Eustace in time to see her publicist, Lana, struggling to close her umbrella from within the doorframe. Giving up, she dropped it on the wet ground and closed the door behind her. The musty room filled with a suffocating cloud of perfume as she combed her manicured nails through her bobbed hair to put it back in place. "It's a bit of a drive but I think it's a stroke of genius on your part, Fate. Having the convention here in this atmospheric old building? So much better than the Paramount."

Fate wiped her tears and glared at the woman. Time had not removed the irritation she felt toward Lana after sharing her with Eustace during the thirty-day book signing tour. The cougar had tried to get her claws into her father during the whole trip. It had been nauseating. She frowned at her father. "You brought her *here*?" He knew Gran's bookstore was special to her.

Eustace looked uncomfortable. "Well, she was worried too."

"Right."

Lana flashed a glossy, cherry-red smile. "Let's have a look at the place, shall we?" Her high heels tapped loudly over the worn cedar floor as she made her way over to the green velvet curtains. She stopped and turned to Eustace. "Coming?"

"In a minute." There was a bite in his voice as he removed his glasses and cleaned the rain off his lenses with a handkerchief. Something he always did, regardless of whether it was needed, but more often when he was ill at ease.

Intent on keeping Lana from exploring, Fate stepped around Eustace. "Uh, it's a total mess out there. Lots to trip over." The last thing she needed was Lana discovering Brune's stinky undead corpse near the front of the store. "It's not going to work here. I say we head back to Seattle."

Lana's mouth dropped open in horror. "We can't leave. Your fans are on their way right now."

"What? How?" Fate looked at her father. "You couldn't have known I was even here."

Eustace returned his glasses to their proper place and smoothed his thick silvery bangs off his forehead. "It would appear your movements today were carefully monitored."

"By who, Sherlock Holmes?"

Lana waved her cell phone. "No, that would be @InAnguish. A rather depressing person who loves complaining about being sad, but who was extremely determined to follow you along I-5. That is until your taxi got lost in thick traffic."

Overwhelmed by this bizarre development, Fate stared at Lana. After surviving six long months in a deadly world filled with magic and monsters, this place and everyone in it, seemed more unreal than anything the *Book of Fables* could throw at her. Her old life as a writer and author felt even more alien. It didn't matter that writing had been her passion since she'd first learned how to spell. She hadn't had a single writerly thought from the moment she'd been trapped inside the *Book of Fables*. Unless she counted the times she'd used the Words of Making to conjure something, but that had only been out of pure necessity.

"Who exactly is this stalker?" Fate asked.

Lana tapped the screen of her phone and showed them a

picture of a cosplayer dressed as Anguish, the dark foreboding angel from her book.

She suddenly remembered the cosplayer she'd run into when she'd snuck out of her book signing. She hadn't known it at the time, but Brune's summoning spell had kicked in, forcing her to come to the bookstore. At the time, she'd blamed her desire to leave on a major skirmish between a warlock and three demon goblins in cosplay. She'd been so excited about her readers dressing like her characters from *Magic Brew*, but also unsettled by how much they'd thrown themselves into their roles. The most disturbing of the bunch had been @InAnguish.

Fate wrinkled her nose at the picture. "Ew, what a creeper."

"Indeed," Eustace agreed. "But when Lana told me where your were last seen–"

"Through the hashtag I made: Find Fate Floyd," Lana chimed in.

"I knew where you were headed," Eustace finished.

"You let her leak the location to everybody and their dog?"

"That's what you pay me for." Lana cheerily typed on her phone. "The whole thing's trending as we speak."

Eustace shook his head in disapproval. "I didn't want any of this–"

The delivery door banged open, interrupting him. "Is she here?" Jessie quickly closed the door to the foul weather. When she put her back to the door, Fate noticed the annoyance in her friend's frown. Jessie hated being wet, messy or windblown, which was exactly the uncomfortable condition the trek between the car and building had put her in. When her gaze landed on Fate, her warm, hazel eyes rounded with surprise. "You're here!"

They met in the middle of the room, bending forward over some boxes to hug.

"Yeah, just playin' a little game of hide and seek." Fate tried to match her best friend's radiant smile and failed miserably.

Raindrops beaded over Jessie's skin, the color of coffee with cream. Being part Malaysian and Swedish had given her the exotic, natural good looks of a Hawaiian girl enjoying sun and surf all year long. Nothing could be further from the truth. Jessie shied away from outdoor activities, unwilling to share space with bugs, dirt and the cold northwest coastal weather. Many a day had been spent with Jessie in the safety of home watching cartoons, beading bracelets, doodling and daydreaming. Something Fate had always been quite fine with.

Until now.

As much as being around Jessie and her dad made her happy, and somewhat eased the pain of missing Finn, an urgent sense of duty was growing inside and getting stronger by the minute. Fate glanced at the Keep Lock anchored on the janitor door. She needed to go.

"What made you come here? And what's with the warrior get-up?" Jessie eyed her up and down.

Fate sighed in defeat. "Lana guessed it. I wanted to have the convention here."

Jessie gave Fate her lie detector squint, but before she could start the inquisition, Lana jumped in. "Oh! Your fans are almost here! They organized this whole crazy convoy, and the ones who rented the limo for you have been going on about what an awesome ride it's been. The Twitterverse is blowing up!" She messaged them back. Looking up with a triumphant grin, Lana slipped through the velvet curtains before Fate could stop her. "Follow me everyone," she called out. "Let's have a look at the rest of the place."

Fate's heart thudded with panic. She was rapidly losing control of the situation. What would Brune do when they found her? What if she used the Orb to hurt Eustace and Jessie? She'd never forgive herself if anything happened to them.

Fate moved to go after Lana, when Eustace caught her by the

arm. "Hold on, what's really going on here?"

"Oh my god!" Lana shouted from inside the bookstore.

He let go and Fate bolted from the storeroom, terrified Lana had discovered Brune. When she entered the bookstore, she skidded to a stop. The lights were on, casting a warm glow over the tall bookcases and cozy reading nooks. There wasn't a cobweb or speck of dust in sight and the rounded cashier's counter now gleamed with a fresh polish. The boards nailed over the front doors and the big windows were gone, allowing full view of the brightly lit parking lot outside.

It was as if the spirit of the bookstore had been breathed back into the place. Fate had always assumed Gran had been that life spark, but this miraculous transformation indicated otherwise.

"This place is gorgeous!" Lana twirled around as she gestured at the brick walls. "Rustic yet elegant. It's absolutely magical!"

"Something like that," Fate muttered as Eustace joined them.

Eustace gave Fate a questioning look, but before she could offer any sort of answer, the publicist bustled over and pulled him into the center of the store. "They don't make them like this anymore, do they?" she crooned, tucking a hand in the crook of his arm as he glanced around in confusion.

Fate grabbed a few random books off one of the shelves and shook them for paper dust. They were completely intact. What had happened in the last few minutes? Had all the old and rotting things been restored to new? She could only hope so as she looked for the zombie in the room.

Seeing that Lana was hauling Eustace off to look at something else, Fate rounded the bookcase over by the stairs to see if Brune was still seated in the reading chair she'd left her in. She was gone. And so was the *Book of Fables*. She didn't know if she should be relieved or worried.

Jessie appeared behind Fate. "Time to spill. What's going on with you?"

Fate jumped and gasped. "Jeez, lurk much?" She peeked around the bookcase to make sure Lana was still keeping Eustace busy.

"Boy, are you jumpy. Whatever this is, it must be huge."

"You don't know the half of it."

Jessie rubbed her hands together in excitement. "So tell me. I'm dying to know. This armor is crazy cool by the way. Did you buy it when you were in New York? It totally makes your boobs look way bigger than they really are."

Fate glanced down at the molded breastplate. "Really?"

"And your hair's way longer." Jessie stretched one of Fate's long auburn tresses out in front of her. "Are these extensions?"

"No."

"A clip on?" Jessie gave the thick ringlet a sharp tug as if she expected it to come loose.

"Ow, stop that! It's not fake."

Letting go, Jessie stared where Fate's hair hung at her waist. "Okay, that's weird. Nobody's hair grows that much in one month. Start talking. Tell me everything."

"I, uh–"

"Wait." Jessie dug in her purse. Drawing out a bag of corn nuts, she popped the salty snack in her mouth, her eyes wide with anticipation, like she was eating popcorn at the movies. "Okay, go ahead."

"I've been–"

"This involves a guy doesn't it?"

"How'd you know?"

"Because only a guy could make you take hair-growing drugs and take off out of town without saying a word. Did you come out here to meet him?" Jessie looked over her shoulder. "Oh my god. Is he here right now? Is he hiding?"

The dull hollow ache Fate had grown accustomed to

intensified to a gaping wound. "No, he couldn't make it."

Jessie looked horrified. "He stood you up? Who is this jerk?"

"He'd be here if he could, but I totally blew it." Fate blinked back the sting of hot tears. How could she possibly describe her relationship with Finn? Trying to explain how she'd met the real-life, fictional boy of her dreams, unleashed the most excruciating pain. But Jessie wasn't about to let this go, and Fate couldn't risk bursting into tears. Not with all this commotion going on with her fans. She'd have to be careful, meaning no mention of a Scottish boy named Finn. After years of listening to the countless stories Fate had written about him, Jessie would recognize whom she was talking about in an instant.

Fate grabbed at the ribbon around her neck–the one Finn had given her–once white but now gray with the stubborn stains of a horrifying experience. Her fingers trailed down the silk until she touched the pouch of Finn's holy blend tobacco tied to the end of the ribbon. Squeezing it, she inhaled the earthy scents wrapped inside the soaped leather. The soothing smells fooled her senses into believing he was near, at least enough to help her get a grip on her emotions.

"Okay…" Jessie said, munching on another salty bite with much less enthusiasm. "Then what's–"

"I want to tell you everything." Fate chewed worriedly on her bottom lip. "But first you have to promise you won't repeat a word of this to Eustace. And don't ask any questions until I finish, no matter how insane I sound."

"Lips are sealed."

"I left the book signing and came here because I was under a spell." Fate paused for Jessie's reaction, certain her friend would end the conversation there. Instead, she kept her expression carefully blank and remained quiet.

"When I got here, this place wasn't all clean and new with the electricity running. It was dark, dusty and dank. And the

Fables sign, which has always hung on the outside of the building for the past one hundred years, was over there by the stairs. It's gone now, but–"

"It's on the building. I saw it when the lights came on." Jessie made a face, obviously feeling awkward she was already punching holes in Fate's story. "Sorry, keep going."

Fate's frustration increased. Her only piece of evidence to prove the truth of her story was drilled into brick and hanging thirty feet off the ground. How had the *Book of Fables* gotten back onto the building? Obviously, magic was afoot. She wondered if she should be watching for house elves sneaking around the bookstore. Fate shook her head. Maybe it was best. That big bad book was dangerous to anyone ignorant enough to open its cursed pages and read them out loud.

"Either way, it doesn't matter. The Fables sign isn't a sign. It's a real book with real pages full of stories. Eight to be exact. And they're like Grimm's fairy tales before Disney got hold of them and added cheerful songs and birds that help you get dressed every morning. I know, because I didn't just read them, I was *in* them, and my only escape was to turn them into happily-ever-afters. Which I did. Walt would've been proud. But I had to do some horrible things to make that happen. It was one long, terrifying nightmare."

Disbelief formed plainly on Jessie's face.

Anger flushed hot in Fate's cheeks. "I knew you wouldn't believe me."

"It's just that you've told me wild stories before," Jessie hedged. "It's what you do. You write about stuff like this all the time. Listen, you've got to be tired after your book tour. You probably just fell asleep and pulled an Alice in Wonderland."

"That's what I thought at first too. But I'm telling you, it wasn't a dream, Jess. I was *really there*. I swear. I've been gone for over six months!"

"That's where you're wrong. It's only been a few hours since you left Seattle."

"Time passes differently in Oldwilde."

"Oldwilde?"

"That's where I was. The stories in the *Book of Fables* take place in Oldwilde. There was a time when it was part of this world. It's where all our myths and legends come from. But then science and religion edged out magic and some sort of divide separated the two worlds. Now the only way to cross the divide is through portals like the *Book of Fables*." Fate fell quiet, her thoughts turning to the Keep and its promise of gateways back into Oldwilde. Urgency coursed through her limbs with renewed fervor. She needed to go there. But first she had to figure out how to get everyone in the building to leave.

"Well, I guess that would explain why your hair's so much longer." Jessie bit her nail, visibly deciding whether she would deem Fate completely bonkers or not. "Okay, call me loco but I believe you." Excited, she popped another corn nut in her mouth. "That's where you met this guy you're so hot about, isn't it? Oh! Was he a prince? Please tell me you fell in love with a prince!"

Fate relaxed a little. Finally, Jessie was on side. She could count on some help now. "He's a prince at heart," Fate said, allowing her friend to assume she'd met one of the characters from the Book of Fables.

"Did you kiss?"

Fate closed her eyes. When she allowed herself to be open to the pain of remembering what once was, she could feel the ghost of Finn's kiss on her lips. Warm. Sweet. "Yes," she breathed the one word.

"Wow, I always thought I'd be the winner. You were always so much pickier than me, since no one could live up to your perfect dream boy, Finn," Jessie said, referring to their who-would-get-the-first-kiss-first contest. A pathetic pastime for two fantasy geeks who hadn't made it a priority to cultivate exciting social lives.

"Do you want to hear about my trip to Wonderland, or not?" Fate needed desperately to change the subject. The more her thoughts revolved around Finn, the more the gaping hole in her heart ached.

"Shoot." The package of corn nuts crinkled as Jessie dug for more.

Fate hardly knew where to begin. So much had happened. "It was wild, Jess. When I first got there, I was on this sorceress's island, where all the animals could talk and were part human. It was so *Island of Dr. Moreau,* only without the getting eaten part. I even became best friends with a winged snake."

"Ew, gross."

Fate smiled as she pictured Sithias. She missed him terribly. "He was a beautiful ivory-colored snake when I first met him. But I conjured a glamour so he could shapeshift. Most of the time he was this adorably clumsy human. You would've loved him."

Jessie gave her a doubtful frown. "I don't know about that. But tell me more about this conjuring business. Were you a witch?"

"No. I had the power of the Words of Making–something that happens to the Reader who comes into Oldwilde through the *Book of Fables*. Anything I wrote down and spoke aloud instantly happened or appeared out of thin air." She curled a lock of hair around her finger, thinking back to a night when she'd wanted to look irresistible to Finn. "That's how I grew my hair so long."

"Oh, that's off-the-hook."

"Yeah, I thought so too." Fate grew quiet. *But I made a terrible mistake. I wasn't careful enough,* she wanted to say.

Swallowing her grief, she continued. "I even gave myself the power to fly."

"Whoa! What was that like?"

"Super convenient."

"What? That's the best thing you can say about your Peter Pan impression?"

"Well, after awhile it was as normal as walking."

"Show me. I want to see you fly!"

Fate shushed her. "No way! Not here. Later. I promise. But that was nothing compared to the wicked kick-ass powers I got from a war goddess. I was totally indestructible and Spiderman strong. I even had a sword super-charged with lightning and a killer wind shield."

"Wow," Jessie whispered in awe. "Did you kill anyone?"

Guilt squirmed in Fate's stomach. "What makes you ask that?" she snapped. "Do you really think I could kill someone?"

"Whoa, chill." Jessie pouted. "I was only asking."

Eustace rounded the bookcase they were hiding behind. "Asking what?"

"Uh...what character she's playing," Jessie blurted.

"I was going for Lightning Farron, but I think I missed the mark." Fate glanced down at her armor to avoid her father's probing stare.

Eustace crossed his arms. "Mmhmm."

Lana poked her head around the corner. "Hey, your fans are here. Let's open the doors and get this party started."

Fate whipped past her father, feeling his stare burning into her back. She would deal with his questions later. Right now she had a large group of cosplayers waiting to be let in so they could meet her.

Lana unlocked the front entrance and stepped to one side, allowing the boisterous crowd to flood into the bookstore. Suddenly a building that had stood empty and silent for the past seven years was filled with sounds of life and laughter. In her old life, Fate would've been overjoyed by the idea of so many people going nuts over what she'd written, and she would've been thrilled to have them milling about her grandmother's bookstore after being vacant for so long.

But this wasn't her old life anymore. As much as she wished she could pick up where she'd left off, she knew in her heart there was no going back.

Besides, a dangerous zombie was hiding somewhere in the building. And then there was the call of the Keep…pressing on her with an ever-increasing siren of alarm, an urgency that warred with the ever-present ache of missing Finn and her desperation to get back to him at any cost.

4
THE UNHOLY PIPER

FINN MCKEEN TUGGED THE hood of his cloak further down over his eyes as he moved through the crowded corridor of merchants heading toward the market. From the moment he'd stepped into the kingdom of Asgar, he hadn't been able to go forty feet without seeing a warrant posted for his arrest. Everywhere he looked, his crudely drawn face stared back with a malicious scowl. They were calling him the Unholy Piper–the evil sorcerer who'd used his enchanted music to make Empress Moria dance into the fire and kill herself.

Finn growled under his breath. As gruesome as Moria's death had been, and at his hands, he'd done it to save the people of Asgar. The Dragon Empress had cast a veil of illusion over the land, fooling her citizens into believing they were in a bountiful, rich kingdom, when in reality they were starving and feeding on their own dead.

He shuddered as visions of the squalor and decaying corpses arose unbidden. That had been one of the darkest nights of his life. So many truths had been revealed. He'd willingly become a ruthless executioner, an abhorrent act that had nearly caused a permanent wedge between him and Fate.

His chest tightened at the painful memory. It hadn't mattered that he was under the sinister influence of Mugloth at the time. Fate had witnessed how he'd taken delight in his ability to strip Moria of her power and seduce the empress into killing herself in front of everyone. How could he blame Fate for the revulsion she'd shown him afterwards? She'd only ever known him to be a peace-loving druid and a vigilant protector of life.

Well, he intended to prove he could be that person again.

A man carrying a stack of crates bumped Finn's shoulder. The rough wood caught the weave of his cloak, raking the hood from his face. Hunching with his head down, Finn yanked the garment back in place and ducked through an archway leading into the castle's inner bailey. He surveyed the courtyard, where a few dozen servants were cleaning the scummy pond, hauling weeds away and tilling the ground for replanting.

Finn shook his head at the risk he was taking. He was a wanted man with a hefty bounty on his head. He must be mental to be going inside the castle. But O'Deldar was in there. The druid priest had helped him devise the plan to destroy Moria. He was also the only person who understood that the *Book of Fables* was a direct portal into this godforsaken place, from the one Finn had first met Fate in. A world he desperately needed to return to.

Fate was waiting for him there.

He knew this without requiring evidence. He'd probed the ether as far and wide as possible with his heightened senses, questing for the warmth of her spirit's red-gold flame. But he hadn't been able to feel her presence anywhere in Oldwilde. She'd crossed the fiery divide between worlds, the mystical barrier O'Deldar had once spoken of.

Finn crossed his arms, pressing them tight to his chest. Her absence ached inside him, deep down to the bone. Even his skin hurt with the want of her touch. Not knowing how to get to her was killing him little by little.

And that's why he was willing to risk everything to find the only man who could point the way to finding his sweet lass.

5
THE LETTER

FATE WALKED OUT INTO a sea of red leather jackets. Most of the crowd had dressed as the main character's gang from *Magic Brew*. A handful of others were dressed as the rival gangs of witches, warlocks, pixies and shadow elves.

Jessie stepped in next to Fate. "Holy crap. It's like your book exploded in here."

"Yeah," Fate said under her breath. "Make sure you watch out for the dark angel. That's the nut bar who stalked me."

Jessie looked above Fate's head. "You mean the one standing behind you?"

Fate turned, her gaze traveling over a gauzy, gray gown to a grim face painted white with eyes darkened into sunken hollows. "*You*," she hissed as she once again tried to figure out the sex of the androgynous character standing before her. "I take it you're @InAnguish."

The angel nodded solemnly.

"You followed me out of the library, chased my cab and ratted me out!"

The angel's black wings bounced as he or she shrugged and smiled sheepishly.

"What do you have to say for yourself?"

"Please forgive me?" The angel's voice was so hushed Fate still couldn't tell if she was talking to a skinny guy with a pretty face or a freakishly tall girl.

Fate huffed. "Only if you tell me your real name and say it in your normal voice."

"Mortemer," the angel confessed, his voice deep and

unmistakably male.

"Mystery solved at last. You're forgiven, Mort." Giving him a smile, Fate sidestepped away awkwardly, until Jessie extracted her fully by taking her by the arm.

"Whoa, geek alert," Jessie whispered as she glanced back at the angel. "And that's saying something in this room."

Fate shook her head. "And this coming from the person who dressed like a Powerpuff Girl all through the third grade."

"Excuse me? I wasn't the only one, *Blossom*."

"Fate!"

Fate turned and waved at a girl dressed like a Goth witch who was pushing her way through the crowd.

"Who's that?" Jessie asked.

"She's the one who organized this inopportune shindig."

Jessie stared at Fate in disbelief. "Don't tell me you're *not* happy about all this!"

Unable to pretend any longer, Fate dropped all efforts at appearing like everything was normal. "You have no idea what I've been through since I've been gone."

Jessie rolled her eyes. "Oh, you mean I can't relate to your celebrity life, flying all over the country, signing books for fans who are dressing like the characters from your book and wanting to throw you a big party? Boo hoo, it must be awful."

"That's not what I'm talking about."

"Oh sorry, I guess you're referring to your *other* trip. The one to Neverland."

Hurt by the remark, Fate studied Jessie, trying to figure out if she really hadn't believed her story.

The Goth witch strolled over to them, her entourage following in her wake, carrying camera equipment, food trays, beverages and folding tables. "Set up over there," she ordered her underlings. Removing her sunglasses, she revealed blue-gray eyes, and a love for heavy eyeliner and charcoal eye shadow. She pursed her perfectly lined ruby-red lips as she regarded Fate. "Love the digs, Fate. Could've done without losing the deposit on our room at the Paramount." Flashing a brief smile, she smoothed the Cleopatra-style bangs of her wig with a long black fingernail. "But hey, we know how to go with the flow. Right, Mason?"

She elbowed the Japanese guy dressed as a shadow elf standing next to her, jolting him out of staring at the generous curves of Fate's leather breastplate. He nodded his head so hard his anime-spiked hairstyle wobbled. "Sure. This place is dope."

Impatience burned in Fate's chest. How could she feel bad about mundane problems like losing a deposit when she was duty-bound to go to the Keep and protect it from being destroyed? She forced an apologetic smile. "Sorry about the last-minute switch. Uh…I never caught your name."

"Darcy."

Jessie gave Darcy the thumbs up. "Cool witch costume. The wig and tattoos really sell it."

Darcy shot her a cold smile. "The hair and tats are real, sweet thing. This is how I roll all year round."

Jessie's face flushed red. "Oh, sorry. I thought..."

Darcy placed her full attention on Fate, her pale expression fixed into a smooth, stony stare as she looked her up and down. "Now *this* is a kickass costume. Real leather and custom-made."

"Real armor for a real warrior," a smooth, flirty voice interjected.

Everyone turned toward the guy with long black hair dressed in a dark overcoat and wearing a dented top hat. Fate remembered him. His name was Steve and he'd come as a warlock. The last time she'd seen him, he'd been rolling around on the floor, wrestling with three demon goblins. He'd since fixed his smeared eye makeup and was back to being his self-composed, good-looking self.

Fate nodded. "Hi Steve."

Taking his top hat off, he bowed. "That's Rade Silverhand to you."

She shook her head, easily resisting his charms. "How about we stick with Steve. Wouldn't want you getting all warlocky on us again."

He replaced his hat with an odd expression, faintly amused and a little disdainful. "No, you wouldn't want to see the real warlock in me come out. As for that barbaric display earlier, you can blame the triplets."

Fate searched the crowd for three bald, green heads, bad makeup and purple boxing robes. "Is it too much to hope they skipped tonight's event?" She caught sight of the demon goblins the same time they spotted her. They all waved to make sure she couldn't avoid seeing them. Fate waved back.

"Thish is aweshome!" one of them lisped through his plastic vampire fangs as he bounded over to her. His eyes grew round as he took in Fate's armor. "Dude, check out the threadsh on thish chick. She'sh lit!"

The other two bounced around Fate like champion boxers, whistling and grinning. "Woo, you slay, girl!"

Fate smiled uncomfortably. "Good to see you guys again."

"You remember ush?" the first one asked.

"How could I forget?"

"What'sh our namesh then?"

Caught off guard by the question, Fate scrambled to remember their names. She quickly gave up. The book signing seemed so long ago, like a dream long faded from memory.

He elbowed her playfully. "Jusht messhin' with ya. I'm Lincoln. Theshe losersh are my brothersh, Roooshevelt and Jeffershon."

Fate couldn't tell them apart under the green makeup, warty noses and skin caps. "I'm sensing a theme here."

Lincoln grinned. "Yeah, our mom'sh a freak for the dead preshidentsh."

"Time to quit hogging the guest of honor and give her some space." Steve stuck his walking cane out to keep them from crowding Fate–the very action that had started the last fight between them.

In one swift movement, she grabbed the cane with an uppercut swing, catching the silver end of it in Steve's armpit. Digging it in, she forced him to stand on his toes. His look of shock matched her own.

The others jumped and backed away in awe.

"Whoa, she'sh got shome sherioush game!" Lincoln laughed. "What ish that? Karate or shomething?"

"Or something." Fate smiled secretively as she thought back to the intensive training she'd received during her time in the *Book of Fables*. Until this moment, she hadn't realized she'd honed her instincts to the point of acting without thinking. She let go, leaving Steve to catch the cane before it fell.

"Nice save, Fate." Darcy threw Steve and the three demon goblins a warning frown. "We wouldn't want a repeat of what happened at the library. Right?"

They all nodded their heads like kindergartners.

Jessie grabbed Fate by the arm, pulling her away from her fans. "What the heck was that? You went all Black Canary on that guy! Minus the fishnet stockings, of course."

"That would be leather pants now, but the comic book likeness works. Believe it or not, I got really good at hand-to-hand combat and sword fighting." Fate sighed with longing for her lost super powers. "I even had the sonic scream. I could shatter bones with a war cry."

"Did you?"

"Well, no, I never got the chance." She was about to say thankfully, but she kept that to herself. The only person she ever used the destructive power on was Finn. Fortunately, he'd been able to protect himself enough to survive, though the impact had flung him across the room.

Jessie stared at Fate in disbelief. "Okay, I can't do this any longer."

"Do what?"

"Go along with this fantasy of yours."

Fate tensed. "You said you believed me."

"Oh come on. I thought you were playing around. Making stuff up like you've always done. I kept waiting for you to drop it, but seeing what you did just now." She lifted her hands. "You could've hurt that guy."

"Only if I wanted to."

"You need to talk to your dad about this. I don't know what happened to you on that book tour, but I think you've had some sort of mental breakdown."

Panic flushed through Fate. "No. You can't tell him."

"Tell me what?" her father said from behind her.

Fate whirled round. "That I've got a…a big crush on…that warlock." She pointed at Steve with a grimace.

"Doodles." He shook his head.

She usually got upset when he used her baby name in public, but she decided to let it slide due to the abnormal amount of distress showing in his face.

"I think I know what's going on with you, and it's time to deal with it." Eustace glanced at the second floor landing. "We'll talk upstairs. You too, Jessie." Taking each girl by the shoulder, he steered them toward the staircase.

They were near the first step when Lana blocked their way. "Fate, where are you going? You need to get in there and mix it up with your fans. They're setting up the mic so you can do the Q & A."

Eustace brushed past her and unlatched the gated partition

leading to the upstairs private quarters. "Not now, Lana. I need to speak to my daughter."

Fate couldn't help smiling with satisfaction as Lana went stiff and stared at him with lips pressed tightly together.

As they climbed the stairs, movement on the right side of the wraparound landing caught Fate's attention. She glanced over in time to see Gerdie give her a nod before quietly closing the door to the upstairs apartment. Fortunately, Eustace chose the sitting area at the top of the stairs to have their chat.

Jessie stood next to the chair Fate sat down in. As Eustace took the seat opposite her, he reached into his breast pocket and retrieved his wallet. A grim frown formed on his face as he drew out a folded envelope.

Fate gulped. "Are you mad at me?" She wasn't worried about being in trouble. Eustace had never been one to admonish or punish. He preferred to help her realize her mistakes and find ways of making fair amends. But seeing him with this unfamiliar black look filled her with shame. Could he somehow see her for the killer she'd become?

He looked at her, his slate gray eyes examining her face, hair and leather armor as if she was nothing more than a stranger. "You've changed." His voice was flat with disappointment.

"I just wanted to fit in with the other cosplayers. I know I should've talked to you about my costume and coming here, but I wanted to surprise you." She hated herself for her inability to stop lying.

His gazed returned to the envelope. "I never thought I'd see the day when the truth would be so hard to face."

His words cut deep. There was no denying he saw her for what she was. He was disgusted by her bloodstained soul. "Dad, I–"

"No, wait. I have to get this out." He opened the letter-sized paper, worn and heavily creased from being in his wallet. "Your

Gran left this for me in amongst her will and testament. She hoped you'd be spared from her family legacy, but looking at you now, I'm fairly certain you've been affected."

Fate's pulse was beating so loud in her ears, she wasn't sure she'd heard him correctly. But it sounded like he was talking about a family disease. She glanced at Jessie. Had she been right? Had she inherited some sort of genetic psychosis? Had she completely imagined her journey through the *Book of Fables*?

When she'd first found herself inside the book's hidden realm, she'd questioned her sanity completely, but Finn had helped her adjust and she'd eventually come around to accepting the unbelievable. But now it looked as if none of it had ever been real, not even Finn.

Her heart imploded and tears filled her vision. "Just give it to me straight," she croaked. "Is it schizophrenia? Is that what it is?"

Eustace looked up from the worn letter. "No, it's nothing like that. This is much more complicated."

"Oh no." Fate wiped at the tears. "It's some sort of rare thing nobody knows what to do with. What happens to me now? Are you going to lock me away for the rest of my life?"

"Well, it's not up to me."

Fate jumped to her feet. "What? So you're just going to hand me over as a ward of the court?"

Eustace took Fate by the arm, pulling her gently back to her seat. "Doodles, calm down. I'm here with you. We'll face this together."

Fate sniffed. Her whole life she'd thought her overactive imagination had been a good thing, a fun way of escaping the harsh realities of everyday life. Instead, what she'd thought was a gift, had proven to be a curse–one that had caused her to lose her mind.

Eustace handed her the worn letter. "I want you to read this.

It'll help you understand what you're in store for."

The letter shook in Fate's hand as she blinked through tears. She recognized Gran's writing immediately and cried even more at the sight of it.

Eustace reached over and pulled her in for a hug. "Do you want me to read it to you?"

Fate gulped back a sob and nodded.

He took the letter and began reading.

My dear sweet Fate,

It is my deepest regret you have been given this letter. From the moment your mother was born, I prayed that she be saved from this terrible curse upon our family. Losing my daughter on the same day my granddaughter came into this world was the worst and best day of my life. I can at least be grateful your mother never lived long enough to have this curse touch her. But you are next in line, Fate. I have told your father to watch for signs that you've been affected by the curse. He will know them by your odd behavior and inexplicable occurrences. I have left proof to prepare him and I've provided everything he needs to deal with the change that has come upon you.

Fate's heart hammered against her ribcage. Her skin was on fire. She felt trapped and wanted to run away, but there was no escaping this. She was stuck inside a body that had some horrible disease of the brain.

This family curse will defy all logic and you will feel you've lost touch with reality. Stay strong, dear heart. Trust in yourself and know that all is right with you.

I have always said that magic is real. I should've told you how I came to know magic is more than fiction, and for this, I am truly sorry. I know this because our family comes from a long line of guardians who have served the Keep for over five hundred years.

Fate sat straight. "Dad, did you just say the Keep?"

Jessie's confused gaze darted between Fate and Eustace. "Does this mean Fate's not crazy?"

Eustace lifted his gaze. "No, she's not."

Fate stared at her father in disbelief, still half expecting him to dismiss Gran's letter as the ravings of an old lunatic. He was a science guy. In what world did her egghead dad believe in the stuff of fantasy?

"Really?" Fate whispered.

"Really," Eustace answered, though there was a terrible sadness in his expression.

Fate fell back in her seat, her muscles relaxing and pulse steadying with relief. She wasn't stark raving mad. "What else did Gran say?"

Eustace cleared his throat and continued reading.

By now you know that the Keep is a storehouse filled with magical objects and gateways that lead to many different worlds of magic. If your father has given you this letter, that means you have not yet entered the Keep. It is my hope that I can now convince you to not take the oath of the Keep Guardian.

Fate's heart plunged to her stomach as Eustace folded the letter with a hopeful expression. Nervously running her hands over her thighs, she shook her head.

Eustace tilted his head, staring at the ceiling. "Oh Fate, tell me you didn't."

Fate bit her lip. How could she tell him she would even sell her soul to the devil if it meant saving Finn? If Eustace knew she took the oath because of a boy, he'd never forgive her. "I...I didn't know–"

"How could you not know?" Eustace said, his tone sharp. "What part of sacrificing all your worldly ties and dedicating the rest of your life to protecting the Keep until the day you die, did you not understand?"

"You forgot about the part where I get to retire when I'm 90," Fate added.

Eustace stood, towering over her, radiating anger like never before. "Fate, this is serious. This is your life we're talking about."

Fate rose to her feet and met his furious gaze. "You're right. This is more serious than you'll ever know, and it's my life and my decision." She took a deep shaky breath. "As much as I hate to say this, Dad, there's nothing you can do to save me from what I have to do."

6
THE PRIEST IS GONE

FINN BREATHED A LITTLE easier once he reached the east wing of the castle. There wasn't nearly as much foot traffic in the halls to navigate. Merely a few chambermaids, who scurried past him with fearful gazes cast downward, as if he might scold them or add to their duties. He looked like a nobleman to them. He still wore the kilt and jacket from when he'd been knighted by the king of Beldereth.

His first inclination had been to run straight to Beldereth to seek the comfort of the king's company. Rudwor had become like a father to him, but his good friend did not hold the answers to crossing the fiery divide. O'Deldar was the only one who could help him solve that dilemma.

All the same, it was terrible being stuck in Oldwilde without Fate by his side. At least when the Green Man had trapped him inside the oak, he'd had no awareness of time. He'd been at peace and at one with all of nature. When the old god had first released him, his determination to find Fate had spurred him on and given him strength. But nothing could have prepared him for the loss of being separated from the Earthmind, and his longing for Fate only worsened his low spirits. Loneliness chipped away at his resolve with each passing hour. What if he never found his way to her?

Grief seized his heart.

"Buck up, boyo," he muttered. "It's too early to go losing it already."

A door opened toward the end of the long corridor and the early morning sunlight splashed across the floor as a chambermaid stepped out with a basket overflowing with thick coverlets and dirty linens. Finn studied the doors lining the hall, trying to remember which one led to O'Deldar's chamber. He knew it looked out over the ocean, which meant the priest's rooms were on the right. But which one? He couldn't risk entering the wrong chamber. His face was too recognizable.

Finn caught the attention of the chambermaid as she hurried toward him. "I'm looking for O'Deldar."

She stopped, her face flushed as she shifted the weight of her heavy burden to the other hip. "Oh, you won't find the king's counselor here. Haven't you heard? The priest is gone."

"Where did he go?"

"No one knows. His chamber was found in ruins and there was blood everywhere. Many think him dead, poor soul."

Reeling from the news, Finn grabbed the wall for support. He instantly knew what must've happened. Fate had killed O'Deldar. There was no forgetting the crazed state she'd gone into the first time she'd met the priest. If O'Deldar hadn't interrupted Brune's spell at that moment, there was no telling what would've happened. No wonder Fate had looked so guilty every time Finn had asked her how she'd gotten the Rod from O'Deldar.

"When?" Finn choked, his throat constricting.

"It was late winter when it happened."

Finn scrambled to do the mental math on how long ago that had been. He'd been encased within the oak in the early spring, the day of Alban Eiler. It had only been two days since he'd been freed from the tree and the weather was now quite hot. The wheat fields were tall and would be ready for reaping in about a month. By all accounts, O'Deldar had gone missing about six months.

"Point me to his room," Finn said, unable to keep the gruffness from his voice.

"Two doors down, m'lord." She squinted to see his face within the shadows of his hood.

"Carry on." Finn's chest burned with frustration as he watched her hurry toward the stairs. He'd been counting on O'Deldar's help. What the hell was he supposed to now? He stood rigid, clenching his fists. He wanted to punch a hole in the wall, but this was no time to lose his cool. He couldn't afford to draw undo attention.

Taking a deep breath, he called upon everything he'd learned from the monks during his time at the Springs of Almsdeep. "Stay Whole," he whispered. "Stay Whole."

After a few moments of repeating the mantra, a thin veil of peace came over him and he entered O'Deldar's chamber. The room was dusty and neglected. Someone must've instructed the chambermaids to leave his belongings alone. Good. That meant he wouldn't have to worry about being discovered. He would have the freedom to comb through everything, read every book and parchment until he found what he needed to cross the fiery divide standing between him and Fate.

7

HOW WILL WE EXPLAIN THE REEK?

"WHAT'S NEXT?" JESSIE ASKED in an obvious attempt to break the tension between father and daughter. "Where do we go from here?"

"*We* don't go anywhere," Fate said. "This is something I have to take care of."

Eustace thrust the letter into Fate's hand. "No, that's where you're wrong. Your grandmother left an entire library behind of grimoires, scrolls and tablets, some of which outline warnings about the *Book of Fables* and the history behind the Keep. I've been studying these texts for the last seven years, and I can tell you right now, you're going to need someone along who's knowledgeable about–"

"What? You know about the *Book of Fables*?"

"I know enough to want to stay away from it. Why, what do you know about it?"

Fate dropped her gaze and stared at her boots. "I...I sort of got caught inside the book as a reader."

Eustace's face paled in shock. "What?" He looked her over again, studying the length of her hair, the defined muscles of her arms and the hand-crafted leather armor. Closing his eyes, he swallowed, his expression pained. "Oh god, what happened to you in there?"

His concern shattered the thin veneer surrounding her grief. Tears stood in her eyes as memories of Finn and everything they'd been through crashed in. Curling her fists, she pressed her knuckles against her eyes, forcing the sadness away. "I'm fine, Dad. I got out."

"All so you could jump back into the lion's den?"

"Don't worry about me. I'm stronger now… and more grown up. I was gone for over six months. Technically I've had a birthday, I'm eighteen now."

Eustace looked horrified. "Well, you're still seventeen as far as I'm concerned, and you have no idea what's ahead. Finish reading the letter. Your grandmother warns against going into the Keep without at least knowing what you might be facing."

Fate skimmed through the last paragraph. "I already know about Brune. Not exactly on my list of favorite great-aunts, by the way."

"She's dangerous," Eustace insisted.

"And she's here."

Eustace frowned. "What? Here in the bookstore?"

Fate nodded.

Eustace paced the landing as he glanced down at the crowd. "We've got to get all these people out of the building."

"Good luck convincing Lana to shut the party down without a good reason," Fate said. "I say we sneak Brune out of here."

Eustace gripped the railing so hard his hand shook from the pressure. "Why would she cooperate?"

Fate waved an antique key at her father. "Because I have the Key to Brune's precious Keep and she's desperate to get back there."

Jessie's eyes grew round with fear as she glanced over her shoulder. "Where is she?"

"Hiding." Fate walked over to the apartment and knocked on the door.

Gerdie cracked the door open and peeked out.

"Is she in there?"

Gerdie wrinkled her nose. "You can't tell by the smell?"

"Who's this?" Eustace asked as he stepped in next to Fate.

"This is Gran's twin sister, Gerdie." Fate smiled. "She,

however, is on my list of favorite great-aunts."

Giving Eustace a lopsided grin, Gerdie reached to shake his hand. "Glad to meet ya. Feels like we already met though. Fate talked about you a whole lot."

Eustace stooped to shake her small hand. "Hi Gerdie. I recognize you from Berdie's box of family photos." He straightened. "But how is it you're still…?"

"A kid?" Gerdie finished for him. "Time passes differently in Oldwilde than it does here."

"But you've been gone for," Eustace paused to do work the numbers in his head, "about seventy-five years. That would mean you experienced upwards to hundreds of years passing by."

Gerdie's little shoulders sank, along with the spark in her eye. "You don't have to tell me. I lived it."

Fate hurried to change the subject so Gerdie wouldn't have to explain the tragedy she'd experienced. "How come I never saw those pictures you mentioned?"

Eustace looked relieved to be moving beyond the uncomfortable moment. "Your grandmother kept the photos of her missing sisters locked away. She didn't want to give you or anyone else a reason to investigate the family history in case curiosity led to accidentally coming across the secret she'd been protecting her entire life." He sniffed and cleared his throat. "Sorry, but something smells terrible in there. I think we've got a dead animal situation."

"Nah, that's just Brune," Gerdie said.

"Excuse me?"

Gerdie opened the door all the way and stepped aside so they could see Brune sitting at the kitchen table.

Eustace took one step forward, then stopped. "Oh my, there's something horribly wrong with her."

Jessie peered around Eustace. "Ew gross, she looks like…"

"A zombie?" Fate asked.

"Yeah. But she's not, right?"

"No, she's for sure a zombie."

Jessie squealed and ran out of the room.

Eustace drew out his handkerchief and held it over his nose. "You actually expect us to get her past that crowd downstairs?"

Fate waved him off. "Everybody's dressed up. She'll fit right in."

"And then she'll promptly clear the room. How will we explain the reek?"

"We'll tell them she's going for realism," Fate offered.

"You expect everyone to buy that?"

"Hmm...a roomful of hardcore cosplaying fantasy geeks? Yeah, pretty much."

Folding his arms, Eustace frowned at Brune with open distaste, then turned to Fate. "Lana's bound to come looking for you any minute now. I think it's best you go downstairs and start that Q&A she was going on about. While you're keeping everyone distracted, Gerdie and I will sneak Brune down to the janitor closet."

"Wow, you really do know all about the Keep." Fate stared at him in wonder. She was grateful to have her father helping to tidy this awful mess. But more than anything else, she liked not having to lie to him anymore.

Lines of sadness formed near the edge of her father's eyes. "That's what I've been trying to tell you. I've been praying this day would never come, but I've been preparing for it all the same." Turning away, he covered his nose and ducked into the apartment.

Fate strode over to Jessie. She was standing at the opposite end of the landing, putting as much distance as she could between herself and the zombie. "Come on, Jess." Fate hooked her hand in the crook of her friend's arm and turned toward the stairs.

When they reached the bottom, Jessie looked at her with eyes wide. "This is nuts."

Fate nodded. "And it's only going to get nuttier, which is why I want you to go home, where it's safe."

"No way! I can't go home after what I know!"

"Who's going to take care of Oz? You are my cat sitter, after all."

Jessie rolled her eyes. "Oh please. Mom's been babying him like you wouldn't believe. He likes Indian food now. A lot. He won't touch his cat food anymore."

"Great. You spoiled my cat."

"Don't blame me. Mom's the one who–"

"There you are!" Lana called out as she trotted over. "Come, come, everyone's waiting."

Fate followed Lana over to where Darcy was standing next to some tech guy at a table with his laptop, speakers and mic. He handed Fate the mic as Darcy smiled coldly. "Nice of you to finally show up." Her tone was upbeat but laced with tension. Before Fate could say a word, Darcy turned to the loud crowd milling about the main area of the bookstore. "Everyone, can I please have your attention."

Faces turned to them as conversations died down and silence filled the room.

"Our guest of honor is here to answer all your burning questions. But first, let's give her a big hand."

Everyone clapped and hollered.

Fate waved. "Thanks guys," she said into the mic.

"We're recording this for our site, so raise your hand and I'll bring the mic over to you," Darcy instructed as everyone quieted down and raised their hands eagerly.

Fate's smile felt wooden as she stole a glance at the stairs. When would Eustace and Gerdie get Brune on the move? Her impatience was building to an excruciating level. Her need to go to the Keep had become as physical as hunger. An urgent sense of duty was pressing on her, becoming intense with each passing moment. It was all she could do to not throw the mic on the floor and race out of there.

Someone nudged Fate. Darcy's boyfriend, Mason, was staring at her. "You gonna answer the question?"

"Oh, uh..." Fate glanced out over the audience. Darcy gave her a glare that could curdle milk as she held the mic for a blue-haired girl dressed as a pixie. "Can you repeat that?" Fate asked.

The blue pixie jumped with excitement, making her sparkly dragonfly wings bounce. "If you haven't guessed, I love the pixies in your book. Where'd you come up with the idea to make their saliva an aphrodisiac?"

It seemed like a decade had passed since Fate had written her book, or even thought about it, for that matter. There was a time when she would've loved discussing her characters with interested readers, but she'd been through too much. She'd been changed irrevocably. Sadly, none of this seemed very important anymore. "Hmm," Fate mused aloud, "I don't exactly remember how I thought of that one. It just sort of dropped in my head, and it seemed to work for the story."

The girl's shoulders sagged with disappointment. Darcy held her lips in a tight angry line as she moved to a guy wearing a red leather jacket.

"I really dug the main character, Edge. He's chill," the guy said into the mic. "You really got into his head. How is it you were able to sound like a dude? You know, being a chick and all."

"Oh." Fate grasped for a more interesting answer than the last. "I suppose I'd have to blame that on being raised by my dad. I ended up playing with action heroes instead of dolls."

Grinning, he nodded his head as a light chuckle ran through the crowd.

Darcy's tense expression relaxed as she brought the mic to a girl dressed as a ghoulish harlequin. "I thought the Ghost Market was wicked. Did it bother you to make unicorn heads and mermaid fillets available for sale in the market?"

Fate started to speak, when a movement near the top of the stairs distracted her. Brune was wrapped from head to toe in a bed sheet. Eustace gripped her by the arm, holding her straight as she teetered down each step. Gerdie followed from behind, propping Brune upright whenever she tilted backward.

"Fate?" Darcy's tone was sharp.

"Huh?" Fate muttered as she dropped her gaze to the crowd. "Oh, uh…no I was okay with chopping them up. I've never exactly been a fan of rainbow-farting unicorns or sing-songy mermaids. Unless of course, they're singing to lure sailors to their death." She felt a sharp pang, remembering how Finn had come close to drowning when he'd answered a siren's call.

Laughter and shouts of agreement filled the room.

Fate smiled tensely as she watched Eustace, Brune and Gerdie reach the bottom of the stairs. When she glanced back into the crowd to answer the next question, Darcy was staring back. Then she turned to see what was distracting Fate.

Darcy pushed through the audience toward the stairs. "And what's this?"

"Any other questions?" Fate said, hearing the panic in her voice amplified by the mic.

"What are you hiding from us, Fate Floyd?" Darcy walked over to Eustace and tugged on Brune's sheet. It fell away and everyone gasped. "A zombie? Wow, a really good one too." Curling her nose, Darcy waved her hand in front of her face. "Ew, complete with special effects!"

"It's amazing what kinds of smells the right number of chemical compounds can produce." Eustace shrugged his shoulders, obviously uncomfortable with being discovered.

"Are you a chemist?" Darcy asked.

"I dabble," Eustace muttered into the mic as Lana bustled over.

"What's this?" Lana asked, grinning overly wide to compensate for her confusion. "Nobody said anything about this to me."

Brune hunched in on herself as the audience crowded around to get a closer look. Some poked the gray, flaking skin of her skeletal arms, asking her what kind of makeup she'd used. Others backed away, complaining that she looked realistic enough without the realistic stench.

Jessie stepped in next to Fate. "How are you going to explain this?"

"Haven't a clue. Any ideas?"

"Nope." Jessie dug out her bag of corn nuts.

Fate frowned. "Put those away. This isn't a movie. It's my life."

"Yeah, and it's way more entertaining than a movie."

"Thanks for nothing." Fate turned to the audience and tapped the mic. "Hey everyone, listen up. I've got an announcement to make."

Crunching on her snack, Jessie smiled. "Can't wait to hear this."

Faces turned in Fate's direction, every expression filled with high expectation. "I was going to wait until the very end of the evening before we did the big reveal, but you're way too on the ball for that." She wagged her finger at Darcy.

Darcy folded her arms, her chin held high as she smiled smugly at Fate.

Fate paused for a moment, struggling to think of something believable to tell everyone, but all she could focus on was the sound of Jessie's munching and the crinkling of the plastic bag as she reached for another corn nut.

"Don't keep us all in suspense," Darcy prodded.

Fate laughed. Sort of. It was more of a choking sound. "I uh…I thought I'd announce the title of my next book." She gulped dryly as she scrambled for a catchy title. "It's called…Diary Of A Zombie."

The room was dead quiet for the longest minute.

"Yeah!" someone called out. "I like it!"

With that, everyone started asking questions all at once. As Darcy brought order back to the room, Fate nudged her chin at Eustace, gesturing for him to get Brune to the back room. Nodding, he and Gerdie slowly steered Brune away from the crowd.

After an hour of non-stop questions, Darcy finally concluded the Q&A session. "Help yourself to food and drink, everyone." She turned to the tech guy and signaled him to start playing music.

Breathing a sigh of relief, Fate set the mic down and looked at Jessie. "Come on, let's go find Eustace." Checking to see that Darcy was otherwise occupied, Fate led the way, inching through the crowd toward the back of the bookstore. Just as she caught sight of the green velvet curtains leading into the storage room, Darcy and her boyfriend appeared in front of them.

"Hey Mason, look who's trying to sneak out." Darcy was talking to him, but her eyes were fixed on Fate with an air of suspicion.

He didn't say anything. He was too busy staring at Fate with an awestruck grin.

Darcy stepped forward. "What's the hurry? The party just started."

Fate clenched her fists. This girl was really getting on her nerves. "I'm not going anywhere. My publicist just called a little confab in the back room is all. She's waiting for me right now, so if you don't mind, I'll–"

"You mean her?" Darcy narrowed her gaze and stared past Fate.

Fate glanced over her shoulder to where Lana was interviewing a group of cosplayers and snapping shots of them. "Oh, she obviously got distracted."

"Mmhmm." Darcy wasn't convinced.

Fate stepped around her. "Yeah, well, I'll just go and wait for her."

"You do that," Darcy said as Fate and Jessie slipped through the velvet curtains.

"What's her damage?" Jessie asked.

"I guess she's still mad about me switching locations on her. Can't exactly blame her. If I didn't have such an unbelievably crazy excuse, I'd be feeling pretty crappy about it." Fate blinked to adjust her eyes to the darkness. She'd braced herself for the assault of Brune's stink as soon as they entered the small room, but all she smelled was the musty odor of old boxes. Had they gone outside? She called out to Eustace.

He flipped the light on. "Hey, Doodles. We've run into a bit of a problem."

Gerdie stood next to him, wringing her small hands together. At her feet was Brune's prone body, fully covered by the sheet.

"What happened? Did Brune do something?" Fate asked in alarm.

Gerdie shook her head. "That's just it, she hasn't moved for the last twenty minutes. We think she might be dead. For good."

"That's a bad thing?"

"It is if you wanna get into the Keep. And other stuff, if you know what I mean." Gerdie gave Fate a conspiratorial wink.

Fear squeezed Fate's heart. She knew exactly what Gerdie meant. Brune was the only one who knew how to find the gateway leading back to Oldwilde and to Finn.

Fate whipped the sheet off Brune's body. Her corpse was now a dried husk. The rotting flesh had shriveled against the bone and looked as hard and tough as beef jerky. Whatever putrid sludge had filled her veins had most likely turned to dust, which would explain why she no longer stunk. Fate looked at them. "She's all mummified. She was still squishy only an hour ago. How could this have happened?"

Gerdie shrugged. "I don't know. I figured the Orb would keep her alive, but Brune must've gotten herself in trouble with some pretty heavy-duty magic for her to rot out this fast."

Fate grabbed Brune by the neck in a panic and shook her. "Wake up, you witch!"

Eustace took Fate by the arm. "Fate, what's gotten into you? Calm down. Trust me, we'll figure this out."

Feeling ashamed about her outburst, Fate let Brune's head drop to the floor with a dull thud.

A thin moan filled the room.

Gerdie kneeled next to Brune, placing her ear next to her mouth. Another moan followed and Gerdie looked at Fate. "I was wrong. She's still in there."

"Oh thank god. Come on, let's get her up and out of here." Fate slid her hand inside her boot to retrieve the Key and stepped in front of the janitor door. With the Key poised near the keyhole, she stared at the Lock.

Her pulse raced with anticipation. She was finally ready to take that first step back to Finn. If only she knew what was waiting behind the door. Fear gripped hold. Not for herself but for Eustace, Gerdie and Jessie. This all-consuming sense of duty toward the Keep and endless longing to be with Finn fueled her like nothing else she'd ever known. There was no turning back for her. But it wasn't too late for the others.

Fate put her back to the door. "Dad. Jessie. Gerdie. This is where we say goodbye."

8
THE FIERY DIVIDE

RUBBING HIS TIRED EYES, Finn set aside the scroll he was reading and looked out through the bank of windows to where the sun hung low above the ocean's horizon. He stood and stretched his stiff limbs before walking out onto the balcony. Where had the time gone? He'd started going through O'Deldar's library in the early morning. He figured it must be well past eight in the evening.

The sinking sun spilled fiery sparks over the calm sea. Finn gripped the stone balustrade until his knuckles turned white. The last time he'd looked out over these waters, Fate had been with him, and for one precious moment, everything had been perfect.

The ever-present ache in his heart climbed into his throat and tightened into a painful lump. He couldn't stop the sweet recollections from surfacing, even if he wanted to. Every detail of that night was etched into his soul. He closed his eyes, remembering how his touch had made Fate shiver with desire. For a split second the memory came to life and he saw her lips, slightly parted, waiting expectantly for the kiss they'd both been craving. He'd been completely unprepared for the honeyed taste of her mouth, and with it, her wild unabashed response. She'd innocently offered herself then and there. God knows he'd wanted to. Even now his body hungered for her skin against his, their two hearts beating as one.

But there'd been too much darkness surrounding them. Just as there'd always been, from the second their lives had first collided.

Swallowing the pain, Finn opened his eyes and frowned at the dusky sky.

He'd defeated the darkness Mugloth had cast over him. The shadow was gone now. There should be nothing keeping them apart. Yet here they were, two worlds apart. Separated by a magical barrier of sentient fire.

Finn let out a weary sigh. He'd spent the entire day searching for answers and had barely finished the first stack of books. There were at least a few hundred more left to investigate, and too many scrolls to begin to count. If only there was a way to zero in on the right texts.

He turned, setting his back against the railing as he stared at the mountain of knowledge resting within the dusty chamber. "The answer's in there. I know it." He narrowed his gaze on the daunting pile. "Where is it hiding?"

The sound of seagulls and waves crashing against the cliffs below were the only response to his question. Giving into exasperation, Finn shifted his weight to the other foot and sighed. As he did so, the last rays of the sun shot past his legs, reflecting off something shiny sitting on one of the bookcases lining the back wall. His grandfather had taught him to heed all signs, regardless of how small or insignificant they might seem.

Finn crossed the room, careful not to block the sun as he closed in on the sparkling object. It was a large sapphire embedded within the spine of a leather bound book lying on its side, buried at the very bottom of a huge pile of other books. Kneeling down, he grabbed the books on top and set them aside.

"Hmm, *Immram Brain*," Finn mused as he held the book and slowly translated the Gaelic title. "*The Voyage of Bran*."

He knew this one well. Grandda had recounted the ancient Irish tale more than a few times. A man named Bran Mac Febail is visited by a woman from the Otherworld, a place of eternal summer, where the people are forever youthful and healthy, and food and water is endlessly abundant. She invites him to voyage across the sea and visit her land. Bran gathers a company of men and leaves Ireland for the Otherworld. After happily staying there for what seemed only a year, Bran grows homesick and decides to return to Ireland. The woman wishes he would stay, but when he insists he must leave, she warns him not to set foot on the shores of his homeland. When Bran and his crew sail back, the people who gather along the water to greet them do not recognize his name except in legends passed down through many generations. This upsets one of Bran's men. He jumps off the boat and swims ashore. But the moment he steps on dry land, the man turns to ashes. Seeing this, Bran turns his ship away from Ireland, sails out of sight and is never seen again.

"He turned to ashes," Finn said under his breath as he thumbed through the last pages of the book, stopping when he came to a penned drawing. Spread across both pages was a wall of fire stretched without end between the people on the shores of Ireland and Bran's ship.

"The fiery divide," Finn whispered with a grim smile. He'd finally found evidence of its existence, which meant there had to be something else in O'Deldar's library that would show him how to cross the divide without being burned into a pile of ash.

9
THIS IS THE KEEP?

"GIVE ME THE MUMMY." Fate reached for Brune.

Eustace held tight to the stiff carcass. "No."

Jessie crossed her arms. "I second that."

Gerdie kicked a box. "What do you expect me to do? Enroll myself in the first grade?"

Fate had to admit, Gerdie had a point. The life she'd left behind had died over seventy-five years ago. There was nothing here for her now. If anything, Gerdie was probably more prepared for what was to come than Fate was. "Okay, you can come. But that's it."

Eustace frowned. "Since when do you give me orders?"

Fate smiled nervously. "Since now?"

"Not happening, Doodles. But I'm in full agreement with Jessie staying behind."

"No way! I'm not staying in Boringville after all this!"

"You can, and you will," Eustace said in his parent voice.

Tears filled Jessie's eyes as she stared at Fate. "How can you do this? What happened to besties all the way?"

"That was before I nearly died five or six times. You have no clue how dangerous it is."

Eustace shifted Brune to the other arm. "Not what I want to hear, Fate."

"Sorry. I might've exaggerated. It was probably only two or three."

Eustace tightened his lips.

"Go!" Jessie pouted. "Just go!"

"Jess, please don't be mad at me."

Gerdie tugged on Fate's hand. "We gotta go. Time's tickin' down on Brune."

Unable to face Jessie's anger, Fate turned to the door and slipped the Key in the Lock.

As soon as she turned the Key, the door sprang ajar, the hinges creaking as it swung all the way open. A cool draft swept past them. Fate peered into the darkness. Any janitor supplies that had been inside the closet were gone, replaced by a long corridor with a faint pinprick of light at the end. Something about the radiant glow of light beckoned.

Holding onto Gerdie's hand, Fate stepped through the threshold. As Eustace followed lockstep behind them, the whole world tilted without warning. Gravity pulled on her, causing her to lean forward at an alarming angle. Reaching for something to hold onto, Fate had no way of righting herself. The gravitational pull yanked her off her feet.

Fate screamed as she hurtled through space. A circular tunnel of neon-blue lightning churned around her, bolts zapping and burning from every side. As the G-forces increased, pain tore through Fate's body as if she was being stretched across the universe. Just when she feared she would burst into a cloud of atoms, it was over and she was tumbling over a stone floor.

Still in shock, Fate rested her face against the cool surface of the floor, grateful to have something solid beneath her again. She started to rise, when a blow between the shoulder blades flattened her.

Gerdie rolled off her. "Sorry about that. Again."

"Yeah," Fate groaned. "This really needs to stop. I'm not a mattress."

Gerdie hurried from the spot. "Speakin' of which, you better move before your dad comes flyin' thorough the portal."

"Oh, jeez." Fate scrambled out of the way on all fours. She no sooner cleared the area, when Eustace shot through the portal and landed in a heap. Brune's stiff corpse whipped past him and slid to a stop a few feet away.

Fate stood and rushed to her father. She'd never seen him look so astonished and out of place. "You okay?"

Eustace straightened his tie and smoothed his thick bangs back in place. "Bit of a bumpy ride. Other than that, I'm quite fine." The tightness in his voice said otherwise as he rose shakily to his feet and glanced around at their surroundings.

They were in a large circular room with a domed ceiling that, by all appearances, looked to be a library. The curved bronze metal walls were lined with tall bookcases, broken here and there by portraits of strange lands, a few statues of mythical creatures and a stuffed, furry alien creature in a cage. Some kind of lab experiment bubbled away amidst ancient tomes stacked all over a huge wooden table, which hovered a foot off the floor in the center of the room.

Fate walked over to the table and stooped to see what was holding it off the ground. Was it magic or science? Eustace did the same. When he straightened, there was a curious glint in his eyes. "Interesting," he mused.

Fate nodded. "Curious for sure. But I was expecting something much bigger and more impressive than this." She glanced at Gerdie. "Are you sure this is the Keep?"

Gerdie stared at the ceiling with a confused frown. "Somethin' tells me this ain't all of it."

A leather book embossed with a grotesque face encircled by tentacles caught Fate's attention. "*Necronomicon*. Wasn't that a fictional book by H. P. Lovecraft?"

"I would not touch that if I were you. Otherelse, you risk calling the Great Old Ones."

Fate backed away from the table, searching for the owner of the crackly voice with an East-Indian sounding accent. Sounds of gears and clanking metal had her turning in the opposite direction.

The cage housing the stuffed creature was moving toward her on mechanical crablike legs. The animal's devil-pointed ears twitched, letting her know it was not stuffed with sawdust as she had first assumed. It had the face of a fox, but its body was more like a monkey, with practiced hands smoothly navigating its portable prison away from the wall. Looking equally dumbfounded as Fate felt, Eustace and Gerdie stepped in next to her as the cage came to a full stop in front of them.

Pulling on what looked like the brake, the creature parked its cage, hopped off the seat and stuck its whiskered snout through the bars. "And who would you be?" For some reason it spoke through a device, which amplified its voice to an annoying pitch.

Fate winced at the sound. "I'm Fate, the new Guardian. And this is my dad, Eustace, and Brune's sister, Gerdie."

Mischief sparked red in the creature's eyes as it ignored the others and studied Fate. "Ah, Brune found her successor, though I'm not accustomized to a guardian who comes with escortendants." Its ears drooped slightly. "I gather she didn't make it."

"No, she's here." Fate stepped around the table and dragged Brune's wrapped body to the other side.

The creature's ears shot straight up. "Is she expirated?"

Fate flung the sheet back. "If you call being undead and mummified expirated, then yeah."

"You say she's undead? That would be the doing of the Orb. The only way to nullivoid such a condition is to combinate it with the Rod. Do you have it?" The creature extended an eager hand through the bars of its cage.

Fate regarded the strange-speaking animal with cautious curiosity. As jumbled as some of its words were, she was surprised she was able to understand the meaning behind them.

Gerdie stepped in front of Fate. "Who wants to know?"

The animal's gaze dropped to Gerdie and its slanted eyes narrowed to slits. "Move aside, pesky little beast."

"Who you callin' pesk–"

"I agree with Gerdie," Eustace interjected. "We won't be handing anything over until we know more about whom we're dealing with."

The creature's eyes widened as it studied Eustace. "If you must know, my name is Farouk. I am the Keep caretaker, and have been so for thousands of years." It directed an arrogant smile at Fate. "I have seen hundreds of guardians come and go, some of which I supportorated, and not so much with others. You would do well to get on my pleasantful side."

"Noted," Fate said.

"Splendillent. Now. Back to the matter at hand. We have an iron-eating scavenger loose within the Keep. It's already eaten through the subsurface and its size has doublfied over the last twenty-four hours. The bigger it gets, the more likely it is that it will want out and either breakture the Keep's seal or attempt to perforgrate the breaching door into this sanctuary."

The duty-bound sense of urgency that had been with Fate since she first took the oath intensified. Her months of army training kicked in, instantly shifting her into soldier mode. "Breaching door?" she asked.

Grabbing a gear, Farouk steered his cage over to a large hatch. The iron iris of the door was shut tight for the moment. The creature waved its hand over a screen displaying a series of geometrical patterns. Glimmering particles of light shot out from the panel, spreading over the wall like liquid soaking into cloth. Wherever the shimmering light moved, the solid bronze wall became translucent, revealing the Keep. Nothing in all of Fate's experiences, not even those within the *Book of Fables*, had prepared her for the sight unfolding before her.

The Keep stretched out as far as the eye could see. On first glance it appeared to be made entirely of massive gears and moving parts. Miles and miles of ancient structures filled the flat plains of the gears, each slowly rotating in opposite directions. Gigantic revolving hoops encompassed the complex system, sweeping in circular rotations, which appeared to be generating a crackling force field around the Keep. Beyond the protective sphere, lay the glittering stars of deep space, interrupted only by a smoldering red planet and a gaseous green nebula.

Eustace and Gerdie edged close to the transparent wall, both staring wide-eyed and slack-jawed. "Where are we, exactly?" her father asked after a moment of stunned silence.

"We are in the Chaos Region, the birthplace of multi-dimensional magic," Farouk explained as he walked his cage back over to stand next to Brune's body.

Knowing they were on the other side of the universe should've been entirely unnerving, yet Fate felt as if she knew this place, like she belonged there. The barely audible thrum of the revolving hoops and slight vibration within the walls and floor were all comforting sensations that made her feel strangely at home.

She unclasped the chain holding the Rod and placed it in her palm. The spell Brune had cast to force her to get the Rod–at any cost–had driven her to do the unthinkable. She'd spilled blood to take it and she'd been obsessed with keeping the Rod for herself ever since. But now something had changed. Possibly the spell had waned with the last of Brune's life ticking away.

Whatever the reason, the Rod's hold over her was gone. As much as Fate resisted, she knew she had to restore Brune to life. She would need her help to rid the Keep of the scavenger. That was her first priority as the new guardian. Then, and only then, would she be able to return her attention to finding a gateway back to Finn.

Fate dangled the Rod in front of Farouk. He grabbed for the chain, but she jerked it out of reach. "It's best you tell me how to use it."

"That is secretential information, and is unfit for any human."

"Well I'm not about to hand it over to you," Fate said. "Besides, what makes you fit for the secret?"

Farouk's eyes narrowed into angry slits as he squeezed the bars of his cage. "You'll have to take my wordbond for it."

Eustace pulled Fate aside. "You shouldn't tease him. You're going to need his help and he's already said he wouldn't give you any if you got on his bad side."

"I can't go kissing up to him either. He'll never respect me if I do."

"Well, there must be a better way to go about this. This requires diplomacy. Maybe I can negotiate this for you."

"Sure, you can try. But first, are you up to speed on the whole Orb and Rod deal?"

Eustace scratched his chin thoughtfully. "I did read something about the Orb of Aeternitis. If I remember right, it was a small, gold object made of interlocking rings engraved with magical symbols and numbers. By turning the rings in specific order, one could activate alchemical formulas, which would summon forces powerful enough to bestow life or death."

Fate stared at him in surprise. "Bingo, only its power is faulty without the Rod." She held the gold bar between two fingers. "This tiny hunk of metal is the only thing that'll unlock the Orb's full power and make it work the way it's supposed to. Meaning, whomever combines the Orb and Rod is the one who gets to have all the godlike powers that go with it."

Gerdie stepped in between them. "And that ain't happening on my watch."

"I see," Eustace said. "Then we must tread carefully. Where

is the Orb?"

"Hangin' around Brune's neck. It's the only thing keepin' her alive," Gerdie explained.

Eustace removed his spectacles and brushed the lenses over his sleeve. "Well there's a conundrum. We'll have to leave it on her while we unlock it. Does that mean she'll be the one endowed with the power once she's brought back to life?" He replaced his glasses. "Given Brune's shady reputation, I can only imagine the trouble such a power in her hands will bring down."

"Exactly," Fate agreed. "I say we cut our losses, rip the Orb off Brune and draw straws for who's going to be the next immortal around here."

"For your information, I have supremable hearing and I know what you're saying," Farouk informed them from the other side of the room. "I have already previsionated this dilemma and made all the obligessary arrangements."

The three of them turned to Farouk as he steered his cage over to the table. He reached for a small brass contraption made of springs with weighted arms and a scoop that swiveled from a clockface. "I call it the combinator. It will unite the Orb and Rod with absolute neutrality for everyone in the room."

Fate flung her hands in the air. "Why didn't you say that in the first place?" She and the others joined him next to the table.

Farouk avoided her gaze. "I was testing your knowledge."

"Testing my ignorance is more like it." Fate took the combinator from him with a frown. "What do I do with it?"

"Place it on Brune's body."

"Ew, do I have to?"

Farouk huffed. "You'll have to grow a thicker skin than that if you are to be an effectful guardian."

"Fine," Fate grumbled as she kneeled down next to Brune and placed the combinator on her bony chest. "Now what?"

"Remove the Orb from the chain and place it on the arm

with the spoon. But you must be quick. The Orb must remain in contact with her by the chain or the combinator, to maintain whatever life-force she has left."

Tense with revulsion, Fate pulled on the chain around Brune's desiccated neck until she found the clasp and unhooked it. Then she dragged the Orb over Brune's body, bumping it against the combinator, before quickly depositing the gold sphere onto the spoon. "Done. What do I do with the Rod?"

"Slot it into the hole of the second arm. Good, now wind both arms counterclockwise until the springs are tight and no longer move."

Fate stopped to look at Farouk. "You do mean counterclockwise, right? No offense, but you've got that word salad thing going on."

Faruouk's back stiffened. "Of course I insinufy counterclockwise."

"You just did it again."

Faruouk's ears pressed against his head. "Do as I say."

"Alright," Fate muttered as she wound the springs. When the mechanisms tightened, the clock started ticking. She let go and stood. "Why do I feel like I just set a bomb?"

"In essence, you have," Farouk said. "You may want to step away a fair distance. Oh, and look away. You don't want to be blinded by the God spark."

"Well, there's an afterthought to fill you with dread." Eustace gestured for Gerdie to follow as he put a protective hand on Fate's shoulder and guided them to the far wall. "None of this was in your Gran's notes," he muttered to Fate.

"Sorry, Dad, but that'll probably be the case from here on out."

The sound of the ticking clock grew louder as everyone fell silent and waited nervously for the bomb to go off. The arms holding the Orb and Rod slowly rotated into alignment, one tipping over the other as they inched closer. The moment the Rod pierced the Orb, light blasted from both objects.

Covering her eyes, Fate turned away. A hot wind slammed against her, followed by a terrible shrieking noise. Eustace grabbed her hand, squeezing to reassure her, as he had always done throughout her life. Little did he know that she was more afraid for him than she was for herself. She'd already walked through hell and back. That changes a person, and in ways she didn't want her father to know about.

What worried her most was that he was entirely new to all this. Eustace had no idea what he was in for and she could not bear the thought of anything ever happening to him. In that moment, she vowed to keep him safe. She'd been forced to live without one parent and she wasn't about to lose the only parent she'd ever known.

The power built around them, charging the air with energy thick with the smell of ozone. Pressure weighed on them in the form of a glittering, gaseous cloud. Fiery micro sparks seared Fate's face and hands. She wanted to swat the pain away and fight. Instead, she tensed every muscle and held still. This was something they'd have to wait out.

The blazing light snuffed out in an instant, taking the ear-piercing shriek with it. Thankful for the silence, Fate checked on Eustace and Gerdie, then cautiously glanced over her shoulder at Farouk. "What the heck was that?"

"The impersonal supratemporal power of discreation," he answered.

"Yah, whatever that means." She edged toward the cloud of smoke hanging over Brune's still form. "All I want to know is, did it work?"

Waving the smoke away, Fate spotted Brune's face, now youthful as she stared at the ceiling. Thick, wavy blonde hair splayed over the floor as her hazel eyes moved and focused on her. Fate was shocked by her beauty. She appeared to be only a few years older than Fate–nineteen or early twenties–and had the flawless aesthetics of a model. Fate had been so focused on Brune's cruelty she'd never expected anything other than a warty witch. In fact, the stinky zombie would be almost preferable to her impossible good looks. At least then she'd find it easier to keep hating her.

Gerdie barreled past Fate and stooped over Brune. "I see you've got your pretty face back. Just remember, Brune, pretty is as pretty does."

Brune rose to a sitting position, knocking the combinator to the floor. The arms broke, sending the Orb rolling over the floor. She reached for it, but not before Gerdie snatched it from her grasp.

"That's mine," Brune said in a tone filled with authoritative rage.

Gerdie shoved it in her dress pocket. "Not anymore."

Brune's gaze shifted to the Rod, still stuck in the arm that had broken off the combinator. Fate lunged and grabbed the piece. "Oh no you don't. I'll hold onto this, thank you."

Glaring at them both, Brune rose to her feet. "I need the Orb. Without it, I'll just start aging. I can't go through that again!"

Farouk moved his cage closer. "No, Brune, we combined the Rod and Orb to bring you back. The restorstruction is sound. You'll age, but at the rate you humans are meant to."

Relief softened Brune's anxious expression. "That's good to know. Old age is a scary, scary thing. But being undead…that's an unholy nightmare." She fell quiet as a haunted look filled her eyes.

Fate couldn't imagine being trapped in a rapidly rotting body. She wondered what she would do if she'd been turned into a zombie. Would she be desperate enough to send an innocent girl into absolute danger just to save herself? She liked to think she'd never be that selfish, but she couldn't be a hundred percent sure.

Brune regarded her ripped, bloodstained clothes with a look of disgust. Without a word she walked over to a large cabinet, pulled out a fitted military jacket with pants and proceeded to shed what she was wearing to put the uniform on.

Always the gentleman, Eustace cleared his throat and turned away to afford her some privacy.

Once she was dressed, Brune visibly shook off what lingering trauma she'd been feeling and turned to them with a look of all business. "First things first. We need to lock the Orb and Rod away. I hardly think pockets are safe storage."

Gerdie folded her arms. "It's safe enough for me."

Fate threaded her gold chain through the rounded top of the Rod and clasped it around her neck. "Ditto."

Eustace shook his head. "Fate, you've seen what these things can do. I agree both pieces should be put under lock and key."

Fate could hardly believe her ears. He was siding with Brune. She opened her mouth to argue, when a loud hum suddenly interrupted, and the inner rings of the portal they'd come through started rotating.

Brune looked at Farouk. "Did you activate the portal?"

"No, I certainly did not." He marched his cage over to the tunnel of spinning blue light.

Brune watched him frantically wrenching on the lever next to the opening. "You never closed it!"

"That was always your job," Farouk argued.

"Did you forget that anything can jump into the stream?" She walked over to the table, grabbed a laser gun and aimed it at the portal. "Get ready, you idiots. I guarantee you won't like whatever's coming through that door."

10
EVERY ACTION HAS A CONSEQUENCE

"BOLLOCKS!" FINN THREW THE last book from the pile against the stone wall with a loud thud. The ancient tome's fragile spine cracked. Yellowed pages broke free and fluttered to the floor. Turning away from the table, he paced back and forth, furious and frustrated that he'd spent the whole night scouring through the last remaining books in O'Deldar's collection. All that was left were the mounds of scrolls, most of which had proven to be simple healing recipes, love and beauty potions and wealth spells.

The druid priest had obviously been forced to be the empress's nursemaid, rather than attend to the more important duties of being the king's counselor. What a waste. No druid worth his salt would lower himself to such mundane work, but then again, O'Deldar had to feign his allegiance to Moria all those years.

Every muscle in Finn's body coiled tight as panic set in. What if he never figured out how to leave Oldwilde? Every part of his being screamed no. That was a reality he couldn't live with.

Finn stormed over to a large chest and kicked it. His boot punched a hole in the wood and his foot got stuck.

"Bloody hell," he muttered as he struggled to pry his foot free. Giving it another good yank, he broke loose, stumbling backward as something inside the chest clicked and a shallow drawer pushed open near the very bottom.

Regaining his balance, Finn bent to have a look. "What have we here?" He reached for the thick, rectangular object wrapped in red silk. The moment the slippery cloth fell away, a nauseating wave of darkness washed over him. Pain spiked his brain and his limbs weakened. Unable to hold onto the object any longer, he dropped it and stared in surprise.

It was a book bound in weathered wood and held together by leather straps. Embedded within the center of the cover was an iron ornament in the shape of a trident crossed with an arch, or possibly a bow. The title was scorched in the language of the Sidhe near the bottom of the cover. Finn's Sidhe was a bit rusty, but he was fairly certain his translation read, *Feadh-Ree Triad*. The Feadh-Ree were the faery folk, but he'd never heard of any triad in connection with them.

Still reeling from the book's harmful emanations, Finn backed away until his strength returned. What the hell was O'Deldar doing with a sorcerer's grimoire concerning the Sidhe? Druids keep to the earth and are strictly forbidden from interacting with the fae. The Order's rules were in place for good reason. Finn had learned that lesson first hand when he and Fate had been captured by the dark faery in the *Book of Fables*. Why would O'Deldar have such a book? Had he been dabbling in the dark arts?

No. Finn refused to believe the druid priest was anything less than honorable. He would've sensed if the man had been an oath breaker of the Druidic Order when they'd first met. There had to be a sensible reason for holding onto the book.

Finn stared at the grimoire with increasing revulsion, but also with reluctant curiosity. What if the answers he was searching for were inside the book? The thought of opening it made his skin crawl.

But desperate times called for desperate measures.

Finn grabbed the silk and sniffed it. He recognized the pungent smell of juniper and the sweet citrus scent of agrimony. Both plants were used for fending off evil. Smart. O'Deldar had soaked the cloth in the plant oils to keep the dangerous energies from leaking out of the book.

Feeling slightly more confident, Finn used the cloth like a pot holder and lifted the book off the floor onto the table. But he'd need a lot more protection than the cloth could provide. Scanning the shelves filled with herbs, incense and talismans, Finn gathered his arsenal together and placed all the necessary items around the grimoire. After the last candle and incense were lit, he wrapped his hand in the silk and unlatched the strap holding the book closed.

As soon as he pried the cover back, a shadow filled the room and a hiss, like that of many snakes, emanated from the pages. Fear streaked along Finn's spine. He hated snakes, but even more than that, he loathed exposing himself to any kind of evil.

Especially after his recent battle with the darkness he'd been possessed by. He'd come horribly close to succumbing to the dark side. His actions toward Fate during that time had been unforgivable. Even now, he could barely face what he'd done. Was all this really worth the risk?

The first of the Order's moral codes asserted itself: *Every action has a consequence that must be observed and one must be prepared to compensate for the action*. There was no way of knowing what he might set loose if he delved too deep. Some actions can never be remedied.

"Stay Whole." Finn ground his teeth as he shoved the warning aside. He didn't see any other option. He had to forge ahead.

Bracing himself, he flipped each page, scanning illustrations of plants and the making of dangerous tinctures and potions, skimming the details of questionable rituals, all while being careful not to read any of the text aloud. Finn knew too well the power of the spoken word. Fate's use of the Words of Making, and the trouble they had caused, were proof of their power.

Finn had no idea of what he was searching for, but he felt certain he'd recognize it on sight. Unfortunately, that meant going through the entire book page by page.

Somewhere around the halfway point, Finn stopped when he came to a diagram of two worlds with a wall of fire between them. At the center of the firewall was a gateway in the shape of a triangle. Each point was marked by a Sidhe symbol. Was this the Triad?

A queasy feeling came over him as he turned to the next page. He read through an exhaustive description of how to prepare the summoning and ultimate negotiation with the Triad, the gatekeepers in charge of opening the portals between worlds.

The ball of dread forming in his stomach eased slightly. Surprisingly, the author of the book didn't appear to be an evil sorcerer. He was a monk who once walked both sides of the old world and the new. He called himself a keeper of the Holy Magic, a very dangerous magic that invoked creatures of fae to do his bidding in the name of truth and light. He went by the belief that humankind was made in the image of the one true god and therefore had the right to command all other creatures. Only there was one major catch. The spell caster must be beyond reproach and be someone of pure heart, who had thus far remained untouched by any invasion of evil.

Finn gulped. "Guess that rules me out."

11
THIS CAN'T BE FOR REAL

BRUNE TOOK AIM AS something hurtled into view.

"No wait!" Fate shouted.

Brune wasn't listening.

Fate leaped at her, knocking the laser gun's beam straight up. The deadly red ray scorched the bronze ceiling, melting metal, leaving a deep glowing groove in its wake.

Recovering her balance, Brune swung around with a punch to Fate's ribs. The blow hurt, but it wasn't enough to knock the wind out of her, thanks to her leather armor.

"Hey!" Eustace yelled.

Fate waved him off. "It's okay, I'm fine." She would've returned Brune's invitation for a good fight, but Jessie slid into Fate's legs.

Blinking in shock, Jessie gave her a little wave. "Hi."

Fate offered a hand to help her onto her feet. "Jess, I told you to stay behind."

Jessie teetered in place. "That's what I did. But the door never closed." She glanced away with a guilty look. "On account of my foot being in the way. All I did was take a look inside. When nothing happened, I sorta walked into the janitor closet and still nothing happened. But then Darcy and the others came into the storage room. I was trying to hide from them to keep your secret. When it looked like they might find me, I took one extra step backwards, that's all. Then blam, I was shooting through some crazy wormhole." She rubbed her arm. "And it wasn't fun at all. It was really scary. And painful."

"I know. But you've got to go back." Fate turned to Farouk.

"Fire it up again, Jessie's going home."

Brune barred her way. "Nobody's leaving."

Jessie shrank from her. "Who's she?"

Fate stepped in between them. "Jessie, meet Brune, best remembered as the zombie."

"Really?" Jessie looked Brune over. "Who Dorian Grayed her?"

"I did."

Jessie's eyes grew huge and round as she took in her surroundings. When she saw Farouk, she gasped and pointed. "What's *that*?"

"Not really sure what *that* is," Fate said, "but it's calling itself Farouk. And it talks weird."

"I'm not an *it*. He will suffice," Farouk snapped as he continued to struggle with the lever for the door.

Brune pointed her laser gun at Jessie. "I can't allow you to leave. We have a secret to protect."

Eustace placed his hands on Jessie's trembling shoulders and moved her behind him. He held his chin high as he glared at Brune. "You will *not* harm this girl."

Adrenaline shot through Fate's heart as Brune aimed the gun at Eustace. "You shoot my dad, and I'll have you wishing you'd died of old age."

Eustace looked at Fate with renewed fear in his eyes. "Fate, don't–"

Gerdie stomped over to Brune and kicked her hard in the shin. "Drop the gun or I'll swallow the Orb." She popped the Orb into her mouth.

Brune stared at Gerdie in horror. "You wouldn't."

"I would."

Brune dropped her aim. "Alright, but she's here for good now. There's no letting her leave. If the world finds out about–"

"I think it already has," Farouk yelled. "There are more

coming through!"

All eyes turned to the blazing, churning portal as it spewed a clump of bodies into the sanctuary. Groans of pain came from the tangle of limbs before Fate recognized one of the voices.

"Get off me, jerk!" Darcy yelled as Lincoln continued to lie on top of her.

Mason lifted his head off the floor, but he couldn't move. He was pinned under Steve. "You heard her. Get the hell off my girl." He jerked his shoulder to jar Steve. "You too. Move your junk before I lose it on you."

Steve shifted onto all fours and hovered over Mason as he shakily glanced around.

Fate shot Jessie a frown. "You told them?"

Jessie's mouth dropped open. "No, I swear I didn't!"

Brune grabbed Lincoln, jerking him to his feet. "Hands on the wall!" She waved her laser gun at the others to do the same. Within seconds, she had the demon goblin, warlock, witch and shadow elf facing the wall with their hands raised. Each of them looked confused and a little nervous, but not nearly as scared as they should be.

Brune stormed over to the portal, grabbed the lever and thrust it down. The iris spiraled inward until it ground to a tight stop. She sneered at Farouk. "And that's how it's done."

Crossing his furry arms, Farouk dropped into his seat, silently mimicking her smug expression.

Darcy twisted around as far as she could, while still keeping her hands pressed to the wall. "I demand to know what's going on. This is America, we have rights."

Brune strolled over to her captives. "That's rich. You couldn't be further from the truth, or America, for that matter. And let me tell you about your rights. You lost them the moment you stepped into my domain."

Anger stirred in Fate. If the Keep belonged to anyone, it

belonged to her now. She was the new guardian. Not Brune. Yet her great aunt was acting like the changing of the guard had never happened.

But it had. Fate had signed her life away and taking the oath had changed her. Something new boiled in her blood. She felt protective of the Keep, and with it, a terrible sense of imminent danger that was growing worse.

Still, there was much she had to learn about this place and her new position. It was painfully obvious she needed Brune to at least teach her the basics. She would have to tread lightly. "Brune, you don't need to be so heavy handed about all this."

Brune turned to her. "Heavy handed?" she scoffed. "Look, greenhorn, you have no idea what's at stake here."

"Farouk filled me in about the scavenger."

"That's only part of it. There are other things loose in the Keep."

"Like what?"

Brune glanced at Farouk. In that instant, Fate detected a hint of shame in Brune's eyes. "We'll get into that later. Right now, we need to figure out what to do with these intruders."

Darcy dropped her hands and turned all the way around. "Intruders? It's not our fault your portal thingy sucked us up and dumped us here."

Brune turned to her with an icy stare. "It's not my fault you stuck your nose in where it's not welcome."

Darcy threw up her arms. "Fate, WTF?"

Steve snorted. "I think in this case, the abbreviation lacks a certain punch."

Darcy ignored him. "This can't be for real. Are we being punked? Like, really. What's going on?"

The others dropped their arms, chiming in with questions, some laughing nervously.

Lincoln removed his vampire fangs and skin cap, revealing a

cropped afro gelled into random spikes. He looked to be about sixteen, a lanky version of a young Will Smith. Right down to the mischievous grin. "Dude, thish ish one crazay prank," he said, surprising Fate with a lisp she'd blamed his plastic fangs for. "Were we on a shlide? And thoshe lightsh! Talk about trippy. My brothersh will be jelly when I tell them about thish!"

Mason snapped shots of Farouk with his phone. "And what about this little dude? Killer animatronics, man. I gotta blog this!"

Steve squeezed his cane as he studied the sanctuary with nervous excitement. "Guys, I don't think this is an amusement park. The books in here look like collectibles. Expensive ones." He glanced at Fate. "This is a secret vault inside the bookstore. It's where you keep all the really good stuff, right?"

Their reactions reminded Fate of her own initial response when she'd first been thrown inside the *Book of Fables*. She'd thought she was dreaming, or worse, insane. It had taken a long time to accept the unbelievable. "Guys, you're all way off base. This isn't some elaborate hoax or fancy amusement park, of which I could never afford to build. Steve's the closest to what this is, but it's nowhere near Fables Bookstore. Or Earth. We're on the other side of the universe. This is really happening."

"Ooh, so scary," Darcy said, faking a shiver. "Come on. You expect us to believe that? We all know your motto: *Reality sucks. Make-believe rocks.* But really, enough's enough."

Mason frowned at his cell phone. "Hey, I've lost service. You got wi-fi here? What's the pass?"

Fate walked to the breaching door. "Fine, if you won't believe me, believe your own eyes." She swept her hand over the control panel as Farouk had done. The others gathered around as the glimmering light spread over the wall, turning it transparent to reveal the sprawling Keep down below and the glittering stars beyond the gigantic sweeping hoops.

Silence fell over the group and mouths gaped open as they stared out at the incredible sight. Fate couldn't help staring either. She didn't think she'd ever get used to what she was seeing.

Mason pocketed his cell phone. "How are you doing that? It's gotta be some sort of projection." He glanced over his shoulder, searching for the source.

Jessie stomped her foot, startling everyone. "Guys, this isn't being faked. I had a hard time swallowing it all too, but believe me, everything's for real."

"Nobody's talking to you, sidekick." Darcy's glower fixed on Fate. "Look, you've proven yourself to be the ultimate queen of cosplay and larping, all rolled up in one big fancy package. We bow to you. But it's time we get back to the convention. I've got people waiting for an awesome night and the only way to do that now is to let them in on *this*. Plus, it's the only way I'll forgive you for hijacking my venue."

Fate threw her arms up in exasperation. "You got me. This is all one big joke. And if you try to leave, Brune is only going to laser tag you with her plastic ray gun. She's a real hog for points."

"Count me in. I've been thirshty for a game of lasher tag," Lincoln said.

Darcy folded her arms and scowled at him. "We're not playing laser tag. I've got a cosplay contest to judge as soon as we get back."

"I'm down for some laser tag," Mason said, avoiding his girlfriend's glare.

"Give me a gun, let'sh do thish." Lincoln bounded across the sanctuary, pushing books aside, tipping jars over and poking around the bookshelves in search of laser guns.

Brune stormed over, grabbed him by his purple robe and slammed him against the table. "Stay out of my stuff."

"The name'sh Lincoln, beautiful. But you can call

me Lincbaby."

"I don't care if you're name's God, keep your mitts off my things." She turned to everyone else. "That goes for all of you!"

Lincoln raised his hands in surrender and laughed. "Whoa, I like how you're gettin' into your role." He looked her over appreciatively. "I reshpect that. Go ahead, rough me up all you want."

Brune's face wrinkled with disgust. "You're nothing more than troll slop to me."

He laughed again. "Game on, girl." He glanced from side to side. "So where'sh the gunsh?"

Brune whipped her laser gun out and stuck it under his chin. "Right here, little boy. How'd you like your skull aerated. One hole, or two?"

"How about a kish firsht?"

Mason stepped in next to Fate with worry in his eyes. "The gun's not real, right?"

Fate flapped her arms in defeat. "Yeah, no worries. It's only lethal if she pulls the trigger."

Mason shot Lincoln a concerned look. "Dude, quit messing with her."

Brune shoved Lincoln and stomped over to Fate. "Do something with these…pests, or I will."

Fate stared her down. "What do you expect me to do? You won't let them leave."

A sneaky sort of smile spread on Brune's face. "I say we let them loose in the Keep. Let them get their game on out there."

Fate fumed silently as she stared into the face of the person who had so callously thrown her into the *Book of Fables*. She already knew Brune didn't hold blood relations in high regard, which made everyone else nothing more than bugs to be squished.

Gerdie appeared next to Fate and pointed. "Uh…I think

somethin's out there."

Fate followed the line of Gerdie's hand, staring into the distance as she stepped closer to the transparent wall. A dark shape skimmed over the rotating landscape. At first glance, it looked like a small helicopter, except that it didn't move right. The sweep of gigantic wings heaved the body through the air. Was it some sort of enormous bird? But even as she thought the question, her gut clenched with fear. A distant roar echoed across the Keep, muffled only by the walls of the sanctuary. "What the heck is that?"

Brune stepped in beside her. "That would be a Chimera."

"As in fire-breathing lion with a snake for a tail and big bat wings?"

"Pretty much, give or take a little goat and hawk."

Everyone clustered close to the wall, watching the beating wings of the beast as it flew straight for the sanctuary. Within seconds it was upon them, filling their field of vision. The beast growled and flames splashed against the wall, before it rammed against the breaching door. The deafening impact and terrible scrape of claws resounded through the metal walls.

Screams filled the sanctuary as everyone scrambled away from the sight of the thrashing beast. Darcy clung to Mason as he shakily filmed the monster with his phone, while both Steve and Lincoln dashed for the back wall of the sanctuary and hid behind the table.

"Game over, man! I want off thish ride!" Lincoln screamed.

"Is it gone?" Steve asked as he peeked over the table's edge. He slowly stood when he saw that the Chimera had retreated.

"Promptdictable as always," Farouk said, 'It's been doing that every hour, since you first led it to the door, Brune."

"Don't give me that look," Brune snapped. "I was running for my life. It's not like I sent it an engraved invitation."

Farouk's eyes glazed over with boredom. "Yes, yes, we've

already been over your monumantic messbacle. Disfortunately, that does not undo the fact that you unleashed a host of monsters, while also failing to termiclude the scavenger."

"Host of monsters?" Fate asked. "There's more out there besides that thing and the scavenger?"

"Oh yes." Farouk's furry chest heaved like he was tired. "There's a pack of Fomorians slithering and sliding about down there."

"I've never heard of those before."

"Fomorians are an ancient race that have eludevaded historical accounts with any real exacturacy, because of the chaos and confuddlement they cause anyone who crosses their path. It will be tricksome dealing with them."

Fate groaned. "This just gets better and better. Anything else I should know about?"

Farouk grew quiet as he studied each face staring back at him. His slanted gaze slid to Brune. "I've been running diagnostifications–both surface and subsurface. The readings are registering a disturbtion we've never seen before. Gears are slowing and some have even begun to turn in the opposite direction."

Brune shifted her feet and looked the other way. "It must be the scavenger. God only knows what it's eaten into by now. Have you been tracking it?"

Farouk seemed insulted by her question by the way his ears stood straight and the whiskers of his snout twitched. "Of course. The scavenger is in Quadrant 56 as we speak. So far it's been staying on the surface, though it did destructalize a moving belt, which is attached to several gateways. Seven to be exact. Each one has remained open. Maintenance bots have already repaired the belt, but as you know, they are ill equipped for knowing the perplexacies of closing and restructifying the gateways. Nothing has come through them so far, but it's only a matter of time before some sort of nastilence makes its way out."

"Doesn't sound like anything too unmanageable. I assume you already have a supply of materials needed for welding the gateways shut." Brune strapped on a belt of glass bullets filled with glowing red liquid.

"Of course, but you miscomprestand." Farouk's tone grew impatient. "This is not the disturbtion of greatest concern. I've been getting readings from the core."

Brune stopped shoving her supply of radioactive-looking bullets into the chamber of a long rifle wrapped in copper tubing and stared at him in disbelief. "What? That's impossible. We never get readings from the core. Isn't it supposed to be made of solid crystal or something like that?"

"We've never known for certain what the core is composulated of. Or what's inside…until now."

Fate waited for Farouk to continue, tensing with each second he remained quiet. Something in his tone set her nerves on edge.

Brune cocked the rifle. "Well, are you going to tell me or wait 'til I die of old age again?"

Farouk leveled his slanted gaze on Brune. "The readings are picking up signs of movement inside the core, and of an organtic nature."

"You mean signs of life?"

"Yes," Farouk said in a hushed tone. "Something else is down there."

12
DRAGON EYE ME

"WHOA, THAT WUSH SHOME uber shuspenseful dialogue jusht now." Lincoln stepped out from behind the table with a swagger. "Who'sh writing the shcript on thish? Cuz I gotta shay, bravo."

"Dude, stay woke. This is all for real." Mason pointed at Farouk. "Including that talking Franken hamster."

Steve came out from behind the other end of the table. "Yeah, so stop strutting around like you're all that. We all know you lost it and screamed like a little girl." He looked at Gerdie. "Even the little girl in the room didn't scream as high as you did."

Lincoln pushed him. "You throwin' shade on me? I wushn't down there on the floor by myshelf."

"Oh shut up!" Darcy fumed. "I'm with Linc. We can't go swallowing this hook, line and sinker. None of this is scientifically possible. Putting aside what we've seen, do you actually believe we're not on Earth anymore and that we've been thrown across the universe?"

Steve and Mason were silent a moment. Then Mason laughed. "She's right. That's ridiculous. Cancel what I said."

Steve nodded and shook his head. "Ditto."

"Idiots," Brune muttered. She strapped some kind of jet pack with dragonfly shaped wings on her back, slung her rifle over her shoulder and walked over to Fate. "I'm going out there to weld the broken gateways shut. I estimate it'll take me anywhere between four to ten hours, barring any serious interruptions. If you don't have every single one of these stowaways whipped into shape by the time I get back, I'll personally feed each one of them to the Chimera."

Fate scowled at Brune, but kept her lips pressed tight. She wasn't about to give her the satisfaction of arguing. "Aye, aye Captain."

Brune chuckled silently and slammed her fist on the button above the breaching door's control panel. As the hatch spiraled open, she turned to the others. "Did you hear that? You either soldier up and start falling in line, or you're all breakfast, lunch and dinner for whatever comes a-knockin'." Sneering at their confused expressions, she jumped, freefalling out of sight before she rose into view, the wings of her jetpack an invisible blur as she turned and flew into the heart of the Keep.

Mason covered his mouth and pointed at Brune. "Did you see that?"

Lincoln was right next to him, his head bouncing up and down. "Oh yeah, where can I get me one of thoshe?"

Mason let out a low whistle with a dreamy look on his face.

Darcy pulled Mason away from the hatch. "Forget it. You'd kill yourself on that thing."

Eustace stepped in next to Fate. "Well, Brune's a real breath of fresh air."

"More like a bag of hot air." Gerdie crossed her arms as she watched Brune become a tiny speck against the massive surface of the Keep.

Fate walked over the table and leaned against it. "She's got a point though. These guys don't stand a chance if I don't figure out some way to prepare them for–"

"For what? Fighting mythical beasts?" Eustace frowned with disapproval. "I hardly think these kids could fight cranky kittens, let alone what we just witnessed outside these walls." He shook his head as he perused the clueless group: Lincoln bouncing in place and punching the air, Steve sneaking around the bookshelves, Mason holding his cell phone high over his head to get a signal, while Darcy nagged at him to be a man and demand their release. It was obvious they still hadn't accepted the truth of their situation. "I say we send them all home. Brune's not here to stop us anymore."

"But I am." Farouk raised his cage to its full height and charged it over to the portal."They cannot be allowed to leave. They will broadcast the positionality of the portal, and once they do, the whole world will come rushing in."

Fate could hardly argue. The footage Mason had just recorded would be all over the internet within seconds of his return. "If they have to stay, then you better have some suggestions for turning them into at least bicycle police, if not soldiers. I certainly know Brune's crazy enough to make good on her promise."

"You've got that right," Gerdie agreed.

Farouk lowered his cage to eye level with Fate. "I may be able to offer a fixlution that can instasuddenly turn anyone into a master warrior. But I must warn you, anyone who is weak-willed may suffer side-effectuals."

"What is this…'fixlution'?" Fate rolled her eyes at the ridiculous word.

Farouk leaned close, his small hands rubbing together as his devil-pointed ears leveled out, giving him a sly expression she didn't like. "I've been tinkering with an ancient form of martial alchemistry over the past thousand years. All that's been missing are my test subjects, but now it appears I finally have some."

"They're human beings, not lab rats." Eustace's normally calm voice cracked with anger.

Farouk's ears popped back up, his eyes wide as he nodded. "Of course they are, and I respect that."

Jessie raised her hand. "I'll go first. I've always wanted to be a ninja."

Fate lowered her friend's hand. "Uh-uh, no way. We'll try it on Darcy first. She's been getting on my nerves all night."

Eustace admonished her with a frown.

"Just kidding. Mostly."

"I assure you, the procedure is perfectlessly safe. In theory." Farouk muttered the last part.

"Test it on me first," Fate offered. She missed her super powers and desperately wanted to replace them with something that would give her more confidence. "If all goes well, we'll ask the others if they want to be ninjaed. I don't care what Brune says, we're not enlisting the draft here."

"No, Fate, I will not stand by and watch you risk your life," Eustace argued. "I'll be the first test subject."

Fear drilled through Fate. He didn't know it, but he was her Achilles heel. If anything happened to him, she wouldn't be able hold it together anymore. "Dad, you can't. Somebody's got to make sure this caged rat doesn't pull anything funny."

Farouk's snout wrinkled at the insult.

"Besides, I'm the Keep Guardian. It's my duty to take the lead on this."

Farouk shook his head. "That may be so, but experitesting on you is too riskylous. The Keep needs its guardian. That's why test subjects have been in short supply around here."

"Well, that leaves me." Jessie smiled wide.

Eustace frowned. "I can't let you.

"Dad's right, Jess," Fate jumped in. "It's way too risky."

Jessie's smile vanished. "Why? Because you think I'm weak willed and won't make it? Well, it's not up to you. This is my decision."

Gerdie tugged on Fate's arm. "You should really let her make up her own mind. Nobody likes to be treated like a helpless little girl. I should know."

"No, I can't. I just can't." Fate turned to Farouk in a panic.

"Give us another option."

"There is none. If you want to arm these lambs, follow me." Farouk turned his cage and steered it across the sanctuary toward a set of five large metal doors lining the far wall of the domed room. Each door was engraved with symbols that made Fate think of alien alphabets from movies. Farouk stuck an odd looking key into the hole in the center panel of a door marked with a series of squiggles, lines and circles.

Eustace, Gerdie and Jessie followed him inside, and just as Fate brought up the rear, Darcy called out to her. 'Hey, where're you guys going?"

"Just getting the five-minute tour," Fate called back. "Carry on with whatever you were doing over there. We'll be back in a sec."

Darcy grabbed Mason's hand and dragged him along behind her as she marched over to Fate. "Oh no you don't. You're not leaving us here to wait around with nothing to do."

Fate wondered if that glower Darcy was so fond of wearing was normal for her. "Fine, just–" she stopped as Lincoln and Steve crowded in as well.

Darcy set her fists on her hips. "Just what?"

"Never mind." Fate huffed and turned to follow Farouk down a long hall before entering through another door. When they crossed the threshold, everyone gathered around her, all staring in awe at the massive warehouse-sized room flanked on each side with tall iron columns the size of buildings. A complicated looking engine with lots of gears and moving parts hummed at the end of the mile long chamber. Artificial sunlight poured in through a series of opaque windows, each stretching vertically between the columns, making the place look like an industrial-style cathedral.

Set within the very center was a recessed arena as big as an Olympic pool. The bottom of the round courtyard was inlaid with geometric-shaped tiles in the form of a huge starburst. Farouk walked his cage down the smooth ramp leading into the arena. Fate and the others followed. When they reached the bottom, Fate noticed the walls were a good twelve feet high, much taller looking than when she'd viewed it from the top.

"Whoa," Steve said as he removed his sunglasses to peer at the vast ceiling. "I'm beginning to think we might not be in the bookstore again. Or even on Earth."

Fate squinted at him. "You think?"

"Does it matter? This place is off the hook." Mason high-fived Lincoln.

"All of you stop it. We're on Earth," Darcy insisted. "Don't you get it? This is some sort of underground base hidden under the bookstore." She narrowed her charcoal rimmed eyes at Fate. "Tell them the truth."

Fate seethed with frustration. "I've been telling you the truth! Get it through your thick heads already. We're not underneath the bookstore and we're not on Earth. We're floating in the middle of outer space, for crying out loud."

All of a sudden, the gravity of her words hit home and she felt sick to her stomach. She had no idea where they were in relation to Earth. The air caught in her lungs and the gnawing ache in her chest went from dull to painfully sharp. It was bad enough that Finn was caught in another dimension, but now they might be millions of light years away from each other. What had she gotten herself into?

She looked at everyone, seeing that her words had taken effect. Fear had wiped the grins off their faces.

Guilt set in. Had she been too harsh? She needed to remember how hard it had been to accept the impossible. She couldn't count the number of times Finn had talked her down off the ledge when she'd been in total denial of their grim reality after they'd arrived in the *Book of Fables*.

"This really is real?" Steve said, his already pale face growing chalky with fear. "What's happening here? Where the hell are we? I want to go home."

Suddenly, they were all talking at once in a panic, bombarding Fate with demands and questions she couldn't answer.

Eustace stepped forward with a stern expression. "Calm down, everyone."

The others fell quiet and turned to him, happy to have the only seasoned adult in the room take charge and help them make sense out of their insane situation.

Eustace continued, "Obviously, we're being faced with circumstances that have only been the stuff of fiction up until this moment."

Lincoln bobbed his head. "You got that right."

"And isn't that why you're all here?" Eustace asked. "You're seekers of adventure. You're open to the impossible. If you weren't, you wouldn't be here dressed as the fantastical characters you admire."

Relief set in as Fate watched her father do what he did best–keep her world safe, calm and manageable. The others no doubt sensed his grounded nature, because they were nodding, hanging on his every word.

"If you didn't have the same courage and strengths those characters embody, you wouldn't have been drawn to them." Eustace paused as he gauged their reaction. "You each need to trust that you're stronger than you think and that you have what it takes to face what's ahead."

"I don't know man," Lincoln interrupted. "I'm sho shketched right now, I'm ready to drop mud."

Eustace grimaced at the description, but quickly restored his composure. "That's alright. Having courage doesn't mean you're fearless, it means you're brave about facing what scares you."

Lincoln looked at Mason. "Man'sh got a point."

Eustace smiled. "If there's one thing I've learned, being prepared is the best way to face your fears. So who here wants to learn martial arts? Matrix-style."

Lincoln's and Mason's hands shot up in an instant. Steve and Darcy kept their hands down.

"Good." Eustace ignored Fate's look of alarm. "I'll leave it to the Franken hamster here to take over."

Farouk stomped one leg of his cage. "The name is Farouk. Anyone who addresses me otherelse will suffer severible consequences." His tone was low but his voice blared. He'd turned the volume up on the device he spoke through and it further tortured everyone's ears by echoing throughout the massive chamber in waves.

Fate sidled up next to Eustace as Farouk ordered his two test subjects to line up in front of him. "I don't know about this. Something tells me this could backfire horribly."

Eustace pushed his glasses to the top of his nose. "People need to feel they have a choice, Doodles. Besides, if we keep them powerless and unable to help themselves your job as guardian will be that much harder."

"Well, you're right about that. Just not for Jessie. We need to protect her from herself." Fate turned to look at her friend who was sulking and watching Farouk.

He was marching his cage back and forth in front of Lincoln and Mason like a drill sergeant. He finally stopped and pressed a few buttons on the small control panel set between the gears he used to steer his cage. One of the geometric stone tiles slotted loose from the floor and rose, becoming a short pillar the size of a public mailbox. A thick slab slid out of the top half. Embedded within its surface were a dozen round slots holding mechanical devices.

Farouk retrieved one of the gadgets and held it high. "This is a Dragon Eye tempora."

"Shounds like one of the daily shpecials from Poo-Ping Palashe," Lincoln said, causing Mason to burst out laughing.

Farouk ignored them. "Wearing it will imbue you with absoplete knowledge of dragon style Kung Fu."

"Oh, little dude, that's the bomb." Mason high-fived Lincoln yet again. "Lay it on us."

In their excitement, they both headed toward the pillar.

"Get back in line." Farouk's voice amplified to such a pitch, they clapped their hands over their ears. "These are not cupcakes I'm handing out. You must first comprestand what the effectuals will be. Your chi will be elevated to super human magniportions. Physical skill, strength and speed will be doublefied. Mental alertness and reflexes will be highly acute. If the chi is raised to ideal levels, any latent supernatural abilities you have will surfmerge."

Lincoln bounced around, gyrating his fists like he was dancing at a rave. "Dawg, even better! What're you waiting for? Jack ush in."

Farouk's gaze slid to Fate and Eustace then back to the boys. "There are risks," he confessed begrudgingly. "One of you may develop less than desirable side-effectuals."

"Do any of them include bleeding from the eyes, coughing up an organ or instant death?" Mason asked.

Everyone tensed as Farouk paused a touch too long. "Nothing along that line. They will be much worse. If your chi rejects the Dragon Eye, you may suffer severe confuddlement, perturbitude and phantascinations to the point of violent behavior or suicide."

Mason looked surprised. "Oh, is that all? We hear warnings like that on TV all the time. Let's do it. Dragon Eye me." He gave Darcy a peck on the cheek, then turned to bump fists with Lincoln.

Darcy scowled at them. "Fools."

13
THERE'S NOTHING CIVILIZED ABOUT FAERIES

FINN PLACED THE LAST of the ritual items on the corner of the purple cloth he'd found in the main part of the chest that had held the grimoire hidden. Everything he needed had been carefully packed away inside the wooden chest. He was familiar with most of the ingredients for the ceremony–crystals, feathers, holy blend tobacco, incense, sacred lamp and wand. Except for the cloth, which was embroidered with a circle of Sidhe symbols.

Finn slipped the white cloak made of flax over his shoulders, clasping the hook at his neck before donning the hood. It was clear to see by this ready supply of ceremonial tools that O'Deldar had performed several of the grimoire's rituals. The druid priest had obviously managed to come through them unscathed. If he hadn't, Finn would've sensed the presence of darkness in the man when they'd first met.

If only he could be as sure of his own ability to pull this off. He desperately wished O'Deldar had been present to do this for him.

Finn clenched his jaw. Dwelling on if-onlys was a useless waste of energy. He needed to trust that the time he'd spent encased within the oak and his connection with the Earthmind had thoroughly cleansed his spirit. He'd known without a doubt he'd been fundamentally changed for the better. It was time to start believing in himself and the purity of his intention to reunite with Fate. If nothing else, his love for her would surely protect him against the deadly fae he was about to invoke.

Taking a deep breath, Finn glanced down at the open pages of the grimoire and began reading the invocation aloud. With each word spoken, his mouth grew dry and his tongue seemed to thicken. As he neared the end, speaking the incantation became difficult.

The moment he spoke the last word, a murky brown haze formed above the ceremonial cloth. As the haze expanded, a sickly yellow glow gleamed at the center, growing brighter, spreading until it became a dull golden circlet surrounding a blue-green expanse shot through with veins of dirty brown. Dark formless shapes snaked within the portal's deep folds of space.

Finn's nerves stretched thin as he watched a frenzy of movement disturb the aquamarine clouds. They were coming. The shadows seemed to be coagulating, growing denser, larger. Within seconds, something pushed through the outer membrane of the portal. Before Finn could make out what it was, he did as the book instructed and turned his back to the portal.

An icy breeze raked past him as the sound of hooves clopped onto the stone floor. Clawed feet clicked, and something slithered off to other parts of the chamber, while the hoofed thing stepped close and sniffed his head. Stifling a shudder, Finn tightened his grip on O'Deldar's wand.

"Who is it that presumes he has the authority to summon us?" a deep grating voice asked next to his ear.

"Your master." Finn's voice sounded more like a choke. His mouth and throat were as dry as chalk.

A condescending chuckle filled the room. "Master of none is what you are. How can you be our master when you have no control over yourself? Remember what you wanted to do to Fate?"

Finn's face flushed hot with shame. The book instructed that the Triad would sense his weaknesses and seek to fill him with self-doubt and confusion.

The slitherer snaked along the wall Finn was facing, ruffling the heavy curtains. He closed his eyes before it could show itself to him. The book warned against looking upon the Triad, since doing so caused paralyzing terror and guaranteed insanity.

"I am endowed with the authority of the Lord of Light," Finn answered.

More laughter. "You are a filthy pagan and worship the old gods. What do you know of the new god?"

The book had said he'd be tested on his faith and character. He was to answer questions and challenges with politeness and moderation to keep the conversation civilized, which to Finn seemed ridiculous. There's nothing civilized about faeries. They are wild and unpredictable. Despite his dislike of them, he wasn't about to go against the book's advice while they were in the same room with him.

"Aye, you'll have to forgive me. I've never observed the laws of the new god. But as you know, I'm druidkind, which means I know your history with the Lord of Light and how He cast you down to earth."

Silence.

Finn almost smiled, knowing he'd stunned his inquisitor with secret knowledge.

"What is it you wish from us?" the hoofed one asked.

"I want to leave here and cross the fiery divide into the other world," Finn answered.

"What is this fiery divide you speak of? We know nothing of such things."

Anger burned hot in Finn's chest. What a lie! "Don't act daft with me. You know about it. I command you to speak the truth!"

"Very well, but the location is unknown to us. The Djinn

took control of the divide eons ago and have kept it cloaked ever since."

Hearing this made Finn want to go into a fit of rage. Fuming silently, he pressed his lips together. This was supposed to be a quick, simple transaction. He didn't have time for complications. "If I find the divide, can the Djinn open the gateway?"

"The Sidhe constructed the divide and it can only be opened by the Triad."

"Bloody brilliant," Finn swore under his breath. It was bad enough being forced to deal with faeries, but the Djinn too? He knew very little about them. "Send me a guide. One who knows where to find the Djinn."

"Fae do not deal with Djinn. Payment for such a request will exact a high price."

"Remember whom you're dealing with." Finn's voice pierced the room with an air of authority. "You may've hidden the truth from the rest of mankind, but I know you've been condemned to serve us. I owe you nothing for this."

The impatient stamp of a hoof against stone resounded directly behind him as something rough snaked across his foot.

Finn tensed. Holding the wand tight in his fist, he whispered an incantation, igniting the tip with a blinding white light. Growls and hisses filled the air as he listened to the fae creatures retreat to more shadowy corners of the chamber.

Letting out a sigh of relief, Finn loosened his grip on the wand, when suddenly a clawed hand slid over his shoulder, snatching away his only defense.

14
XENA'S IN THE ROOM

EUSTACE SLOTTED THE KEY Farouk had given him into the door marked with the Greek symbol for knowledge. It was the only mark they'd been able to recognize so far. Fate, Jessie, Gerdie, Steve and Darcy followed him inside.

"Now this is more my speed." Eustace stopped just inside the door and glanced around at the massive library.

"Oh, yeah." Steve walked over to a shelf and ran his fingers over the leather spines of a row of books.

The heels of Darcy's lace-up Victorian boots clicked over the marble floor as she strolled into the center, turning slowly as she took the place in. Somehow, she still managed to look unimpressed.

The library took Fate's breath away. Romanesque architecture housed countless books with walls stretching in half-mile lengths on either side. The shelves were stacked six stories high, each level divided by wraparound terraces. Intricate arches laced across a curved ceiling painted with frescos rivaling Michelangelo's Sistine Chapel.

"Sure thing, a bunch of dusty old books are so much more exciting than getting super powers," Jessie grumbled.

Fate tried to hide the hurt she felt. "Jess, we're just watching out for you."

Jessie's glare landed on Eustace. "What happened to your big speech about making our own choices?"

Eustace looked apologetic. "I'm sorry you're upset with us, but your mother will kill me if I allowed anything to happen to you."

"How's she going to do that if she's not here?" Jessie yelled, surprising both Fate and Eustace. Fate couldn't remember a time when Jessie had lost her temper with an adult. She was all about manners.

Jessie paced back and forth like a caged animal. "I know what's at stake here. We might never make it back home. This place is dangerous. I get that. But how am I supposed to defend myself when I'm stuck in a library? What am I supposed to fight those monsters with? Harsh language?"

Steve held a book with occult symbols embossed all over the cover. "You could use magic against them." They turned to look at him. All of a sudden he looked very warlocky to Fate.

"Put that away," Gerdie scolded him. "Nobody dabbles with the magics without my say so."

Jessie dropped into a leather chair with a loud huff. "Great, I can't even do that much."

"If you haven't noticed, I didn't get to be Dragon Eyed either," Fate reminded her.

"And you don't need to." Resentment darkened Jessie's expression. "Look at you. You're all muscled arms and kickass armor. And you already know how to fight. Watch out everybody, Xena's in the room."

Fate clamped down on the urge to tell Jessie to grow up. Her patience was wearing thin. Smoothing Jessie's ruffled feathers and worrying about how the others were faring with Farouk's questionable tactics at turning them into super soldiers was not what she should be focusing on. If anything, she should be out there with Brune, fixing what was broken and corralling the monsters that had been set loose.

Then she'd be free to do what she really wanted. Find a gateway back to Finn.

Eustace's voice interrupted her thoughts. "Jessie, I

understand your frustration, but there's another line of defense you may want to consider. Knowledge is every bit as powerful as brute force, if not more so."

Jessie folded her arms. "Yeah, that's what they all say, until somebody gets punched in the face."

Eustace placed both hands on the table between them and leaned forward. "You don't see me picking up the sword. Instead, I'm choosing to arm myself with knowledge about the monsters outside these walls. I want to know their strengths, and most of all, their weaknesses. If I do my job right, Fate and the others will have a better chance at defeating them. And surviving the attempt."

Jessie shot Fate an anxious look.

"But as you can see, that's a task far too immense for just me and Gerdie." Eustace waved his hand at all the books in the enormous library. "So I'd like to suggest we assemble a different sort of team here in the library. Jessie, Steve, Darcy? Will you join us?"

Steve hurried over. "Count me in. I haven't been playing a warlock just to look hot in these high rollin' threads." He sniffed and puffed his chest. "I've always been into the magics. Anybody want to have their cards read?"

"Not by some dabbler," Darcy grumbled.

Steve's back stiffened. "I'll have you know I'm a student of the mystical arts."

"Oh really? Then you must be up on all the history too. So answer me this. What are the Tarot's origins?"

"Hmm," Steve mused, his blue eyes glinting with mischief. "You probably think the Tarot started with a mystical sect of the Knights Templar. I believe they were located in Syria at the time."

Darcy's eyes widened. "Hardly anybody knows that."

"What's even less known is that the Tarot was introduced to

Southern Europe from India, via the Arabs."

Darcy opened her mouth, but she seemed to have nothing to counter what he was saying and promptly tightened her lips.

Eustace watched the silent war between them. "Uh…well, it's good we've got that settled." He looked at Jessie. "And how about you? Can we count you in as part of the team?"

"I suppose," she muttered.

"Excellent." Eustace winked at Fate.

She mouthed a silent thank you.

He nodded, before turning his attention back to the others. "Time to get to work then." He glanced around at the walls of books. "But where in the world do we begin?"

"Good question." Gerdie tapped her foot impatiently as she glanced around. "It's not like we can ask a librarian."

Suddenly, the sound of grinding stone echoed throughout the expanse. Everyone turned as the two giant roman pillars flanking the entrance to the library rotated, spinning a full turn before revealing a long, narrow doorway. When the pillars came to a full stop, out stepped two twelve-foot tall, wispy figures. They each had six flesh-colored arms, and might have looked like spiders, except that they were equipped with two inhumanly long legs attached to mechanical torsos. They had pale, expressionless faces made of the same flesh-colored plastic. The unsettling masks ended at the ears. The rest of the skull was made of brass machinery, blinking with gold lights, coils and sparking circuits. Their heads swiveled in unison upon long necks of copper tubing and wire as they gazed vacantly at Fate and the others. "What is it you seek?" they both asked in soft, modulated tones.

Shaking his head with a smile, Eustace laughed. "Everything you've got on the Fomorians please."

The robot librarians split off in separate directions, each easily scaling the bookcases to the upper levels with the ease of spiders, due to their many arms.

"And throw in whatever you've got on Chimeras!" Fate called after them. Ever since the fire-breathing creature had rammed itself against the sanctuary walls, she'd been dreading going out into the Keep.

After ten minutes of watching the librarians crawling over the walls of the library, they returned with several large stacks of books. Upon delivering the goods, the willowy robots stood by, towering over everyone as they gathered around the large table.

Eustace went through the volumes. "Hmm, it appears the Fomorians go as far back as Babylonian times. We have the seven tablets of Enuma Elish here. Correction. Eight tablets. How very curious."

"If you say so." Fate was entirely clueless on the subject. "Anything there on the monster who can't decide what it wants to be when it grows up?"

Eustace shoved three thick tomes across the table. "Try the Bibliotheca. The Chimera will be in there."

Fate grabbed one of the books and flipped through the first few pages. "What is it, some sort of dictionary?"

"More like an encyclopedia of myths and legends." Eustace didn't bother to look up from the volumes he was studying.

"I don't know…it all looks Greek to me. Literally. You do know I can only read English."

"Look again," Eustace told her.

Fate glanced down just as the Greek letters shifted to English. "Oh, that's too cool. But there's no table of contents. Please tell me I don't have to comb through all three of these humungous books. And here I forgot to take that speed reading course last year."

Eustace didn't answer.

"Dad?"

"The others can help you," he answered absent-mindedly.

"Okay. Which one of you book soldiers wants to pitch in?" Fate asked.

Steve chose one of the volumes. "I'll dig in."

Fate looked at Darcy, Jessie and Gerdie.

Darcy sat down next to Eustace. "Don't look at me. I'm on Fomorians with your dad."

Jessie held out her hand, though begrudgingly. "Fine, give me the other one."

Gerdie backed away with a sneaky smile. "I'll leave you to it. I'm gonna keep the librarians busy with some other stuff."

"Like what?" Fate asked.

Gerdie was quiet a moment. "I'll let you know if I find it."

"Sure." Curious as to what she was eluding to, Fate watched her head toward the other end of the library with the two robots following her. It wasn't like Gerdie to not roll up her sleeves and help. Whatever mission she was on must be pretty important for her to take a pass.

Sighing, Fate went back to skimming pages. Not too long ago, she would've devoured the epic myths inked on the pages of the ancient Greek tome in front of her. But her experiences inside the *Book of Fables* had changed her on so many levels. She'd grown far too accustomed to picking up the sword and charging into battle.

Impatience skimmed along her nerve endings. The restless warrior she'd become fought to be let loose. But it wasn't just that. She feared the oath she'd taken as Keep Guardian had permanently sealed a penchant for warfare. As far as Fate was concerned, she should be getting her ninja on with Farouk and the others. Not thumbing through books like the nerd she used to be.

"Found something!" Steve flipped his long hair off his shoulder with a proud sniff.

Fate slammed her book shut. "Thank the gods, cuz I gotta

say, Zeus's family soap opera is tired. I mean really, how many times do we have to hear about his dad wanting to eat him and his sibs? You'd think a peek at the original version would have a few surprises."

Steve stared at her with a big grin. "Well, I found it fascinating reading."

"I'm with Fate," Jessie agreed. "Mine's a snore too. Book Three's mostly about a bunch of characters who've never made it into any of the really good books and movies. I haven't heard of half of these jokers."

Steve sagged in his seat. "Guess that makes me the biggest geek in the room."

"No, that would be my dad." Fate's remark garnered no response from Eustace. He was too engrossed in his reading to hear her. "So whatcha got?"

Steve leaned eagerly in toward them. "There's a few ways you can take on the Chimera. The first is the obvious full on attack with whatever weapons you've got in hand. Apparently, arrows and spears will pierce the hide. There's a story in here about how Bellerophon used a lead-pointed spear to–"

"Not gonna happen," Fate interrupted. "I'm not risking third degree burns by getting close enough to spear that thing. I'll snag Brune's laser gun."

"Right, I guess that would be best," Steve agreed. "Well, you can also use magic to weaken the different animal powers and then take them out one by one. Not sure what book we need to find those particular spells in, but I'm sure the librarians can point us in the right direction."

"Is that it?" Fate asked. "Those are my only options?"

"There's one other, but it's trickier." Steve turned the page. "If you confuse and scare a Chimera, the different animal parts will turn on each other."

"You mean like make the snake strike the lion?"

"Exactly. Make that happen and you can just sit back and watch it self-destruct."

Fate frowned. "I don't know about that one. It's going to be hard enough getting past my own fear and confusion. How am I supposed to scare it? Jump out of the dark and say boo?"

Steve's enthusiasm flagged. "Sorry, the book doesn't say."

Fate realized her negativity wasn't helping. "Well, at least that's more than we knew five minutes ago." She gave him the thumbs up. "Nice work, Steve."

Jessie slumped in her chair and rested her chin on her hand.

"And you too, Jess," Fate added quickly. "Steve nailed down a few key solutions and you eliminated a whole bunch of other stuff."

Jessie flung her head back and stared at the ceiling. "You're welcome."

"What's wrong with you?" Fate asked. It wasn't like her sweet-natured friend to be so sullen. But then again, these were outrageous circumstances.

Jessie let her head roll slowly to where she could see Fate and studied her with an icy stare. "You know what."

Fate held her hands up, staring questioningly.

Jessie kept her cold gaze leveled on her. "Remember how long we worked on our Nightingale armor for last spring's Comicon? And the kickass routine we came up with for the contest?"

Fate smiled at the memory. "Uh huh, we totally crushed it."

"We worked on our look for an entire year. That's all we ever talked about. Like how much we wanted to be real wood elves with all those killer skills: archery, sneak, pickpocket, alchemy…" She looked Fate up and down. "Now you're all that for real. I'm not."

Fate's stomach twisted in a knot. She finally understood why Jessie was so upset.

"You know, I think maybe I should check on Farouk and make sure everything's Kosher over there. Want to come with?"

Jessie's hazel eyes widened with surprise. "What about all the research we're supposed to do?"

Steve put a finger on the page to hold his place and looked up from the book. "You two go ahead. I'll search for the Chimera weakening spells."

"Thanks a bunch." Jessie all but sprinted for the door.

"Yeah, thanks, Steve." Fate stood and waited for Eustace to argue against them leaving, but he continued to read without interruption. She'd never seen him so completely absorbed before. It troubled her a little, but she needed to remember how she used to be about her love of books and the fascination they once offered.

She glanced around for Gerdie so she could tell her they were leaving. Fate finally caught sight of her on the third level of the library with the robots. How had she gotten all the way up there? There weren't any stairs or ladders anywhere. Had she piggy-backed on one of the librarians?

Fate continued to watch Gerdie, wondering what she was doing. Her heart fluttered with hope. Gerdie had promised she'd find a way to get her back to Finn. Was she looking for some kind of map showing which gateway leads to Oldwilde? Fate wanted to climb the book shelves and hound her with questions.

"Where're you going?" Jessie called out.

Fate stopped and looked back at Jessie. She hadn't realized she was walking in Gerdie's direction. "Nowhere special," she replied before turning to join her. "Yet."

15
HE'S PAPER THIN

"THERE'S SOMETHING NOT RIGHT about this human," a feminine voice crooned next to Finn's ear as she tossed O'Deldar's wand to a neglected corner of the room.

Finn's pulse raced with fear. He'd done his best to hide the darkness he'd been touched by, yet this one seemed to have found him out. He desperately wanted to open his eyes, but he heeded the grimoire's warning and kept them closed.

She tugged the hood of his cloak away from his face and scraped a talon along his rune-marked temple "He's been marked by the Elder race."

The hoofed creature clopped back into the center of the room. "Hmm…unfortunate."

"Yesss, he's protected," the slitherer hissed.

Finn listened in surprise. The runes his friends, Grysla and Tove, had inked into his skin had increased his strength and speed to super human levels, but it had never occurred to him they would protect him against the fae as well. Gratitude toward the tree troll and her daughter rushed in. He owed them so much. First, for saving him from freezing to death in the Twisted Bone Forest. Second, for making him part of their family. And now they'd given him a shield in one of his greatest hours of need.

Did that mean he could look at these creatures without going insane? Possibly, but this was no time to be testing such things out.

The female drew closer to Finn, so close the heat of her breath fanned his face. It smelled of damp earth and moss.

"No, the Elder race runes aren't what make him…different," she continued.

Finn's heart skipped a beat. She was narrowing in. He had to stop her from probing. Otherwise, he'd lose his leverage in the negotiation.

"He's paper thin." Her talons clicked against the stone as she circled him.

Her comment astonished Finn. What was she getting on with?

Stopping in front of him, she tapped his chest with the point of her claw. "This one did not come from a mother's womb. He was conceived and born from pure heart's desire."

Finn stopped breathing. How could she possibly know he was Fate's creation come to life, a character she'd invented and fallen in love with? When he'd first found out he was merely the sum of meaningless words strung together on paper, his world had been ripped out from under him. His whole life had been a lie, the offhand daydream of a bored girl. The amount of grief and rage the awful discovery had caused him had been almost unbearable at the time.

In the end though, Fate's love and his own efforts to redefine himself had given him the foundation he'd needed to carry on. Yet, now that the wound had been reopened, the old anguish rose to the surface.

"Such a beautiful boy and so much pain," she whispered as she trailed her claw lightly down the length of his arm.

Swallowing the lump in his throat, Finn drew breath again and pulled away from her touch. He hated this emotional manipulation. It was time to put a stop to it. "I command you to find my guide immediately and take your leave of me."

"Bring forth a guide and let's be done with this," the hoofed one said, his tone impatient.

Finn breathed a sigh of relief.

"No. We must *all* agree that this almost human has authority over us," the female argued. "I contest his right."

Wanting to punch her, Finn clenched his fists.

"His humanness is not at issue. I sense a righteous mission, therefore we must obey," the hoofed one replied.

Finn nodded in agreement.

"It's true, a strong love lies at the heart of his mission, but pain distorts the purity of his intent," she said. "As sweet as this lovely boy smells, he reeks of loneliness and longing."

A queasy sense of defeat churned in Finn's gut.

"Are you sensing a stain on his soul?" the hoofed one asked.

The female fell quiet for a moment. This had been Finn's main worry all along. Once she probed deeper, she'd discover he'd been possessed by evil at one time. After that, it would only a matter of seconds before he lost whatever clout he had over the Triad. Then all would be lost as far as finding Fate.

"Possibly," she said at last. "I'll need more time with him."

She had to be lying to the others. Finn frowned with confusion, then cracked his lids to have a peek at her. He needed to see what he was up against. For a split second, he glimpsed a pair of shapely bare thighs and delicate kneecaps, which turned into flesh-toned feathers near the shins and the rough, gray scales of a raptor's claws at her feet. Before he could raise his gaze to view the rest of her, she jerked his hood down over his eyes.

"You really don't want to look upon my true form," she warned. "I promise. Your mind will break."

"What the–?"

"I'll stay and be his guide until I know for sure there's no mark on his soul," she told the others.

The room filled with silence.

"Very well," the hoofed one said as he clopped across the room.

The slitherer followed and Finn heard the crackling of the

portal as both creatures slipped through the gateway. He stood still, nervous and unsure about how to deal with the one that had stayed behind.

"Alone at last," she purred near his ear.

Needing to put some distance between them, Finn walked over to the heavy curtains and drew them back. The night sky was clear and moonlight splashed across the black ocean. "Why are you doing this?"

"Because the only way you're going to find your Fate is if you have a proper muse." She turned him around to face her. "Open your eyes and look at me."

Keeping his eyes shut, he shook his head. "What is this, some kind of trick?"

The voice she used next sent shivers over his skin. "Finn? Look at me."

"No," Finn croaked, barely able to speak for the wave of emotions crashing in on him. "Please, don't do this."

A hand touched his and fine-boned fingers laced through his own in an all too familiar way. Finn's heart hammered against his ribcage. He fought against looking at her, knowing that once he did, it would be the end of him. Yet, he could not resist. He desperately needed to see her face again. And with that, he lifted his gaze and drowned himself in the deep pools of Fate's cinnamon brown eyes.

16
KILLER UNIFORM

"HOLY CROW," JESSIE MUTTERED under her breath as they walked across the expansive chamber and stopped at the edge of the sunken arena. "It's the freakin' Borg."

Fate was too shocked to reply. She couldn't believe what she was seeing. In the span of a few hours, the goof, Lincoln, and Darcy's mild-mannered boyfriend, Mason, were almost unrecognizable. They were no longer dressed in their costumes. Farouk had provided them with burgundy military jackets, leather pants, gloves and combat boots. They were now soldiers who were sparring with astonishing expertise.

"Wow, those Dragon Eye gizmos actually work," Fate commented, while trying to hide her envy.

"Uh huh, and they look super cool. And kinda hot," Jessie added.

Fate didn't disagree. Their movements were confident and the headgear gave them an edgy futuristic look she found appealing. The Dragon Eye wrapped around the head, covering the forehead with an elaborate array of mechanisms, which circled down around one eye. Embedded within the cybernetic machinery clustered over the covered eye, was a gleaming, reptilian eye, which upon second thought, was disturbing.

"Ew, did I just see those Dragon Eyes move and look around?" Fate watched for a few minutes. Concern coiled tight in her stomach. Who was running the show? The soldier or the headgear?

Jessie waved her off and headed down the ramp. "I didn't see anything. Come on, let's get down there."

Fate followed lock step. She and Farouk needed to have a conversation. He was sitting back in his bucket seat chair, arms behind his furry head as he watched his test subjects with apparent satisfaction.

Fate banged on his cage. "I'm not comfortable with this."

Farouk gave a start and scrambled off his chair clenching his heaving chest. He caught his breath and frowned at her. "What are you doing here?"

"Checking up on you."

His ears angled back as he narrowed his gaze on her. "Unbligessary. Everything is working as calcumated."

"If by working, you mean you expected your Dragon Eye doohickeys to turn these guys into the Borg collective, then we have a problem."

"The tempora merely locks onto the nervous system and connectifies with the reptilian brain, allowing the Dragon Eye stone to governate the physical movements."

"Those aren't stones," Fate argued. "Those are creepy, blinking snake eyes."

Arrogance smoothed Farouk's frown. "There is much you miscomprestand. The Dragon Eye stones were mined by Shaolin monks of the Sui Dynasty and empowered with positive sheng chi energy and the honorable thought forms of Kung Fu masters."

Fate had to admit that sounded impressive, enticing even. "If they're all that, then I should be able to strap one on too."

"No, we cannot risk the guardian."

Frustration set in. She'd had months of intensive training with the best warriors in all of Oldwilde. The training had at least stayed with her, even if her supernatural strength and speed had abandoned her. She wasn't about to admit it out loud, but being shown up by a bunch of cosplayers who hadn't earned their training was really getting under her skin.

"I want to try the Dragon Eye on," Jessie pressed. "Along with a uniform."

"Jess," Fate warned, "We talked about this–"

Jessie stopped the words in Fate's throat with a sharp glare. "You just said you'd like to try it. And now you're stopping me? What's your malfunction? Why are you always trying to keep me down? Are you afraid I'll be better than you for once?"

The accusation stung. "No, why would you say that? Is that really what you think?"

Pressing her lips in a tight angry line, Jessie took the headgear Farouk handed her. "Where do I change?" she asked him.

Farouk pointed to in the direction they'd just come from. "Back up the ramp and all the way to the left wall to the weaponry room. The uniforms and swords are in there."

Hurt and confused by Jessie's outburst, Fate watched her best friend storm away. How long had she been harboring all that anger and resentment? The pain of it made her miss Finn all the more. Suddenly, the ache of him not being there, mixed with Jessie's hurtful words were more than Fate could face. She desperately needed a distraction from the compounded pain.

"Is there something I could be doing?" she asked Farouk. "Maybe I should go out and help Brune."

Farouk looked her over, as if measuring her worth. "Not before you have gone through your final initiation."

"Oh goody. And what horrors does that involve?" Fate stared back at the creature suspiciously. "This isn't like a college sorority hazing, is it? I don't want any food dumped on me. Unless it's chocolate syrup. I suppose I could handle that, but no marshmallow fluff. Got it?"

Perplexed, Farouk wrinkled his snout. "I knew you had pequirkuliar customs on Earth, but that one is nonsensical."

"Says the nonsensical sounding varmint. Which begs the

question. Why do you mix your words like that?"

Farouk stood still. Only his eyes moved, and for a split second Fate thought she glimpsed a flash of light, like the glow of smoldering embers. In that instant she felt fear without knowing why, but then the light blinked out and she wondered if she'd imagined it.

Farouk let out a sigh and tapped the device amplifying his voice. "The transmodulater mixes my words. The device is not always exacturate in its translation."

"You're speaking a different language?"

He smiled slyly. "You could say that."

He sounded Indian, but she was fairly certain he wasn't from Earth, let alone India. "What's the language? What are you?"

"Someday, if you've proven yourself uprightable, I might tell you. For now we must address your initiation. This is no small thing, and it should already have been done." He glanced at his small army of two. "I was not previsionating these others to have to deal with."

"You and me both."

"Wait for me in the sanctuary. I will join you, but first I must leave them with sword techcedures to master."

Fate fought the feelings of resentment rising as she climbed the ramp. She could see how Mason and Lincoln had given over to the power coursing through them. Their faces were emotionless, except for the glint of excitement in their eyes at the superior ability they'd been suddenly blessed with.

She remembered what that had felt like when she'd been inducted into Murauda's army. The war goddess's power had consumed her mind, body and spirit. Lightning, wind and untold strength and speed were all that had existed. She'd been made invincible. Most of all, Murauda had freed her of all emotional ties. The kind that weakened warriors.

The kind that weakened her now. Fate really had to wonder

how she was going to do her job when she was missing Finn more and more with each passing day, all the while worrying about everyone else's safety.

Jessie arrived the same moment Fate reached the top of the ramp. She was dressed in full gear, her dark hair slicked back in a ponytail and sword in hand. For the first time since she'd known Jessie, Fate felt as if she didn't recognize her friend. As gorgeous as Jessie had become, since she'd first hit puberty, she'd been self-consciously hiding her good looks behind her hair, wearing oversized fluffy sweaters with smiley faces and kittens, and always jeans, never skirts. For some reason, Jessie had always found it impossible to radiate any sort of confidence. Yet here she was, standing in front of her thoroughly self-possessed.

If circumstances were different, she'd be happy Jessie had finally gained some confidence. But this was artificial, and she especially didn't care for the disturbing look of detachment in her friend's face.

"Killer uniform. It totally suits you," Fate said. Unlike the others, who were wearing deep red military jackets made of canvas, Jessie had chosen a fitted, high-collared leather trench lined with two rows of silver buttons down the front. "How's the head piece feel? Are you all like…I know Kung Fu?"

Jessie thrust her sword forward, slicing the sharp tip within inches of Fate's nose in a figure-eight pattern. The blade whipped enough of a breeze to move the hair around her face. Before Fate could react, Jessie retracted the sword, bringing it down by her side in one swift movement. "I don't know, you tell me." Jessie's expression was indifferent as she brushed past Fate.

Fate stared in stunned silence as Jessie clomped down the ramp in her new combat boots. Heartache filled her chest and she turned away quickly to hide the tears welling in her eyes. She hurried to the exit, and by the time she pushed through the sanctuary door, she was sobbing.

She slid to the floor and hugged her knees. Why was this happening? If there was one thing she could always count on it was the constancy of Jessie's friendship. They'd known each other since kindergarten and had been inseparable ever since. Losing her best friend was every bit as excruciating as losing Finn.

The door to the sanctuary opened. Farouk clambered across the room and stopped in front of a glass cabinet. Hastily wiping her eyes dry, Fate gulped back the last of her tears and stood. Relieved that Farouk hadn't seen her crying, she walked over to stand beside his cage as he thumbed through a set of keys.

"What's the fancy helmet for?" Fate sighed, grateful for the distraction. She liked the look of the gleaming bronze helmet with its fawn-colored wings fanning out from polished disks of gold on each side.

Farouk unlocked the cabinet and stepped aside. "This is the helmet of Hermes."

"The Olympian god, Hermes? Aka, Mercury?"

"The very one." Farouk's tone was flat, almost bored. "Every guardian must pass the helmet's test as the final rite of passage."

"Hold on. Nobody said anything about passing a test. What about the oath I took? You know, the one where I signed my entire life away?"

"There are three rites. The first was agreeing to separate from your previous life by taking the oath. Passing through the Keep threshold was the second. The third is assuming your position as guardian through the absorbalation of Keep knowledge. Given that you survive the download," he added rather hurriedly.

"What the…?" Fate's breath stalled in her lungs. "I don't get it. You weren't willing to risk me getting suped up on Dragon Eye powers, but you want me to wear this death helmet?"

Farouk's ears stood less straight as he nodded. "This is how it's been done for thousands of years. But it should come as a comfortment that everyone in your bloodline has survived the initiation."

Fate swallowed the wave of fear rising beneath her skin as she removed the helmet from the cabinet. "Thanks, I feel so much better now." The metal was colder than it should be and sent a rash of goose bumps over both arms. "Can you at least tell me about the helmet and what I'm in for?"

Farouk glanced over his shoulder at the breaching door as if he worried someone might catch him telling secrets. "Hermes used this helmet to receive messages the gods wanted passed onto mortals. When the helmet came to the Keep it was retroquipped with discs encoded with all that is known about the Keep because the metal happens to be a splendillent conductor of information. We have used the helmet as a means of transhifting information to the guardians ever since."

"Okay, that doesn't sound so bad. What makes this thing so dangerous?"

"Hermes was a god and the helmet was never made for mortals to wear. Adjustifications have been made, but the download remains extremely invasive. While this can be painful, it is not lethal. The real danger lies in the abstract nature of the Keep knowledge. It has been known a time or two to push the human mind beyond what it can accept and it was rejected."

"And by rejected, you mean they died?"

Farouk nodded gravely.

Fate gulped. "Skipping past the possibility of my dying, how about we fast forward to the fringe benefits. And they better be pretty stellar, because I've got to be honest here, I'm thinking of stepping down and letting Brune have her position back."

Farouk's whiskers twitched with agitation and looked as though he might argue with her on that last point. But then he surprised her with a calm explanation. "The information is transhifted to the subconscious mind in the form of symbols and universal archetypes. Each time you have a question about the Keep, an archetype or symbol unfolds and is then filterated through the memory centers of your brain. Your answer will come to mind as if it has always been part of you."

Fate glanced out over the slowly rotating landscape of the Keep and the revolving hoops creating the artificial stratosphere. She could live a thousand years here, study every book in its massive library and still not know everything about this mysterious structure. Burning curiosity mingled with the ever-increasing sense of duty she felt toward the Keep. She wanted to know more and doing this would at least make her the guardian the Keep needed.

"Alright, let's do this."

Farouk's snout curled with the faintest smile as he gestured for her to have a seat. Taking a deep breath to calm her nerves, Fate sat down, raised the helmet over her head and held it there. "Farouk, if the worst happens, I want you to let my dad take all the others home."

"That will not be obligessary."

She frowned at him. "That's not an answer, especially when I'm not even sure what that means."

Farouk gave her a playful but dismissive wave. "I have no doubt you will return a fully initiated guardian."

Fate wasn't so sure and considered making a threat in case she didn't survive, but decided it would be an empty one at best, since she wouldn't be around to to enforce it if the worst happened. Squirming in the seat with nervous energy, she slowly lowered the helmet, surprised when the visor slid over her eyes and darkness swarmed in.

17
WE'RE DOOMED

THE DOWNLOAD HIT HARD, like a spike to the brain. Blinding light filled Fate's vision. Noise like the squeal of a boiling kettle and blaring horns pierced her ears. Fiery pain drilled down her spine, shooting scalding waves through her arms and legs.

Terror, like nothing Fate had ever felt, exploded in her heart. She reached to remove the helmet, but her body wouldn't respond. She was paralyzed, forced to endure the pain that had turned to a billion pins and needles pricking the surface of her skin, driving deep into her bones and organs.

The high-pitched sounds reached a crescendo, edging out every thought. All that existed was the stabbing pain and endless screech. She tried desperately to remember what had come before the torturous existence she now found herself in, but even her brain was beyond reach. Flashes of memory came and went, until all at once, her entire sense of self fell away.

Then merciful silence descended.

A kaleidoscope of vibrant colors, symbols and geometric patterns bloomed into view, becoming what looked like the mandalas of Eastern cultures. Hues of red turned to shades of violet. Turquoise mixed together with emerald lights shifted into brilliant tones of gold. This went on and on, each mandala exploding anew from the center, unfolding into an unending array of uniquely different shapes and colors.

The speed in which the mandalas shifted in color and design increased, each encoded with ancient knowledge held in secret for untold eons. They rang out musical notes one at a time, building into a celestial symphony.

An eternity flowed away in the span of seconds as mysteries unraveled. Systems of magic and universal truths unlocked. Veils drew back from time itself, until all that remained was the essence of forever.

The mandalas divided. First into two then four, eight, sixteen, until hundreds of them formed a grid of countless radiant dots. The grid reordered into crisscrossing, rotating ovals. The pixilated image solidified into a crystal clear scene of the Keep, viewed from a vantage point somewhere on the outside. Six giant rings whipped in opposite directions, creating the force field protecting the round metal structure that was the Keep. The cycles of each day played out. Powered by an ancient, magically infused technology, the massive gears on the surface turned, moving miles and miles of elaborate vaults with clockwork precision.

Time suddenly stopped and played backwards.

Fate's detached vantage point shifted to the Keep interior, where she observed the changing of the guard from the moment she herself entered the Keep, to Brune and her disastrous mistakes, to her great grandmother's time and down through hundreds of other guardians, all the way to the very first Keep Guardian.

Her journey backward showed how every girl lived solely to fulfill her duty to the Keep. Each was a lonely existence filled with careful routines, studies in magic, weaponry and relentless training. Very few had the opportunity to use their well-honed skills, but on the occasion when a creature escaped, or if scavengers grew out of control, the battles were bloody and often lethal. A grievous injury such as Brune's ended her time of duty and the next guardian was promptly summoned. This went on through thousands of years with Farouk in attendance, a constant presence and the only companion to each lone guardian.

But then the timeline shifted abruptly to one without Farouk and his human charges. Mechanical spiders crawled beneath the subsurface of underground cogs and wheels, repairing and maintaining the complex system. Gigantic robots with forklifts for arms were stationed near major portals, where a myriad of exotic looking vaults arrived from unknown locations on a regular basis.

Each was an architectural wonder made of rare and unusual materials. Most vaults were as large as temples, though some were as massive as pyramids, others as small as mausoleums. Regardless of size, each vault was unloaded by the robots and bolted to the main conveyer belts by worker robots to begin its century long journey through the Keep's orderly rotation along the surface, before sinking down into the underground and back to the surface again. This went on for an indefinite period of time without any sign of who or what had created the Keep.

Time suddenly reversed, thrusting Fate swiftly to the present. Her own self-awareness rushed back as she approached her own timeline. The further she moved from the distant past, the more she resisted. She hadn't learned everything there was to know about the Keep. There were still too many unanswered questions. How old was the Keep? When had it been built? Who were its builders?

Most importantly. Why had such a thing been built?

Fate watched the perpetual motion of the Keep increase as the years ticked by. She was literally running out of time. Somehow, she had to figure out how to put the brakes on. She already knew that whatever she focused on was what she'd been able to zoom in on. As images sped past in a blur, she searched for one constant to put her attention on.

Against the blue cast of the Keep's iron surface, she finally saw what she was looking for. Burning deep beneath the gargantuan gears slowly turning the grouping of vaults was the red glow of the furnace fires. Time began to slow as she focused on the radiant hot spot and her consciousness dropped into the bowels of the Keep.

The subsurface was dark and grimy. Steam belched from rows of pipes snaking endlessly over oily panels filled with complicated machinery. Cranes lowered robots down into the shadowy depths. Others were being hauled in large waste bins, their mechanical arms filled with slimy debris.

The roar of the furnace filled the cavernous expanse, its hellish fire casting a blood-red light over soot-stained surfaces. Beneath the incessant noise of the furnace were the constant thrum of countless moving parts and the grinding of giant gears.

She came upon a place where the machines were assembling the robots she'd been seeing. After running along a conveyor belt, each finished robot was dunked inside a vat of glowing aquamarine liquid–an infusion of magic that brought them to life. Every once-in-a-while the infusion failed and the dysfunctional robot was disassembled and sent to a scrap yard, which was filled with damaged, worn out robots and magical runoff.

Blue sparks came from these disparate parts. A few pieces came together, rebuilding into something new, though crude and unrefined. The sight was unsettling, but since any further information was not forthcoming, she lost interest altogether.

Feeling momentarily directionless, Fate felt herself lifting away from the scene. Her awareness was returning to her body. But she wasn't quite ready to give up. Once again, she searched for something to anchor her.

Glints of blue light sparking in the red murk caught her attention. Streaming in a single line, were thousands of spider robots. They were carrying what looked like glowing sapphires and disappearing with the gemstones through a hole the size of a bowling ball. Allowing her consciousness to follow them, Fate traveled the long winding tunnel into the very core of the Keep. At last, the spiders spilled out into a round chamber. It was a laboratory of some sort. Complex systems of glass beakers and vials, connected by reams of copper tubing bubbled with a luminous sea green colored liquid.

A robot Fate hadn't seen before until this point, was manning the laboratory. It was spindly in design like the many-armed librarian robots, but this one's head appeared to be made of flesh and bone, though not of a human. Faintly blue, wrinkled skin covered a large, bulbous skull. Flat facial features narrowed into a pointed chin.

Its round, bulgy eyes radiated light, which it used to zap the vials it was holding. The robot turned its electric gaze to the buckets of gemstones the spider robots were delivering. Scooping the stones out with a metal cup, the robot poured them into a blender, crushing them into a fine powder, which it added to the first of a long line of boiling beakers. The robot hurried over to the end of the line, where the liquid had become condensed, glowing neon blue, as it filled a tiny vial drop by precious drop.

Putting a cap on the vial, the robot rushed across the laboratory, pushed through a round hatch and juddered down a passageway lined with nothing but rusted pipes dripping with condensation. The robot stopped in front of the next hatch, pressed a code to open it and entered what appeared to be a utilitarian chamber with walls as tall as a hundred-story building. Slotted through massive notches in the walls were gears that stood still. Oily water lay in shallow pools over the eroded floor.

Fate's interest began to wane. As far as she could tell, all she'd managed to do was follow robots attending to routine maintenance of the Keep. They did not appear to hold the mysteries she'd hoped to unlock about the Keep's builders. She started drifting higher, giving the robot one last cursory glance, where it was fiddling with something in a shadowy corner.

Lights suddenly illuminated an elaborate shrine built into the dark corner. What Fate had assumed was merely another vacuous room that was somehow integral to the functions of the Keep was actually a temple to something or someone very important. Could this be a shrine to the original builder?

She pushed her awareness closer. The shrine was sculpted from metal, though now tarnished to a dull black. A master metal worker had crafted the piece to perfection. Sharp flourishes in the shape of wings radiated from a throne flanked by scaled tigers frozen in a vicious growl. Fierce, hawk-faced men wielding spears and shields stood guard next to the back of the throne. Women with the bodies of snakes entwined themselves at their feet.

But the central focus of the masterpiece was the most astonishing part. Sitting with a straight spine on a rigid throne was a woman dressed in intricate layers of armor and a helmet of lotus-style petals climbing into a decorative peak. Like the librarian and the robot she'd followed there, this regal woman also had six arms.

Something about this seemed familiar, but Fate couldn't pinpoint why at the moment. She was too drawn to the woman's face. She was sculpted from a pale blue stone. Perhaps Angelite, like the gemstone necklace Fate had at home. The woman's expression was peaceful and her eyes were closed. The artist had dabbed faint pinks on her lips and painted a light feathering of lashes on her lids. The soft, realistic touch gave the impression she was alive, while her body was encased in the sculpted armor that was part of the iron sculpture.

Or was this a tomb?

The thought saddened Fate. Especially when she noticed two small sculptures worked into the design of the throne. Just above her left shoulder was a man and woman embraced in a kiss. Over the right shoulder was the same couple, but the woman looked ill and he was holding her in his arms. How terrible. The woman must've died, leaving her grieving lover to build this lasting monument in her memory.

The tragedy of the two lovers triggered thoughts of Finn. Fate couldn't help wondering if she too was destined to be forever apart from him. Just thinking this brought about the most unbearable grief.

No. She refused to give up. They would find each other again.

The robot leaned in toward the woman with a vial in hand. The glowing liquid illuminated her blue face as the robot pressed the glass against her lips. Much to Fate's surprise, her mouth parted and the robot emptied the vial without losing a single drop.

She was alive!

More curious than ever, Fate pushed closer as the woman's six upturned hands began glowing with the same aquamarine color the robot had fed her. The energy turned to liquid, filling her palms to overflowing. The luminous liquid spilled and traveled along pathways sculpted into the sides of the throne, running to the floor, where it split off into several troughs. Within minutes, lines of aquamarine lit the expanse, becoming a complex geometric design, which touched the edges of the room. The massive gears notched within the walls began to turn, each rotating in opposite directions.

Fate didn't understand exactly what she was observing, but she wondered if this otherworldly being was the source of the magic running through the Keep. But who was she? How long had she been in this state of everlasting sleep?

Without warning, the woman's eyes opened. Black as night, they stared straight into Fate.

The robot was every bit as startled and staggered backward,

jabbering with excitement in an alien language. Ignoring the robot, the black-eyed woman ensnared Fate in her steely gaze. "*Who dares enter my Obiectis?*"

Her mouth never moved, but her words invaded Fate's consciousness like someone busting down a door. Shock reverberated painfully through Fate's awareness. She recoiled. The chamber shrank from view in an instant. The laboratory, furnace fires and grinding gears blurred by.

The second Fate's consciousness slammed back into her body, she felt the heaviness of her physical form as if it weighed hundreds of pounds. After experiencing the lightness of moving wherever her attention took her, the simple effort of lifting her arms seemed Herculean. Pain drilled along the length of her right forearm to her hand. She pulled the helmet off her head and let it fall to the floor in her hurry to inspect her burning palm.

She let out a small gasp when she saw what had been lasered into her upturned hand. Glowing beneath the surface of her skin, a round symbol spun within moving interlocking rings. It looked like a tiny version of the Keep. "What's this?"

Farouk pushed his snout through the bars of the cage, his eyes wide with concern. "The guardian seal." His tone was dismissive as he stared at her intently. "What happened?"

"Other than what appears to be this unsettling brand under my skin?" Fate struggled to catch her breath. "Nothing."

"I don't believe you. That helmet is only supposed to be on for one minute."

"How long did I have it on?"

"Nine minutes. Nine very prolingered minutes."

As Fate took in a shaky breath, her pulse began to steady. "What're you complaining about? It seemed like a hundred thousand years to me."

Farouk shook his head. "Did you see something you

shouldn't have?"

"How would I know? It was all new to me."

Farouk looked unconvinced. "Why did you stay in longer? No one has ever done that before. Did you deliberaposely seek something out?"

Fate chewed on her bottom lip. "Is there anyone else here in the Keep besides us? And I'm not referring to the monsters Brune let loose."

Farouk's grip tightened on the bars of his cage. "No. Why do you ask?"

"Sorry to drop a bomb on you, but we're not alone. There's someone else here and she seems to think she owns the place, except that she didn't call it the Keep. She called it the Obiectis. Why'd she call it that?"

"The Obiectis is what the original builders called the Keep." Farouk flopped back in his chair with his hand to his chest like he'd been shot.

"I don't know how, but she somehow knew I was there." Fate stared into space, seeing the woman's face as clearly as if she was in the room. "And let me tell you, she wasn't pleased. There's going to be trouble. Trust me, I know. I've run into her type before."

She thought back to Elsina and Moria, two dangerous sorceresses from the *Book of Fables*. For some reason they were extremely territorial and had a penchant for punishing trespassers. Fate frowned at Farouk. She was growing more uncomfortable with his stunned reaction by the minute. "I'm getting the distinct feeling you know exactly who she is, so start filling me in."

When Farouk didn't respond, she rattled his cage and he jumped in his seat. "She's awake!" he moaned. He grabbed the gears, shifting them haphazardly in an attempt to throw his cage into motion but they jammed and the cage lurched and crashed into the wall.

"Whoa, where's the fire? Why are you in such a panic?"

Farouk's furry little chest heaved as he worriedly wrung the tip of his tail. "We're doomed." His ears drooped and his shoulders slumped. "We're doomed."

18
CALL ME YOUR FAERY MISTRESS

FINN STOOD RIGID AS he looked at the faery who'd taken on Fate's form. She was an absolute duplicate down to every perfect detail. The same auburn hair that fell in wild waves to her waist, the pale skin blushed with the faintest touch of rose on her cheeks, and the wide questioning eyes that splayed his heart open every time. He began to shake from head to toe as she stepped closer. The heat of her body drew him in.

He couldn't keep himself from swaying toward her.

Lifting her chin, she smiled sweetly, then dropped her gaze to his mouth and ran her finger over his lips. "Kiss me," she whispered.

Her touch sent shivers through him as he stared at her mouth, softly pink and irresistibly moist. As wrong as this was, he leaned in, desperate to taste those lips. Before he could stop himself, he grabbed her by the waist and pulled her against him, pressing his mouth hungrily against hers.

Responding with a soft moan, she coiled her fingers through his hair. As Finn reveled in the softness of her lips, he probed deeper, when suddenly he met with something rough as sandpaper. Alarmed, he held still, as the awful realization came over him. She had the coarse tongue of a cat.

Pushing her away, he wiped his mouth with disgust.

She stared back, wide-eyed and innocent. For the first time he glimpsed something ugly lurking beneath the surface of Fate's lovely face. He hated this creature for using her beauty as a weapon against him.

"Finn, what's wrong?"

He turned away from her. "What's wrong, is you're not her."

"But I can be," she insisted. "Having her with you will inspire you. You're going to have to do whatever it takes to cross over to her and you'll need something to keep you strong during those times. Especially when all seems lost. Let me be your muse."

He shook his head. "No, I can't have you looking like her. It's not right. You're not worthy. You're some hideous thing and she's..."

"Your angel?"

He didn't answer, but she'd hit the mark. Fate was everything he'd ever wanted–beautiful, smart, funny, kind, and most of all, entirely unpredictable She was always surprising him. Sometimes in ways he could do without, but deep down, he liked that she kept him on his toes. As far as he was concerned, Fate was perfect for him.

"I can be everything she is and more." The faery touched his back.

Keeping his gaze averted, Finn jerked away from her. "Leave me alone! I don't want you here. Go back to the Triad. I'll summon you once I've located the divide."

"If you find it."

"Oh don't worry, I'll find it. Even if it kills me."

"A very likely outcome," she warned. "The Djinn live in the Mirajaran Desert. The name means phantom expanse. Without a guide, you won't know the difference between reality and illusion. Only the most seasoned humans know how to navigate that desert."

Finn turned to look at her again, his heart twisting painfully against the false vision standing before him. "How are you able to do this?" he asked, barely able to choke out the words. "How is it you can look exactly like her...sound like her?" He closed his eyes against the pain welling in his chest. "You even move like her."

"Your unusual connection with her makes it easy for me," she answered. "Her essence is part of you, yet without her, you are incomplete. Your longing for her will be your undoing. I must say, I haven't felt this kind of passion, desire and pain in a very long time. Whether you're willing to admit it or not, you need a muse to keep you going."

Bunching both fists at his sides, Finn fought against her offer. Everything about this was wrong. He should banish the faery. As her summoner, he had the power to do it. But seeing Fate here in front of him, even as a lie, had awakened something weak and greedy inside him.

"You can stay." Shame churned in his gut. "But you can only look like her when I need you to. And when you're not looking like her, you'll keep your true form. I need to know what I'm dealing with."

"Your small human mind can't handle what I look like."

"Beg to differ with you, love. I suspect the Elder race runes will protect me just fine."

He caught the recognition of truth in her eyes before she glanced away. "Very well."

The words were no sooner out of her mouth when the air wavered around her, distorting the image of Fate's face and form. Finn gulped down his revulsion as an oily black swamped the brown of her eyes in glistening darkness, while an angular bone structure replaced the soft planes of Fate's features. Her auburn hair gave way to a wild main of straw-colored hair shot through with feathers. The texture of her clothes became yellowed skin covered in down. Quills daggered her arms, thighs and shins. Her hands and feet curled into bird claws.

"What are you?" Finn asked, watching in horror as a pair of large, membranous wings unfurled from her back.

"Some would call me your faery mistress."

Chills ran over Finn's skin as his grandfather's warnings surfaced from the past. This was a faery known on the Isle of Man as the Lhiannan Shee. Her sole purpose was to find a human man to love her by becoming the woman of his dreams. And while she inspires him to great heights, she feeds on his life force energy.

Fear iced through Finn's veins. He'd just signed a deal with an energy vampire, and as far as he knew, his only way out of the agreement was to die.

19
THE MORTCARION APOCRYPHA

"YOUR PANICKING IS MAKING me panic," Fate told Farouk.

He pushed himself off his seat and smoothed down his fur. "Indubiously. We must preperate ourselves." Farouk shifted the gears and walked his cage swiftly across the sanctuary without crashing it this time.

Fate followed him over to the wall of bookcases, where he retrieved a myriad of boxes, opening each before discarding one after the other. "I can't see how whatever it is we're supposed to fight her with–and every other threat out there–is going to fit in any of these boxes of yours. Unless of course, you've got an upgraded Dragon Eye gizmo in one of them."

She waited for Farouk's response, but he continued with his frenzied hunt in silence. "Uh, the history lesson I just got was good and all, but it didn't exactly turn me into Wonder Woman. Silly me for thinking it might, but the only way I see us getting on the winning side of this, is if I level up somehow. You know what I mean?"

"You've absorbalated the collectiplied knowledge, experience and skill of every guardian that has come before you on a cellular level. Is that not enough of an advantage for you?" He grunted as he pulled a lever to raise his cage and grabbed a box on the top shelf.

"Really? Other than this subdermal seal I've been branded with, I don't look or feel any different." She rubbed her palm to test the sensitivity of her skin. Much to her relief, the burning sensation was beginning to ease.

"Ah! Here it is." He turned to her with a relieved smile and held out an odd looking ring.

"No, really, we just met. I think it's a bit early for engagement rings, don't you?"

Farouk's ears slanted as he frowned at her. "Take it."

Fate plucked it from his grasp and turned it this way and that. The gold band was decorated with colorfully painted cherubs on each side. Between them was a thick oval cap painted a royal blue enamel with gold flourishes. She wrinkled her nose. "Do I have to wear this? Vintage is cool and everything, but this?"

Farouk's glare remained unchanged. "You have no idea what you hold in your hands."

"The world's tackiest Victorian jewelry?"

"Why did you go down into the Keep's core when you were wearing the helmet?"

His question caught her off guard. "I don't know. I was curious. I suppose I just really wanted to know who built the Keep."

His hand shot through the bars as he jabbed a finger at her. "Exacturacy. No other guardian has ever done that during the initiation. Not even Brune. If anyone was going to do such a thing, it would've been her. But she was, as well as all the others, quite fine with knowing only the history of the Keep guardians.

"Which is?"

He looked uncomfortable. "You witnessed the paradelcade of the changing of the guard over the last five hundred years."

"I did. But how exactly did you become the caretaker? You did say you've been here for thousands of years, right? Yet, when I went further back, before there were guardians, I didn't see hide nor hair of you. Or should I say hide nor fur?" She chuckled then stopped short.

Farouk narrowed his eyes on her as he shrank in on himself,

his head sinking between his shoulders. She'd hit a nerve. Not that she'd been trying to hit anything in particular. What was he hiding?

"My story is of no importinance." He was standing stiff with his little hands clenched. "Our focustrate is best placed on what you discovered within the core. Put the ring on."

Fate stared at him as she tried the ring on several fingers before finding the one that fit. "Fine, we'll put a pin in this conversation. For now." She held her middle finger up and smiled. "It's on. What next?"

"There's a little latch on one side. Push it to open the lid."

"Oh, so is this some sort of locket ring?" She ran her fingertip along the edge of the oval and stopped when she felt the tiny latch. "Wait. Given where I am and the hell I've already been through, what happens when I pop the lid? This isn't the Ark of the Covenant and full of wispy ghosts that'll melt my face off if I look at them, is it?"

He looked at her like she was insane. "No, you will not have your face melted. And yes, the Arc is here and safely tucked away in one of the vaults. The ring you hold is a telepathicgram projector. It contains the origins of the Keep you're so curious about."

Fate studied the ring with more interest. "Hmm, sounds good. Unless it hurts like the helmet did."

"Viewing a telepathicgram is quite painless. You'll hear the narrator's voice as if she's with you and see what she saw."

"I suppose I can handle that." She ran her fingertip back and forth over the latch with growing excitement. "Okay, here goes nothing."

Pressing the latch, she jumped as the lid flipped open and an arrow clicked in a counterclockwise direction. A round dial filled with symbols rotated in the opposite direction as a gold starburst-shaped gear began to spin, slowly at first, until its speed became a blur. A cone of sparkling light and mist shot from the center.

A cloaked form flickered over the illuminated mist like a movie. The person walked closer and drew the hood of the cloak back, revealing the face of an elderly woman. Her wrinkled skin was covered with scars carved over her face in distinct tribal patterns. She had the opaque, vacant eyes of the blind, and Fate might've taken her for human, save for the three eyes blinking on the woman's forehead.

The woman bowed her head and looked straight at Fate, which sent a chill down her spine. When she finally spoke, her voice sounded like the scrape of dry leaves rustling over sand. "*I am Vasha,the last surviving member of the Galactic Psionic Counsel. This is the Mortcarion Apocrypha, unofficially transcribed against the Counsel's wishes and compiled in secrecy by me.No other living being knows of its existence. The contents of these scriptures are a complete record of events comprising the history of the building of the Obiectis and the resulting Chaos Region War.*

As the accounts to follow will reveal, the fate of those who come after I am long turned back into stardust, will depend on a full understanding of the early history of the Obiectis Builders and their ultimate fall to the chaos power known as Kali."

The woman inched closer with a palpable sense of urgency. *"She will wake again one day, and without this knowledge, I fear for the existence of all life throughout the universe."*

Fate's heart thudded hard in her chest. She wanted to shut the lid on the projector ring. She didn't want to hear how much worse everything could get. But she needn't have worried, because circumstances decided for her. The sliding sound of iron against iron as the door of the sanctuary hatch opened like the dilating iris of a camera lens. Fate glanced up in time to see Brune shoot through the opening and land in the middle of the room.

Slapping her hand over the projector ring, Fate snapped the lid shut and shoved her hand in her pocket. "Welcome back."

Brune slipped the aeronaut pack off her shoulders and set it down none too gently. Dirty, tired and covered in sweat, she dropped into a nearby chair and ran her hand through her messy blonde hair.

Fate exchanged an anxious look with Farouk. Her instincts told her to keep the ring and its contents a secret between them, at least for now. He gave her a furtive nod as they both turned to Brune, each staring at her in uncomfortable silence.

Brune eyed them both with suspicion. "What's going on? Did I interrupt something?"

Farouk steered his cage into the center of the room. "No. We're just surprised to see you back so soon. Were you unable to reach the breatktured gateways?"

"Of course." Brune's tone grew condescending. "I'm not some greenhorn. Remember who you're talking to, Farouk."

Fate pressed her lips together to keep from arguing. She wasn't anywhere near as unseasoned as Brune accused her of being, but something told her she'd be wasting her breath if she tried to defend herself.

Brune released Fate from her cold gaze and looked at Farouk. "Your readings must be off, or you gave me the wrong coordinates, because the gateways were repaired and closed when I got there."

Farouk's back stiffened. "My diagnostifications are never wrong."

"What are you so upset about? At least we know nothing else came through the portals."

Farouk's gaze flicked to Fate. "I'm more concerned with who or what fixed the flawmage."

"Maybe it was the robots," Fate offered quickly, in an attempt to steer the conversation away from her recent discovery. "Isn't that their job?"

"It is to a restrictured degree. Any repairs outside their programming would have to be input by me or a guardian."

"She should know that," Brune interjected. "Did you even bother to take her through the final initiation?"

"Uh, standing right here. And yes, I took the data spike in the brain and got lasered." Fate raised her hand to show Brune the seal glowing in her palm. "I'm all caught up."

"Hmph, that's what you think," Brune snickered.

Fate opened her mouth to speak, when suddenly a terrible roar reverberated through the sanctuary walls, followed by the thunderous crash of the Chimera slamming against the open hatch. Fate and Brune each dove out of the way as a stream of fire poured through. Being closest to the control panel, Fate scrambled on all fours and slammed her hand over the screen to close the breaching door. The iris spiraled shut, dousing the flames as the Chimera rammed the hatch, clawing at the iron barrier with renewed frenzy.

With her heart pounding, Fate turned to Brune. "You were saying?"

Brune stood and walked across the sanctuary to the set of doors leading to other sectors. "That's nothing. Wait until you're out there and face to face with that thing."

"Well I pretty much was just then!" Fate yelled. "I mean really, were you born in a barn? Do you not know how to close doors behind you?"

Brune gave her a patronizing smile as she stepped through the door marked with the residence symbol. "Yes, ma'am, I do." She kicked the door shut behind her with a loud bang.

Fate threw up her arms and looked at Farouk. "Well that was mature. What is she, three-years-old?"

"Ninety-four, to be exacturate."

"Is she always like that?"

Tilting his head, Farouk thought about it. "Yes. You might say she's grumptankerous."

"There's a fitting word I think I'll add to my growing list of descriptives for Brune."

Farouk grinned wide, which made him look disturbingly sly. "You're welcome to it. I have others if you're fascenticed."

"I'm good for the moment." Fate toyed with the projector ring. "Right now, I think it's best I get back to this. I've been dreading what's on here, but it feels good to have information Brune doesn't know anything about." She gave Farouk a conspiratorial smile, but he was already navigating his cage over to the exit.

"I'll leave you to it while I check into the diagnostification equipment." He pushed through the door marked for the science lab and let the door slam.

"Sure," Fate muttered, feeling slightly rebuffed as she opened the lid of the projector ring. Light and mist brought the narrator, Vasha, back into view and Fate settled in to watch and listen.

"*To fully understand this story, we must begin our journey in the deep past, with a thorough understanding of the Chaos Region. There are two planes of existence. The physical plane is made of the celestial bodies we call galaxies, stars and planets, all of which are bound by the laws of physics. The plane of multidimensional magic, on the other hand, is an infinite cosmic ocean composed of pure potentiality that permeates and flows through every living thing. This sea of magical energy reflects back all thoughts and emotions, which are brought into physical form when made strong enough.*

"Primitive civilizations were sensitive to multidimensional magic and they could see past the material plane. These were the shamans who used magic for healing, communication with spirit and minor demonstrations of manifestation from nothing. As society progressed and intelligence increased; sorcery, wizardry and alchemy emerged, in what is called the Age of Miracles. Later, science reigned

supreme and technology was used to harness multidimensional magic, effectively severing the connection between the living and the magical plane.

"When life forms are directly linked with multidimensional magic, they create a harmonious, unifying force, which produces smooth currents throughout the magical plane. Likewise, separation from magic, leads to inharmonious thoughts and emotions, which generate psychic energy storms. These disturbances rush in waves to the outer edge of space, where they pool in a roiling sea of wild magic known as the Chaos Region.

"When psychic storms increase in frequency and intensity, the negative energies of the collective grow and develop consciousness. Born of the collective cauldron of fear, greed, lust and rage, they become entities of both the material and magical plane.

"Since the beginning of time, the Chaos Region has spewed forth these beings of immense power and magnitude, known throughout history as gods, demons, faery and djinn–to name but a few. They are unpredictable beings, many of whom have taken ownership of young planets to help shape the terrain and atmosphere while guiding life forms as it suits them. When the energies are particularly strong in negativity, monsters are spawned, and these seek only to toy with mortals and destroy the worlds they inhabit.

"The Chaos Region has always been a forbidden zone for this reason. Until one race thought themselves above all rules.

The Obiectis Builders were once a highly intelligent race known as the Golandon. They were a tall, blue-skinned species, humanoid in appearance, with six arms instead of two. Having reached the peak of their evolutionary potential, the Golandon had achieved the ultimate in cultural, psychic and scientific development, especially in technology infused with multidimensional magic.

"With such achievements came a bloated sense of superiority. The Golandon thought themselves better than all other races and jealously guarded their advancements. They refused to share their

knowledge with the Galactic Federation and kept their inventions under heavy guard. Their hoarding behavior engendered bad relations and invited thieves. After a time when too many of their secrets were stolen, the Golandon decided to build a barricade, which would put an end to all such thievery for good.

"After assembling their best minds, they took their blueprints and advanced technology to the furthest regions of space, straight into the heart of the Chaos Region, where they knew they could not be followed. It was there they built a structure, which to this day defies all logic and every scientific law known to the collective pool of universal knowledge.

"The whole of the Golandon race abandoned their home planet and moved to the Obiectis. Over time, the civilization as a whole perfected the original design, tearing out all that was substandard, while adding layer upon layer of improvements, until at last there was nothing left to improve. They had created a marvel, a construct the size of a small planet with its own sustainable ecosystem and defensive shield.

"Having reached the pinnacle of their goal, the Golandon began to devolve.

"Had the Golandon lowered their pride enough to consult with the Psionic Counsel, rather than retreat from society to live in the darkest edge of space, we would have warned them of the dangers of their actions. With all their intelligence and knowledge of multidimensional magic, the Golandon never once realized that living so far away from the Great Central Sun–the source of all enlightenment–would be a giant step backwards.

"Ideas no longer flowed in the way they once took for granted. Innovation and ingenuity dried up, and with the structure running on its own, there was very little to be done. The Golandon had designed the perfect prison and they were its inmates. They had built it in the middle of a churning ocean of negative energy, which was slowly seeping into their prison's structure.

"Their civilization collapsed as depression, rage and apathy settled upon them. The fall began with those who first succumbed to their darkest emotions. Thousands grew violent and went on killing rampages. Those few who still had their wits about them, programmed the robots to police the insane and imprison them underground. In the meantime, they worked feverishly to design a shield. One which would allow the wild magic needed to fuel the Obiectis, but would filter out the harmful energies affecting them.

"This is how the six colossal hoops revolving around the Obiectis came into existence. Each hoop sweeps round and round, generating a force field that protects from the harmful psychic energies, while collecting wild magic within filaments embedded along the outer shell of each ring.

"Unfortunately, the revolving hoops took over a hundred years to build. Only a small percentage of the Golandon descendants were left by then and an even smaller number of them remained sane. Needless to say, the Golandon paid a heavy price to keep their precious technology a prized secret.

"As word traveled from world to world on the Golandon's technological wonder, jealous eyes cast greedy gazes upon the Obiectis. War broke out within the Chaos Region. Unlikely alliances were formed between scavengers, mercenaries and federations in a futile attempt to take the impenetrable fortress by storm. But the harmful emanations within the Chaos Region brewed distrust and infighting among alliances, eventually dividing them.

"A thousand year war was fought over the right to occupy the volatile patch of space around the Obiectis in the hopes of breaking through its shield. Not one was ever able to infiltrate the Obiectis.

"The endless plotting, the bloody battles and the incessant greed which drove an entire galaxy to war caused massive disturbances throughout the Chaos Region. Tidal waves of turmoil rippled along the magical plane, coalescing into untold numbers of bloodthirsty

entities which ravaged countless planets like a plague. Historians of old named this terrible time the Age of Monsters.

"The screams of the tortured echoed across the galaxy. Terror rolled toward the Chaos Region in crashing waves, where the building energies created another monstrous consciousness. For centuries it slumbered, growing in size beyond any other being which had come before, its food the nightmares of the innocent.

"When the war finally reached an apex of violence and slaughter, the colossal entity awoke. Its bloodcurdling shriek reverberated throughout the region as it turned its gaze on the fleets of ships battling in and around the Obiectis.

"The war ended in that one moment with a feeding frenzy of absolute destruction. The chaos entity tore through every ship like a massive hurricane, devouring the life force of all passengers while absorbing their spirits into its gargantuan body of roiling energy. It fed and fed until the space around the Obiectis turned into a sea of wreckage and hollowed out ghost ships.

"The titan then turned its ravenous appetite upon the Obiectis. Screeches of fury resounded throughout the inner walls as it hammered the structure. The force field generated by the revolving hoops deflected the entity, but the Golandon knew it was only a matter of time before the rings weakened under the relentless barrage–"

As soon as Fate heard the door open, she punched the lid of the projector ring closed against the palm of her other hand, cutting short the terrifying images and sounds playing out in front of her. Fear jittered along her nerve endings as Jessie and the others entered the sanctuary. They were still in full uniform, but they'd removed their Dragon Eyes and seemed more back to normal.

Lincoln attempted a kick that fell markedly short of what Fate had witnessed earlier. "That wush legendary! Did you catch the palm shtrikesh I wush layin' down?"

"How could I?" Mason flailed his arms in poor form. "I was too busy amazing myself with my high-speed arm blocks."

Lincoln scratched his nose and looked around. "Where'sh that bosshy blonde? Ish she back yet? I'm ready to show her my new movesh." He laughed and swiveled his hips. "If you know what I mean."

"Better not let her see you doing that," Mason warned. "You might be ready to kick some monster ass, but I'd take bets she'd kick yours, and good."

Jessie turned a cool gaze toward Fate. "Nah, I'd take a bet against her. Being a guardian doesn't make you all that. We've got stuff they don't." Her tone was forceful and directed solely at Fate as she patted the Dragon Eye headgear attached to her belt

Fate looked down at the floor. She should be angry with Jessie for being so blatantly competitive, but she was too frightened by the images in Vasha's story. None of them knew the danger they were actually in and their arrogance could get every one of them killed, including her best friend.

20
THE BLACK-EYED GODDESS

FATE STACKED THE BED pillows behind her and sank into them with a heavy sigh. Her room was nothing less than luxurious. The walls were lined with warm woods carved in intricate arches framing beautifully painted frescos. Ornate lanterns glowing with amber light hovered near the tall ceilings. A sitting area offered several over-stuffed chairs and a sofa, each of which floated in the air a foot off the floor. Even her bed floated like an air mattress on a still pond. She had no idea how the furniture was made to defy gravity, but she liked the light rocking sensation beneath her whenever she shifted her weight.

She smoothed her hand over the massive bed's cream-colored linen coverlet, feeling like royalty in the lap of luxury. The Golandon definitely knew how to live in style. Apparently, every living area within the Residence Section was furnished every bit as lavishly. And each suite came with its own chamber robot, which had been lightly humanized with pleasant faces. Her chamber robot had been outfitted with a round grandmotherly face–comforting, until it turned away and revealed the blinking circuitry behind the mask. But Fate wasn't about to complain. Not when it meant she didn't have to make her bed in the morning. She could even leave her clothes on the floor.

Fate wriggled her toes and let out another deep sigh. Now that she was alone and able to relax with her own thoughts, she realized how completely exhausted she was. So much had happened in the last twenty-four hours. She'd literally gone from being bounced out of the *Book of Fables*, to landing in the middle of a fan convention, to catapulting across the universe, and finally, downloading thousands of years of Keep knowledge into her brain. All in one day.

If that wasn't enough to put her into a weeklong coma, there was the added stress of knowing the Keep was swarming with vicious monsters. Not to mention, the constant juggling of everyone else's delicate feelings. Especially Jessie's.

At the moment, Eustace, Brune and Farouk were strategizing some sort of plan to eliminate the Chimera. She'd insisted on being part of the planning, but fatigue had won out and she'd had to excuse herself. There'd be time to find out what the three of them had hatched up in the morning. Leaving did nothing to soothe her nerves though. After coming so close to the heat of the Chimera's flames, the reality of facing the fire breather without a wall standing between them was downright paralyzing.

Shivering, Fate hugged her arms. She was too tired to face the next day with any amount of confidence. She felt fragile to the bone, like the tiniest bump would shatter her into a million pieces. As much as she needed and welcomed the quiet and solitude, a terrible sense of loneliness crashed in. The heartache she'd been able to beat back with all the distractions returned full force. Tears welled in her eyes and fell on the sheets.

"Finn, I miss you so much," she whispered. "I need you here with me."

Cruel silence answered back.

"Why?" Fate cried out. "Why can't we be together? Are we cursed?"

She knew the answer before she even asked the question. They weren't together because of one thoughtless mistake. Her mistake. She had no one else to blame but herself. If she hadn't conjured the Green Man with her Words of Making, Finn wouldn't be trapped inside a tree.

Fate punched the mattress as anger burned in her chest. She couldn't picture her life without him. He'd always been with her, first in her imagination and then in the flesh. He was everything she'd ever wanted, and more. Finn was part of her, and she was part of him. It hurt in a thousand different ways to be apart from him. Surely they were meant to be together.

Using the edge of the sheet, Fate wiped her eyes dry. "I won't give up. I'll die before I give up." She reached for the tobacco pouch holding Finn's Holy Blend tobacco and inhaled the earthy scent. She tried to imagine he was near, but the emptiness was too great, filling fast with a monstrous pain that tore into her chest and ripped a sob from her throat.

She gave in and cried until exhaustion finally wrung her dry. Rolling onto her side, Fate stared into space, wanting desperately to abandon her duties as guardian to go in search of the gateway to Oldwilde so she could find Finn. Being with him would give her the strength she needed to confront the monsters waiting for her inside the Keep. With him fighting by her side, she could face anything. He was more powerful than anyone else here. Finn was the destroyer of the mightiest destroyer. She'd once seen him use his power over the elements to embed a war goddess, into solid rock. What more did she need?

Fate sat straight up, remembering the recording on the projector ring and the carnage the chaos entity had wreaked upon those ships. She'd been dreading whatever was left of the remaining footage. She knew it would somehow connect to the sorceress she'd come face to face with inside the core. The woman terrified her. Finn was the only one who could fight someone that powerful and win.

The idea of bringing him back to the Keep before she took care of anything else energized her. She had planned on viewing the last part of Vasha's message when she felt emotionally and physically stronger. But now she wanted to know exactly what she would be facing.

Without wasting another second, Fate flipped the lid on the projector ring. A spray of light and mist streamed from the ring. Images of the surface of the Keep flickered over the shifting screen and Vasha's voice filled the quiet room.

"Since the time of their societal collapse, the surviving team of Golandon scientists and engineers had been installing portals to other worlds in case another disaster forced them to abandon the Obiectis. But not as swiftly as they would've liked. The portals would take only six at a time and not all of them were accessible, because of each portal's one-hundred-year long rotation. Only a small percentage of the portals moved along the surface. The majority were located deep below the gigantic turning gears.

"They evacuated people of importance first, those who could carry with them the technological secrets of their civilization and continue on with the Golandon legacy in other worlds. Their best scientist was chosen to stay behind. Before leaving, the scientists cybernetically enhanced him to prolong his life indefinitely. They then placed him in stasis deep within the core. If the invasion damaged the Obiectis and it could not self-repair, he was programmed to wake and oversee the repairs himself.

"The last and most crucial part of their plan to save the Obiectis was the role of the High Priestess. Her knowledge of multidimensional magic exceeded even that of the Golandon scientists. She was a Sensitive, in tune with the astral forces and able to manipulate dark matter to do her bidding without the need for technology. In other worlds, some would call her a witch or sorceress

"The High Priestess feared the chaos god. The entity was powerful beyond anything she had ever encountered. The only way to stop the behemoth was to contain it within something she could control. But no manmade structure would hold it. The container needed to be a living vessel with the strength of will to dominate the

wild beast and ultimately tame it.

"As the last of the Golandon fled through portals to parts unknown, the High Priestess took her position and gazed at the churning mass of darkness swarming over the revolving hoops as it burst through the last remaining shreds of the force field. Black writhing clouds swamped the artificial atmosphere, filling the immense space with the terrifying howl of a thousand storms, questing for the life force energy it craved.

"The High Priestess closed her eyes and commanded the entity to enter her. Nothing could have prepared her for the massive onslaught of the being's immense energy invading her. She knew her own smallness in that moment, like a ship swallowed by a tidal wave. Every horror and atrocity that had created the monster, consumed her whole and blazed into existence. All the old truths and ancient magic she'd clung to abandoned her.

"Dark wrappings of power seeped into her cells, down to the molecular level. As the last vestiges of her spirit struggled to hold on, she realized her own secret longing for power and surrendered to the darkness. In that instant, she willingly merged with the entity, a choice which transformed them both into the fearsome, black-eyed goddess, known in that moment of manifestation as Kaliena.

"Her changed form overflowed with rivers of darkness, which sought to spread across the universe. The black tendrils of smoke curling around her body lashed toward the portals, slipping through before fully closing behind the departing Golandan, flowing into hundreds upon hundreds of other worlds. Thus, spreading the seeds of her power throughout untold galaxies, where she has since become deified as a mighty goddess of both creation and destruction. She has been called by hundreds of names–the Cosmic Mother, the Devourer Of Him Who Devours, the Great Sorceress and Kali, to name but a few.

"Kaliena took full ownership of the Obiectis. For a time, she slept, dreaming of her omnipresent self and the power she wielded

over the many worlds she now possessed. When she finally woke from her long sleep, the connection to her many selves became severed and she found her consciousness limited to her physical body. Unfortunately, this division left her trapped within the residual negative energies of the chaos being. Her wisdom and reverence for life had moved on with the other parts of herself now scattered throughout the universe.

"For hundreds of thousands of years, she used the portals in an attempt to reunite with the missing pieces of her greater soul. When this proved fruitless, she turned to seeking out powerful objects of magic in the hopes more power would offer a solution. She stole these instruments of magic from countless worlds, hoarding them like treasures within the Obiectis. When none of these objects gave her the power to do what she desperately craved, her thirst became insatiable.

"A time came when a powerful sorcerer named Wodrid discovered a gateway into the Obiectis through a mystical lock, a trespass which nearly ended his life. The wizard was no match for the sorceress, Kaliena. For some unknown reason, she allowed him to live and held him prisoner. When he regained his strength, she tortured him, partially for her own amusement, but mostly to discover how he'd found a way into her impenetrable fortress.

"Wodrid withstood this torment in a way that surprised her. She soon came to admire his strength and endurance. Having been alone with only her mechanical servants as company, she eventually softened and allowed him a modicum of freedom, though his life wholly belonged to her. She would never allow him to leave. But as decades passed, something changed between captor and captive. They fell in love and Wodrid had no other choice but to join in her quest to rebuild her original power.

"Unbeknownst to Wodrid, Kaliena was not the immortal she claimed to be. She'd been secretly relying on magical elixirs and amulets she'd stolen from other worlds to maintain her youthful life

force. But she finally came to a point where she could no longer hold back her bodily decline. She needed stronger remedies, and her supply of ancient amulets had finally been drained of power.

"When at last, she confessed her weakness to Wodrid, he helped integrate her mortal form into the magically infused technology deep inside the heart of the Obiectis to keep her alive. He stayed by her side as she slipped into dreamless slumbers, each of which lasted a little longer with each passing day. Desperate to give her hope, Wodrid broke his oath to The Order of Druids by revealing a sacred secret. There were two objects which could restore her to godhood. He told her of the Orb and Rod of Aeternitis, two instruments of incredible magic, when combined, would give her the power to call anything into existence.

"Her last words to him as she fell into a permanent sleep were to find the Orb and Rod and deliver them back to her. Before Wodrid left, he brought the scientist out of stasis and instructed him to monitor Kaliena's life force until he returned with the means to revive her.

"As of this last entry, I observed the passing of two centuries without any sign of Wodrid's return. As my own life nears the end of this existence, my Sight dims and I do not See as much as I once did. What I can See, is that the revolving hoops of the Obiectis continue to turn. The portals still fill with magical wonders and Kaliena sleeps through it all. But of one thing I can be sure, the Golandon scientist will find a way to wake her. It's in his blood to make broken things work. The problem is, he knows not of what he is waking and I fear for the future of the universe when his task is complete."

As Vasha's face vanished from the misty screen, Fate hastily shut the lid of the projector ring. Her mind was reeling. She could barely breathe, knowing she'd witnessed the moment the Golandon scientist achieved his goal of waking Kaliena. The frightening images of the black-eyed goddess, Kaliena, shrouded in writhing darkness and her ultimate, downward spiral into a greedy, power-hungry sorceress would haunt her. Yet for some reason, her fear had become hair-raising terror when Wodrid entered the picture with his beautiful elfin face, delicately pointed ears poking through his long silvery hair and eyes the color of ice.

By the time the recording played to the end, Fate's terror had increased to an irrational level. She couldn't shake the feeling she knew Wodrid. His face had been disturbingly familiar. She was certain their paths had somehow crossed, and not in a good way. Yet surely an unpleasant encounter with him would've scorched itself into her brain. Not to mention, given his mission to revive Kaliena, he would've used everything in his power to take the Rod from her if they had met.

She grabbed at the chain of her necklace to check if the Rod was still attached. Her panic eased when she felt the warmth of the thin gold bar between her fingers.

Her head was spinning. "Wodrid." The name felt foreign on her tongue, yet familiar at the same time. "Wodrid. Why do I know that name…and that face?"

Squeezing her eyes shut, Fate reached back in her memory, recalling as much as she could from her time in the *Book of Fables*. But too much had happened. Pinpointing how she knew Wodrid proved to be impossible. It was like looking for a polar bear in a snowstorm, and every bit as nerve wracking.

"Oh, screw it," she muttered. Tomorrow, she'd ask Farouk what he knew about Wodrid. Or maybe she should hold off. Any conversations she had with Farouk needed to be about enlisting his help to locate the portal to Oldwilde so she could bring Finn back to the Keep.

Her heart raced at the thought of seeing Finn. It was almost too much to hope for. She shook her head. There was no room for doubt. She had to believe it was possible. For a split second, she allowed herself to imagine his face when they reunited–the passionate glitter in his green eyes, the irresistible curve of his lips and the dark golden strands of hair falling artfully across his forehead. She smiled in spite of the bittersweet ache spreading through her chest.

Fate scooted down into the bed and hugged a pillow. A good night's sleep was in order. She would need her wits about her tomorrow.

"Lights out," she said through a yawn, her eyelids already drooping as the light of the lanterns dimmed to blackest night.

21

HIS MOTHER'S SON

THE LHIANNAN SHEE GAVE the nearby tables in the tavern a sidelong glance. "You shouldn't overstay your welcome," she warned Finn.

Ignoring her, Finn sopped up the last of his mutton stew with a wedge of bread and stuffed it in his mouth. After a solid day spent in O'Deldar's room without eating, he was weak with hunger. "We'll leave as soon as I'm good and full." He chewed his food slowly and swallowed. "You may not need to eat, but I can't go any further without refueling."

He looked up from his empty plate, wincing at the sight of the faery. To keep her from taking on Fate's form, he'd made her wear a glamour of someone he detested. In this case a young gangly boy with a freckled nose and red hair, an evil kid who'd come frighteningly close to killing Fate by sacrificing her to a bloodthirsty oak.

Finn swigged back the last of his mead, barely able to stomach what he was looking at. "Other than men, what is it you actually eat?"

"Love is what feeds me." A frown darkened the faery's ruddy complexion. "A bite of which I'm desperately craving at the moment."

Anxious knots twisted in Finn's gut. He was playing a dangerous game allowing the Lhiannan Shee to join him on his quest to locate the fiery divide. But the loneliness he'd been plagued with had only gotten worse and his temptation to see Fate again was more than he could resist. He told himself he needed this reminder to keep him from giving up, but he knew he was fooling himself. His desperate desire to be with Fate had made him weak-willed.

He reached into his sealskin sporran for a few coins and laid them on the table. "Let's be off then." He stood to leave.

Finn's movement turned heads in the room. He'd been careful to keep his face hidden beneath the hood of his cloak, but looking back, that in itself may have drawn suspicion. Tensing as he reached the door, he heard the faery scream his name.

There was no time to react. Something thick and hard smacked into the side of the head. The blow dropped him to the floor in a flat second. A blast of fractured light filled his vision and with the last shred of his dimming awareness, he caught sight of the Lhiannan Shee.

She'd morphed into Fate.

As Finn struggled to keep his eyes open, the faery with Fate's face fell to her knees next to him. "Stay with me, Finn. Get up and fight. I know you can do it."

The conviction in her voice filled him with renewed strength. Growling with effort, Finn pushed himself off the floor, only to be knocked back down as a cracking sound filled his skull and plunged him into darkness.

Finn woke to screams of misery. A pounding headache cut through his fogged brain. Groaning with pain, he opened his eyes to a dark cell. Beyond the bars imprisoning him, the light of a torch flickered over greasy stone walls stained black with years of filth and old blood.

Some sort of wooden knob had been jammed in his mouth to gag him. Someone must've guessed by the Elder race runes inked on his skin that he could invoke the elements and bring a hurricane down upon them. He tried to force it out with his tongue, but a strap held it firmly in place.

Finn moved to take it out with his hand, when he realized his wrists were shackled and solidly anchored to the wall. Panic flooded his veins as he jumped off the scummy floor. His ankles were bound as well, and he could go no further than a standing position. He strained against the iron grip of the manacles with every ounce of power he could muster. But there was no breaking them, regardless of his extraordinary strength.

Why had he gone into that tavern? Fate had given him the ability to fly with her Words of Making. His raging hunger really could've waited the extra hour or two it would've taken to get to a village well outside of Asgar. But no, he'd allowed himself to get careless. All because he'd been able to stroll in and out of the castle so easily.

A furious scream tore from his lungs, his cry muffled by the plug in his mouth. He went berserk, kicking and wrenching his arms against the restraints. The shackles bit deep into his wrists and ankles until his bones throbbed, but he couldn't stop himself. His own stupidity infuriated him.

His raging ignited a series of howls and shrieks from other parts of the dungeon. Out of breath from the painful struggle, Finn dropped his fists and hung his head as he listened to the other prisoners. The loudest of them sounded insane, some like caged animals, while others cried out in horrible agony.

Finn gulped and glanced down. They'd stripped him of his Beldereth uniform and the sporran holding all his worldly goods, including his flute, of course. He was dressed in rags. This must be some kind of torture chamber. No doubt, it wouldn't be long before it was his turn on the rack.

He no sooner came to his grim conclusion, when a guard appeared, unlocked the door and stepped aside, allowing a cloaked man to enter. His face was in shadow, but judging by the cut of his clothes and fine fabric, he was someone of nobility.

"Leave us," the man said to the guard as he removed his hood.

As dim as the light was in Finn's cell, he recognized Prince Tynan immediately, though he must have been crowned king after Moria's death. The young man took after his mother. He had the same ivory complexion, dark hair and red glint of the dragon in his brown eyes.

"I knew it was only a matter of time before I would look into the eyes of my mother's killer." Tynan's mouth twisted into a hateful line. He held Finn's flute high for him to see. "I suppose you came back to finish what you started. Was it not enough for you to take my mother? What kind of animal are you that you need to end her bloodline?"

Finn's throat tightened around the grief he felt for Tynan. This was a good man who believed he was facing the murderer of his innocent mother. The king would never know what a truly evil woman Moria had been, which left Finn with nothing he could say in his own defense, even if he could speak.

Tynan's fist shook with anger as he tightened his grip on the flute Finn had used to enchant Moria into throwing herself into the flames. The muscles in his jaw tensed as he clenched his teeth. "What did my mother ever do to you?"

Looking the king in the eyes, Finn shook his head. He wanted to tell Tynan that he did it to end the suffering of his people, but the king obviously had no desire to hear what Finn had to say. Not that he'd allow him to speak. The king knew Finn could use his rune power to invoke the elements that could bring nature's wrath down upon his kingdom.

"We were the most prosperous kingdom in all of Oldwilde," Tynan seethed. "That is, until you killed our empress. It was she who blessed our people with endless wealth. Her death cast a shadow over the land, bringing death and decay down upon us all!"

Finn steadied his gaze on the king. It didn't matter that he was gagged. There was nothing to be said. How could he ever prove that Moria had plotted revenge against Asgar by marrying Tynan's father and giving him the perfect son and heir? Her patience had known no bounds. Over a span of seventeen years, she'd manipulated the king into relinquishing his rule to her authority and had allowed the kingdom of Asgar to fall into rot and ruin. The most cruel part of her plan was the web of illusion she'd woven over the people. She'd made them perceive only prosperity, where no one ever grew sick or died. In actuality, the castle had been crumbling down around them and their bountiful harvests were that of the dead.

Tynan would never know his mother had intended to use him against Asgar as her final act of vengeance. If Finn hadn't stopped her when he did that night at the great bonfire, Moria would've awakened Tynan's Serpen blood and turned him into a dragon that would finally raze the kingdom to the ground.

Finn understood Tynan's blindness. No loving son could ever believe his mother was so evil and vengeful. Not unless he personally witnessed her despicable actions. All the sorrow Finn felt for the young king welled in his eyes.

A fleeting look of surprise passed over Tynan. "What's this? Tears? From the Unholy Piper?" He stared at Finn, confused for a moment. Then rage returned, turning his pale face red as he held the flute in both hands, straining until the hollow reed snapped in half.

Finn winced. His grandfather had carved that flute for him. He'd lovingly scored it with Druidic inscriptions, and later, Tove had inscribed the Elder race runes into the wood, transforming the flute into a powerful weapon. Finn had used it as a wind sword to fight his greatest opponent, and of course, on Moria as a seductive instrument of death.

The king shoved the broken end of the flute against Finn's

jugular. The red spark of vengeance lighting his eyes quickly reminded Finn that Tynan was every bit his mother's son when it came to holding a grudge. "I could easily bleed you out right now," he snarled.

Finn held his breath as the king jabbed the sharp splinters into his skin.

Tynan abruptly flung the two pieces of the flute against the wall. They clattered onto the grimy floor. "I won't though. I wouldn't want to deny the executioner his due. And it's important for my people to witness the axe coming down upon your neck. Justice will come when I slide your head onto a pike and send your rotting skull on a tour throughout my kingdom so every man, woman and child can see that the Unholy Piper is truly dead."

The king punctuated his promise with a slug to Finn's gut. Gasping from the sudden blow, Finn watched Tynan turn and leave. The pain spreading through his belly became a sick feeling of dread as the guard slammed his cell door shut and locked it.

Finn hung his head, staring at the broken flute lying near his feet. Somehow, it was no surprise he'd meet his end this way. It didn't matter that he'd committed his crime when he'd been overtaken by Mugloth's darkness. He'd done too many unforgivable things. Most of all, he'd enjoyed destroying the empress.

For that alone, he deserved his punishment.

22
WE CAN'T ACT ON THIS PLAN

FATE RUSHED INTO THE sanctuary. She'd fallen asleep without instructing her chamber robot to wake her in time to make the morning meeting. Now she was late and had missed her chance to talk to Farouk about her plan to save the day by bringing Finn back to the Keep to help them. More than likely now, she'd have to fall in line with whatever plans everyone had arrived at without her. Unless she could get him alone, the chat with Farouk would most likely have to wait until after she completed her first mission.

If she survived.

She skidded to a stop as everyone in the room turned to look at her. "Uh, sorry I'm late." She inched into the room, feeling weird and sheepish as frowns formed on the faces of Farouk's new army. Jessie, Mason and Lincoln were wearing what appeared to be cybernetically enhanced armor over their uniforms. They also had their Dragon Eye headgear on. The usual goofing around was now replaced by a serious, somber mood.

Steve acknowledged her with an easy smile and Darcy at least nodded to her. Fate was glad they had at least chosen to work in the library. She wished she could say the same about Jessie.

Brune's expression held an air of annoyance. Fate walked stiffly by, expecting to be berated for her tardiness. Much to her surprise, Brune refrained, and instead, held out a set of armor. "Put these on. We'll be heading out right after the meeting."

Fate took the heavy pieces, which consisted of a helmet,

gloves, contoured breastplate, shoulder pads and arm and leg bracers. Each was outfitted with a mysterious menagerie of brass and copper discs, gears, wiring and what looked like hydraulics.

Everyone was gathered around the huge mahogany table, which had been cleared of all the lab equipment she'd first seen on their arrival. Eustace smiled and opened a space for her. "We were just about to familiarize ourselves with the different quadrants of the Keep," her father explained as she stepped in between him and Gerdie, who stood on a stool so she could see better.

"I've got some good news," Gerdie whispered to her.

"Really? What is it?" Fate whispered back as she strapped the leg bracers onto her thighs.

Farouk cleared his throat with a stern glance in Fate's direction. "As I was saying before the bargeruption, Quadrants 148, 29 and 537 are hot zones."

Gerdie gave her a wink. "Tell ya later."

Fate nodded as she pulled the breastplate down over her head and buckled the sides. Feeling rushed, she hastily slipped the arm bracers on and locked the shoulder pads onto the breastplate. When she pulled the gloves on, she stopped to study the mechanics attached to them. Curiosity got the best of her and she tested the gloves by squeezing the edge of the table. The wood groaned beneath her fingers and broke off in her hand.

She looked at the others in surprise. "Sorry." She placed the jagged piece on top of the table before giving Farouk her full attention.

Farouk eyed the damage with irritation then tossed a large scroll out onto the table's polished surface. The scroll unfurled, revealing a detailed map of the Keep's two hemispheres. He tapped each of the circles with an ornate bronze pointer stick, triggering the appearance of 3D projections of both halves of the Keep, each an exact replica in every way.

He pointed at one of the halves. The spot lit with a red glow, spotlighting a much smaller and less scary duplicate of the Chimera. "This is Quadrant 29. The Chimera's taken up occupendence there because it's closest to the sanctuary, which is positionated here, within the axis point of the revolving hoops." A tap on a schematic tucked in the corner of the scroll produced a 3D image of the Keep and the rings sweeping around it.

"Are you saying the other rooms, like the library and residential suites, are built inside the rings?" Eustace asked.

"Not at all. We would never withstand the velocity generated by the motionment of the rings. We are positionated within the connection point between the rings."

Eustace nodded and Fate could see his engineer's mind working out the logistics. "Makes sense, though I have to wonder why we're not down there on the surface of the Keep, where there would be more options for structural expansion."

"The Keep is strictly for housing all magical objects of dangerous quantportions," Farouk answered, though impatiently. "Shall we move on?"

"By all means." Eustace gave Fate a playful shrug.

Farouk pointed at another section of the same 3D hemisphere and lit the area with another red glow. Everyone leaned in as the light illuminated a host of deformed humanoids. Some had the heads of animals, others the bodies of sea creatures, while most were grotesque distortions of humans, slithering and scrabbling between the architectural vaults. "These are the Fomorians, currently located in Quadrant 148. From what I can gatherclude, they seem to be searching for a way out of the Keep. They've had plenty of chancetunity to escape through any one of the gateways–all of which open during twilight–but so far they've bypassed every one of them."

Fate screwed up her face at the repulsive creatures. "What are they?"

Brune leaned forward. "Only an ancient race of chaos-makers. Get near just one of those bad boys, and your brain turns to mush. Confusion and terror take over. Time distorts, and before you know it, you're sucking your thumb in the psych ward for the rest of your natural life."

Fate stared back in horror. "If that's the case, how do we fight them if we can't go near them?"

"We'll come to that, but let's not get ahead of ourselves." Farouk aimed his pointer at the other hemisphere of the Keep. The area lit up and a figure appeared. At first glance it appeared to be a knight in spiked armor, but a closer look revealed a creature comprised of twisted metal, shrouded in blue mist. It loomed over a huge cathedral, while tearing into the cast-iron dome and gorging on mangled scraps.

"This is the scavenger," Farouk continued. "As you can see, it's growing in size as we speak. I calcumate it to be growing at an amplinential rate of two hundred percent a day."

"Then let's dismantle the thing before it gets out of control," Mason said.

Farouk looked at him with barely contained patience. "It's already out of control. Ordinaturally, scavengers never get this big, but this one likes iron, which most of the Keep and many of the vaults are made of. It has plenty to eat. Every vault made of iron in Quadrant 56 has been destroyed and now it's gone through half of the ones in Quadrant 537. It's also extremendously strong because it ate Thor's Hammer."

"Really?" Eustace exclaimed. "Thor's Hammer actually existed?"

Farouk's gaze slid to the librarian section of the table. "Yes, that and many other things you thought were myths." He huffed with annoyance. "Now then, any battle with the scavenger will draw the Chimera's attention, and most likely the Fomorians. The chance for survival goes down if you have to face all three at once. Therefore, termicluding the Chimera is our first order of business."

Fate watched for any sign of nervousness in Mason and Lincoln, and especially Jessie, but there wasn't a trace. They either didn't understand the gravity of what they were about to do, or the Dragon Eye was giving them a false sense of invincibility. Most likely it was the latter.

"What's to keep the scavenger from coming after us while we're facing off with the Chimera?" Jessie asked.

"Scavs are only interested in one thing," Brune answered. "Consuming whatever material it is they need to build themselves up with."

"Shweet, it'll be focushed on eating when we come down on it. Lead the way and I'll blow it to piecesh." Lincoln aimed his hands like a gun and made an explosion sound.

Brune laughed. "You better make that shot count. If you miss, it'll come after you like a mad hornet. Scavs have strong survival instincts, which makes them very hard to kill."

That silenced the military section of the room.

A burst of restlessness came over Fate. "Okay, let's do this by the numbers. We focus on the Chimera first." The sooner they got this first scary mission out of the way, the sooner she could talk to Farouk about Finn. "What's the big master plan?"

"I'll leave this to the research team to explainate." Farouk handed the pointer over to Eustace before making himself comfortable in the cushioned bucket seat of his cage.

Fate stared at her father in surprise. He'd been part of the strategy meeting the night before, but she hadn't expected him to be given the lead in planning the attack. Farouk and Brune had certainly embraced having unwelcome guests in their midst

"Certainly." Eustace appeared a bit uncomfortable. "Steve here discovered some key points about the Chimera, which I'll let him explain."

Caught off guard, Steve glanced one way and then the other. "Uh, sure. Um…well, the Chimera is made of about twenty different animals. It has the talons of a raptor for ripping its prey to shreds and the forelegs of a primate, which gives it incredible upper body strength. It's covered in the nearly impenetrable hide of a dragon. It has the wings of a bat and the horns of a ram and hindquarters of a–"

"Maybe we should just focus on the two main animals, Steve," Eustace interjected politely.

"Right, more to the point that way," Steve agreed. "Well, the Chimera's got the head of a lion and the tail of a snake. This means the Chimera is one organism controlled by two brains, each of which is dominated by very different instincts. Generally, this isn't a problem for the creature, unless it's disoriented enough to see its two heads as separate from itself. In which case, the lion would see the snake as a threat, or even a competing predator, while the snake might see the lion as prey–"

"Yeah, yeah, we get it." Lincoln shifted back and forth. Like everyone else in the room, he was anxious about the mission. "The shnake and lion shtart tearing each other apart."

Steve nodded. "Exactly."

"How do we make that happen?" Mason added. "Blow magic confusion powder in their noses?"

"We lead the Chimera to the Fomorians," Brune answered.

"What? Are you nuts?" Fate looked from Brune to Eustace. "First we have to offer ourselves as bait and then we fly into the lose-your-mind-zone?"

Eustace raised his hand in an attempt to calm her concerns. "I know it sounds like a crazy plan, but we've come up with protections." He turned to Darcy. "Show them."

Darcy gave everyone a smug smile as she placed seven brass gadgets the size of flash drives on the table. "These are chromatic amplifiers." She sent them sliding across the table.

Fate reached for hers, but Darcy swiped it out of reach. "You can have yours as soon as I demonstrate how it works." She held the amplifier for everyone to see. "All you need to do is press the button on the bottom."

The crystal encased behind the tiny round window of glass gleamed with a bright blue light as electrical strobes danced over the copper coil surrounding it. A clear hum filled the room, the notes shifting methodically along a simple musical scale.

"Really? That needed demonstrating?" Fate held out her hand with an eyebrow raised.

Darcy shrugged and dropped the amplifier into Fate's open palm.

Eustace placed a large ancient tome on the table and opened the yellowed pages to a section filled with handwritten text. "We found this *Book Of Conquests* when we were researching the Fomorians yesterday. It says here, '*Truly, to fight against Fomorians was all the same to punch a wall by head, to hold an arm in a snake nest or place a face to flame*'."

Fate tried her best to smile, so as not to sound too negative. "Oh, that's encouraging."

"I know it sounds gloomy," Eustace agreed, "but what it's saying here is the Fomorians cannot be defeated by anything other than their own might."

"Except maybe this tiny secret weapon?" Fate waved it at him. "What's it supposed to do, bore them to death with lousy music?"

"No, it's not a weapon." Eustace's eyes shone bright with fascination for the subject. "We discovered something very interesting about the Fomorians. They emit sounds, undetectable to the human ear, which distort reality and the very fabric of time. But, thanks to Darcy and her findings in the Builder's records of sound technology, we've come up with a way to disrupt their emanations. Farouk assembled the devices last night, and voila, we have the chromatic amplifiers."

Fate had never heard her father use the word, voila, before. He was more excited than she'd previously guessed.

"The amplifiers will allow you and the others to safely inhabit the same space as the Fomorians," Eustace continued.

"I like the sound of that, pardon the pun." Fate's smile was pained as she turned off the annoying sound of her amplifier. "But how do we fight them if they're so indestructible?"

A loud thump at the other end of the table grabbed everyone's attention. "With this." Brune shook the end of a thick chain attached to an ornamental, octagonal-shaped box the size of a grapefruit. It was silver and covered in symbols. "The Eye of Balor."

"Brune was kind enough to risk her life last night to retrieve this from one of the vaults inside the Keep," Eustace explained. "Apparently, Balor was once king of the Fomorians. He was known to have one eye that was always shut, because to look upon his venomous gaze was to die a terrible and instant death."

Fate grimaced. "Ew, are you saying his eye's in that box?"

"Short of looking inside for myself, it would seem so," Eustace said. "Suffice to say, we have our weapon against the Fomorians. If the stories are correct, neither gods nor giants could save themselves from the baleful glare of Balor's eye. Hence, the reason for its extraction, and why it is kept in a box. We can now use their own might against them."

Fate nodded as she listened. "No offense, but all this sounds like theory. Words like, 'it would seem so', and 'if the stories are correct', don't exactly fill me with loads of confidence."

The light went out of her father's eyes and his brow furrowed with worry. Fate felt terrible for calling him out in front of everyone, but it needed to be said. This was life and death.

"You're right, none of this is tested." Eustace looked at Farouk. "We can't act on this plan. Uh, hello?"

Farouk was slumped in his chair, his head falling to one side as he snored softly.

Gerdie rapped his cage. "Hey, wake up!"

Farouk jolted awake. "Wha–what?" His ears shot straight up as he looked around.

The worry in Eustace's eyes turned to horror when he saw that Farouk had fallen asleep. "I was saying we cannot act on this plan when nothing's been tested. We don't know if the amplifiers will actually work. And what if that's not actually the Eye of Balor? It's not like we can look inside to confirm."

Brune rounded the table and walked toward Eustace. "This is how it's always been done. We trust in the system the Builders left in place. They were nothing if not precise about recording every item stored inside each vault. The same goes for the Library. We trust that every scrap of information found there is every bit as accurate and true. It has to be, there's too much at stake."

Fate looked down at the projector ring on her finger. Why was Brune referring to the Builders? They weren't responsible for the collection of vaults and magical objects in the Keep. This was Kaliena's collection. Was Brune really that in the dark about the history here?

Eustace pressed his fists against the surface of the table. "Well, I for one will not send anyone out there based on theory alone."

Fate put her hand on his arm. He was shaking with sheer tension. "You're not, Dad. We each need to decide for ourselves if we're going to do this." She looked across the table at Jessie, Mason and Lincoln. "How do you guys feel about the plan? Do you think it'll work?"

Her friend's expression remained unperturbed. "It's better than winging it. I'm in."

"No problem here," Lincoln chimed in.

Mason hesitated for the briefest moment as his gaze moved to Darcy. Her eyes filled with hope and Fate could tell she was waiting for him to back out.

"Yeah, I'm ready," he said at last.

Darcy glared at her boyfriend with a look of utter disappointment. "Fools." Her mouth turned down as she fought to hide her fear.

For once, Fate understood how Darcy was feeling. Fate was terrified for Jessie. Her best friend and the others had no business going out there to face those monsters. Their courage was false. Any bravery they felt was being artificially pumped into their brains by the Dragon Eyes. What would happen if their headgear got knocked off? Would they be able to defend themselves, or would they be paralyzed by fear?

Eustace pushed away from the table and paced. "This is insane. What was I thinking going along with this? I can't allow any of you to go. You're just kids."

"How different is this from governments drafting eighteen year olds into the army and sending them to war?" Fate asked.

Eustace stopped and looked at her, his jaw clenching as he shook his head. "No, it's not like that. Everyone here has a choice."

"Yes, they do." Fate looked at the seal glimmering bright beneath the skin of her palm. "But I don't. I took an oath to protect the Keep. I want so bad to leave here, but…"

She trailed off, realizing she'd been fooling herself into thinking she could actually leave to go find Finn. Her place was here, defending the Keep. As much as she wanted to go to him–*needed to*–she knew deep in her bones she could not turn her back on her responsibilities. Taking the oath had changed her on a fundamental level. Whatever this part of her was now, it rose to the surface and refused to be ignored any longer.

She took a step toward Eustace. "I'm sorry, Dad, I have to

do this, and there's nothing you or I can do to keep any of this from happening."

23
HERE KITTY, KITTY

"TAKE THE AERONAUT PACK before I throw it at you." Brune's jaw flexed as she stared Fate down.

Fate backed away with her hands up. "I told you, I don't need it. I can fly on my own."

"Since when?"

"Since I gave myself the power with the Words of Making."

A look of surprise replaced Brune's scowl and she set the pack down. "Wow, you actually gave yourself the power to fly? Huh, I never thought to give myself that one when I was inside the *Book of Fables*. Smart."

Fate nodded proudly, and with excitement. She was looking forward to a good flight. It had been awhile.

Brune relaxed and rested her hands on her hips. "Let's see."

Fate glanced around at everyone, suddenly self-conscious. "You'll see soon enough. Open the hatch."

"I'd rather see it in here."

"Why?"

"I'm mostly just curious, but we should probably make sure you're not rusty, or something."

"It's like riding a bike. You never forget."

Jessie stepped in next to Brune. "Do it, Fate. I've been wanting to see you fly since you first told me you could."

Fate's insides squirmed with discomfort. Something wasn't right. Why was Brune egging her on this way? She glanced at Eustace. His confused expression wasn't helping. "Well there's not a lot of room in here, but if you insist," she muttered.

Steve, Darcy and Mason cleared the center of the room,

while her father and everyone else stepped back against the walls.

Feeling edgier by the second, Fate shook it off as best she could and leaped into the air with her arms extended. She caught air for a nanosecond then plummeted, crashing to the floor with all the elegance of a belly flop. The blow came like a punch to the gut, knocking the wind out of her as she rolled on her side, curling in on herself and cradling her stomach. The pain of her fall turned to nauseating shock. She understood why she and the other warriors had lost the supernatural powers Murauda had given them. With the death of the war goddess, their powers had slowly waned to nothing. But she'd always assumed that whatever power she'd gained from the Words of Making would be permanent.

The heat of humiliation scorched her face when she heard the guffaws and snickers in the room. Eustace was suddenly crouched next to her. "Ignore them. Are you alright?"

"My ego's maimed, but I'm fine," Fate groaned as she allowed Eustace to help her stand. She turned to Brune. "You already knew my power to fly hadn't stuck. You could've just told me."

"And miss seeing you flop on your face?" Brune chuckled with satisfaction.

Eustace moved into Brune's space with one step and towered over her. "I hardly think that was called for."

Brune's smile vanished as she edged back. "Hey, you got a problem with making people laugh? It's a morale booster and eases the tension before going on a mission that might get them killed."

The laughter in the room died. Eustace remained silent as well, but Fate could tell by the tension across his shoulders that he was still furious.

Fate walked over to the aeronaut pack Brune had been forcing on her and picked it up. "Okay, how do I wear this thing and how do I drive it?" She frowned at the tangle of straps and flimsy set of wiry, dragonfly-shaped wings attached to the motor.

Brune didn't bother to look at her. She was busy inspecting the straps on the aeronaut packs Jessie, Lincoln and Mason were wearing. "You should know. You're the new guardian."

Fate's jaw dropped. "Really? You helped them, but you're not going to help me?"

Brune cinched the straps crisscrossing her torso, walked over to the hatch and punched the button. The grinding sound of metal filled the room as the iris of the hatch spiraled open. She stuck her head out, looking this way and that. "Nope," she finally said. And with that, she revved the gears on her aeronaut pack and jumped.

Mason gave Darcy a quick peck on the cheek–she'd already refused to kiss him goodbye–and followed behind Lincoln, bumping into him when he hesitated to jump. "What're you waiting for?"

"Jusht makin' sure the Chimera'sh not around."

"Brune already checked." Mason glanced back at Fate. "Didn't she?"

Lincoln punched him in the arm. "A double check never hurtsh. Yup, all'sh clear!" he yelled as he leaped into a freefall.

"Idiots! All of you," Darcy shouted.

Mason made an about-face and jumped before he had to listen to another word.

Jessie paused at the opening before turning to Fate. "Hurry up. And *please* get it together. Our lives depend on it." With a shake of her head, she jumped and vanished from sight.

Fate's heart hammered in her chest as she hooked the pack's curved bars over her shoulders. How was she supposed to figure out how the straps worked? If she didn't get it right, she could slip out of the pack and fall to her death.

"Here, let me help," Eustace offered.

Farouk trundled his cage over to them. "No, the guardian must do this herself." His slanted eyes slid to Fate. "You have all the knowledge you need for everything the Keep holds. All that's required is a question."

"All I've been doing is wondering how the heck I'm going to untangle this mess of straps."

"Be exactitude with your question. The answer will come."

Gerdie encouraged her with a nod.

Taking a deep breath, Fate closed her eyes and asked for instructions on how to wear and operate the aeronaut pack. She no sooner asked when a deep knowing came over her. Her hands moved of their own accord, crossing the straps with precision, buckling in and tightening the give as if she'd done it her whole life.

She turned the ignition. The wings whirred and vibrated across her back. "Guess this means I'm ready to go." She grabbed her helmet and pulled it on.

Eustace and Gerdie followed her over to the hatch. "Be careful," her father said, his eyes filled with fear.

Gerdie put her small hand in his. "Don't worry. She can take care of herself."

"She's right, Dad. I can do this." Fate mustered a smile that shook at the corners of her mouth.

Fearing she might lose her nerve entirely if she gave into Eustace's concerns, she turned and launched into space. The brief yet sharp tug of gravity startled her before the aeronaut pack kicked upward, thrusting her forward with surprising speed. Relief flooded her limbs, though she was still nervous about relying on a machine to keep her in the air. What if it broke down or ran out of fuel?

She glanced down at the intricate network of architectural wonders far below. A dizzying moment of vertigo gripped hold, frightening her. Flying had become second nature and heights had never been a problem, until this moment.

Her confidence was shaken. She still hadn't recovered from finding out she'd lost her power to fly. That was an ace she'd thought she would always have up her sleeve. She'd have to play it cool in front of Jessie and the others though. None of them had any problem diving from a height that made the Empire State building look like a tiny toothpick, and she'd already made a fool of herself.

Unfortunately, she was in jeopardy of furthering their low opinion of her if she didn't figure out where the others were located soon. She glanced around, trying to spot them, while also watching for signs of the Chimera.

Brune's voice crackled in the headphone built into her helmet. "Fate, we can see you. Continue veering left." She paused. "No, your other left."

Fate corrected course before she caught sight of Brune, Jessie and the boys hovering in the distance. She'd no sooner caught up with them, when they all turned and continued moving ahead.

"Stay alert, people," Brune ordered. "We're coming up on Quadrant 29. Keep an eye out for–." Her voice cut out to a hissing sound.

Frustrated with the fuzzy reception, Fate tapped the earpiece. If it wasn't for the fact that she could see Brune flying up ahead, she might've thought something had happened to her. She'd have to talk to Farouk about updating their equipment when they got back.

If they made it back.

Fate's nerves jittered with heightened tension as she fell in line with the others and followed Brune's descent until they were skimming above the seemingly endless maze of vaults below. Now that she was closer, she was struck by the sprawling landscape of diverse structures, whether they were temples, mausoleums, towers, castles, cathedrals, pyramids or enormous statues. The surface of the Keep looked more like one huge exotic city unified only by moving walkways snaking in and around them.

Curiosity stirred in Fate. Under any other circumstances, she would've welcomed the opportunity to explore every one of the unusual structures. But too much was riding on being on guard and this was no time for distractions. They were in Chimera territory.

"Nearing the end of Quadrant 29," Brune informed them.

"Shouldn't we've seen the Chimera by now?" Fate tried to ignore the hairs rising on the back of her neck. The words were no sooner out, when a distant roar sounded from behind them.

"Crap!" Lincoln yelled. "It'sh coming up from behind! How'd we get thish far without sheeing it?"

Adrenaline shot through Fate, lacing her veins with panic as she glanced over her shoulder. The flapping of huge, multi-jointed bat wings crested the rooftops before she saw the entire body of the creature land on a towering jade statue of a rearing unicorn. With another terrible roar, the Chimera leaped back into the air, breaking off the horse's head beneath its tremendous weight as it pushed off.

"Don't look back. It'll slow you down!" Brune shouted. "Follow me and stay the course. We have a ways to go before we hit quad 148."

Brune was right; Fate shouldn't have looked. She'd almost come to a standstill. Jessie and Lincoln were already speeding past her. But Mason was turned toward the beast and hovering in place.

"Mason!" Fate yelled. "Move! Get out of here!"

He spun around and started towards her, but the Chimera had already closed the gap between them. Rising just above Mason, the creature's snake tail lashed out, coiled round his torso and flung him against an enormous granite gargoyle. Mason's body crumpled on impact and fell to the ground like a rag doll. With a fiery growl, the Chimera began to descend, no doubt to finish the kill.

Fate sped toward the Chimera, yelling at the top of her lungs to distract the monster. Both heads turned to look in her direction. Fate cranked the gears into full throttle and darted away to reach Jessie and the others.

"Mason's down," she reported. "We need to go back for–."

A blow from behind flung her off course and she plummeted head over heels. Not knowing up from down, she gripped the gears and revved the engine. The aeronaut pack kicked in, righting her enough to catch her bearings.

A few hundred yards away, the Chimera grappled the side of a spiraled tower, the lion's head turned in the opposite direction, searching for her. Fortunately, she'd been knocked through the air like a stray baseball and it didn't seem to know which direction it had so carelessly batted her. But then the creature's scaly tail snaked upward and the serpent locked eyes with her.

With heart pounding in her throat, Fate turned, weaving her way through a series of spires topping the dome of a crystal cathedral. She'd barely reached the other side when she heard the crush of the spires behind her as the beast gave chase.

Brune's voice broke through the sound of Fate's pulse drumming in her ears. "Fate, you're leading it the wrong way!"

"Well, I'm sorry!" Fate shouted into her mouthpiece as she darted around the corner of a gilded Parthenon-style temple. "What do you want me to do? Stop and give it directions?"

"Take cover between the –" Brune's voice cut out.

Fate hovered in place, slapping the earpiece. "Between the what?"

The Chimera burst from the middle of the temple, toppling five of its massive columns. Screaming for her life, Fate dodged out of the way to avoid being crushed by a falling column and dipped in between an ivory castle and dark monolith etched with symbols. She felt safer in the lower regions of the Keep. Given the Chimera's size, she hoped it might avoid chasing her in the confined space.

Brune's voice returned. "That's good. Stay low. I'll tell you where to go."

Clinging to Brune's commanding voice, Fate nodded silently as she gazed skyward. Growling flames surged from above as the Chimera swooped low before sweeping high to come around for another pass. She cringed from the heat. "Which way do I go?"

"Straight ahead and to the right."

Staying close to ground level, Fate sped through the narrow space between the different structures then veered to the right and ducked under the archway of a stone bridge.

"Can you see the twin obelisks yet?" Brune asked.

Fate flew a little higher and squinted at the distant horizon. "Yeah, I think so."

"Make sure your amplifier is on when you get there. The Fomorians are camped out in the coral coliseum right next to the obelisks."

The sound of smashing stone jolted Fate back into panic mode as she turned to see the Chimera bulldozing through a pagoda. She launched skyward and rocketed over the varied skyline. The monster's furious roar echoed throughout the expanse as it closed in from behind. Claws sliced the air next to her head. Gasping with shock, she ducked low, zigzagging between a bell tower and the peak of a silver pyramid. A snarling inferno surged at her back as she pushed the aeronaut pack's speed to its limit. Leaning her head into the wind, she raced to the obelisks and jetted between them, her heart hammering, flooding her body with adrenaline.

She'd made it to the finish line. The Fomorians could take it from there.

Suddenly, the hot slice of the Chimera's claw drove into her calf, hurtling her sideways through space. Unable to self-correct, Fate smacked against a wall. Pain exploded through her back as she crashed to the ground. The air slammed from her lungs and her leg throbbed. Her vision filled with stars as she fought to keep from passing out.

The Chimera's roar resounded above her. Fate looked up, eyes wide as the creature pitched downward, its wings catching the air like a ragged kite. She scrambled to her feet, but her leg gave out and she fell. Not that there was an exit. She was hemmed in on every side.

Fate drew her laser gun and pulled the trigger. A blinding stream of red light blasted the Chimera in the chest. The beast landed in front of her, rearing back with a pained roar as smoke rose from a deep bloody gash. But it wasn't enough to kill the behemoth.

With arms shaking, Fate shot again, this time missing its body. The laser beam sliced into a wing instead. The lion's head jerked, eyeing the shredding membranous skin of its wing with a snarl. Its gaze snapped back to Fate at the same time the snake's head arched with a hiss over the lion's head.

Terror froze Fate in place.

Brune's voice jarred her to attention. "Fate! You need to move. Now!"

Fate cranked on the gears, expecting to lift off. The pack's engine wasn't running. She turned the ignition with no response. "Oh no, the fall wrecked my pack! What do I do?"

No answer from Brune, her voice had cut out again.

"I'm coming, Fate!" Jessie's voice screamed in her ear.

"Stay away!" Fate yelled as she fired at the approaching Chimera with a steady stream of red cutting light.

The creature writhed and growled, swiping at the laser beam like a cat swatting flies. The laser seemed to be more of an irritation than anything else, but Fate didn't know what else to do.

The Chimera lashed at her, knocking the laser gun from her hands. Dizzy with fright, she staggered backward and turned her head, expecting to be incinerated on the spot. But the flames never came.

The enclosed space rumbled with a shriek of pain. Fate opened her eyes as Jessie drove her sword deep into the monster's back.

An even greater fear filled Fate when the snake struck Jessie from behind. "Look out!" she screamed.

Jessie whirled round, blocked the snake's bite with her protected forearm then launched skyward. "Here kitty, kitty," Jessie said, her tone playful, "Come and get me."

The Chimera leaped into the air, its leathery wings flapping furiously as it chased after Jessie.

"Jessie, no!" Fate cried, choking on her tears. Her heart was racing and her breath had accelerated into short, painful bursts. Panic had set in. After seeing Mason swatted out of the air like an insect, she feared Jessie would meet the same end. She'd never felt more helpless than at that moment.

Fate drew her bloody leg to her chest and pressed on the gash. She winced. Not so much from the physical pain. That, she could handle. The grief seeping into her heart was what she couldn't bear. If the worst happened to Jessie, she'd never forgive herself.

Ever.

24
FALL ASLEEP AND NEVER WAKE

"MY QUEEN, THIS IS no place for a lady," the guard warned as he unlocked Finn's cell. "This filthy animal is not to be trusted."

"Open the door and leave me to speak to the prisoner alone," a woman's voice commanded.

Finn struggled to open his eyes, but his lids were heavy and continued to close. Hunger and thirst had made him weak and listless. After Tynan's visit, he'd resigned himself to a swift execution, but the dreaded day had not yet come. He'd even expected to be tortured like the other prisoners he heard screaming throughout the dungeon. Instead, he'd been left alone to rot in his cell. No one came with even the most meager amount of food and water.

As the days blurred together, Finn's strength waned, his mind grew muddled and he lost all track of time. Sleep took over. At first, sweet dreams of Fate rescued him from his hellish existence. His jaw ached from the wooden plug wedged in his mouth. But as he grew more and more parched, his dreams turned to dark roiling waves, forever thrashing him in a heaving ocean as he gulped thirstily, only to vomit buckets of brackish water afterwards.

Since then he'd been plagued with hallucinations of being carried to a public courtyard, where the executioner waited. He'd lay his head on the block and just as the axe came down, the waking nightmare ended and he'd find himself back in his cell. Now and then his delirious visions shifted to Fate appearing in his cell. They would hug and kiss and she would say she was there to use her Words of Making to take him away. She'd write down his escape in her little notebook, speak the words aloud and vanish without him.

Those were the worst dreams.

Finn buried his face against his arm. He'd rather die than be tortured by false hopes again and again. Yet his spirits had already lifted at the thought of someone wanting to speak to him. Or was this just another trick of his dehydrated brain? What woman would actually come into this cesspool to see him? Unless it was the Lhiannon Shee. Had she finally come to help him escape?

The swish of silk and the scent of flowers washed over him like a fresh breeze as the woman entered his cell. He heard the ruffle of her dress as she bent down and touched his forehead. Her hand was soft and cool. The kind touch, after so much isolation and hardship, brought tears to his eyes.

"You poor thing. Here take some water." Lifting his head, she did her best to pour water past the plug but he only received a few precious drops. "You must understand, my husband is not a cruel man. He's doing what he thinks is right and just."

Taking a shred of strength from her gentle presence, Finn forced himself to a sitting position. His dulled brain swirled as he tried to focus on her, but his vision was bleary. Through the fog, she seemed to be an angel. Her long hair fell in golden cascades over a dress of silvery blue. She was a brilliant splash of color against the dark, grimy walls holding him prisoner. She was light where there had only been darkness.

Recognition slowly surfaced and he realized this must be Princess Kaura. Though she would be queen now. Was this another hallucination? What reason would she have for coming to this horrible place?

"You know my father, O'Deldar?" she asked.

Hope surged through Finn as he nodded vigorously.

"He explained everything to me before he left us. I know why you had to do what you did. You do not deserve this treatment."

Finn frowned at her in confusion. If she knew the truth, why hadn't she told Tynan? Or had she? Is that why there's been no execution? Did he mean to let him slowly starve to death instead?

"I cannot tell my husband what I know," she said as if in answer to his silent questions. "Even if he could make himself believe the destruction Moria brought down upon his beloved kingdom, he would still insist on having you punished. You killed his mother, and as a king, he cannot allow you to go free."

Finn bit down on the wooden plug, his body shaking with disappointment.

"I dispatched a messenger hawk to my people in the Eldunough Islands as soon as I heard you'd been captured. They have soldiers skilled in ways to free you without my husband knowing who is behind your escape. They're due to arrive in two days."

Finn's pulse raced with renewed hope.

Kaura's gray eyes filled with sadness as she reached out to brush the hair off Finn's brow. "Unfortunately, my husband chose to keep your imprisonment a secret from me until he publicly announced the date of your execution. I'm so sorry to tell you this, but your execution has been set for tomorrow."

Finn stared at her in disbelief. Why dangle hope in his face, only to snatch it away? He closed his eyes, banging the back of his head against the stone wall over and over again.

Jarring pain rattled his skull.

Kaura grabbed his face. "Please stop," she pleaded. "I asked my husband to extend the date, but he's afraid you're too close to death already and he will not risk denying the kingdom of your public execution."

Finn collapsed against the wall, his body quaking with fury and grief. Why had she even bothered to come to him at all? This was by far the cruelest act he'd endured thus far.

"Now that I know you cannot be saved from the executioner's blade, I will not stand by and watch you suffer a minute longer." She pulled out a small vial of red liquid. "This will bring about your end peacefully. You will fall asleep and never wake."

Finn stared at the vial in horror, yet part of him ached for the painless, easy death she offered.

"Do you want it now?"

"No," a voice in his head said, firmly and with instant anger. It was Fate's voice. Finn stared at the poison Kaura offered as shame overcame him. Fate would never allow him to give up this way. He'd almost allowed defeat and self-pity to get the best of him.

It didn't matter that he was destined to die the next day. He would face what was to come head on. He cringed. In this case, head off.

He met Kaura's gaze and gave her a stern shake of his head.

"Are you certain?"

For the first time in weeks, his mind was clear as he gave her a firm nod.

Kaura set the vial down next to him and rose to a standing position. "In case you change your mind. Crush the glass with your foot. The poison is absorbed through the skin." She walked to the door and turned. "May you be blessed in the next life."

Finn waited for the guard to lock the cell door behind her before kicking the vial out of reach. He couldn't risk another moment of weakness.

Resting his head against the wall, he closed his eyes. Her visit had exhausted him, sapping what little energy he had left. As he drifted along the edge of sleep, he heard a scratching noise, followed by a quick little whistle of his flute.

Finn's eyes popped open. An odd looking creature froze under his stare. It held the broken half of his flute in its pink hands, its mouth in the shape of an 'O' as it blinked at him. If it wasn't the size of a cat, and with feathered wings no less, he would've thought it was a field mouse.

The creature's whiskers twitched as it lifted the flute to Finn. "Is this lovely music maker yours?"

Certain the hallucinations were back, Finn blinked a few times, expecting the oversized mouse to disappear. When it didn't, he decided to give into the delusion. It's not like he had anything better to do. "Mmhmm," he replied.

"Oh my." The mouse ran its hand over the Druidic inscriptions. "You're a lucky one, to have such a thing of beauty."

Finn shrugged. "I don't feel very lucky." But with the plug in his mouth the words were unintelligible.

"What was that?" the mouse asked. "Would you mind if I removed the strap around your head so I might understand you better?"

Finn nodded, then quickly shook his head to let the mouse know he wouldn't mind at all.

The mouse set the flute down carefully, flew to Finn's shoulder and crawled around to the back of his head. Nimble fingers felt around for the buckle buried beneath the locks of his shoulder-length hair. After a bit of fumbling around, the leather strap fell free, the weight of it pulling at the wooden plug.

Finn pushed the rest of it out with his tongue, letting the torturous gag fall in his lap. Pain sliced through his stiff jaw as he closed his mouth for the first time since his capture. "Thank you," he croaked.

The mouse flew back down to the floor and picked up the flute. "You're welcome. Now what was it you were saying?"

"Uh…I can't remember."

"No matter." The mouse paused a moment as it went back to admiring the flute before blowing another soft, quick note into the mouthpiece.

"Where did you come from?" Finn's mouth was so dry he could barely speak.

"I live in the southern turret, but I make my rounds through the castle regularly. Today's rounds include the horse stables and the dungeon."

Finn studied the creature. "I thought maybe you were from Elsina's island."

The mouse tore its gaze from the flute and trembled. "Oh dear, is she here?"

"The sorceress? No."

"Then why would you speak of her?"

"It's not everyday I see an overgrown, talking mouse with wings. As far as I know, there's only one person who created creatures like you and that's Elsina."

The mouse shot a worried glance over its shoulder. "Most of us fled when her lover flung himself off the cliffs. Elsina's wail of grief sent quakes throughout the island and scared us away."

Finn was quiet a moment, tracing back to when he and Fate had failed to bring about a happy ending for the fairy tale called *The Lonely Sorceress* in the *Book of Fables*. For a split second, he thought maybe Fate hadn't given Elsina the happily-ever-after she needed to escape the big bad book. But Fate had to have escaped or she'd still be stuck in Oldwilde and he would've already found her.

"Do you remember a snake called Sithias?" Finn asked. Fate had given Sithias the ability to shapeshift. And just like the mouse, the snake had wings as well. If Sithias could get to Asgar in time, he could impersonate Tynan and grant a much needed last minute pardon.

"Elsina's spy? Of course."

"Is there any way you could find him and bring him here?"

The mouse scrunched its pink nose in fear. "I don't dare go back there. I'd be punished for leaving."

"I'll let you have the flute if you bring Sithias back here. But it has to be before morning."

The mouse looked at him then down at the flute. Worry played across its furry face as it weighed the risks. After several long minutes, the mouse set the flute down. "I truly love this music maker, but not enough to make me want to go back to Elsina's island."

Finn's heart hammered with panic as the mouse skittered over to the door and squeezed through the bars. "Wait." The dry rasp of his voice echoed inside the cell.

The mouse pulled its head from between the bars and turned to look at him.

"I have two flutes. Would twice the payment be enough?"

The mouse rose on its haunches and searched the cell. "Where is this other music maker?"

Finn peered into the dim corners, searching for the other broken half. At last he saw the tip sticking out of a deep crack it had rolled into. "There." He nudged his chin toward the flute.

The mouse trundled back across the floor and retrieved the flute. It brushed the dirt off and studied the Elder race runes. "Aw, this one is even more magnificent." It blew into what was the end of the flute but no sound came out. Disappointment overshadowed its smile. "It doesn't work."

"Hold it straight up and down just under your mouth and blow."

The mouse did so and jumped when its efforts produced a flat hollow note. "Oh my! I do like the sound of that!"

"Enough to fly back to Elsina's island?"

The mouse pursed its lips into a tight line and tilted its head.

"You drive a hard bargain, but yes, I'll do it."

"Good. Please hurry," Finn whispered hoarsely as the mouse left the two broken halves of the flute with him and wedged itself back through the bars.

Relief washed through Finn like a heavy tranquilizer. As the tension drained, his body went limp. Unable to hold himself upright any longer, he slipped sideways to the floor, fighting to stay awake. Now that he could speak, he was free to invoke the elements. He muttered the rune power for Earth, certain it would ignite at any moment. When the elemental power kicked in he would shake the walls of his prison, crumble the encasement around the locked door and bust it down.

He visualized himself doing just that. Cracking the dingy passageways, caving them in on the guards, pulling stones from the floor with the flick of his hand, building barricades behind him to keep his pursuers from giving chase. He smiled at the thought, sinking fully into the dream, convinced he had broken himself out of his prison.

"I'm free," he murmured. But sleep had won the battle.

25
DISTORTED REALITY AND FRACTURED DIMENSIONS

FATE LIMPED ALONG THE moving walkway as fast as she could, while keeping her gaze fixed on the twin obelisks towering above the vaults surrounding her. She'd torn her aeronaut pack apart, using the wires to tie one of the brass wings to her leg as a splint. The added support helped, but every step was excruciating and her makeshift tourniquet wasn't enough to stop the bleeding. She needed stitches badly.

"Can anyone hear me?" she shouted into her mouthpiece.

Shortly after Jessie had lured the Chimera away, there'd been a flood of unintelligible shouts and screams from Brune and Lincoln. Then nothing. Complete radio silence had descended. Not knowing what had happened to Jessie and the others tortured Fate beyond all reckoning. She worried what she would find when she reached them. Would there be nothing but torn, bloodied bodies?

She gulped down the urge to scream. "Jessie's fine. They're all fine," she told herself. "We're having technical difficulties. That's all." Her hands curled into fists. "Ooh, I swear when I get back, I'm tearing a strip off Farouk for giving us such crappy equipment."

The throbbing in Fate's leg worsened, forcing her to stop and rest. Allowing the moving walkway to carry her forward, she glanced around. The scenery had changed since she'd moved beyond the confined space the Chimera had cornered her. The grouping of vaults surrounding her weren't the massive structures she'd left behind. These were minimal enclosures filled with vegetation.

A garden encircled within elegant arches advanced to the forefront. At the heart of the garden grew a huge tree filled with blossoms surrounded by soft mounds of grass. She would've liked to enter the inviting scene and wondered what sort of magical object this particular vault housed. The answer slotted into her brain. The tree itself was the object of power. Picking a blossom for someone revealed true friendship if the petals turned into gold coins. Anything opposing friendship turned the petals into worms.

Fate shuddered. She hated worms with a passion. At least she didn't feel the need to pick a blossom to test her friendship with Jessie. Her best friend had proven her feelings when she'd risked her life to save her from the Chimera.

Fate clutched her stomach as panic churned deep within. "Please be all right, Jess."

Another vault rose into view. A ring of nine tall oaks surrounded a large standing stone with an image of a woman holding a disc carved on its surface. Water poured from some hidden source within the stone into a moss-covered well. Fate's history with oaks had been unpleasant to say the least. She should've wanted to turn and run from the scene, yet her reaction was the opposite. She was irresistibly drawn to the grove. Before she could question what she was looking at, the intensity of her curiosity revealed the answer: This was the sacred well of Arnemetia, goddess of spring waters and healing.

Perfect, just what her leg needed.

Fate stepped off the walkway, wincing as she stumbled from the unexpected drop. Favoring her injured leg, she moved gingerly between the oaks, while also checking the sprawling canopy overhead to ensure the branches weren't moving unnaturally. Most of the oaks she'd encountered inside the *Book of Fables* had a nasty habit of grabbing and skewering their victims alive.

Once inside the grove, the rest of the Keep fell away as she waded through thick beds of delicate white flowers. She was suddenly transported back to the island of Innith Tine, where Finn had been interred within the giant oak. She'd spent months sitting at the base of the massive tree, waiting for his release. During that time, she'd watched the barren island return to life at an incredible speed, until at last the forest had returned to its former glory. This grove was like a little slice of those woods.

When Fate reached the well, she sat down on a low ring of stones, the rough edges cushioned by soft moss. The water pouring from the stone was clear, yet the well was filled with a milky substance. Fate dipped her hand into the well and sipped a small amount. The liquid tasted of honeyed cream with a pinch of salt. A thirst like no other came over her and she gulped to her heart's content.

She stopped drinking when a strange tingling overwhelmed her throat, buzzed down her torso and into her injured leg. A cooling sensation eased the hot sting in the wide gash, before sinking into the bone, lifting the sharp ache. Rising to a standing position, she tested her full weight on the leg and smiled when her muscles reacted without pain. She drew her dagger from the sheath and sliced through the wires binding her makeshift splint and let the pieces fall away.

Sheathing the dagger, Fate turned to leave, though with great reluctance. She didn't know if the resistance came from feeling closer to Finn here in the oak grove or if there was some vital detail she was forgetting. Maybe it was a little bit of both, but she didn't need to ponder why she wanted to stay for very long. The answer came unbidden.

Arnemetia's well was not only for healing. This was also a wishing well. All that was required for a wish to be granted was an offering of a treasured possession.

Fate knew exactly what she'd need to give up to have her

deepest wish granted. Removing her helmet and gloves, she pulled at the ribbon round her neck and lifted the small pouch out from under her armor. Squeezing it, she breathed in the aroma of warm leather and the woodsy scent of Finn's sacred tobacco. Tears came to her eyes as she fought against tossing the pouch into the well. How could she let go of the one thing she'd always used to feel connected to him? She highly doubted she would've made it this far if she hadn't had this small but soothing object to keep her going.

But wasn't it worth giving up this last piece of Finn if it meant he could be with her now?

Fate swallowed back the tears and removed the ribbon from her neck. She ran the silk through her fingers and rubbed her thumb over the soft leather. Which one should she offer the wishing well? The scents within the tobacco pouch offered the most comfort, but Finn had cherished his mother's ribbon and he'd given it to Fate as if it had been a piece of his heart.

Decision made. She kept the ribbon and tied it round her wrist.

Closing her eyes, she dangled the tobacco pouch over the well, careful to word her wish silently before daring to say it aloud. She knew all too well the ramifications of careless words spoken in the form of a wish. At last, she opened her eyes and took in a deep, shaky breath. "I wish for Finn to appear before me now." She let the pouch drop into the well, where it vanished in the chalky water.

Seconds ticked by excruciatingly slow as Fate waited for Finn to appear out of nowhere. Afraid impatience would get the best of her, she forced herself to stay rooted to the spot. Much to her relief, the water stirred as a head pushed through the opaque surface, followed by broad shoulders, strong arms and muscled torso.

Fate's heart pounded out of control as she watched Finn's

familiar form rise in front of her, his head bent. At first he was completely covered in the milky substance and seemed made of the stuff. But then the liquid disappeared, soaking into his clothes and skin once he stepped free of the well.

He lifted his head, eyes wide as he stared at her through strands of bronzed blonde falling in careless waves over his rune-marked temple. "Fate? Is it really you?"

She was shaking from head to foot, barely able to breathe. All she could do was nod.

He closed the space between them in two steps, scooped her in his arms and whirled her around in circles. "I can't believe you're here!" His breath feathered against her skin as he nuzzled his face against her neck.

A euphoric thrill passed through her body. "Me either," she whispered breathlessly. She pressed against him, inhaling the masculine scent of his skin.

He pulled back to look at her, his eyes roving over her face. A smile curved his mouth as he moved in for a kiss. Afraid she was dreaming, Fate stopped him by putting her hands on each side of his face, taking in every detail–the golden stubble shadowing the strong line of his jaw, the enticing curve of his mouth and the green of his irises flaming bright with excitement.

Finally convinced he was real, she coiled her fingers in his hair and pulled him close. The moment their lips met, Fate lost herself in the sweet taste of his mouth. Buried desire erupted to the surface like a raging fever. Trembling, she slid her hands along his back, kissing him with wild abandon. She pressed her body against his, but the armor she was wearing formed a wall between them.

"Wait, hold on." She hastily unbuckled the shoulder pads and breastplate. Letting the pieces topple to the ground, she fumbled with the arm and leg bracers and tossed them aside. Crooking her finger with a playful smile, she invited Finn to pick up where they'd left off.

He gladly stepped forward, circling his arms round her waist as she wriggled close. The heat of his body soaked into her, tipping her into a dizzying fall of sweet oblivion.

If ever there was a more perfect place or time to surrender herself completely, it was here and now. Their past had been riddled with obstacles, but there was nothing in the way anymore. Finn was free of the darkness. They were free to be together without fear of being torn apart by anyone or anything.

Fate pulled him down into the field of flowers. Finn followed eagerly, leaning over her with a look of wonder on his face. She traced her finger over his mouth. "I love you, Finn."

He kissed her fingers. The warmth of his lips sent delicious shivers along her arm. "And I love you." His voice was hoarse with emotion. "I've always loved you, Fate, even before we met."

Tears welled in her eyes. "I've missed you so much."

"And I you." He gently kissed away the tear escaping down her cheek.

She closed her eyes as his mouth trailed over the line of her jaw, down to the length of her neck and along her shoulder. Unable to contain the fire building inside, Fate arched against him. Finn responded in kind, his limbs interlocking with hers in a surge of unbridled desire.

A state of pure bliss pulsed through Fate's veins. Her body hummed with joy as she opened her heart and soul. Nothing else mattered than this moment. Heaven could wait, if this wasn't it.

Suddenly, Finn's body went rigid in her arms and he lifted off her.

Fate's eyes flew open. "What's wrong?" she cried out. But he stared at her, mute with a stunned look of pain darkening his face. Her mind reeled as she tried to make sense of what was happening. That's when she noticed the claw sticking out of his chest. She screamed as Finn's body dissolved into liquid, splashing over her feet and pooling in a puddle of white water beside her.

Standing in the empty space above her, with clawed hand still extended, was a hideous creature with a fleshy bulbous head of writhing eels for hair. Sickening emanations of power radiated from its beady red eyes.

Gasping, Fate scrambled back on all fours. Unbearable grief edged with raw terror descended upon her like a vicious storm. What was this monster and what had it done to Finn?

The answer slid into her brain. She was in the presence of a Fomorian, a being whose mere presence distorted reality and fractured dimensions. She glanced past the branches and spotted the twin obelisks. She'd lost complete track of time and the vault had already passed into Fomorian territory without her realizing it. Her gaze darted to the utility belt holding the chromatic amplifier she needed to disrupt the Fomorian's mind-bending effects.

Eel Head was standing on the belt and her holstered laser gun was tickling its blubbery toe.

Just then two more Formorians entered the oak grove. One trundled in at a slow pace, the bulk of its deformed body carried forward on long spindly arms with mangled knuckles for feet. The other being was more human in form, except for the thick quills radiating from its temples, skin as rough and wrinkled as an elephant's hide and chilling, blood red eyes. When they joined Eel Head, some form of silent communication seemed to pass between them before they turned their full attention on Fate.

Immense power radiated from their presence, a grating energy that agitated the very air and scraped along the edge of Fate's nerves. The Fomorians stared at her. The combined force of their attention crashed over her like a dark tide, sucking her into an undertow of despair. Fear stabbed her heart. She tried to remember what came before this wave of anguish, but all that existed was the pain of having Finn ripped from her arms and the dread that he might be dead.

Forgetting all else, she edged over to the puddle and cupped her hands in the milky water. "Finn, come back to me," she begged as tears rushed freely. "Please, I need you."

The water rippled in response before giving way to a head that formed from the creamy liquid and pushed out of the shallow pool. Fate's sobs turned to hysterical laughter as the masculine, dripping, claylike form rose in front of her, before the chalky water dried back and revealed the man. But this was not Finn.

Fear locked the air in Fate's throat as she looked into the stone-faced expression of the sorcerer, Wodrid. He gripped her by the neck and lifted her to eye level. Fate grabbed at his wrist, flailing her legs and struggling to breathe. "You!" he said, his voice a low scream. "You're the one who stole the Rod of Aeternitis from me!"

Confusion caved in on Fate. Her memory of how she'd come into possession of the Rod had always been lost to her because she'd been under Brune's spell at the time. But now the memory cracked wide open. She'd stolen the Rod from O'Deldar and it was Wodrid's blood she'd been covered in when she'd returned after three forgotten days.

Wodrid threw her to the ground. "And you took my leg too!" He glowered as he swiped his red cloak aside to show his false leg. It was cast in silver and molded in the form of armor.

Fate scrambled to her feet. Dizzy, she shook her head, unable to see straight. The space between them seemed to buckle. Light guttered on and off, and nightmarish shapes crept along the edges of the trees. "I don't know you. We've never met," she lied, hoping he'd leave her alone.

Amusement smoothed the scowl from his fine, elfin features.

If not for his contemptuous gaze, he was almost beautiful. "Hmm, come to think of it, you're not the vicious warrior who sliced my limb clean out from under me. She was inhumanly fast and strong. You're nothing but a weak, mewling coward."

A sick squirming sensation in Fate's stomach confirmed the truth. He was right. She'd left that fierce warrior behind in the *Book of Fables* and had since turned back into a wimp in need of saving. Her fall from supernatural to ordinary had left her more vulnerable than she'd been willing to admit until this moment.

Wodrid stepped forward with his hand outstretched. "I'll be taking the Rod now. You have no right to what has always been mine."

A familiar possessiveness surfaced from Fate's hindbrain. She grabbed at the chain and gripped the Rod hard in her fist.

"We can do this the easy way or the hard way." He took another step toward her and stopped when she inched away. "Oh, is that how it's going to be?"

Fate went very still as dark folds of power writhed around him. The overwhelming pressure sucked the air away as he raised his arm and flexed his hand. A storm brewed in his upturned palm, building into a churning black mist shot through with sparks of electricity.

He smiled, then flung the energy. Twisting tendrils of power curled around Fate, simmering her flesh until she screamed with the pain of being boiled alive. Falling to the ground, she thrashed at the creeping vines of scorching darkness covering her. Wodrid bent down, grabbed the chain and tore the Rod from her neck.

"No–" The suffocating swarm of heat and dark energy snatched away her cry. Fate gasped for air. She couldn't breathe, couldn't breathe. The thick metallic tang of searing black magic filled her throat and lungs. She was choking to death. The weight of it dragged her down, down, down, where light ceased to exist.

26
COPIOUS AMOUNTS OF CHOCOLATE

"ISH SHE DEAD? Oh man, I've never sheen a dead body before. It'sh uber creepy."

"She's not dead!"

"Are you sherious? Nobody alive ish that pale. That girl'sh takin' a dirt nap."

"Out of the way, you idiot. Fate, wake up."

Pain sliced across Fate's face. She grabbed her cheek and opened her eyes to Brune hovering over her. Raw misery flooded into Fate's aching head. "What's going on?" She rubbed her dry grainy eyes, trying to focus. Lincoln crowded in close to Brune, staring like a rubber-necker at a train wreck. But where was Jessie?

"You passed out." Brune's tone implied Fate had inconvenienced everyone.

"Where's Jessie? Is she alright?"

"I'm here." Jessie appeared over the top of Fate's head and knelt down. "Can you sit up?"

Fate teared up at the sight of her friend. Too emotional to speak, she let Jessie help her rise to a sitting position.

Jessie cringed. "Looks like the Chimera got your leg pretty good."

"It was just a scratch. It's all better now. I drank from the well."

Worry crossed Jessie's face as Fate shakily rose to her feet, but as soon as she put weight on the leg, pain shot through her calf. "Ow, ow, ow!"

Jessie grabbed her by the arm to keep her from tipping over.

"You drank that? No wonder you're sick. You've got to be more careful. You could've died."

Fate glanced over at the well water. It was murky and covered in pond scum. "I don't get it. The well was…" She trailed off, her mind jumping to the sweet creamy water she'd enjoyed and her deepest wish come true, which had turned into the most terrifying nightmare.

"Not a watering hole for birdbrains," Brune finished for her. "It's a wishing well. No healing involved."

"Uh…I, uh…" Fate stammered, now thoroughly confused. If her leg wasn't healed, where did that leave Finn? Her chest tightened with grief. She refused to believe he'd been taken from her again.

Brune waved her off. "Don't sweat it. The Fomorians messed with your head."

"Oh my god, that's right." Fate looked around nervously for the monsters. "They were here. What happened? Where are they?" And where was Wodrid? Her hand flew to her neck. She was still wearing the necklace with the Rod. He hadn't actually taken it. Had she hallucinated the entire thing?

"All gone." Brune swung the chain holding the silver box containing the Eye of Balor. "Worked like a charm too."

"Yeah, it was shick!" Lincoln added. "The Eye wush like a ninth-level shcorching ray with bonush to fire damage on each ray."

"No way," Jessie argued. She scooped a handful of silt piled next to her. "Did you not see how those freaks broke apart? That was ninth-level disintegration damage if anything."

Fate sighed with exhaustion. "Does it really matter? This isn't a video game."

"No it'sh even better." Lincoln grinned.

Fate made a face at the ridiculous direction they'd gone in. "You might want to ask Mason if he agrees with that. Has anyone heard from him or is our substandard equipment still on the fritz?"

"The gear's fine," Brune said. "The Fomorians scrambled the frequencies, even before we reached this quadrant."

"Mason's all right," Jessie assured Fate. "He sounded pretty banged up, but he's alive. His pack's totaled, so we'll have to pick him up on the way back."

Fate nodded with relief. "What about the Chimera? Did you manage to lead it to the Fomorians before they paid me a visit?"

"Oh yeah, talk about epic!" Lincoln cut in. "That thing shtuck to Jeshie like white on rice. But you should've sheen her, she Shpideyed her way out of it and got the Chimera down into the colisheum."

Fate stared at her friend in awe. "Wish I'd seen that."

Jessie's face lit up. "You wouldn't have believed your eyes. The coliseum was filled with mutants, all squishing and crabbing around. Talk about gross."

"The mind blower wush when the Chimera hit their air shpace," Lincoln added. "It totally shpazzed. You should've sheen how the shnake went to town on the lion. It shank itsh fangsh in right up until it croaked."

Fate grimaced. "Yeah, too bad I missed that."

"All right, time to pack up and jet." Brune had obviously grown bored with the conversation.

Fate limped over to her armor and started strapping on the leg bracers.

Jessie followed her over to the strewn pieces. "Why'd you take your armor off?"

Fate winced as she tightened the strap around her injured calf. "That's a story best told over much pizza and copious amounts of chocolate. You in?"

Jessie glanced down at the Dragon Eye headgear, turning it over in her hands. She almost seemed to be thinking twice about her offer and Fate began to worry she might say no. Then Jessie looked at her. "Sure. I'm in."

"Enterprise replicator, this is not." Fate swallowed the so-called popcorn the food simulator had produced. "Where's the crunch? Salty yes, but spongy mystery curd is not what I ordered."

A knock on the door of her bedchamber had her setting the bowl of sponge balls down and skipping across the room. "I hope you're up to the challenge of describing popcorn in minute detail. Otherwise we're in for a–" Fate stopped in mid sentence when she saw it wasn't Jessie waiting behind the door, but Gerdie. "Oh, hey."

"Heard about your run-in with the Chimera. How's the leg?" Gerdie asked as she entered the room.

"Like it never happened." Fate poked her head out and glanced down the empty hallway for Jessie. She closed the door, trying to ignore the twist of disappointment in her gut. "Didn't Eustace tell you? He was hovering like any good, overly-worried parent when Farouk poured his sparkly, magic potion over my wound."

Gerdie walked over to one of the over-stuffed chairs, which lowered slightly to allow her to climb on easily. The chair rose to its normal hovering height as she settled in with her feet dangling over the edge. "He did. Not that he's takin' any comfort in how fast you healed up. Poor man's kickin' himself for puttin' his only daughter in harm's way."

"It wasn't up to him. He needs to get it through his head I'm not a helpless little kid anymore." Fate chewed on her bottom lip, not wanting to admit out loud how helpless she'd felt when the Chimera had cornered her. Not to mention the freaky fiasco she'd gotten herself into with the Fomorians.

"Doesn't matter. He's your father. He'll always want to protect you," Gerdie reminded her. "But that's not why I'm here." Her brown eyes widened with excitement as she kicked her small feet together. "Remember the good news I told you about?"

Fate sat down across from her. "Oh yeah, in all the almost getting charred and eaten earlier, I forgot about your news flash. Lay it on me."

"Yesterday, I had the librarians search through the records for a portal into Oldwilde." She waited a second to let the information sink in. "I found out what quadrant the gateway's in."

"That's great!" But something like a cold fist closed over Fate's heart and squeezed the joy from her. She slumped in her chair. "I can't leave here, Gerdie. I want to, but I can't."

"I know. You're Keep Guardian. The oath won't let you." Gerdie produced a piece of paper from her pocket and unfolded it. "But you can leave with this. It's a spell to either summon or appoint a proxy guardian in your place."

Fate took the rumpled sheet of paper and skimmed over the words. "This'll release me from my oath?"

"Not exactly. It'll free you from feeling duty bound, so long as your proxy's in place. But if somethin' happens to your stand-in, the oath kicks in and you're back to being emotionally chained to the Keep again."

"Wow, Gerdie, that's huge." Fate's pulse raced with anticipation. This was exactly what she needed. Now she'd be free to find Finn. "Can I do the spell any time I want?"

"Sure, there's no special time you need to do it." Gerdie squirmed in her chair. "Um, there's just one thing. You have to appoint Brune."

Fate stared at Gerdie in shock. "What? You can't be serious! How can I possibly trust Brune after she chucked me into the *Book of Fables*? I almost died in there. Not just once but several times. And how can you trust her? Anyone who would leave her defenseless six-year-old sister in the clutches of a child-eating monster is just…I don't have a word bad enough to describe her!"

"No arguments there, but that was the deal we made. Remember? She said she'd find a way to get you out of your oath, so long as she got to be Keep Guardian again. Well, this is her holding up her end of the bargain."

Fate could not stop shaking her head. "No, no, no. This is insane. What's to stop her from doing something even worse to us once she's got what she wants?"

Gerdie lifted her legs and stared at her toes. "Nothing, I guess."

Fate stood and stormed across the room. She felt torn in half, wanting more than anything to run straight to Finn, but entirely unwilling to surrender her position of power. She stopped in her tracks. Since when had she ever desired power over love? It had to be the oath. It was making her feel this way. She turned back to Gerdie. "I say we squelch on the deal we made with Brune and summon a random proxy."

"Don't you think that's kinda risky?"

"Riskier than appointing Brune? No."

"Think about it. You'd be summoning some innocent girl away from her life the way Brune summoned you."

Twinges of guilt kept Fate from arguing.

"Besides that your proxy needs to be someone with experience. Someone who won't get herself killed her first day on the job like you almost did."

Gerdie had a point, but Fate's distrust of Brune was too great. "Is this the only way Brune can be Keep Guardian?"

"That's what she told me."

"Huh, so that's why your evil sibling was so helpful when the Chimera was ready to chow down on me. She needed to keep me alive." Fate paced back and forth. "We know what happens if my proxy meets an untimely end, but what happens if the untimely ending is mine after I appoint someone? Does that mean the proxy gets to be Keep Guardian on a permanent basis?"

Gerdie thought about it a minute. "I'm not sure."

"You need to find out."

"Done." Gerdie slid off the chair.

"Don't let on that you're noodling around for information. Be subtle," Fate warned her.

Gerdie marched over to the door. "As much as I can, but you don't have a whole lot of time."

"What do you mean? I thought you said I could do the spell anytime."

"The spell yes. It's the portal you gotta worry about. It's going underground in roughly three days, so if you don't go through it before then, you're gonna have to wait a hundred years before you get another chance."

Fate started to complain, when a knock on the door stopped her. Gerdie opened the door to Jessie, who held out a platter full of fudge brownies. "Copious amounts of chocolate at your service. This stuff is the bomb. Waaay better than anything you've tasted on Earth," she said with a wide grin.

Her smile was infectious, causing Fate's worries to recede for the moment. The promise of chocolaty goodness and the tremendous relief at having her best friend back were exactly what she needed to take the edge off.

Gerdie took the brownie Jessie offered. "Mmm, that *is* good." She stepped out into the hallway before turning back to Fate. "I'll let you know when I've got that thing you wanted."

"Thanks, Gerdie." Fate closed the door and followed the aroma of freshly baked brownies into the sitting area.

Jessie set the platter down and flopped on the sofa. "That sounded ominous. What's she talking about?"

Fate grabbed a brownie and curled up on the other end of the sofa. "Just some boring guardian business."

"Oh." Jessie's relaxed demeanor suddenly stiffened.

All the recent hurts rushed back in and Fate tensed. "Do you want to hear about it?"

Jessie rose from the pile of pillows and stared at Fate. "Of course. Why would you even ask? It's not like we haven't shared everything since we were in kindergarten or anything." She crossed her arms and frowned. "I don't know why you keep shutting me out."

Fate's throat went dry. She set the brownie down and pushed the platter away. "Me? You're the one shutting me out."

"Hardly. I've always been the one on the sidelines while I watched the charmed one being showered with one miracle after another. Like the treasures you always stumbled on without the hunt. God, it's so annoying! While you're finding diamond bracelets in purses from thrift stores, I'm finding petrified jellybeans in mine. And the quarter of a million dollar comic book from the garage sale–"

"Which I sold for $10,000 before I knew what it was really worth," Fate reminded her.

"Oh, boo hoo, cry me a river."

Fate stared at Jessie, shocked by this sudden attack. "Do I need to remind you of my nickname at school?"

"So a bat got tangled in your hair at one of the games and you freaked out in front of everybody. Could've happened to anyone."

"I don't know anyone else who's been called Batty since ninth grade. Not exactly the self-esteem builder I was looking for."

"You've got to admit, it's better than what they used to call you in third grade after the worm incident."

Fate bit down on the tears stinging her eyes. Out of those closest to her, Jessie knew how badly traumatized that experience had left her. She still had a worm phobia.

Jessie's expression hardened. "Suck it up, Fate. You turned out all right in the end. You're the gifted one, the bestselling author with droves of fans coming to your book signings. I have no idea what I'm going to do after high school, unless I do what my parents want. Do you see me as a veterinarian? I fall apart when I see a perfectly happy three-legged dog." She shook her head. "But you…your career's set for life. Do you know how many articles of authors I've read who said they struggled for decades before they got where you are? And you got there by *accident*."

"That's because I'm cursed by my name. You know what the dictionary says. Events are beyond my personal control and usually determined by a supernatural power. Look around you. If this doesn't prove it, then I don't know what will." Fate waited for Jessie to absolve her, but she remained stubbornly quiet. Fate sighed. "As for all that hype over my book, I don't even care about that anymore. Not after everything that's happened lately."

"And there's the rub." Jessie laughed, a harsh sound that rang through the room. "I wouldn't let your fans hear that. They'd follow you anywhere. Hell, they did. They're here right now, risking their lives to help you."

"I never asked them to come here!" Fate shouted.

"But they came, and you need to appreciate that they've sacrificed everything for being drawn like moths to the bright light that is you."

Tears welled in Fate's eyes, blurring Jessie's angry face. "You sound like you hate me." She swiped the tears away with the back of her hand. "Do you?"

Jessie dropped her heated gaze and grew quiet.

"How long have you felt this way toward me? Since grade school? Since forever?"

"No." Jessie's voice was so low Fate barely heard her. She lifted her gaze. "Since you became this big deal author. I've been jealous ever since."

"Why? Is that what you want to be?"

"I write stuff," Jessie admitted.

"You do?" Fate fell speechless for a half second. "Why is this news to me? I thought we knew everything about each other."

"I was too embarrassed to show you. My stuff's never been as good as yours."

Fate was flabbergasted. "You've been writing this whole time and never showed me?" She thought back to all the afternoons and weekends they'd spent together thinking up ideas for Fate's stories. Jessie's imagination had always outstripped Fate's. In all that time, she'd never once suspected that Jessie had been interested in writing her own stories. "Okay, when we get back, I have to see what you've written."

"No way, I couldn't stand the humiliation."

"Oh no, you don't. It's happening. And you know what?"

"What?"

"I know I'm going to love it all," Fate assured her. "After all the crazy ideas we've dreamed up together, yours were always the ones I ran with in my stories."

Jessie nodded shyly.

"When this is all behind us and we get back to Earth, we should write something together."

Jessie's eyes lit up. "Yeah? I'd like that."

Fate held out her hand. "Deal?"

Jessie shook her hand. "Deal."

"So, are we good now?"

Jessie let go and squirmed in her seat.

"There's more?" Fate's stomach tightened with dread.

"It's just that ever since you've been back, you've been so careful about what you tell me. Especially about what you don't. It makes me feel like you think I'm too stupid to handle whatever it is you're not telling me."

"I've only been trying to protect you."

"From what? The Chimera? News flash. That was me who saved you from the monster." Jessie tensed, and Fate could see the anger sizzling on the surface. "If anyone here needs protection, it's you."

"You couldn't be more right," Fate admitted. "I'm not brave. I'm scared all the time. Scared for myself, scared for you and Dad. And I…"

"What? Say it, I can take it."

Fate drew her legs to her chest and hugged her knees. "And I hurt all the time. It never stops."

Concern edged out Jessie's frown. "I thought your leg was healed."

"It's not my leg, Jess. It's my heart. I left someone behind and I can't stop missing him. I have this terrible ache in my chest. The pain's always there and I can't tell anyone about it."

Jessie leaned forward. "Tell me. Tell me everything."

The tears stinging Fate's eyes ran freely as she began filling Jessie in about her history with Finn. How she'd first met him at the bookstore and her initial refusal to believe he was her written character come to life. Fate sobbed all the more when she described the day she told Finn the truth about his origins. She relived the painful rift his shock and disbelief had caused them at finding out he was the product of a young girl's offhand daydream.

Jessie listened quietly as Fate went on to describe the

darkness Finn had become infected with. She recounted the insidious changes Finn had gone through when he destroyed the Dragon Empress and Old Mother Grim. She choked on her tears as she described his battle with the darkness and the need to protect her by staying away from her.

As Fate relived her bittersweet reunion with Finn after he had learned to control the dark influence inside him, she calmed down somewhat. Until she came to the part about how she'd carelessly used her Words of Making to summon an ancient nature god to solve a dilemma in one of the earlier fables. She fell back into tears, her body shaking as she told Jessie she was to blame for the nature god returning to inter Finn inside a giant oak in order to restore life back to a barren island.

"I left him, Jess," Fate confessed. "I just left him to rot in that tree."

Jessie rushed over and hugged her. That was all it took to break the dam Fate had so carefully constructed to hold the pain at bay. A flood of sadness and regret washed over her and there was no stopping it. Fate collapsed against her friend, crying an ocean of tears she feared would never stop.

Jessie sat with her, quietly, patiently holding her until her sobs finally subsided. After awhile, Fate drew away and wiped her eyes dry. "So there you have it. The good, the bad and the ugly."

Jessie smiled sadly. "I'm so sorry. I completely misunderstood. It's just that you'd changed so much. You traded in your plaid pants and argyle sweaters for leather armor and I was afraid you wouldn't think I was cool enough to hang out with anymore. Not that I ever really was, but you know what I mean."

"Are you kidding? You saved my butt today! I still can't get over how brave you were. Unlike me." Fate slumped against the pillows. "I'm a total coward without my super powers."

"Don't talk like that. Who wouldn't have a hard time with being normal again? It's so…limited. If I didn't have the Dragon Eye, I never would've gone out there."

They both fell silent.

"I just wish you would've told me how much you were suffering over Finn," Jessie said after a minute. "If I'd known, I never would've been such a brat about my own feelings."

Fate shook her head. "No, it's my fault. I wanted to tell you about him, but there literally hasn't been any time since I got back. And mostly, I couldn't risk falling apart in front of Eustace."

Jessie raised her hands. "I get that. This is not the kind of thing you share with your dad, or any dad, for that matter."

Fate sniffed and nodded.

Jessie grabbed two brownies and handed one to Fate. "So we're good?"

"Better than good."

They bumped brownies and bit into them. Fate swooned when the sweet, buttery chocolate melted over her tongue. "Oh my god. Did I just die and go to heaven?"

"Told you," Jessie said through a mouthful.

Fate finished the brownie and reached for another. "We're in for a doozy of a sugar hangover in the morning."

"And hardly any sleep." There was mischief in Jessie's smile. "There will be no ending the night until I have the complete lowdown on Finn. I need my vicarious thrills and chills, so start talking. I want details–every smooch and cuddle, and other stuff." She eyed Fate with curiosity. "Was there other stuff?"

Fate squirmed under the intensity of Jessie's gaze. "Sort of, but not what you're thinking," she said, her answer muffled by brownie as her thoughts touched on the hallucination of Finn and the free fall she'd taken with him. Had the encounter been real and not some delicious dream that had twisted into the most horrible of nightmares, she would've had 'other stuff' to tell Jessie.

"Don't tell me yet. Lay the groundwork first." Jessie grabbed another brownie. "Okay, go. What's his hotness factor? Mid to high? Or record breaking? He sounds like a sizzler to me, even when he was going through his bad boy phase."

Fate's face flushed with heat. "Oh, you have *no*idea."

27
IT'LL BE OVER QUICK

FRIGID WATER SCORCHED FINN'S skin like fire, ripping him from a comatose-like sleep. Gasping with shock, he checked his surroundings, confused and disoriented. Half a dozen guards stood over him. They'd moved him into a larger room, which wasn't clean by any standards, but seemed spotless compared to his cell. They'd stripped off his soiled rags. He was on the floor, naked as they doused him with another bucket of icy water. Finn curled in on himself, shivering uncontrollably. He wanted more than anything to fight back, but he barely had the strength to lift his head.

One of the guards, who stood out from the others as a royal guard, tossed some clothes at him. "Put these on," he ordered.

Still shaking, Finn grabbed the clothes, his hands fumbling with the legs of the pants as he tried to shove his feet into them and missed.

"For god's sake. You idiots turned him into a bloody invalid," the royal guard complained as he knelt down to help Finn into his clothes.

"The king's orders were to leave him to rot," one of the dungeon guards retorted.

Finn looked away, humiliated by the low level of degradation he'd sunk to. Clenching his teeth to keep them from chattering, he let the royal guard lift him off the ground and heave him over to a table and chair.

"And you took that literally?" the royal guard asked as he helped Finn sit down. "Did it not occur to any of you that we needed the prisoner alive enough to be executed?"

Finn leaned against the table as another guard set a bowl full of gruel in front of him.

"Your last supper," the man grumbled.

The sight of the gray lumps made Finn nauseous. He shook his head and pushed it away. "Water," he rasped.

The royal guard brought one of the buckets over and emptied the last dregs of water into a scratched pewter cup. Finn gulped the water, tipping his head back when he got to the end, waiting for the last precious drop to hit his tongue. But within seconds of drinking the water, his body rejected the sudden influx of life-giving liquid and cramps doubled him over.

"Use your heads. We don't want the Unholy Piper garnering any sympathy by looking pitiful." The royal guard shook his head. "He's thin and can't stand on his own two feet. There'll be no hiding the fact that you've starved the prisoner so close to death, it'll look more like a mercy killing than an execution."

The dungeon guards muttered complaints under their breath, but none of them spoke up.

The royal guard huffed angrily. "Well, there's nothing to be done about it now, short of postponing the execution and all the celebrations that have been planned around it. Get him up and bring him down into the courtyard. And make sure you gag him. We don't want him whistling any of his black magic."

The wrenching inside Finn's gut seized him with pain. He cried out as two guards grabbed him by each arm and lifted him. Another guard came from behind, hooked a rag in his mouth and tied it tight.

"Are there no priests to walk with him to the gallows?" one of them asked.

The royal guard shook his head. "Not for this one. The king will not be giving him a chance to save his soul before he goes."

The guard gave Finn a pitiable look. "Sorry for you, mate." They dragged him down the stone steps. Finn tried to stand between them but his legs trembled and gave out beneath him. Unable to hold his head up any longer, he rested his chin on his chest as they carried him through a long corridor.

The sounds of the crowd outside the castle walls filtered in, bursting in volume when the guards pushed past a heavy door and hauled him across the mud to some wooden steps. As soon as they reached the top of the platform, the noise from the crowd grew louder. Finn raised his head, squinting into the sunny day. His eyes ached from the bright light after being kept in darkness. He blinked, focusing his bleary vision on the huge courtyard filled from wall to wall with people. They must've come from every region of the kingdom. Thousands of angry faces stared back at him, yelling curses and shaking their fists.

From the moment they'd first woken him, he'd been numb to what was happening. But being surrounded by a mob radiating absolute hatred had unearthed the terror he'd been stifling during his incarceration. He'd hoped to escape this by some miracle, but the mouse had obviously failed to find Sithias in time. The grim reality finally hit him. He was about to die.

He could handle this, at least a little better, if the last face he saw was Fate's and not a multitude of hostile people.

The guards locked the shackles on his feet to an iron ring and pushed him to his knees in front of the chopping block. The wood was dark and polished. The deep gashes marking the flat surface between the two hollows where he was to lay his neck had been washed of all blood and gore. Plainly, the executioner took pride in keeping the tools of his trade clean. Hopefully he could count on his blade being sharpened to a razor's edge. History books were full of grisly accounts of an executioner's dull blades and the need for multiple strokes before severing the head. The thought of a clumsy execution made Finn sick with fear.

Wanting to look anywhere but at the vicious crowd, Finn

lifted his gaze to the clear, blue sky. If they hadn't tethered his manacles to the platform, he'd try flying into that beautiful sky, even though that would be just another death sentence. The parapets were lined with Asgar's best. He wouldn't get past the castle walls before he was taken down with a shower of arrows.

He dropped his gaze to the balcony decorated with Asgar's royal blue banners. King Tynan stood there, stiff and staring coldly down at him. Kaura was there too. She gave him the slightest nod, but nothing more, lest she draw her husband's attention.

Finn fixed his gaze on the wooden planks of the platform. A red rose landed in front of him. He would've expected maggoty meat before he'd believe a flower had been thrown at him. He glanced down at the front row.

Standing dead center, just below him, was Fate. Deep down, he knew it was the Lhiannan Shee, but he didn't care. He'd gotten his wish. Her face would be the last image he saw before he died. Nothing else mattered anymore. The knifing pain in his belly waned as a sense of calm took over. He could carry on now, and die with what little dignity he had left.

Footsteps sounded on the stairs behind him. The executioner had arrived. He took his place next to Finn, towering over him with a face hidden behind an iron mask covered in spikes. Finn couldn't see the man's eyes. They were cloaked in shadow, no doubt a purposeful design to hide his humanity and make him all the more terrifying. Finn conceded it was working. Terror seized hold as he dropped his gaze to the enormous axe the man carried in one hand.

A much smaller man moved in beside the executioner and faced the crowd. He appeared to be some sort of scribe, because the crowd grew quiet as he unraveled a scroll. "We present the Unholy Piper to the people, who has been found guilty by the high justice of King Tynan for the murder of Empress Moria.

Having found this sorcerer of black magic to be against all laws of the Asgar Empire, my Lord has decreed and given sentence that he shall be condemned to death by means of decapitation."

The scribe turned to Finn. "Are you ready to give your judge thanks and absolve his majesty of any guilt the endorsement of this violent death may bring him?"

The question shocked Finn. Fear made him want to curse the king and every single soul who'd come to watch this barbaric act. The instinct to survive made him want to rail against them, to destroy them. But he'd been down that road. It was best he didn't have the strength or means to invoke the elements to bring down an avalanche of pain on these people. He couldn't risk the destruction of his own soul all over again. Other than Kaura, none of them knew the truth. He could never make them see Moria for the evil snake she was.

Desperate to be thrown a life ring to keep from drowning in an ocean of panic, he looked down at Fate's face. She smiled and mouthed the words, *I love you.*

Grief welled in his throat as tears blurred his vision. He wanted more than anything to hold her, to kiss her, to stay with her.

Disgruntled sounds rippled through the crowd and someone close to the platform yelled, "Do this one decent thing, would ya!"

Finn tore his gaze from Fate and looked at Tynan. The executioner bent to remove the gag. "One whistle, or whisper of the wrong word, and this axe comes down faster than you can blink," he warned.

Finn nodded as the man pulled the gag down below his chin. "I forgive the king for making the only choice he could," he said as loudly as his parched throat would allow.

The executioner stuffed the gag back in his mouth.

"Noted." The scribe penned the words onto the parchment.

He then held the scroll high again to quiet the people and repeated Finn's forgiveness for everyone to hear.

Tynan nodded and the executioner stepped into position with his axe held high. "Place yer neck on the block, lad. Make sure yer chin hooks over the other side. My aim's always swift and sure. It'll be over quick. I promise you'll never feel it."

Finn's breath came in ragged bursts as he did as the executioner instructed. With his heart pounding violently, he fixed his gaze on Fate's face. She stared back, and as she held him locked within her soft brown gaze, he was able to fully surrender himself to the end of his life.

28
HOLY SKYSCRAPER, BATMAN

A RENEWED SENSE OF purpose propelled Fate out of bed, despite the stomachache and foggy head she woke with. She hadn't realized how badly she'd needed to share her thoughts and feelings about Finn. And Jessie was the only person in the entire universe she was comfortable confiding in. Having her best friend back made facing the trouble ahead so much easier, especially now that she knew Jessie could take care of herself, and anyone else, for that matter.

She only wished she wasn't so completely exhausted.

After pigging out all night and talking well into the morning, they'd finally passed out on top of the giant bed, until the chamber robot alerted them it was time to wake after only a few hours of sleep.

Jessie yelled and beaned the robot in the head with a well-aimed pillow.

"Come on, Jess." Fate slipped her armor on. "I want to talk to Farouk before the others show up for the strategy meeting."

"Can we cancel the meet?" Jessie whined as she sat up and rubbed her tummy. "I'm not combat ready. I'm bloated and ready to blow chocolate chunks." She stood. "Do I look like I gained five-hundred pounds? Because I feel bigger."

"You're skinny as ever. And no, we can't cancel. Scavengers wait for no one. Unlike us, they can overeat without suffering next-morning-bloats."

Jessie rolled out of bed with her hair matted to one side of her face and staggered toward the bathroom. "I hate you." She closed the door.

"Love you too," Fate called after her.

A few minutes later, Jessie reappeared in the room with water dripping off the end of her chin. She looked a little more awake as she trudged over to the door. "What do you need to talk to the furball about?"

"Go get your gear on. I'll explain on the way."

She patted her belly. "Sure, as long as I can wedge my armor on over my food baby."

Farouk's slanted fox eyes gleamed with doubt and amusement. "You believe you met Wodrid?"

"Well, met is too civilized a word for what happened between us," Fate said. "We duked it out over the Rod when I was trapped in the *Book of Fables*. And I'm pretty sure I won the skirmish by slicing off his leg."

"Ouch. And ew!" Jessie grimaced.

"Don't feel sorry for him. It was either me or his leg."

"You say this memory surfmerged during your illusionation yesterday?" Farouk asked.

Fate nodded. "Which means Wodrid was in Oldwilde at the same time I was there. But I have this sneaking suspicion he'll figure out I escaped the *Book of Fables*–if he hasn't already–and the next place he'll look is the bookstore back on Earth. Once he goes there, it's just a matter of time before he ends up here."

Farouk worried the end of his tail, a nervous gesture that made Fate all the more anxious. "No one can open the portal without the Key, and the Key is here."

"I wouldn't be so sure. Have you forgotten the Golandon records you gave me? Wodrid was Kaliena's lover. He'll do whatever it takes to restore her, and to do that, he needs the Rod and Orb of Aeternitis."

"Thousands of years have passed since Kaliena went into stasis. Wodrid cannot have lived this long. He is not neverendless."

"He's a sorcerer, isn't he?"

Farouk nodded reluctantly.

"Correct me if I'm wrong, but life extension is one of their specialties, is it not?" Farouk's silence sealed her point. "Plus, if pointed ears mean anything, he's of the elvish kind. According to Tolkein, elves are long-lived and as close to immortal as you can get. Right, Jess?"

"Absolutely."

Farouk squinted at them both with annoyance. Then he shook his head, the points of his horn-shaped ears drooping ever so slightly. "Even if he remains alive, Wodrid has no way of entering the Keep. Every portal entrance is virtually unyeildable."

Fate sank against the wall with a huff of impatience. "When was the last time you watched the Golandon records? Ten thousand years ago? Kaliena imprisoned Wodrid because he figured out a way into the Keep without an invitation. Don't you remember? That's how they ended up having that long, dragged out Stockholm syndrome romance. And do I also need to remind you he's the one who cursed the *Book of Fables*? He's the reason readers like me were trapped inside the book and forced into changing the endings of those horrible stories as the only way to escape."

"Wait, who's Kaliena?" Jessie asked, looking totally lost.

"Long story. Remind me to tell you later," Fate said.

Farouk frowned at Fate. "Who told you Wodrid cursed the *Book of Fables*?"

"An old druid priest, named O'Deldar."

"I know that druid," Steve said as he swept into the

sanctuary, his coat tails swishing. When he spied Fate, he tipped his top hat and gave her a smile that held a bit of a smirk.

"Oh really?" Fate looked him over. His long dark hair seemed extra sleek, and his eyeliner and black lipstick were applied perfectly. She hadn't bothered with makeup since she'd first been trapped inside the *Book of Fables*. Steve certainly appeared to be adapting well to life in the Keep. Why did that bother her?

"Does that surprise you?" he asked.

Fate detected a challenge in his expression, and for the first time, she noticed flecks of frozen ice reflected in the bright blue of his irises. Uneasiness rippled along her spine.

Steve laughed. "Don't look so shocked. I came across O'Deldar's name in one of the books I was going through earlier." His gaze dropped to Fate's throat as she swallowed nervously. "Is there something important about him? Say the word and I'll keep digging."

"No."

He continued to stare at her with something akin to disdain. Had she offended him?

"Aren't you supposed to be in the library with Eustace?" She hadn't seen her father since last night after Farouk had healed her wound. Eustace had begged her not to go on the next mission. They'd argued and she'd told him not to come to the sanctuary in the morning to say goodbye. His fear for her was undermining what little courage she possessed.

"He sent me to see you off and report back. He's nervous."

Guilt nagged at her. She hated causing her father undue stress. "Tell him not to worry. I'll be fine."

"I'm sure you will." Steve started to leave, then stopped. "But just in case, is there anything you'd like to leave with him? Something of value you wouldn't want to lose out there?"

She frowned. "Like what? My credit card and last

fifty bucks?"

"Well, the Rod for one."

Distrust squirmed in Fate's stomach. "How do you know about the Rod?"

Steve shrugged nonchalantly. "Came up in conversation with your father. He isn't very comfortable with you carrying it around."

"At last, someone else other than me is talking sense." Brune entered the conversation as if she'd been in the room the whole time. She marched over to a row of guns and ammo belts.

Agitation skimmed along the edge of Fate's nerves. Was this some sort of tag team effort involving Brune and Steve? And what of Eustace? Was he in on it too?

No. Her father may have disagreed with her decision to continue wearing the Rod around her neck, but she didn't believe for one second he would gang up on her with Brune and Steve. "No, you can tell Eustace the Rod stays with me," she said, staring at Brune.

Brune returned Fate's hardened gaze. "Don't worry, Steve. If she kicks it out there, I'll make sure the Rod comes back with me."

Feeling fed up, Fate put her back to both of them, grasping at anything to change the subject. "Does anyone know how Mason's doing?" she asked.

As if on cue Darcy, appeared at the door. Unlike Steve, who seemed to be thriving since they got there, Darcy looked wrung out. Her eyes were red-rimmed and sunken within the shadows of dark circles, not that the heavy Goth makeup helped. "Guess you wouldn't know, since you haven't bothered to come to check on him."

"That's my fault," Jessie jumped in. "I kept her busy with way too much girl talk last night."

"How's he doing?" Fate asked, her tone sheepish. They both

knew she should've paid Mason a visit already.

"He'd be better if he wasn't stuck on this hunk of metal with two broken legs and cracked ribs."

Brune snorted. "Hey, it's better than dead."

Darcy's mouth fell open. "You're heartless. All of you. I hope you die out there!" Turning sharply, she rammed into Lincoln on her way out.

He regained his footing with a look of confusion. "What'sh with her?"

"Mason, of course," Fate said.

"Useless sentiment, is more like it." Brune focused on the gun in her hand.

Lincoln ogled Brune as he ambled over to her. "You're a real hard candy. I like it. Let'sh me know there'sh a shoft gooey shenter in there."

Brune pointed her gun at his gut. "How about I expose your soft gooey center to the outside?"

He held up his hands in mock surrender. "Chill, girl. Jusht havin' fun."

"Have fun on your own time. Everybody load up." Brune gestured toward an arsenal of unusual looking guns with flared barrels. "I want two ammo belts per person. We're going to need all the cartridges of deducting fluid we can get out there."

"What's this stuff do?" Jessie asked.

"Instantly turns metal into a cloud of rust," Brune explained. "And we'll need to come at it from all sides. The scavenger's quadrupled in size since yesterday. To put that in terms you'll all understand, it's as tall as a two-hundred-story building."

"Holy skyscraper, Batman," Jessie said. "Will our packs even fly that high?"

"No, Robin, we'll need the Bat plane for thish one." Lincoln bumped fists with her and they laughed.

Brune shoved her gun in her holster. "Go ahead, joke all you want. We'll see who's laughing after one of you loses a limb. Or your life."

The laughter dwindled.

Fate adjusted the ammo belts on her shoulders and picked up her aeronaut pack. "You ready for this?" she asked Jessie quietly.

Jessie stuffed cartridges into the barrel of her gun and cocked the hammer. "Locked and loaded. How about you?"

Fate grabbed a gun, twirled it on her finger and holstered it, surprisingly smoother than she expected. "Five by five."

They both grinned and high-fived each other, having rehearsed moments like this since they'd first started playing make-believe together.

"Line up, everyone," Brune ordered, popping Fate's bubble.

Time to face reality.

Farouk guided his cage over to stand next to Brune. "You are about to face the largest scavenger ever docuscripted within the Keep." He punched buttons on his control panel, which generated a 3D image that hovered in the center of the sanctuary.

Layers of twisted metal formed the shape of what looked like a hulking knight covered in jagged armor. The face was featureless, save for flaming eyes of ice blue and a gaping mouth of blue mist.

Noticing something different from her last viewing of the scavenger, Fate squinted at the rotating form, unsure of what had changed. Then she saw it, a series of chains hung from its shoulders like a royal cape and a crown of uniform barbs sat upon its head. "Is it just me, or does the scave seem to have more fashion sense than it did yesterday? It looks kind of kingly."

"It's just you." Brune rolled her eyes. "Scavs don't design themselves into anything deliberate. They're mindless pests. Think of them like rats. Voracious eaters of whatever they can get their claws on. In this case, it's whatever element they come in contact with when they first form."

"Where'd they come from?" Jessie asked. "Did they escape from other portals like the Fomorians and the Chimera?"

"No, they're born of the Keep." Fate surprised even herself as the answer popped into her head. "Every once in awhile the magic running through the Keep clogs up and the machinery coughs out a dense tangle of energy to purge it. If the energy doesn't dissipate right away, it starts absorbing whatever it's touching, whether it's crystal, stone, or iron like in this case. Once it starts growing, it just gets hungrier and hungrier."

"If this one ate Thor's hammer, who's to say it hasn't eaten something equally as powerful since then?" Jessie added. "What if Fate's right, and the scavenger's thinking more like a king than a mindless rat?"

Fate gave Jessie an appreciative nod for backing her up.

Brune started to say something, but Farouk interrupted. "We would be unwise to minimalize this scavenger, chiefspecially since this one has been allowed to exist beyond a few hours. We have an unprecedential case here and there is no way to previsionate the evolution of a scavenger that is several days old. I suggest you use utmost caution in your dealings with it."

"Hey, we're the onesh with the big gunsh here." Lincoln pulled out his gun and aimed it at an invisible scavenger. "Jusht show me where and when to pull the trigger."

"Let's hope it's that simple," Fate said, feeling buoyed by his bravado. But it was only momentary. She couldn't ignore the dread lurking beneath the surface, dragging her spirits back down.

29
SOMETHING'S NOT RIGHT HERE

THE SCAVENGER WASN'T HARD to miss, even from several miles away. It towered high above the distant skyline, dwarfing the giant architectural structures sprawling to either side. A murky blue glimmer emanated from the iron titan as it lumbered across the terrain, crushing the huge vaults flat beneath its massive feet. Spouts of faery light and ensorcelled flames spewed from the rubble.

As Fate and the others approached from a safe range, the destruction of so many rare and precious magical objects made her cringe.

Brune signaled for everyone to stop and hover. "Stay out of its vapor trail when we get close. The cloud's corrosive and it'll mess with your equipment. Plus it burns like hell when it gets in your eyes and nose."

"Roger that, Lodeshtar," Lincoln said.

"I told you, no code names," Brune snapped. "It's confusing enough remembering your regular names."

Lincoln moved up next to her. "That'sh cool. Drop my real name and jusht shtart calling me Shtarship, becush I'm ready for you to guide my courshe, Lodeshtar."

"In that case, go to hell."

Lincoln smiled as if she were flirting. "That'sh cute, but I'm not going anywhere. You need me and you know it."

Brune looked away in annoyance.

He waved dismissively at Fate and Jessie. "I've named them Chicken Little and Shtink Bug."

Jessie swooped in next to him. "I'm not responding to

anything that lame. We demand new names."

Fate zipped closer. "Agreed. And who's Chicken Little?"

Lincoln tore his gaze from Brune, his expression bland when he looked at her. "I think you know."

"Me?"

"Who wush the shcared little chicken who needed shaving yeshterday?"

Jessie punched him in the arm. "Hey! It could've happened to anyone. You better hope it's not you who needs saving this time, because we might just think twice about helping."

"Enough!" Brune yelled. "So much for sneaking up on the scav. We've been spotted! Take your positions!"

Fate glanced over her shoulder. Adrenaline streaked through her veins when she heard the screech of grinding metal and saw the colossus barreling towards them. The others spread out and she bolted straight upwards. Positioning herself above the scavenger, she grabbed her gun from the holster and aimed. Her sweating hands shook during the five-second wait it took to move directly beneath her.

She squeezed the trigger. The pistol kicked hard in her hand, emitting a gaseous red cloud that blocked her view. Darting off to one side, she caught sight of Jessie shooting at it from a slightly lower level. Another mass of red particles billowed out over the scavenger's spiked shoulder. Rust formed along its barbed crown, down one side of its head, spreading over the bulk of its arm until huge chunks of metal crumbled away.

The creature's gait faltered and a terrible shriek echoed across the expanse. Brune and Lincoln zoomed in low, blasting the scavenger from both sides. The tangle of metal, which made up its legs from the knees down, disintegrated into moldering rust. The scavenger toppled, smashing into an Indonesian-style temple.

Before hitting the ground, the strips of metal in its back

reshaped into scissor-like wings. The scavenger swept up into the air, dodging clouds of deducting gas before careening off in a new direction.

Cranking on the gears, Fate bolted after the scavenger. Jessie appeared off to the side, her Dragon Eye headgear firmly in place and jaw set in determination. Brune and Lincoln fell in behind them.

The scavenger zigzagged, its head hung low like a hawk hunting for prey. It suddenly descended, zeroing in on an enormous gold statue of a Chinese dragon. That's when Fate noticed the hammer it was gripping in its good hand. At first she thought it was Thor's hammer, but this appeared more utilitarian in design. It had one narrowed end, much like a normal hammer, though enormous in comparison.

Swooping over the statue, the scavenger banged the hammer down on the dragon's head. A shower of red sparks rained down over the statue. The metal heated instantly, glowing crimson as it turned molten. Just when the statue looked like it might liquefy into a blob, the dragon's serpentine body undulated and came to life.

With a spine-tingling roar, the dragon broke away from the marble platform it was anchored on, its golden scales gleaming as it snaked through the air. Fate slowed down, shocked by the impossibility of a solid gold dragon flying. First, because it should be too heavy to get off the ground. Second, it had no wings.

Brune caught up with her. "That's impossible. I've never seen anything like this before!"

"I know, it's crazy," Fate agreed. "How's it able to fly?"

Brune frowned at her. "I don't mean the dragon, I mean the scavenger. It animated that statue!" She shook her head, her eyes filled with fear. "Something's not right here. I think we should–"

"The dragon's coming back around!" Fate yelled, her heart

climbing into her throat at the sight of the dragon swimming through the air toward them, its long whiskers flowing round its fierce head. She drew her gun. "Will this work on it?"

"No, gold doesn't oxidize like iron."

"What do we do then?"

"Run!" Brune jetted off in a hurry. "Everybody scatter," she ordered. "Do your best to make it back to the breaching door."

Fate skyrocketed towards the revolving hoops, where they grazed against the force field with crackling golden tracers. A deep growl from below jerked her attention downward. The dragon's widening mouth rose into view. Instinct took over and she drew her sword. Plunging it downward, she struck the dragon between the eyes. The clash of metal rang out, the impact vibrating along her arm as the sword glanced off its head.

Flinging her sword aside, Fate grabbed her disintegrator gun and shot. Red gas filled her vision. Coughing on the noxious fumes, she throttled her pack's gears and hurtled sideways through the gas, hoping the cloud would block her movements.

The dragon burst through the thick fumes, its mouth snapping at her heels. Dizzy with terror, Fate nosedived, heading for the ground to take cover between the vaults. The dragon plunged after her, matching her movements at a nerve-wracking pace.

Jessie darted in front of her, circled round and came at the dragon from the side. At the same time, Lincoln and Brune swooped in from the opposite direction. They were all suddenly yelling, diving close enough to bang their swords against the metallic beast.

Snarling, the dragon jerked its horned head toward them, its massive jaws biting down on air. Lincoln screamed and raced off with the dragon chasing after him and Brune.

Jessie swerved in next to Fate. "That was close."

Biting her lip, Fate watched the dragon closing the gap on

them. "It's gaining on them."

"Don't worry, they'll shake it off any second now," Jessie assured her. "See? They're splitting off in opposite directions. The dragon won't know which one to go after."

Fate gripped the gears and squeezed. "Wrong, it's going after Lincoln and it's too close." She jetted toward the dragon. "Jess, come on, we've got to help him!"

"Get back to the breaching door," Brune's voice cut in. "Now!"

"No, Lincoln's not going to make it if–"

The words locked in Fate's throat as she let go of the gears and fell into a weightless stop. She couldn't move. Shock had numbed her brain, disconnecting her from all physical sensation, her senses honed in on what she was witnessing.

The dragon's jaws widened over Lincoln and clamped down. Blood spilled over the dragon's gold fangs, spraying as it whipped its head back and forth.

Jessie grabbed her by the arm and shook. "Fate, snap out of it. We've got to go!"

Fate blinked at Jessie, allowing her to lead the way. Halfway to the breaching door, she glanced back. The dragon had returned to its marble plinth, where it resumed its original position, still and lifeless, except for Lincoln's life blood staining its mouth.

30
BLOOD MUST RUN

THE MOMENT THE EXECUTIONER raised his axe over Finn's head, a huge shadow crossed the courtyard, as if the sun itself had been extinguished. A hair-raising roar thundered overhead. Faces turned skyward and screams echoed off the castle walls as the crowd dispersed, everyone fighting with each other to get past the gates. Fate's presence vanished from Finn's sight. The Lhiannan Shee had slipped into another dimension, leaving an empty space of warped air in her place.

Orders were being shouted out to the soldiers along the parapets, followed by the drum of their footsteps racing into position. Another massive shadow whipped across the courtyard, followed by another monstrous growl. Finn chanced a glimpse to one side. The executioner was turned in the opposite direction and the axe hung at his side. Finn raised his head from the chopping block just as an enormous, scaled beast swept low above the gallows, its leathery wings kicking up a gust of wind as it landed in the middle of the empty courtyard.

It was a dragon, and it had plucked the king from the balcony on its way down.

The castle guards lined the walls all the way around the courtyard, bows drawn, ready to unleash a hailstorm of arrows at the creature. But they stayed still for fear of killing the king who was being held loosely within the dragon's mouth.

The dragon dropped the king, clutching him in the talons of its front leg as it eyed the soldiers warily. A low snarl issued from deep within its throat. Finn was struck by its ivory color.

Something seemed familiar in the way it moved its serpentine neck. The dragon let go of Tynan then suddenly shrank in size to morph into a slender woman in a cream gown adorned with pearls.

Finn frowned. He'd seen that dress before. Fate had worn it the night of his coronation, when Rudwor had awarded him the station of First Knight. She'd been an irresistible vision. Every detail of her was burned in his mind–the gardenias woven into her long hair, the gleam of pearls against her skin. That had been the night they had spent together, healing the painful rift that had torn them apart. He'd held her in his arms until sunrise without so much as a kiss, but nothing would ever erase the feel of her body pressed against his and the bittersweet torture that had caused them both.

His pulse raced as he stared at the woman's back, willing her to turn so he could see her face. When she finally did, his blood ran cold. It was Moria.

He suddenly felt sick. This had to be some sort of fever dream. Why else would Moria be wearing *that* dress? The witch was dead. He shook his head, hoping to end the hallucination, but she remained firmly in place.

Tynan was every bit as shocked. "M-mother? Is it really you?"

"Yes, my son." She glanced at the battalion and the hundreds of arrows aimed at her. "Please, call your men off. We must speak on an important matter."

Tynan waved his arms at the castle guards. "Stand down!"

When the captain hesitated to give the order, the king turned to him. "I command you to stand down. Anyone who disobeys will be next on the chopping block!"

Tynan turned back to Moria. "Mother, how is this possible? You died. I saw your body. You were burnt beyond recognition and interred in a tomb. Your sarcophagus is locked behind many gates far beneath the temple we built in your honor."

Moria tucked her hand in the crook of his arm and directed him into a slow stroll toward the gallows, where Finn listened in horror. "I understand your confusion. But there's much you do not understand about our Serpen heritage. We are an immortal race, born of fire and not easily destroyed by the flames of man."

"Are you saying you rose from the ashes as a dragon and broke free of your tomb?"

"You could say that." Moria looked straight at Finn and winked.

Finn blinked several times, certain now that he was hallucinating every bit of this. Or had the axe already come down? Was he in Hell and doomed to relive the day of his execution into eternity?

Tynan's bewildered expression hardened as he lifted his gaze to Finn. "Destiny is at work here, mother. As hard as it is to believe, your resurrection has come on the same day of your murderer's execution. You will now witness justice for what was done to you."

Moria nodded. "That is why I'm here, my son."

Tynan signaled the executioner to come forward. "You may proceed," he commanded.

The executioner stepped in next to Finn. "Lay your head back down, lad."

Finn shook his head, every cell in his body screaming out against this final degradation. He refused to die in the presence of this vile snake.

"Down, lad!" the executioner ordered, his tone having lost all patience. When Finn didn't do as he was told, the executioner grabbed him by the back of the neck and shoved him down onto the block. "We can do this the hard way or the easy way, but I suggest you give in and make this easy on yourself."

Finn continued to struggle. Two guards moved in, holding

his arms and pressing him to the block. Too weak to keep up the fight, he went limp and glared at Moria. He'd managed to surrender to his circumstances when he'd had Fate's presence to sooth him, regardless of how false it had been. But having Moria be the last face he saw was nothing short of cruel and inhumane.

She stared back at him, not with contempt, as he would expect, but warmly, like that of a friend. She turned to Tynan as he lifted his hand to signal the executioner to bring down the blade. "My dear son, I am here to right the wrongs of my past."

"You've done nothing wrong, mother."

"Ah but I have, and I'm here to offer myself in trade for the life of the accused."

Tynan paled. "What?"

"Listen to me carefully. The only reason I married your father and came to Asgar was to ruin him and his people. I designed this kingdom's demise and I used my magic to fool everyone into thinking all was well. After the flames consumed me, I could no longer hold the illusion I had layered over the land. That's when the veil lifted and revealed the true state of the kingdom."

She took a few steps toward Finn and pointed at him. "This young man was the only one who saw through my deception, and he was the only one brave enough to stop me. If he hadn't succeeded, I would've sacrificed you, Tynan. I had planned to awaken the dragon in your blood. Had I done so, you would've killed Kaura and destroyed what little was left of Asgar."

Tynan didn't want to hear it. He staggered back and kept shaking his head.

Finn couldn't believe his ears either.

"No, I don't believe you!" Tynan fell to his knees and grabbed his head. "You wouldn't do that! Why would you save the Unholy Piper? He's evil. He tried to kill you!"

Moria knelt beside him and took his hands. "Look at me."

Tynan stared at his mother, wide-eyed with sorrow and disbelief.

"You've sentenced a hero to death," she pressed. "I've come to stop an injustice that simply cannot take place."

Tynan lifted his tortured gaze and looked at Finn. "The people will never understand a pardon for the Unholy Piper. Blood must run."

Moria was quiet a moment. "Then let them think the Unholy Piper has met his end in the most horrible way."

"How?"

"I will return to my true form and allow the dragon to take him."

Tynan stared at her. "Where will you go afterwards?"

"Home to our people, where the River Torle runs deep within Mount Fargrum."

"If what you say is true, I need to know why you did it?" Tynan's voice grew tight. "What horrible thing did my father do to wreak such devastation upon his kingdom?"

"He trespassed into Serpen territory."

Tynan's back stiffened. "Trespass? No. He told me how you welcomed him and his army into your palace and invited them to a grand feast. It was there he fell madly in love with you. He told me that story more times than I ever cared to hear it."

Moria's expression turned to stone. "We Serpen do not suffer fools who enter into our land. It's that simple."

Tynan clenched his fists until his arms and shoulders visibly shook. "You meted out this vengeance of yours over a course of seventeen years for a simple matter of trespass? It's not like he invaded your land, stormed your palace and killed every last one of you. All he did was take a shortcut home."

"How were we to know that was his intention?" Moria asked.

"You found out at the feast."

Disappointment wrinkled her forehead. "You always did have too much of your father's weakness in you."

"Thankfully, yes," Tynan agreed. He looked her over with growing anger. "Leave, before I tell my soldiers to shoot every last arrow they have into you."

Moria's expression softened. "One day, you'll see I had to make you hate me to undo this one last injustice." She gestured to Finn. "Release him from his shackles and I'll take my leave with him."

Tynan appeared to be beyond words and nodded to the guards.

Finn tensed against them as they unlocked his legs and then his wrists. As soon as his hands were free, he pulled the gag out of his mouth. "You're barkers if you think I'm leaving with this snake." He coughed, choking on the dryness in his throat.

"I said I'd take you, but who says you're going anywhere with me?" Moria's sly smile widened into a serpent's mouth.

Before Finn could say anything, her neck stretched impossibly long, horns thrust from her head and smooth skin hardened into ivory scales as her fragile form violently gave way to a massive beast. Moria rose above him then lunged without warning. The last thing Finn saw before everything went black was the dragon's maw and its deadly fangs snapping down upon him.

31
WHAT'S THE ALTERNATIVE TO GOING BOOM?

THE SANCTUARY WAS DEAD quiet when Fate and Jessie flew through the breaching door. The grinding sound of metal on metal as the iris closed behind them cut through the silence like a blaring horn. Brune had arrived well before them and had already shed her pack and armor. She stood next to Farouk's cage, leaning over the big table studying a map and conversing in low tones.

Anger boiled in Fate's chest. Brune didn't seem to care at all that Lincoln was dead.

"Do the others know about Lincoln?" Fate unbuckled the straps and set her aeronaut pack on the floor.

Farouk looked up from the map. "I told them."

Fate thought about Lincoln's brothers. They were probably wondering where he'd disappeared to by now. Her heart sank. They had no idea he was gone forever. They should be told. But how would she even begin to explain how Lincoln had died? She barely believed it herself. "Shouldn't we be…doing something? Like holding a memorial?"

Brune kept her eyes on the map. "No, I'm busy debriefing. As you should be. We need both of you on point, especially since we just shrunk to a team of three."

Fate stormed over to the table. "Really? Lincoln liked you, something that's in short supply where you're concerned. And now you're just going to act like nothing happened?"

Brune stiffened then pushed away from the table to face Fate. "I *am* doing something. I'm protecting the Keep's welfare by figuring out what we need to do next."

“Lives are more important than all this.” Fate waved her arms at their surroundings.

“Yeah,” Jessie joined in. “People aren’t just getting hurt here, they’re dying. I say we take off, nuke the Keep from the other end of the portal. It’s the only way to be sure.” She turned to Fate and bumped fists with her.

“Aye-firmative.” Fate smiled grimly at the chance to apply a few favorite movie quotes to a real situation. But she felt instantly terrible and guilt shoved all playfulness aside.

Farouk turned around, pressing his face against the bars of his cage. “Your ignorwarness astounds me.” His eyes narrowed on Fate with more meaning than he was saying.

She knew he was referring to the Golandon history he’d shared with her. The Keep was a priceless treasure that must be protected at all costs. Not to mention, the oath she’d taken would never allow her to destroy the Keep, regardless of how much she wanted to be free of it. She sighed in defeat. “Fine. What do we need to do next?”

“I have your father and his team explorating this latest unflavorable development and will know more soon.” Farouk moved to the other side of his cage. Using his pointer stick, he tapped on the map laying on the table’s surface and triggered a 3D projection of one half of the Keep.

“Here’s what we know so far,” he continued. “While you were busy fleeing from the dragon, our worst fears became a reality. The scavenger ate through a copper pyramid the size of the Great Pyramid of Giza. Here, in Quadrant 537. The scarab neck collar inside the vault is lost somewhere in the rubble. Underlying gears were destructalized and the entire quadrant has ground to a halt. Maintenance bots are making repairs, but the scavenger has gone into hiding below the subsurface, where the Keep is most vulnerable.”

“Is this normal for a scav?” Reluctance showed in Jessie’s eyes as she joined them at the table.

Farouk's ears drooped slightly. "No, this scavenger is unlike any before it. When it was being attacked, its motivcentive was to create a distraction by animating a statue. We've never seen this ability, or this level of smartelligence."

Fate rested her elbows on the table. "It must've munched on some sort of smart iron earlier on. Was there anything in that quadrant that could drastically bump its IQ?"

Farouk nodded. "Diagnostifications registered the anvil of the god Hephaestus is missing. Once we have the research–"

"Have it right here." Eustace hurried into the sanctuary with a stack of big books in his arms. His hair was mussed and his shirt was rumpled. Fate could tell he hadn't slept since their argument, and now with Lincoln's sudden death, she knew he was doubly worried about her and Jessie.

Steve and Darcy trailed in behind him. Darcy looked more miserable than usual. Her mascara was smeared from crying. She was plainly reeling from Lincoln's tragedy, especially since Mason had nearly met the same fate. Steve had lost the bounce in his step and there was a droop in his posture as he walked in.

Gerdie strolled in after them, headed for her stool and stepped onto it. "It's not lookin' good." She cast Fate a grim expression, suggesting she wasn't just talking about the scavenger.

Fate leaned close to Gerdie. "Did you find out what happens to my proxy if I bite the dust?" she whispered.

Gerdie nodded. "There's no gettin' around it. Brune has every reason to make sure you die once she's the proxy. It's the only way she'll become the official Keep Guardian again."

Fate's hopes sank. What was she supposed to do now? Time was running out. She needed to somehow free herself from her position and get through the portal to Oldwilde before it moved underground for the next hundred years.

Eustace placed the books on the table with a loud thump, jerking her attention back to the matter at hand. He opened one of them to a drawing of a giant rising from a fiery volcano, a hammer in one hand and molten lava in the other. "Hephaestus was the god of fire and metalwork. He served as blacksmith to the gods by making weapons and fashioning automatons for–"

"Automatons?" Jessie asked. Then her eyes widened, like a light turned on in her head. "Oh, you mean like that mechanical owl from Clash of the Titans, right?"

"There was no mechanical owl in that movie," Steve interjected before Eustace could answer.

Darcy let out a weary sigh. "She's talking about the 1980's version. And you call yourself an aficionado of all things fantasy."

"Yes, well, now that we have that important matter settled," Eustace said with veiled impatience. "Might I continue?"

Steve glanced down sheepishly. "Sure."

"Thank you." Eustace cleared his throat. "Hephaestus, unlike the other gods, was intimately connected to Earth's wealth of minerals. He understood that iron is the life force of the planet. As well, blood smells of iron, so Hephaestus forged his anvil using his own blood and imbued the iron with his vast knowledge of all things metallurgical."

"Does that mean we're dealing with a scavenger that thinks it's now the god of fire?" Fate asked.

Withdrawing his handkerchief from his pocket, Eustace removed his glasses and cleaned them. "I believe that very well may be the case. This would explain why the scavenger now has the mystical prowess of Hephaestus to place enchantments on inanimate objects. Of greater concern, is that it has the power to create sentient entities out of molten metal which will follow its commands, such as the automaton known as Talos." He replaced his spectacles, while avoiding Fate's gaze.

Her heart sank. He was miserable with worry and doing a horrible job hiding it.

"FYI," Steve interjected, "Talos is the bronze giant dude from Jason and the Argonauts, circa 1963." He pointed a heated gaze at Darcy, who at that particular moment didn't appear to care.

"Yes, and we could very well find ourselves facing hundreds of those bronze 'dudes'," Eustace said, his expression carefully tolerant.

"Do we have any secret weapons in mind?" Fate asked, attempting to insert a slightly more upbeat attitude to counter his obvious tension. "I don't suppose we could pull the Eye of Balor out for this one and be done with it?"

Her father attempted a smile, but fear showed near the edge of his eyes and ruined the effort. "Ah, well, that's Darcy's department. She's well versed in Greek mythology and she knew exactly where to look for the solution. Though I fear the retrieval of said item appears every bit as dangerous as facing the scavenger." He gave Darcy a disapproving frown.

All heads turned toward Darcy. She shrugged. "Hey, I'm just the messenger."

Brune rubbed her temples. "Spit it out. We don't have all day. What's the weapon and where is it?"

"If Eustace's theory is right, and the scavenger has taken on the godlike qualities of Hephaestus, that means it's every bit as indestructible as an Olympian god." Darcy paused to let that sink in.

"Hold on," Brune said. "Don't you think we're giving this scav too much credit? They're nothing more than walking scrap heaps. This isn't some immortal god we're facing. We pumped it full of bullets packed with deducting fluid and it worked. We disintegrated nearly half of it."

Darcy didn't look convinced. "Maybe, but this 'scav' has the blood of an Olympian charging up its parts. You might've done some damage, but I'm guessing the regenerative powers alone won't allow death. The way I see it, there's only one way to bring this thing down. You're going to have to disperse its physical molecules to the point where it can't even begin to reassemble itself, and the only thing I know that'll do that is a nuclear bomb. But since we'd go boom with it, that's out."

Brune glared at her but remained quiet.

"What's the alternative to going boom?" Fate asked.

Darcy looked at her. "Are you sure you want to know?"

"Uh, yeah." Fate frowned.

"Well, the gods' weaknesses have only ever come from their own creations. As I'm sure you know, they created the Gorgons, which were the undoing of Atlas and–"

"The Kraken," Steve added in a hurry.

Darcy shook her head. "If you believe the movie. It was actually the sea monster, Cetus, that Perseus turned to stone by using Medusa's head."

Steve swore under his breath.

Jessie bumped her shoulder into Fate's. "Is this for real? We're supposed to rehash that old story?"

"Yes and no," Darcy answered. "Medusa's dead and her head was delivered to Olympus, so that weapon's currently unavailable. But her two sisters are still alive and slithering."

"Here in the Keep?" Fate asked, horrified by the thought.

"No, they're holed up in their cave on the islands of Gorgades." Darcy turned to Farouk. "Hopefully, we can access the lair through one of the portals?"

Farouk tapped the buttons of his control panel. After a few beeps, he looked up from the screen. "There's one in Quadrant 106."

"There you go." Darcy patted the table's surface. "Done."

Fate leaned her weight against the table, her head swirling

with overwhelm as an awful foreboding dampened her spirits even further. There was never going to be an end to this. She'd never be free of the Keep. "For you maybe," she muttered under her breath. "For me, it's just the beginning."

32
NOT THE MONSTER YOU THINK I AM

FATE STARED AT THE vault's stone archway with Medusa's hideous head of serpents carved into its ornate design. "So what happens when we enter the vault? Do we get instantly sucked through some nauseating wormhole and belly flop in front of the Gorgons's feet? Assuming they have feet."

Brune rubbed the back of her neck. "Hard to say. Every portal's different."

"God, is there anything predictable in this place?"

"Unpredictability is about the only thing you can predict around here."

"Terrific." Fate glanced over her shoulder, resisting the urge to radio Jessie and have her come with them. She hated being thrown together with Brune alone. Why had Farouk insisted on sending only the two of them to retrieve the Gorgon's head? Was he hoping they'd bond on the mission? Because that was *never* going to happen.

Brune removed her aeronaut pack and adjusted her gear. "Something on your mind?"

"To be honest, I don't think we've got enough back up."

"I know I don't."

"Right. Wait. What's that supposed to mean? Are you saying I'm not back up for you, but you are for me?"

"Pretty much. I'd take your friend Jessie over you any day."

"Then why didn't you?"

"She's not a guardian."

"Neither are you."

"But I used to be."

"So that's the price of admission around here?"

"You should know that. Stop being lazy. Focus on proper questions and you'll get the download." Equal measures of disappointment and arrogance played across Brune's features. "The vaults are only configured to open for guardians. Unless of course, you happen to be out here during twilight when all portals open automatically. But I wouldn't recommend it. The levels of magic released during the gloaming will kill you."

"Right." Fate focused on calling the guardian rules to the forefront of her mind. "Rule number one: *Never remain inside the Keep during twilight when the gateways unlock.*" Feeling smug all of a sudden, she crossed her arms and looked Brune over. "Wait, is that how you got zombified? Gerdie said the Orb was the only thing keeping you alive when you were all shriveled and stinky."

Brune's expression darkened. "Let it go already. I made an honest mistake. I thought I could terminate the scavenger and be out in plenty of time before twilight."

"Yeah, yeah." Fate checked her watch. "Hold on, twilight's only six hours from now. Cutting it kind of close aren't we?"

"The time difference works in our favor. For every hour that passes here, it's a month there."

"Well, that's…convenient." Fate smiled. Time was finally on her side for once. She could go on this gruesome mission without worrying about missing her only opportunity to enter the portal to Oldwilde. Plus, there'd be time to straighten out her affairs before–

"There's something off about you." Brune stared at Fate, studying her like some oddity. "I've been trying to figure it out since you first came back. It's obvious you're not happy with your new position, but there's more to it than that. It's like you're not completely here. You're always distracted. Thinking of something else. Or should I say someone else?"

Fate grew rigid under Brune's probing stare.

"Could it be that handsome young buck I conjured out of thin air when I summoned you to the bookstore?"

"*You* made him?" A sickening knot formed in Fate's stomach. Gerdie had suspected Brune was the ultimate source of Finn's origin, but hearing it straight from the horse's mouth made it *much* worse to accept.

"Yes and no. I merely used the *Eyes of Eros* spell to summon you, but it was your heart's deepest desire combined with the creative forces of the Orb, which produced what I'm guessing was the boy of your dreams."

Fate clenched her fists. What was Brune fishing for?

"So where is he?" Brune made a point of looking around. "Why didn't he return with you? Did the *Book of Fables* get the best of him?" She mocked a sad face. "Did your paper boyfriend die in there?"

"He's not paper! He's real!"

"Are you sure about that?"

Fate's heart thudded out of control.

"He's a product of the Orb. Without the Rod being part of his initial creation, there's a lot that could go sideways."

All the memories of Finn's struggle with the darkness he'd been possessed by flooded in. How many times had Fate wondered if there was something much deeper wrong with him? Something on a more fundamental level.

Brune registered the fear in Fate's eyes. "Oh, so the golden boy wasn't so golden after all."

"No, we ran into some trouble. He's fine now."

Brune looked doubtful. "For the moment maybe, but will he stay that way? I don't know, I think now that you've got both the Rod and the Orb together, you should probably bring him here so you can use them to make sure he stays the way you like him."

Fate's heart latched onto Brune's suggestion as panic took over. Brune had awakened worries she'd been trying to ignore for a very long time. "I'm Keep Guardian. As much as I'd like to, you and I both know I can't leave."

Yet. But Fate wasn't about to let Brune in on just how much Gerdie had educated her on the subject and the options she'd recently discovered.

Brune wagged a finger at her. "Now that's just plain stubborn on your part. You know your contract has a loophole. Why haven't you used it yet? Make me your proxy and I'll let you off the hook for this mission and every other one after that. I can handle this all by my lonesome. I've got an excellent track record of seventy-five years to show for it."

"Right up until you didn't."

Brune leaned within inches of Fate's nose, her hazel eyes flashing with anger. "Don't play self-righteous with me."

Fate stood her ground. "Or what? You'll feed me to the Gorgons? FYI, if you get rid of me, there's no guarantee the next girl you'll have to summon will make you her proxy."

Brune withdrew, her body shaking with rage as she worked to control herself. "Why the resistance? It's obvious you don't want the job. Not with boy wonder tugging at your heart strings." A cold smile spread over her face when she caught the truth on Fate's expression. "Sorry, kid, but you really don't have any other options. I'm the best deal in town."

Fate couldn't take it anymore. "Forget it. I'm onto your diabolical plan. Gerdie dug into this whole proxy thing. If I die while you're my proxy, you get to be Keep Guardian. Permanently. Or should I say forever. It's no secret you'll do whatever it takes to get the Orb and Rod from Gerdie and me so you can use them to make yourself immortal. Even if that means having to pry them from our dead hands."

Brune's jaw twitched.

That was all Fate needed to see to know her suspicions were correct. "I knew it. Word of warning, Brune, it's time to come to grips with your new reality. The only reason you're here is by my good graces."

"Oh? And how's that?" As much as she tried to conceal it, Brune seemed truly puzzled. And possibly a little worried.

Fate relished in it. "I guess you didn't know, since this whole situation is unprecedented–you carrying on with your old guardian duties while the position's already been filled by the new guardian. Well, thanks to Gerdie, it's come to my attention that I have the power to deport you from the Keep. Not sure if deported is the correct word in this case. It's not like this is a country and you're an illegal immigrant, but you catch my–"

"Oh get to the point, would you?"

Fate planted her fists on her hips. "Rude. I was getting there before you interrupted. Let's see, where was I? Oh yes. According to Rule #2,783 of the Guardian Handbook: '*A former guardian who resigns her position to a chosen successor forfeits all rights to said position, regardless of applicable age and eligibility. It is at the discretion of the new guardian, whether the former guardian is of use to the mission or should be expelled.*' There you go. The proper word is expelled."

"Thanks for clarifying. So?"

"What?"

Brune stamped her boot. "Are you going to expel me?"

Fate didn't answer. She wanted to watch Brune squirm a little longer.

"Well?"

Fate tapped her chin. "Hmm, I'm not sure. Maybe it's time we reviewed your attitude of late. Let's see, you've been helpful and instructional, but mean and condescending in your delivery. You've been cool in the face of danger and able to lead during chaos. Though you were cold, brutal and downright bitchy to the survivors of the injured and departed. Hmm, you're not exactly the team player we need around here, so I'm thinking..."

"Look, I know my social skills need scrubbing up." Brune's breathing came in anxious bursts all of a sudden. "I've been living without people for so long I've forgotten how to be...nice and compassionate. Yes, I'm impatient and short-tempered, but like you said, I'm useful and you can learn from me."

"Do I actually need you here to teach me stuff?" Fate patted the top of her head. "Nope. I've got it all right here in the old noggin. Like you said, all I have to do is focus on the questions and I've got all the answers I need. What it really boils down to is, I don't trust you. As long as Gerdie and I have the Rod and Orb, you're a threat."

"I'm not the monster you think I am. Do you actually think I'm capable of killing my own sister and my niece?"

"Duh. Gerdie told me everything you did when you were in the *Book of Fables*. You used the Words of Making to create Old Mother Grim. And then when your grandmother wanted to undo the harm you'd done, you turned the villagers against her just so you could escape the book. They burned her at the stake for what Old Mother Grim did to their children."

Brune's eyes welled with tears, which shocked Fate. "You have no idea what it was like bringing all that misery to everyone we met in the fables. Having to do such horrible things does something to you. It changes you in shameful ways. And then you have to rationalize your despicable actions, tell yourself over and over that your survival depends on causing tragedies until it becomes the truth."

Fate's anger fizzled. She understood that kind of shame after some of the things she'd been forced to do during her own journey through the *Book of Fables*.

"In the beginning, we fooled ourselves into thinking the

stories and characters were just fiction. Make-believe." Brune's voice grew thick with emotion. "But when the children started disappearing and we found out what Old Mother Grim was doing to them. It all became too real."

"That's because it was. You do realize that, don't you?" Fate stared at Brune. "Every person in Oldwilde is as real as you and me, and we played with their fates to save our own."

Brune nodded sadly. "I came to realize that much later, but I honestly didn't know that at first. I was scared about being trapped inside the book. My fear hardened me to the people we came in contact with. I told myself everyone and everything was make-believe, nothing more than fluffy fairy tales needing a villain." Her eyes filled with shame before she dropped her gaze. "So I played the role, a little too well at times."

As much as Fate hated to admit it, she understood. She hadn't believed anything was real when she'd first entered the *Book of Fables* either. But that didn't mean she was going to feel bad for Brune and comfort her with a hug. "I understand you had to do what you had to do. But that doesn't excuse betraying your grandmother to the villagers and leaving your six-year-old sister to fend for herself against that child-eating monster."

Pain splashed across Brune's face. "Gerdie still hasn't given me the chance to explain. But she has it all wrong. I didn't turn the villagers against Oma. My grandmother was devastated by guilt for playing a part in creating Old Mother Grim. She and I tried to destroy the monster with magic over and over. We came pretty close a few times. But Old Mother Grim was too greedy for life." Revulsion twisted her features. "Her appetite for the blood of the young was bottomless."

Out of all the monsters Fate had faced in the *Book of Fables*, Old Mother Grim had been, by far, the most disturbing. The image of that fog enshrouded, gluttonous creature with her engorged belly and vulturine face would be forever burned in her brain.

Squeezing her fists, Brune fought to hold back the tears. "Oma couldn't live with knowing her freedom depended on Old Mother Grim preying on all those innocent children. As you know, the story needed its tragic ending, because if we didn't make it happen, we'd never escape the *Book of Fables*. So Oma sacrificed herself to save Gerdie and I. She told the villagers she was to blame for their missing children."

The breath went out of Fate. She couldn't imagine the heartache and guilt Brune must have lived with all this time. Fate's own guilt over Finn's sacrifice cut to the bone every minute of every day. But at least she held onto the hope of making it right someday soon. Brune would never get that chance.

"I tried to stop Oma," Brune went on. "She was a strong stubborn woman though, and she wouldn't have it. She dosed me with one of her heavy-duty sleeping potions and left me down by the stream. I guess that's why Gerdie thinks I went to the villagers. I woke up a few days later, sick with a headache. It took awhile before I found the burn site. When I saw Oma's body, I actually considered bringing her back to life with the Orb, or using the Words of Making. You have no idea how close I came to doing it. But I was more afraid of what horrible thing I might bring back than I was of losing my grandmother forever."

Fate nodded as Brune fell quiet. She'd lost count of how many times she'd nearly given into freeing Finn from the giant oak with her Words of Making. The only reason she hadn't weakened was because her reckless use of the power to write anything into existence had been the very reason Finn had been interred within the tree by the Green Man.

A tear escaped and Brune wiped at it roughly with the back of her hand. She frowned, obviously embarrassed by her show of weakness.

Fate watched Brune with growing empathy. There actually was a human inside that hard shell after all. Was it possible Brune had been more impetuous in her youth than calculating? Fate could certainly identify with being impulsive more than a few times. Had Finn not been there to spare her from getting her hands dirty with destroying the villains from each fable, she could easily have come out of the *Book of Fables* every bit as hard and bitter as Brune.

Yet, there was still one question needing to be answered. "What about Gerdie, Brune? Why did you leave her behind?"

Brune's brow furrowed with guilt. "I never meant to leave her there. After I gave Oma a proper burial, I used the Words of Making to find Gerdie. I still don't understand why it didn't work."

"Hmm, that happened to me when Finn lost his memory and wandered off in the snow. The Words of Making were useless once he lost his connection to me. I suppose if Gerdie blamed you for Oma burning at the stake, maybe her hatred broke the connection you had with her."

Brune looked tortured. "It's not like I gave up right away. I searched for Gerdie for months, thinking maybe one of the villagers had taken her in. But after awhile, that stopped making sense. I realized I was fooling myself into believing the villagers would ever help her. They were too distrustful and superstitious of outsiders."

"I remember," Fate agreed.

"The hardest thing I ever had to do was admit Gerdie was dead too. Most likely at the hands of the villagers. If I'd known she was alive and all by herself, I never would've left."

Fate regarded Brune with a shocking sense of warmth. "You have to tell Gerdie this. I'll speak to her on your behalf. She needs to listen to what you have to say."

But Fate's guard had been up too long and this newfound

compassion made her feel vulnerable. She must never forget what Brune had done to her. Resentment seeped back in. "Just don't go thinking this changes anything between us just because I'm willing to help you mend things with Gerdie. You spelled me, made me your butt monkey and chucked me into the *Book of Fables.* You didn't care what happened to me. I was expendable, justa piece of garbage you discarded."

The sadness in Brune's eyes faded. "Anyone in my position would've done what I did. I had no other options. I was decaying faster than you can say zombie. If I'd died before summoning my successor, the guardian line would've ended and there'd be no one to set things right in the Keep. You do know if the scavenger causes too much damage in the Keep, the rotations will come to a grinding halt, right? Countless monsters will come pouring through those gateways. I'm talking angry gods, demons, vampires, shifters, you name it. The list is endless. You thought the Chimera was bad? There's worse. Things you can't even begin to imagine. After that, it's only a matter of time before they make their way to other worlds. Including Earth."

Brune wasn't exaggerating. Fate had felt this impending threat deep in her bones since she'd taken the oath. Hearing the possible dangers spoken out loud only renewed her fears. It didn't matter that she understood Brune's motives. She still hated her for using her. "I could've died in there. I almost did."

A hint of empathy softened the hardened plane of Brune's features. "I get it. The *Book of Fables* is every bit as dangerous as the Keep is. I came close to dying in there once too."

"Once? Try several times."

Brune sighed with frustration. "Fine, you win the contest for who almost died the most. Happy now?"

Fate didn't feel any better.

"Let me ask you this." A smile curled Brune's lips, but the smile didn't touch her eyes. "If you could go back in time and stop yourself from being spelled and sent into the *Book of Fables*, would you do it?"

Fate stared back at the woman who had been her puppet master for the last six months. She wanted to yell yes with all the resentment she'd been living with. But they both knew the answer to that question. If it hadn't been for Brune's summoning spell, Finn wouldn't exist. Fate would never have met him in the flesh or kissed his lips and known the bliss of being held in his arms. How could she erase Finn and everything they'd shared together? Imagining a life without him caused her the most unbearable pain.

Brune didn't wait for Fate's answer. Instead, she gestured towards the archway leading to the Gorgons' lair. "So what's it going to be, Keep Guardian? Are we going to do this, or are you going to expel me and face the Gorgons on your own?"

33
MR. ROMANCE HAS TO GO

FINN WENT BERSERK WITH panic, punching and kicking the inside of the dragon's mouth. A growl resounded from deep within its throat, vibrating the spongy wet tongue beneath him. Choking on the fetid, clammy air he was trapped within, Finn did his best to calm down by breathing into his sleeve and silently repeating his mantra.

When Moria had first chomped down on him, he'd thought he was dinner. He was beginning to think he was wrong. Had that been her intention she would've chewed and swallowed him by now. As his racing pulse steadied out, he remembered what she'd told Tynan. *Let them think the Unholy Piper has met his end in the most horrible way*. He supposed the scene needed to look convincing to the soldiers. It really was the only way to let the king off the hook, but he certainly didn't appreciate the petrifying experience.

So here he was, locked inside a dragon's mouth that stunk of honeyed ham gone bad and heading god-knows-where. Moria had said she would go home to the Serpens. Fear jumped his pulse back into high gear. Had he just traded one prison for another? He certainly couldn't see himself shaking hands with her and going his merry way. She may have risen from the ashes, but he was certain she wasn't going to thank him for burning her into a charred lump.

All her talk of injustice and him being a hero had been for Tynan's benefit. There was no room for forgiveness in Moria's cold reptilian mind. That would require a heart, and she hadn't been born with one.

A sudden pitch had Finn sliding down the tongue and banging into the front row of fangs. As he righted himself and shook saliva from his hands, he felt the tug of gravity. Moria was going in for a landing, and at a great speed. Another abrupt dip threw him against the side fangs, but the lack of g-force told him she'd landed.

Daylight shot past the cracks of Moria's fangs as she opened her mouth. Finn edged closer to the front, when her tongue promptly shoved him out. He tumbled through the air, hitting the hard ground. Groaning with pain, he rolled over in the tall grass and looked at the dragon. For a split second he considered launching into the air, but with his stamina being next to zero, she'd no doubt chase him down and snap him out of the sky. And then she would probably make a meal of him.

But wouldn't that be better than rotting away in her dungeon? He couldn't stand the thought of being locked in the dark again. "I don't know what you're waiting for," he croaked. "Just finish me off."

She tilted her horned head and looked at him with one eye. "You don't know who I am, do you?" The voice coming from the dragon was more of a snarl.

Finn wiped the thick slime of her saliva off his face with disgust. "Oh, I know who you are. A soulless snake straight from the bowels of Hell."

"Well, you've got the snake part right."

Finn frowned at the dragon, and then he saw it–the amber eye staring back at him. "Sithias?"

The dragon bowed its head as its body swiftly narrowed into an ivory snake with brown speckled feathery wings. He stood six feet tall when coiled– enormous by normal snake standards–but so much smaller than the dragon he'd shifted out of. "Well done, sir. It only took you about an hour to catch on." Sithias's amber eyes sparkled beneath the shadow of his hunter's cap.

"But then I suppose you're not as sharp, what with the whole lack of food and water ordeal."

Weak with relief, Finn fell back into the grass and laughed until it hurt. "Your acting's really improved," he rasped. "You had me fooled."

Sithias rose on his coils with pride. "Why thank you, sir. I've been practicing my craft every day since I've been back on the island. No time for writing new plays though. My audience can't get enough of my current productions. They're calling my plays timeless classics."

Finn pushed himself to a sitting position. "You've lost the hiss in your speech too. What happened to that? A few well placed *hintsss* would've tipped me off."

"Elsina put an end to that. She doesn't care for the fact that I'm a snake and has forbidden any such reminders."

"Why would she care?"

"Oh. Well, Elsina and I are together."

"As a couple?"

"Don't look so shocked. Is the idea *that* outrageous?"

"Aye, more than a little," Finn admitted. He shook his head in disbelief. "How did it happen?"

"It was all Fate. She turned me into this gorgeous specimen." And with that, Sithias morphed into a handsome, well-muscled man with long, golden brown hair and wings the same color.

Finn's heart skipped a beat at the mention of Fate's name.

"Sometimes I go without the wings and wear a shirt like this." The wings shrank away as a white flowing shirt unfurled out of nowhere and covered his tanned, muscular torso. "What do you think?" Sithias twirled, a gesture that made him considerably less masculine.

"You look like one of those flouncy fellows on the covers of those drippy romance novels."

Sithias shrugged. "Apparently, this is the man I am deep

down inside. That's how Fate described me with her Words of Making. It's how I became the flesh-and-bone man that Elsina recognized as her true love."

Finn clenched at the sudden ache in his chest. "That's how Fate created a happy ending for the fable?" His voice was nothing more than a dry whisper.

"Yesss, though I wouldn't call it a happily-*ever*-after. Oh my, did you catch that? I slipped with a hiss."

Finn stopped breathing. What was Sithias saying? Had Fate failed to escape? He'd always assumed she'd crossed the fiery divide and that's why he hadn't been able to sense her presence in Oldwilde. Had Elsina done something to her? Was Fate…? He couldn't bring himself to think the worst. "Sithias, did Fate make it out of the *Book of Fables*?"

Sithias sighed and flopped down beside Finn. "Yes, Fate went home and she left with the urchin. I know it's selfish but I miss her terribly. Not so much, Gerdie. She's awfully stubborn for such a small person. But I'd tolerate her again if it meant having Fate back."

Finn grabbed him by the shirt. "Don't go scaring me that way." He let go of him. "If she got out, why'd you say it wasn't a happily-ever-after?"

Sithias attempted to smooth out the wrinkles in his shirt. "I was referring to my rather precarious love life. Elsina is a challenge, to say the least. One minute she's all coos and kisses, and the next she's all thorns and shrieks. And at a pitch only dogs can here, mind you. There's no pleasing the woman. To be honest, I was quite happy to have a reason to leave, though who knows what I'll be returning to." He worried his hands together. "I didn't exactly tell her in person. I left a note."

Finn slumped forward, resting his chin on his hands. "That's good, Sithias. I'm relieved Fate–" A dizzy spell stopped him short. His arms gave out and he collapsed onto his side.

"Sir, are you alright?" Sithias helped him up.

"Just a little starved is all," Finn muttered.

"Oh dear, I can take care of that. And here I was prattling on about my love life." Sithias produced a small notebook and pencil. "What exactly would you like, sir?"

Finn frowned at the notebook. "What are you going to do? Sketch a picture of a fruit bowl to help me imagine what I won't be eating?"

"Oh, there's so much you've missed, sir. Fate gave me the power of the Words of Making before she left. So go ahead, order whatever your heart desires."

Finn's heart desired Fate, but his body was in desperate need of sustenance. "Some water to start. And Howtowdie with Drappit eggs, Rumbledethumps and Dundee cake. And throw in some marmelade."

Sithias stopped writing and looked at him. "Other than the marmelade, I have no idea how to describe those other… dishes, sir."

"I wouldn't know the ingredients. My Granda used to make them." Finn sighed. "I'll settle for roasted chicken, mashed potatoes and carrots with gravy and apple pie."

"Those I can more easily describe."

"Oh, and while you're at it, draw me a bath or something along that line. I smell like rotting ham. No offense, but you could use a breath mint."

Sithias breathed into his hand and sniffed. Wrinkling his nose, he gave Finn an apologetic shrug. "Sssorry for that. I'll have you cleaned up in a jiffy." He scribbled in his notebook then recited the written words aloud. "*Finn is now bathed and dressed in a handsome change of clothes.*"

A cool, breezy sensation swept over Finn's skin as his ragged clothes transformed into a pair of army pants and long-sleeved shirt, followed by thick socks and hiking boots appearing over his bare feet. "I almost forgot how refreshing, yet truly disturbing that is," Finn said, remembering the first time Fate had given him an instant shower and washed clothes with her Words of Making.

Sithias smiled. "Disturbing, yesss, but highly convenient. Now, to get your meal prepared." He bent his head as he wrote each item of the menu Finn had ordered and spoke them aloud. The air wavered as the food emerged from the mysterious ether it was made from.

Finn grabbed the water first and downed the glass as fast as his parched throat could bear. Twisting a drumstick off the roasted chicken, he cleaned the meat from the bone in two bites. He stuffed his mouth with potatoes and carrots, barely chewing in his need to feed the hunger he'd endured for so long. He went back to the chicken, tearing chunks of meat from the breastbone, shoveling them in as fast as he could chew.

He was halfway through the meal when his stomach revolted. He pitched forward on his knees and vomited. When the violent bout was over, he wiped the sweat from his brow. "Sorry about that. I swear it had nothing to do with how anything tasted. The meal was mighty good. I guess my stomach's forgotten how to handle large portions of food. Maybe you could conjure something easier to digest, like a cup of chicken broth instead?"

Sithias was already writing a note to clean the mess and promptly produced a cup of hot broth. He handed it to Finn with an uncomfortable expression.

Finn sipped on the broth tentatively. The hot liquid spread welcome warmth through this core and he let out a sigh. "Is something bothering you, Sithias?"

"Uh, well, I was wondering what you plan to do now that you know Fate's not here."

Finn set the cup down, stretched out onto the grass with his hands crossed behind his head and stared at the blue sky. A soft breeze whistled through the tall stalks and swayed gently around him. "I'm going to find my way back to her." He finally believed it this time. With sustenance in his belly and his back to the good earth, he could feel his strength returning already. In a few more days, he'd be able to take on anything that came his way.

"You should know Fate was inconsolable when you were locked away inside the oak. We spent months on Innith Tine waiting for her broken legs to heal. She hardly ate. She wouldn't talk to us. She was like a ghost. All she did was sit at the base of that tree waiting for your release, pining away and growing thinner by the day. All the while, we watched the forest grow at an incredible rate. And when the birds returned to the island, and it looked as though the forest had been restored to its former glory, we thought surely the Green Man would let you go. We even waited another two months after she was healed. But after that, when nothing happened, Gerdie and I began to believe you'd be part of the tree forever."

Hearing about Fate's suffering filled Finn with unbearable grief and sadness. He sat up, his stomachache growing worse as he thought of her. "How did you finally get her to leave?"

Sithias stared off in the distance. "I'm ashamed to say it, but Gerdie and I grew impatient. We knew Fate would never leave, so we pushed her to move on."

"It's what I asked you to do. I made you promise."

"I know, sir. But clearly, we left much too sssoon. If we'd stayed just a little longer, you'd both be together. Instead, you're worlds apart from each other. And if I know Fate, she's moving heaven and earth to find her way back here to Oldwilde."

"How the hell would she get back here?" Finn began to panic. "Please tell me she's not planning to return through the *Book of Fables*. You know what that would mean, don't you?" He didn't give Sithias a chance to answer. "She'd have to go through each fable again. But this time she'd have to turn the endings into bloody tragedies. Do you have any idea what that would do to her? There's no coming back from that. Bringing misery to others changes you. I should know."

"Not to worry. Gerdie told her about another way back. Had I known I'd be seeing you again, I would've paid better attention to the details. Unfortunately, I was love struck and utterly blind to the mantrap I so willingly tumbled into. Rest assured though, Fate was determined to return here with a way to free you from the oak." He shivered with fright. "She would be furious if she knew she missed you by such a short time."

"It's best she doesn't know." Finn smiled, remembering Fate's fiery temper.

"I suppose you'll now have to stay in Oldwilde until she returns. What will you do until then? Where will you go?"

"Time runs differently between the two worlds," Finn mused, more to himself than to Sithias. He knew this from O'Deldar's account of Oldwilde's history and how the two worlds had become divided. He looked at Sithias. "Time passes much longer in Oldwilde, while hardly any time goes by in the other world. I should be able to cross the divide between worlds and get to Fate long before she's ever able to find her way back here."

"Do you really think so?"

"Aye, I do, especially now that you're here. You can use the Words of Making to take us straight to her."

A troubled frown formed on Sithias's overly handsome face. "Oh no, sir. I dare not use the Words of Making so carelessly."

Finn scowled and grabbed him by the shirt. "What? You can't be serious. I need you to do this. And now!"

Sithias held up his hands, shaking with fear even though, in his current form, he was much bigger than Finn. "Sir, with all due respect, you of all people know the trouble we could unleash with this power if we overstep our bounds. You weren't the only one affected by the Words of Making. Before Fate used them to play cupid for me, she rashly invoked Poseidon's wrath upon Elsina's island. Now to be fair, she managed to stop the leviathans of the deep from eating us, but her reckless actions started a war with the God of the Sea. Apparently, he did not appreciate his precious minions being summoned by someone other than himself. I'll spare you the horrid details, but suffice to say, my honeymoon was cut short while Elsina and I attended to the unpleasantness of defending our island from being swallowed by the ocean."

Finn let go of Sithias, his shoulders slumping as he shook his head. "Aye, I suppose you're right. Sorry, I've been so obsessed with getting to Fate I lost sight of what's right."

"All's well, sir. I'll help in anyway I can. As you well know, the Words of Making, when used carefully and in moderation can give us quite an advantage. And the timing is perfect. I've been craving an adventure. Plusss I'm afraid to go home." He muttered the last part.

Finn smiled with relief and slapped him on the shoulder. "Thank you, my friend. I'll take whatever help you're willing to give. Come to think of it, you can start by replacing the flute I lost."

"I'll get right on it." Sithias bent over his notebook.

"It can't just have the Elder race runes carved into it. It needs the Druidic marks as well," Finn reminded him.

Sithias nodded, then muttered the description aloud and produced the flute.

Finn looked it over, marveling at how much the flute matched the one he'd lost. "Perfect, thank you. And while we're at it, there's one thing that's got to go before we set out."

"Is it my hiss?" Sithias asked worriedly. "Its been slipping back in again, and I know how much you detessst snakes."

Finn didn't bother to disagree. When he'd first met Sithias, he'd hated the snake on sight, due to the fact he'd lost his mother to a snake's poisonous bite. But how could he hold onto that when every piece of his personal history before he'd met Fate was fiction? None of it had actually happened. Needless to say, he'd gotten off to a rocky start with Sithias. It had taken him a long time to come around to trusting the amber-eyed snake. Finn couldn't have been more wrong about him. Sithias had proven himself time and again. Though that didn't mean he wanted him to take the form of a serpent while they were together.

"Rest assured, I'll stop this very minute," Sithias continued. "You'll not hear another long 's' from thisss mouth." He gasped and slapped his hand over his mouth. "Oops."

Finn shook his head at the muscle-bound sissy sitting across from him. "No, I can live with that. It's this Fabio thing you've got going on. It might be what Elsina wants to look at, but it's a mismatch in my mind and it's making my head hurt. Mr. Romance has to go."

"Oh that's easily remedied. Hmm, what shall I be?" Sithias tapped the deep cleft in his square chin. He sat straight, his eyes wide. "I know. I'll be the distinguished Dr. Benjamin Weathersby! Remember what a convincing physician I made? Or how about the svelte, charismatic storyteller who took Asgar royalty by storm? That is, before you set our gracious hostess on fire." He mumbled the last part, but Finn heard it loud and clear.

"Is that a complaint?"

Sithias rolled his eyes. "No, of course not. Although, it would've been nice to see how high I could've soared. I'll have you know, a taste of stardom is not a meal."

Finn folded his arms. "So sorry I got in the way with the whole saving-the-kingdom-from-being-scorched-to-the-ground-by-a-dragon thing."

"No hard feelings," Sithias assured him. "Now, back to what I should change into. I say something new, something edgy and exciting." He thought about it a minute and sighed. "So many choices..."

The burst of energy Finn's small meal had given him dropped away and weariness slammed back in. He yawned and stretched. "I'm still wrecked. You think on it while I catch a wink for the next few hours." He curled onto his side and closed his eyes.

"But I need your help. I wouldn't want to choose something equally upsetting."

"Too sleepy," Finn murmured. "Surprise me."

34
AS YOU WISH

"THAT'S YOUR CHOICE? CRUSTY old blind man with more hair for eyebrows than you've got on your head?" Finn stared at Sithias, whose lanky form was wrapped in a long blue robe and stooped over, leaning on a staff for support. "Did you forget we're going into the desert? You need to be strong and able to see. Not to mention, that shiny dome of yours is asking for a 3rd degree burn."

"There's this wonderful invention called a hat." Sithias ran his weathered hand over the entwined, winged snake crowning the top of his carved wooden staff. He turned his head in Finn's direction, with clouded eyes gazing blankly and his elderly features wrinkled in disappointment. "You really don't see the geniusss in my disguise?"

Finn shrugged and shook his head. "You'll have to enlighten me."

"Allow me to introduce myself. I am Asclepius, born of Apollo and the mortal woman, Coronis. I was taught medicine and healing by the wise centaur, Cheiron. You can think of me as the god of healing whenever I appear before you with my magical, snake encircled staff." He winked. "The wings are my own personal touch, not to be confused with the Caduceus of Hermes."

"Impressive resume. Does any of that mean you're not going to pass out after your first fifteen minutes of extreme desert heat?"

Sithias waved his bony arm at him. "Of course, sssilly. Just because I look ancient, doesn't mean I am. I'm as spry as ever."

He dropped his staff and did a little jig, ending with a jump and kicking both feet together in the air. "See? I'd place odds I could even beat you in a race."

Finn laughed, despite his qualms. "Doubtful, unless you've been given super speed to match mine."

Sithias reached into the knapsack slung over his shoulder and pulled out a pencil. "Remember, I'm the one with the Words of Making."

"Good point. So I shouldn't worry about your fogged peepers?"

Sithias laughed. "It's all show. I can see you clear as day."

"Alright, but I still don't see the need for your elaborate get-up and back story."

Sithias made a squawking sound, momentarily too flustered to speak. "How can you sssay that?" he finally managed to croak. "This disguise is my masterpiece. My *pièce de résistance*."

Finn held up his hands in surrender. "Sure, if you say so."

Sithias took a deep breath to calm himself. "Since the brilliance of my plan seems to have eluded you, I'll do my best to illuminate your rather limited thinking."

"Please do," Finn said, barely resisting the urge to roll his eyes.

"We're about to enter the Mirajaran Desert, home to the Djinn. After you fell asleep, I took it upon myself to do a little light reading on the Djinn." He shuddered. "Unfortunately, light was not the word for it. I've since discovered the Djinn are extremely dangerous and not to be trifled with. They are unlike anything we've ever encountered together. If you think Mugloth tested your sanity, you won't enjoy meeting the Djinn."

Hearing Mugloth's name spoken aloud sparked a new layer of tension in Finn. "Go on," he said through clenched teeth.

"I'm presenting myself to the Djinn as a demigod to command a necessary amount of fear and respect from them.

But when they learn that I'm a physician as well, they should be less defensive. Practising the healing arts is a shield of sorts. There's an unspoken agreement, even amongst enemies, to remain neutral toward those who minister to the wounded and dying. As for your story, I will introduce you as my apprentice."

"What's this all about? You talk as if the Djinn would kill us, as soon as look at us."

"That's precisely my concern." Sithias huffed as if Finn were a child too young to understand. "Don't you know anything about the Djinn?"

Finn shrugged. "They live in lamps and grant wishes?"

"Oh, if only that was all." Sithias shook his head. "Did you really intend to enter the Mirajaran Desert without any knowledge of the Djinn?"

Finn glanced skyward and didn't answer.

"Well it's a good thing I'm here then."

"Aye, you saved the day," Finn conceded with a sigh. "So tell me, why are the Djinn so hostile towards humans?"

"They were here first. That's mostly what it boils down to. The religious texts I read tell of an ancient race of Djinn who populated the planet and flourished by spreading their culture and government across the lands with God's grace upon them. Unfortunately, they became corrupt and God sent his army of Angels to drive the Djinn behind the veil, where they live upon the earth but are no longer part of it. When humans replaced them, the Djinn waged war upon humanity, secretly attacking from behind the scenes as an invisible enemy creating chaos."

"So we can't see them because they live in another dimension."

"Yesss, a parallel universe, which makes them terribly slippery, especially since they have no permanent form. They're not carbon-based like most life forms. They're elemental in nature, mainly fire. This makes them shapeshifters of the highest order."

"Like you."

"No, not like me. I can't break apart into fire, cross through dimensions, or teleport anywhere I please."

"Aye, but you have the Words of Making. I'd say we're evenly matched."

Sithias's wizened face rumpled into a serious expression. "That's where you're wrong. We're at a distinct disadvantage. We'll never find them. Their kingdoms are hidden behind the veil. Our only hope is if they choose to show themselves to us, which is highly unlikely."

"There must be some way to summon and command one with a spell."

"It's true. The Djinn are susceptible to magic. But we must be careful to call upon the more benevolent amongst them and pray we don't attract the more vengeful sort."

"You just said they're *all* hateful toward us," Finn reminded him.

"I came across hints of a more open-minded faction of the Djinn, who've been helpful to humans. Though I'll need to do more research to determine which ones exactly." Sithias dug around in his knapsack and retrieved his notebook. Opening it to a blank page, he scribbled a quick sentence. "*I have in my possession the book of spells for summoning and binding the elemental beings known as the Djinn*," he said as he held the message out in front of him.

Upon speaking the last word, a violet-colored mist swirled in front of him, coalescing into a large jeweled book, before it dropped to the ground with a dull thud. Sithias reached for the thick tome and began thumbing through the yellowed pages.

"Now, let's see what we have here," he murmured. "*Luring Ghuls to Ruination* spell. No, I don't think we want to be anywhere near those necrotic flesh eaters. Nasty things, those. They like to ssslip into dead bodies and take them for walks. That is, when they aren't eating them, or some poor, unfortunate child."

"Aye, let's pass on those ones."

"*Protections Against the Palis*spell." Sithias shuddered. "Oh my, we'll want these protections when we get to the desert. The *palis*creep up on those who are sleeping and drain their blood by licking the soles of their feet."

Finn gave him the thumbs up. "Agreed, protection for the feet are a must."

Sithias ran his finger over the list. "Oh look, instructions for making a talisman to ward against the *shaitan* of the desert. Apparently, these are the most insidious of the Djinn. They never show themselves. Instead, the shaitan whisper wicked thoughts into the minds of humans. The only means of detecting their presence is through the evil actions that follow between men and women."

"They sound like demons to me."

"Very much so," Sithias muttered as he copied down the materials needed for the talisman.

Finn rocked in place while Sithias proceeded to conjure each item out of thin air. His nerves railed along the edge of panic. This expedition into the desert was becoming more and more complicated and littered with greater risk than he'd expected. Not that he'd allow any of that to stop him. He'd merely assumed having Sithias along would guarantee a smooth and speedy way of locating the fiery divide.

Sithias shaped some red clay into flat round disks, then carved an eye with radiant marks around it into the pliable shape. Lighting a fire over the disks with a few spoken words, he recited an incantation, over and over, until the clay hardened. The fire blinked out and Sithias reached for one of the talismans. "Ouch! Still hot." He blew on his fingers.

"You really think these will help?" Finn asked.

"I'd prefer not to do a test without them. We must keep our wits about us. The Mirajaran Desert is perilous enough without the shaitan poisoning our thoughts. Do you know what Mirajaran means?"

"Phantom expanse."

"Then you know reality and illusion intermix once you enter the desert."

Finn nodded grimly. "We'll need a guide."

Sithias stroked his long grizzled beard. "Where do we begin to find the right one?"

Finn clenched his fists tight in frustration. "I know of one." He sighed. He'd hoped to avoid calling upon the Lhiannan Shee, but it looked like he didn't have any choice. He glanced around, searching for some privacy. "You finish your research and I'll take care of calling a guide." He spotted a copse of pine trees in the far off meadow and headed toward it.

Confused, Sithias frowned at him. "How do you propose you'll do that?"

"Let me worry about it," Finn called back.

When Finn reached the trees, he pushed his way through the dense branches until he reached the enclosed center. The smell of pine and earth wafted around him as he searched the shadows. The Lhiannan Shee was already there, perched on a low branch, her talons digging into the bark like a monstrous bird.

"You're looking for me?" she said.

"Aye, you said you'd guide me to the Djinn after I reached the desert. We'll be going there in the morning."

"With that snake as your companion? I would've much preferred traveling with you alone."

"He's my friend. I need him."

"More than you need me?" The air wavered around her, diffusing her sharp, birdlike features into the familiar soft planes of Fate's face.

The urge to reach out and draw her into his arms was overwhelming. Finn shoved his fists into his pockets. "Stop. I forbid you to take her form! You're never to do that in front of my friend."

The tempting glamour of Fate faded, leaving him with the cold predatory gaze of the Lhiannan Shee. "I told you, Fae do not deal with Djinn. We are deadly enemies. I must exact a high price for crossing over into their territory. I'll be putting my own life at risk."

Finn grew nervous. "What kind of price?"

She stepped off the branch and circled him. Her pale, thin-skinned wings dragged behind her in the dust. "A kiss."

Finn could still feel the sandpaper texture of her tongue when he remembered their last kiss. He swallowed back his revulsion. "Just one kiss? That's all?" He supposed he could do it as long she took Fate's form and he kept his eyes open for inspiration.

Her small, heart-shaped mouth curved into a sly smile. "That's all. But it must be given out of love."

A knot of dread formed in Finn's stomach. "I can give you a kiss, but there'll be no love in it."

She cocked her head to one side, her black eyes tracing the line of his face. "I have a good feeling about you. Something tells me you'll manage to do it right."

Finn frowned. Everything in him wanted to banish her, but his drive to keep moving forward would not allow it. "Very well," he finally agreed.

Her membranous wings trembled with excitement. "I can't wait," she whispered.

He backed away. "I assume you have ways of following me." His voice came out tight, revealing the tension he was trying to hide.

"Always."

"Then I'll expect to see you in the morning as soon as we arrive at the desert's edge. And come as a man. Someone who looks native to the area."

The air around her rippled as she faded away, and all that remained was her voice. "As you wish, my love. As you wish."

35
WE'RE GOING TO NEED A FORKLIFT

A BLACK DIZZYING VORTEX sucked Fate through the gateway the moment she stepped through the arch. Turbulent air knocked her from every side as she hurtled along the portal's length. Frightening darkness engulfed her. Wanting to scream from the pain of being bashed inside the churning energy, she bit down and kept quiet. She had to play it cool after putting Brune in her place and showing her who was boss.

Fate hit the breaking point, but just when a shriek of pain formed in her throat, the portal spit her out. She hit the ground, shoulder first. Pain shot down her arm as she curled inward, rolling with the fall until she slid to a stop.

Seconds later, Brune shot out and crashed against her. Fate jumped to her feet like it was some kind of race. Happy to be the first one standing, Fate smirked at Brune as she slowly stood and rubbed her hip.

"That was fun. Can we do it again?" Fate said with a sniff. She was not about to admit she felt like a walking bruise.

"Have you lost your marbles? That was the worst ride I've ever taken through any portal. And I've jumped through hundreds."

"It was a bit bumpy."

Shaking her head at Fate, Brune turned her attention to their surroundings. "Damn. We landed smack in the middle of the lair. Look at all the statues. Goggles on."

Fear streaked along Fate's spine as she fumbled with the snap on her utility belt. Her hands shook as she grabbed the brass goggles. They were built with layers of reflective glass, enabling them to see the Gorgons' reflection, versus their true image. She strapped them on, swaying dizzily as a series of upside-down and right-side-up images of the cave flashed in succession before stabilizing to the proper orientation. Fate blinked until her vision acclimated then tried to adjust the heavy goggles on her head, but without much success. They dug into her cheekbone and pinched, but it was a small price to pay for protection against being turned into a garden statue.

She glanced at the nearest stone figure. It was a young man with his hand held out against impending danger. When her gaze settled on his face, she shivered with dread. His mouth was open, forever frozen in a contorted, terrified scream. She could only imagine what horrifying sight would cause him that much fear.

More nervous than ever, she turned her attention to the vast cavern. Thick stalactites hung from the ceiling, some of them dripped so low they'd connected to the floor and had become deformed pillars. In amongst them, the stone victims stood like a large crowd waiting for the final moment of an apocalypse that would never come, at least for them.

A greenish light emanated from a tunnel in the distance–the only illumination against the darkness filling the shadowy grotto. Fate didn't want to take a single step further. She wanted to turn around and take the portal back to the Keep, no matter how bone-shaking the ride. But she'd agreed to come on this mission. How could she turn tail and run now? Brune's attitude towards her would be insufferable if she left.

Pride and competitiveness propelled Fate forward. Gripping her laser gun, she headed toward the light, surprising Brune by taking the lead. As they moved through the tunnel and approached the opening, the light grew brighter and an emerald gleam shimmered over the rough walls.

With her heart pounding in her ears, Fate edged her way into another cavern with a lake in its center. The viridescent water appeared to be the light source. Stalactites as thin and sharp as spears clung to the ceiling, each wet with electric green liquid, which rained tiny droplets into the pool.

"Does it seem like we should've seen some slithering by now, or am I just being paranoid?" Fate whispered to Brune.

"Wish I could say it was you, but I have to agree."

"There's another tunnel over there." Fate pointed at a dark hole across the cavern. "Maybe we should–"

Brune gestured for silence, her jaw clenched as she nudged her chin toward the pool.

Tiny waves rippled the water. A black snake, no larger than a cobra broke the water's surface. Fate aimed her laser gun at it. Was the snake attached to the Gorgon's head? Her skull would have to be huge to accommodate a full head of snakes that size.

Fear iced through her veins.

Five more snakes surfaced, then twenty, then hundreds until a swarm advanced toward the water's edge. The gun shook in Fate's hand. Her instinct was to blast away as many of them as she could in one sweep. But they needed the head intact, snakes included.

"We're going to need a forklift to carry that head back," Fate whispered.

Brune took a step back. "Something tells me that's not her head."

The horde of snakes slithered over the rocks, dragging the torso of a female covered in scales. Fate didn't register what she was seeing at first…until she noticed the snakes were attached at the torso, which heaved itself upright, revealing a reptilian head with jagged horns. This Gorgon looked nothing like her snake-haired sister, Medusa. She had a writhing tangle of snakes carrying her forward instead of legs.

While trying to make sense of the creature, neither Fate nor Brune realized the Gorgon was looking back at them, until the moment she grabbed her bow and quiver.

The Gorgon knocked an arrow and shot with astonishing speed. Fate and Brune both hit the ground, the arrow zinging through the air just above their heads. Brune shot back. The red laser sliced the Gorgon's reptilian hide and left a smoldering gash.

The hair-raising hiss of thousands of snakes filled the cavern as the Gorgon let another arrow fly. They hurtled out of the way in separate directions. Brune rolled down the incline, stopping herself near the water's edge. Fate smacked her back against the rock wall. Gasping for air, she aimed her laser gun at the Gorgon's gown of snakes. The beam cut through several hundred of them, chopping a good third of the Gorgan's support out from under her. She teetered sideways as she sniped an arrow at Fate, missing her arm by about an inch.

Following Fate's lead, Brune dove onto her belly, taking a shot from the other side, cutting off the remaining snakes supporting the Gorgon. Screeching in pain, the Gorgon toppled to the ground, a blackish ichor spurting from the flailing severed ends.

Fate jumped to her feet and charged over to the Gorgon who was dragging herself towards her fallen bow. Drawing her sword, she raised her blade over the monster's neck. But Fate hesitated, suddenly squeamish at the thought of chopping off her head.

"Do it!" Brune rose to her feet. "The snakes are growing back!"

Breathing hard and fast, Fate watched in horror as freshly grown scales sealed over the bloody ends and the amputated parts lengthened while forming heads at the tips. Dizzy with revulsion, Fate steeled herself and brought the sword down. Closing her eyes for a split second, she felt the blade strike bone, the impact nearly jarring the sword's hilt from her grasp. But it wasn't bone she'd hit.

The Gorgon blocked the swing of her blade with her bow. Before Fate could counter, the creature twisted the bow against the top of the blade, jerking it from her grip. Fate reached for her gun, but some of the regrown snakes seized her ankle, wrenching her legs out from under her. The gun fell and rolled out of reach.

Fate slammed on her side, pain driving into her ribcage, wind rushing from her lungs. Snakes lashed at her legs, sinking their fangs into her armor. Fate screamed, kicking wildly in a panic to get them off.

A laser blast tore through the Gorgon's chest, knocking her back. While Brune hammered away at the Gorgon, shearing off snakes and searing more holes in her tough hide, Fate unsnapped her dagger and hacked at the snake heads locked onto her armor by their fangs. Free at last, she scrambled backwards, searching for her sword.

Grabbing it off the ground, she raced over to the Gorgon, no longer troubled by the gruesome job. Without missing a beat, Fate brought the blade down, slicing through the Gorgon's brainstem like butter.

The body thrashed, jerking violently in the last throws of death. The Gorgon's arms reached for the severed head, whapping blindly, which sent it rolling down the rocks toward the water.

"Get the head before it hits the water," Fate shouted.

Brune chased after it, grabbing the head by one the horns seconds before it fell in the pool. Smiling in triumph, Brune heaved the hideous head off the ground for Fate to see–the Gorgon's face frozen in a scream of rage, fangs protruding from the mouth and red snake eyes glaring.

"Ew, bag it." Fate grimaced and quickly wiped the black goo off her blade with the carrying bag before tossing it to Brune.

As Brune reached out to catch the bag, her eyes went round with fear. "Fate, behind you!"

Fate turned to see two enormous snakes slithering from the far tunnel. She raised her laser gun and shot, missing the one she was aiming at. The serpents hissed, fixing their gleaming eyes on her as they snaked round the bend. Four more snakes followed and Fate fired again, this time hitting one in the head. It reared back, when suddenly an unrecognizable form ducked low to pass through the tunnel entrance.

The thing entered the chamber, rising to a height of twelve feet or more. Fate staggered back, her heart hammering with terror. It was another Gorgon with an overly large reptilian head. From the neck down, she was human in form, naked and vulnerable in every way. Six serpents the size of boa constrictors grew from the back of her huge skull. Their strong muscular bodies lifted and bore the Gorgon forward like loyal servants who never allowed her dainty, human feet to touch the ground.

Her massive head turned toward her fallen sister. When she saw the decapitated body, she let out an anguished cry, sharp and shrill. She rushed at Brune, who stood there caught like a kid with her hand in the cookie jar, holding the severed head of her sister. Brune threw the head at Fate's feet, then started blasting the Gorgon with her laser gun.

Fate opened fire from the other side.

The serpents veered into the shots, taking the hits to protect its human form. The laser blasts did nothing to stop the Gorgon. She was on Brune in seconds. One of the serpents bit into Brune's shoulder, lifted and pitched her into the pool. The Gorgon moved toward the water, no doubt to wade in and finish the job.

Fate lifted the severed head by the horn. "Hey, over here!" she called out.

The Gorgon swung around. Fate edged toward the opening

leading back to the portal, but not quick enough. One of the serpents lashed out, corralling her into the middle of the cavern. The Gorgon advanced with frightening speed, forcing Fate into the tunnel on the other side.

She didn't get far before darkness engulfed her. Digging in her utility belt, she retrieved a sun disc and clicked it on. The metallic disc whirred and darted out into the darkness in front of her, shining its bright beam over the narrow walls. Terror pooled alongside increasing hopelessness. What if the tunnel was a dead end? How could she defend herself within such a narrow space? She struggled to think, but her instincts and training were clouded by fear.

Hisses from behind pushed Fate forward. Adrenalin flooded her system, jolting her body into a high-speed chaotic run that became suddenly harder. The level ground had turned into an incline. The walls closed in, making it difficult to breath. Was she having a claustrophobic reaction or was the air stale?

Either way, she was in trouble. Her legs were growing heavier by the second. She needed oxygen. Grabbing the wall for support, Fate gulped back the acidic tang of fear creeping into her mouth. She needed to get a grip on her raging terror. Her chances of survival were already low, but this panic was definitely going to get her killed.

Fate rounded a corner. The walls opened into a small cave with a high ceiling. Strewn over the ground, were piles of shedded snakeskin. Shuddering, she directed the light of the sun disc over every part of the cave using the remote control, searching for another opening. Her breath stalled in her throat. She was trapped.

Letting the Gorgon's head fall with a dull squelch, Fate ran to the far wall and put her back to it. "Breathe," she whispered. She called the sun disc back to hover next to her and turned off the light. Drawing her sword, she waited within the inky black.

Not that she was under any delusions of not being seen. She'd watched too many wildlife shows with Eustace to know snakes can detect infrared radiation in the dark, but only within short distances. But by the way she was sweating, she probably looked like one big glow-in-the-dark stick.

Fate gripped the hilt of her sword as the sound of scales slid over the rock. She fought to keep from trembling and held every muscle tight as she could, so as not to give the Gorgon any sound waves or vibrations to follow.

When the dry skins crinkled under the weight of the slithering serpents, Fate stopped breathing, waiting for them to move closer. One of them brushed against her hair. A tongue flicked over her cheek. A rasping hiss sounded near her ear.

Fate turned the sun disc back on, directing the strong beam into the snake's eyes. It reared back, giving her the room she needed to sweep the blade of her sword. The head dropped and the other five serpents descended upon her, striking from all angles.

Fate lopped off the head of two more before another bit into her armor. A long fang punctured the thick leather. Stabbing pain drove into her bicep. Screaming, she swung her blade down on its neck. The body thrashed, swiping away a serpent ready to strike with mouth agape.

Fate's courage swelled. There were only two serpents left to go. Adrenaline fired through her veins, thrusting her into a fighting frenzy. Shrieking with rage, she went berserk, hacking at anything that moved. Slicing another head off, she went after the last one. It rose high above her, its hiss more of a horrible wheeze as it swayed back and forth.

There was no reaching it. The bodies of the amputated serpents jerked and writhed, blocking her way. The raw ends were already healing over and growing back. Shaking from the need to kill or be killed, Fate held still, allowing her training to take over. Distraction was her only weapon in that moment. Holding her sword toward the serpent, she swung it to one side. The serpent tensed, watching the tip of her sword while she reached for her laser gun.

Taking aim, she discharged a steady beam into the heart of the Gorgon's fragile human body. Thin, pale skin turned reddish black. A fleshy hole widened in the chest. Fate didn't stop until she burned straight through. The severed serpents buckled out from under the Gorgon, dropping her to the ground. Her ear-piercing screech filled the cave. The last serpent descended on Fate. Ducking low, she swung round and hewed the head clean off. The body flopped until Fate lost patience and stabbed it again.

Out of breath, Fate stumbled against the wall and leaned on it for support. A terrible fatigue was setting in. Her body begged to sit down, but she wasn't about to rest there. Picking up the Gorgon's head, she staggered back through the tunnel. When she emerged into the chamber, she found Brune lying face down on the rocks with her legs floating in the water.

Fate ran over and touched her face. Her skin was ice-cold. "Brune?"

Brune moaned something.

"Come on, let's get you back to the sanctuary." Fate grabbed Brune under the arms and dragged her fully out of the water. Even with the cybernetically enhanced strength built into her armor, the effort winded her.

"You have to leave me," Brune groaned.

Fate struggled to catch her breath. "No way. I'm not leaving you here."

"I'm contaminated."

"I'd hardly call getting wet, being contaminated," Fate argued.

"There's something in the water. It got into the bite. I can feel it."

Fate waved her off dismissively and then dropped her arm in exhaustion. "We'll fix it. But first we need to get you out of here."

Brune rose shakily to a sitting position. Dark green veins bulged from her neck and were spreading over her jaw.

"Ew…uh you look a little…under the weather" Fate squinted at the infected area. She struggled to her feet and held her hand out to Brune. "Come on. Farouk will patch you up."

Brune looked at her. "I can't go with you."

Fate teetered in place. "You can, and you will."

Brune's chin quivered as her eyes filled with tears. "No, I deserve this."

Fate bent at the waist, leaning her hands on her knees. The mere act of holding her head upright was tiring. "Despite being constantly annoyed by your overblown superiority complex and complete lack of people skills, even you don't deserve to be left behind in a hellhole like this. So don't make me have to drag you and this two-hundred-pound head out of here. Because I will. But it's got to happen now. I'm fading fast. I've got a fang stuck in my arm and I think it might be killing me. I say that because I'm not feeling all that great at the moment."

"Really?" Brune gave her the frown Fate had grown accustomed to seeing. "Are you saying I can't sacrifice myself for the good of all, because you need saving?"

Brune's face dimmed and blurred. Fate rubbed her eyes, but her vision only got darker. "That's not what I meant, but that may be an option we can…" She trailed off. Her tongue suddenly felt thick and her words slurred as she tipped over and blacked out.

36
THIS BEAST HAS NO MANNERS

THE LUSH GREEN OF the meadow melted away into shapeless gray hues before rearranging into the rise and fall of the rolling desert plains. Finn squinted against the glare of the sun bouncing off white sand. Sithias had used the Words of Making to put them on the very edge of the Mirajaran Desert, but from where they stood, there was no way to tell where the Mirajaran began or ended. The waves of sand stretching past the horizon looked the same in every direction.

Heat radiated off the ground in waves. There wasn't even the slightest breeze to make it a little more bearable. Finn could already feel his energy being sapped by the extreme heat and was tempted to invoke Air to call a gentle wind, but he knew it was best not to tamper with the elements for the sake of comfort.

Finn turned to Sithias, who was well shaded beneath a straw, pointed hat with a round brim the size of an umbrella. He looked like a Mexican wizard. All that was missing were the colorful patterns woven into the weave and dingle balls for trim. "I think some major sunblock is in order," Finn suggested. "The burning's already beginning."

"You're eyeing my hat, are you?" Sithias bounced in place, making the overly wide brim of his hat flop. "A stroke of genius really. I'm amazed at how comfortable I am under this manmade shade I've designed." He pulled at the string under his chin. "Although this chin strap could use a little adjusting."

Finn didn't bother to tell him his invention had already been designed centuries ago. He wiped at the sweat beading on his upper lip. "That's because you've got the constitution of a snake.

You need the heat."

"Not when I'm in human form."

"Fine then," Finn gave in, "I'll take one of your sombreros."

While Sithias went about producing another hat, Finn shielded his eyes with his hand and glanced around for the Lhiannan Shee, turning a full 360 degrees before he gave up.

"I assume you're expecting our guide at any moment." Sithias handed Finn the huge hat.

Finn placed the hat on his head, feeling instant relief from the blazing sun. "Aye, I was expecting her–I mean him–to be waiting for us when we got here."

"Are you going to let me in on who this mysterious guide isss?"

"Uh…someone I met in Asgar–a good piece of luck finding him too. This fellow's familiar with the Mirajaran. He'll get us where we need to go."

Sithias narrowed his clouded eyes and stared at him. "You look nervous. Are you certain we can trust this man?"

Finn was about to continue his lie by assuring Sithias they were in good hands, when he spotted a distant caravan of camels rise over a swell and pointed over Sithias's shoulder. "There he is."

"Shall we let your guide in on my disguise, or should I stay in character?" Sithias asked as they started walking in the direction of the camels.

"It's probably best he thinks you're Asclepius. We wouldn't want him slipping up in front of the Djinn." Not that it actually made a difference. The Lhiannan Shee already knew Sithias was a shapeshifting snake. But Sithias didn't need to know that.

"Excellent. Asclepius lives." Sithias slowed his pace and leaned heavily on his staff like the old man he was pretending to be.

The single file formation of camels drew to a halt in front of them. Three of the camels were for riders and the other three carried provisions. The rider was dressed in layers of fabric and wore a red turban. His face was covered with only the eyes showing. Had it not been for the two empty saddles, Finn might have worried this was a desert nomad they'd run into. He couldn't help being impressed by the Lhiannan Shee's authenticity and preparedness.

"Your ships of the desert have arrived," the guide announced.

Confused, Finn frowned. Why did his guide sound female? What kind of game was she playing now? "Who are you? I was expecting–"

"My brother, Hakim?" She removed the veil from across her face, revealing a dark-skinned beauty with raven hair and eyes the color of olives. She smiled seductively. "He couldn't make it, so he sent me in his place. You may call me Alya."

"Alya, this isn't going to work. You need to send for your brother," Finn argued.

"It works for me," Sithias said, his stoop suddenly gone. "Allow me to introduce myself, Alya. I am Sith–" He cleared his throat. "Asclepius, healer and physician, at your ssservice."

Her gaze shifted to him as she bent her head in greeting. "I have heard of you." Her eyes widened, as if in awe. "Is it true you can raise the dead?"

Sithias looked stumped. "I can," he answered carefully, "as long as it doesn't interfere with the natural order of things."

"I would think any such resurrection would be a disruption."

Sithias opened his mouth to speak, but Finn cut in. "Where is Hakim? He said he would be here. He knows where to find the Djinn."

"As do I." Her gaze burned with defiance.

He could see she wasn't going to back down. "So this is how it is."

"If you're that dissatisfied, I can turn around and go home."

"No, it's too late for that. We'll just have to make do," Finn grumbled as he stormed over to one of camels.

The Lhiannan Shee held up her hand. "I wouldn't do that if–"

The camel jerked its head toward Finn, growling with its mouth open. Foamed spittle sprayed from its gurgling throat. Finn stopped in his tracks, not because he was startled; the beast smelled like slimy compost.

"Walking up to a camel that way only disturbs it," she admonished him. "You must approach in a non-threatening manner. And *don't* look it in the eye."

"I don't care about its bloody feelings. I'm more concerned about the assault to my senses." Finn covered his nose as he eyed the grumpy, spitting camel.

"I apologize for my apprentice," Sithias said, playing the blind man by using his staff to step in next to Finn. "We're grateful to have you and your camels–" He slapped his hand over his nose. "Oh! What is that smell? Is that coming from these beasts? It's horrible. No offense to our gracious host."

She bowed her head slightly. "None taken. After a time, you'll grow accustomed to their odor and it won't be as bothersome."

"I'd rather fly than sit on that walking flea carpet of smelly mystery stains," Sithias whispered to Finn.

"Had the same thought," Finn agreed, "but we'd fry to a crisp under this sun, and we certainly can't walk. It's too bad driving an air-conditioned jeep is out of the question, or I'd have you write one up."

"Sounds interesssting. What's a jeep?" Sithias asked.

"Never mind. We'd end up spinning the wheels and digging ourselves in anyway."

Sithias waved his hand in front of his face. "The camels it is then. How long do you think it'll take before we can't smell them anymore?"

Finn sighed in resignation. "Probably longer than it takes to get where we're going."

After traveling most of the day, the stink of camels became the least of their problems. Camel riding proved to be more than a little uncomfortable. It was downright unpleasant. Although, Finn appeared to be fairing better than Sithias.

Sithias had gotten off to a rocky start with his camel. Upon mounting the animal, he'd proceeded to fall onto the camel's neck when it rose to its feet, hind first. Something the camel had not appreciated. The two never got along after that. His camel moaned and growled for hours, and even tried to run off with him.

Worse yet, the Lhiannan Shee had been willing to let him ride off into the horizon. She wanted Finn to herself. The only reason she finally chased after Sithias was because Finn had threatened to break his agreement with her. It's not that he'd been worried about Sithias exactly, since he would eventually have found his way back, either by sprouting wings or using the Words of Making. Finn's main concern had been with showing the Lhiannan Shee he was the one in charge.

For the moment, all was calm. The endless, undulating waves of sand against the clear blue sky had a soothing effect on Finn's mind. He could let go and allow his thoughts to travel where they might, and Fate was where they went. He imagined her sitting behind him with her head resting on his back and her arms around his waist. At times, when he was completely in the moment, all was right with the world.

"My tailbone's throbbing," Sithias moaned. "This animal

and its herky-jerky gait will be the end of me. I'm being thrown about this saddle with each ungainly step. My thighs are chafed and my tush is turning into one big bruise!"

Finn turned in his seat to have a look at him. Sithias was clenching the wooden horn of the saddle for dear life, his legs clamped tightly as he sat atop the camel stiff as a board. "Aye, it's no picnic on this thing, but you need to loosen up. Let your body sway with the movements. You'll find it easier than staying rigid in your seat."

Sithias hunched forward with his wrinkled face pinched into a miserable frown. "I tried to give this beast of burden the respect it's due. I was a caribou once. Remember? I carried you and Gerdie through a snowstorm."

"Aye, I remember."

"But I can't do it. This beast has no manners."

The camel turned its head and growled, its lips flapping and spewing spittle into the air.

Sithias shielded his face. "See? It's doing that on purpose!"

Finn squelched the urge to laugh. "It does seem to dislike you. Maybe you should try some of your healing powers on it."

"What I'd like to do is show it there's a deadly snake on his back." He kept his voice low so 'Alya' didn't hear him.

"You're overstating the deadly part, but it's possible the camel senses a reptile on his back."

Sithias gave him a dismissive wave. "I'd never credit this creature with that much intelligence."

The camel bleated, as if to argue the point.

"We're nearing Djinn territory," the Lhiannan Shee announced as she brought the caravan to a stop. She turned to look at them. "I suggest we make camp here. If we get any closer, we'll be susceptible to the illusions that plague this land."

"Oh thank the gods!" Sithias exclaimed. "Get me off this thing!"

The camels were unpacked and the tents were pitched within minutes, thanks to Sithias and his Words of Making. He limped over to his tent and whipped the flap aside. "I'll be taking a moment to gather myself together before we summon the Djinn. I have some ointments that need to go on places best kept private." With that, he disappeared into his tent.

The Lhiannan Shee sidled up next to Finn. "Alone at last. If I had to listen to another wailing complaint from him, I'd go insane."

Finn ignored her and took a shaded seat under the canopy. Between the Lhiannan Shee constantly pressing him for attention and Sithias's misery, he was feeling a little irritable himself.

She sat down beside him. "Pretending like I'm not with you…always," she added, "isn't going to make me go away."

"Why do you keep on with this?" Finn was growing tenser by the second. "My heart belongs to someone else. Nothing you could do will ever change that."

She stared at him with an open look of longing. "It's in my nature to feed on love. It's what nourishes me. I suppose this leaves me wanting for the kind of love you feel for her. For eons, I've watched mortals and how deeply and completely they love each other. Attachments are foreign to the Fae. We're free spirits. Yet we envy your depth of emotion. We're capable of inspiring the greatest of passion in the hearts of mortals, but we lack the very same in our own hearts."

"I didn't know you had a heart."

"We do. We simply use ours differently." Her olive-toned irises deepened to the cinnamon brown of Fate's eyes.

Finn looked away. "Don't. I ordered you not to do that."

She placed her hand on his. Her skin was soft and cool to the touch. "I'm sorry, it was unintentional. I can't help myself. She's all over you–living under your skin, flowing through your blood.

She's all you see when you look at me, and like the chameleon I am, I respond and become what is in my environment."

Sithias burst from his tent, his arms full of materials for the summoning.

Finn jerked his hand out from under hers.

"What's this?" Sithias asked as he stood over them.

Finn looked at him. How was he going to explain who she really was? He'd hoped to avoid the subject entirely. A scowl formed on Sithias's wizened face, and Finn grew increasingly uncomfortable.

The sound of a loud, groaning gurgle invaded their space.

Sithias stood stiff and nervous. "Is that camel walking over here? Tell me it's stopping. Tell me it isn't heading straight for me."

Finn glanced past him. While all the other camels were sitting in single file where they'd left them, Sithias's camel was on its feet and sauntering over. The Lhiannan Shee jumped to her feet just as the camel stopped behind Sithias and bumped its head against his back.

Sithias squawked and dropped the bundle he was carrying. Bottles, crystals, sage sticks, feathers and candles spilled everywhere. "It's come to eat me!" he cried.

The camel bleated at him, then went back to chewing its cud lazily.

"I think she likes you," the Lhiannan Shee said as she grabbed the reins and pulled the camel back to the herd.

"She?" Sithias yelled. "Well, I fear *she* wants to trample me to death!"

Finn tugged on Sithia's robe. "Calm down, we have work to do. I need you to focus."

Sithias plopped down next to him, but his gaze was fixed on the camel. "It's difficult to concentrate when I'm being stared at with those thickly fringed, droopy limpid eyes."

"Careful, you're in danger of sounding in love," Finn teased.

Sithias gasped with horror. "Never!"

The Lhiannan Shee rejoined them. "Exactly what are we summoning?" she asked as she watched Sithias arrange the ceremonial pieces on the blanket.

"The *jann*," Sithias replied. "Out of all the Djinn, they're the most open-minded about humans, and enemies of the *ghul*, which I see as a plus. They're also well known for revealing the occasional oasis to travelers they deem worthy."

"None of the Djinn are to be trusted," the Lhiannan Shee warned.

"I fully realize that. The *jann* have also been known to hide an oasis from humans they dislike. Unfortunately, my options are extremely limited. There may be many different kinds of Djinn to choose from, but the *jann*are the only ones who'll be open to helping us. As long as we prove ourselves deserving," Sithias explained.

"How do we do that?" Finn asked.

Sithias fussed with a crystal, turning it this way and that. "I'm not sure. All I know is, when the *jann* appear, they take the form of a white camel or a whirlwind. Personally, I'd prefer the latter. I've had quite enough dealings with camels, thank you."

"Fair enough," Finn said. "But we'll be needing to do this alone." He turned to the Lhiannan Shee. "You need to leave."

Anger flashed across her bronzed face, but fear flickered in her eyes. "No, you need me here for this. I can't leave you to the mercy of the Djinn."

Finn fumed silently. He wanted to tell Sithias she was Fae and that her very presence during the summoning would unleash some sort of attack upon them. She'd told him straight out the Fae and Djinn were deadly enemies. But he didn't want Sithias to know he'd made a pact with a creature whose only agenda was to seduce him so she could completely consume his life force energy.

Sithias watched the stare-down, his head turning from Finn and then to 'Alya' and back again, blowing his disguise as an old blind man.

Finn punched his fist into the sand. "Enough with the charades. Sithias, it's time you knew Alya here is an energy-sucking faery. She's part of the *Feadh-Ree Triad*, the only Fae who can open the gate through the fiery divide."

"I knew there was something going on between you two." Sithias blinked with an obvious jumble of thoughts going through his head. "And here I thought it was sexual tension."

Finn didn't bother to confirm there was that too.

"Why send her away when we're just going to have to call her back after we're shown where to find the divide?" Sithias asked.

"Fae and Djinn don't see eye to eye." Finn narrowed his gaze on the Lhiannan Shee. "You knew the Djinn would deny us help if you stayed during the summoning."

She didn't answer.

"Didn't you?" he pressed. He laughed bitterly. "You want to keep me from crossing the divide. Why didn't I see that before?" He shook his head. "You almost had me. I damn near fell for it."

The Lhiannan Shee sat very still.

"Leave, and don't come back," Finn commanded her. "I'll call the Triad when I'm ready and not before. Only then will you get your payment."

The Lhiannan Shee reached out to him, her expression pleading before she was forced to fade from sight in the blink of an eye.

It was the first time Finn knew her to be truly gone. Until this moment, he hadn't realized how much comfort he'd taken in her presence, whether seen or unseen. When he'd been at his lowest, starving and dejected, and in need of the strength to hold on, he'd clung to what the Lhiannan Shee had given him, a real-life vision of Fate, in the flesh. He hadn't known how much he needed that until this moment. Panic fired through his nervous system and anxiety gripped hold. How would he fare without the crutch of being able to call forth the vision he needed to keep going?

Something broke inside and his spirit fractured. A sudden, terrible chill spread over his skin, icing deep into his bones.

The journey wasn't over yet. What if things got so bad he lost his way? What if he needed the Lhiannan Shee to be Fate for him, because one moment of inspiration meant the difference between life or death?

"You will, sir," Sithias said. "You have me now. I'll keep you safe from the Djinn, and especially from that succubus."

"What?" Finn shivered as he stared at Sithias with confusion. "Do you read minds now too?"

Sithias looked at him with deep concern. "No. I thought you were talking to me at first, but it's clear you were speaking your thoughts aloud. This is not a good sign. That vampire has her hooks in you. Look at you, wild-eyed and trembling like you're stuck in a snowstorm rather than this desert." He wrung his hands together. "Oh dear, I believe you've become spiritually dependent on this evil creature and you're now suffering from the sudden withdrawal of her presence."

37
PINKY SWEAR

"THAT'S EVERYTHING. THE WHOLE story," Fate told Gerdie as she smoothed her fingers over the fading snakebite on her arm. She really should talk to Farouk about bottling the rescue potion he'd used to neutralize the Gorgon's poison in her system. So many people back on Earth could benefit from its miraculous healing properties.

Gerdie squirmed with discomfort, slid off the chair and paced back and forth in the sitting area of Fate's bedchamber. She stopped and looked at Fate. "Do you believe her?"

Fate was quiet a moment. "I do."

"What about what she did to you?"

"As much as I hate what Brune did, I can understand why now. She was being driven by her oath as much as I am. I can't really blame her for doing what she needed to do."

"Do you know how long I've lived with thinkin' Brune got Oma burned at the stake, and left me all alone, struggling for survival for hundreds of years? I can't just let that go because Brune twisted the story around to make herself look innocent."

"Maybe so, but all the hatred you've been carrying around is hurting you, Gerdie."

"Feels better than bein' sad all the time," Gerdie muttered.

Fate sat down and curled her feet into the softness of the couch. "You weren't there when she told me. It was shocking. Suddenly, the hard cold Brune we both know was gone, and someone who was sincere and sorry stood in her place. I know you don't want to hear this, but her side of the story sounds like it could be every bit as true as yours."

"Brune always was the best liar in the world."

"But what if she's actually telling the truth? Don't you want the chance to set things right between you two? Especially since Farouk said she might not survive past another day."

Gerdie's tight little shoulders relaxed and her expression softened. "She did save you."

Fate nodded. "She could've done nothing and let us both die in that awful cave." She looked at the ceiling and sighed. "I can't believe I'm saying this, but I don't think Brune's the evil witch I always thought she was."

"Maybe I'll go see her later," Gerdie mumbled.

"I think that's best."

The chair lowered so Gerdie could climb back on. She tucked her knees under her chin, while tugging the hem of her dress down over her legs. "I suppose now that Brune's out of commission, you've lost your proxy. I'm real sorry. I know how much you wanted to find Finn."

"I was never going to make Brune my proxy."

Gerdie brows knitted with confusion. "You're thinking of summoning the next girl? I'm not even sure there is one. I'm pretty sure the Inkwell line ends with you."

"Where is it written that we have to choose someone from our family?"

Gerdie thought about it a minute. "Hmm, you could be right. I didn't see anything that said otherwise when I was lookin' through the Guardian Handbook."

"Exactly."

"Then who?"

"Jessie. She's perfect. She's proven herself to be a natural-born warrior. She's brave and smart. And most of all, I can trust her."

Gerdie nodded slowly. "Sounds like it might just work. Have you asked her yet?"

"Last night. She's all in."

"When do you leave?"

"Tomorrow after we use the Gorgon's head to turn the scavenger into a pile of abstract art."

Gerdie smiled. "So it's all worked out then."

Fate's heart fluttered with nervous energy. "Almost. Now comes the hardest part."

"Telling Eustace about Finn."

"You guessed it, and let's just say, I'd rather face the Gorgons again than tell Eustace I'm in love with my imaginary boyfriend and leaving to go find him. Awkward doesn't even begin to describe what that's going to be like."

A knock on the door set Fate's nerves on edge.

"That's my cue to leave." Gerdie hopped out of the chair.

Fate rose from the comfort of the sofa and blankets. She stared at the door, unable to move toward it.

"You're pastier than Sithias ever was, and that's sayin' something." Gerdie walked over to the door, reached for the handle and stopped. "Just remember, he's your dad. There's nothin' you can say that'll make him stop lovin' you."

She opened the door and Eustace stepped in. "Leaving already?" He smiled fondly at the tiny adult standing before him.

"Yup. Apparently, I've got decades of resentment I have to deal with. Plus, you two have some catchin' up to do of your own."

Eustace nodded knowingly and closed the door behind her. Hesitating a moment, he finally turned around, struggling to maintain a neutral expression as he walked to the middle of the room. He bent and kissed Fate on the forehead. "How are you? I understand the Gorgon's lair was no picnic."

All of Fate's reservations fell away and a flood of emotions rushed to the surface. Eustace had always been her pillar of strength and nothing would ever change that. Sniffing back a tear, she stepped in for a hug. Eustace gathered her in his arms and squeezed back. "How bad was it?"

She rested her head against his chest with a weary sigh. "Horrible beyond words."

He guided her back to her pile of pillows and blankets. "Have a seat and tell me all about it."

She plopped down into the soft cloud of warmth and drew the covers to her shoulders. "No way, you'll ground me for an eternity if I tell you all the ugly details."

He looked as if he was about to argue the point, then he smiled in agreement. "You're right. It's probably best you leave me with my illusions concerning your safety. Especially after the alarming state Brune returned in." He sat down opposite her, regarding her with a curious glint in his smoky gray eyes. "I will say, I couldn't be more proud of you, Doodles. You're strength is...astonishing."

"Thanks, Dad. That means everything to me." She fell quiet, growing nervous again. How was she supposed to bring Finn into the conversation? Eustace had barely adjusted to her role as Keep Guardian. Would throwing a boyfriend in the mix be too much for him?

"What is it? I can tell something's eating at you."

"Well, there's one thing I haven't mentioned since I got back from the *Book of Fables*. I've...been waiting for the right time to tell you, but everything's been so chaotic."

"I know. We've all had to roll with the punches. What is it?" He leaned forward, resting his elbows on his knees. "Whatever it is, you can tell me. Nothing's going to change between us."

Fate sat straight and rigid. "You promise?"

"I promise." He reached his hand out. "Pinky swear."

Fate intertwined her pinky finger with his. "Remember, pinky swear is the most solemn of promises. Break it and you'll have to swallow thousands of needles."

"Yes, and so I've heard since you were six-years-old."

"All right then." She gave his pinky a good shake. Letting go, she flopped back against the pillows and started wringing the blanket in her fists. A flurry of words buzzed in her head as she fought to put together the perfect sentence. "Do you remember the boy I used to write about?" she said at last.

"Finn McKeen, of course."

She lifted her gaze from the blanket she was mangling and looked at Eustace. "What would you say if I told you I actually met him for real?"

Eustace stared at her blankly. "I'd say…how could that be?"

Fate relaxed a little. This part he would at least understand and believe. "When Brune summoned me to the bookstore, she used the Orb with a certain sort of…love spell." She continued to explain the details and Eustace listened without interrupting. She watched for the tiniest sign of distress on her father's face, but he remained calm, merely staring back with his head bent, his eyes displaying interest behind his scholarly glasses.

"My, that's astounding," he said after she was done relating how Finn had come into existence. "I knew the Orb had extraordinary powers of creation, but to produce a sentient being made of actual flesh and bone…well that's far beyond anything I could've guessed possible."

Fate fidgeted with the pillows behind her back, wanting desperately to avoid this next part. She gave up on trying to get comfortable. Nothing about this was comfortable. "I could hardly believe it at first. In fact, I didn't. It was all too impossible. He was exactly as I imagined him." She smiled without meaning to. "Better actually."

It was Eustace's turn to fidget uncomfortably. "I take it you got to know him rather well."

Fate nodded. "I did. He traveled through all the fables with me."

Eustace cleared his throat and tugged at his tie. "Exactly how familiar did you two get with each other?"

Leave it to her dad to get straight to the point. Fate's face grew hot and she suddenly wished the ground would open up and swallow her. She bunched the blanket under her chin, wanting to duck and hide behind it. But she didn't. She wasn't a child anymore. "We fell in love."

The room fell horribly silent, and when she gulped, the tiny noise sounded like it was booming through a stereo.

"Ah, I see." Eustace removed his glasses and turned his attention to cleaning the lenses on his sweater vest.

"Nothing happened beyond a kiss," Fate blurted out. She couldn't allow his fears to take his imagination to places that would embarrass them both.

"Oh, thank god." He put his glasses back on and settled into the chair looking greatly relieved. "So, this young man is your first love. Or should I say second, since you'd already fallen for him when you first imagined him?"

"Pretty much." Fate smiled shyly.

"Tell me about him."

Fate relaxed her grip on the blanket and nestled against the pillows. She described Finn's caring nature and his knowledge of Druidic magic. She explained how the Elder Race runes enhanced his abilities, not only to that of super human strength and speed, but also his power over the elements. When she came to the part about how Finn had become possessed by Mugloth's darkness, she chose her words carefully and tempered the story. After all, this was her overly protective father. Certain details would forever taint his opinion of Finn and she couldn't have that.

"From what you tell me, Finn sounds like a commendable young man. I know something of the Druids, and they honor life above all else. He must've had a terrible war of conscience within himself to take even the life of the monsters you encountered in the fables."

"He did it for me, Dad. He didn't want the darkness he'd become infected with to touch me. He knew if I'd had to do those horrible things I'd be changed by them."

"Yet, he managed to remain honorable and true to who he was in the face of such intense resistence?" Fate detected a hint of doubt in his voice.

"I'll be honest, there were times when he almost succumbed to the evil."

Eustace's grip on the arm of the chair tightened. "And how exactly did those moments manifest themselves?"

The image of Finn's cruel smile and the ruthless black pools of his eyes flashed in Fate's mind. As much as she wanted to forget, there was no erasing the painful memory. Mounting self-loathing mixed with his connection to the evil oak, at the time, had culminated in a distortion of his feelings toward her. In a moment of complete overwhelm, his anger and resentment had careened out of control, driving him to the very edge of doing the unthinkable between them. But in the end, he'd fought the sinister influence rampaging through his system by taking a blade to himself. The physical pain he'd caused himself had cleared his mind. She'd been frightened, but Finn had proved his love for her, not just then, but time and again.

"What did he do?" Eustace leaned forward with intense concern. "It's all over your face. He did something to you, didn't he?"

"No." Fate faced her father straight on. "He protected me against *everything*. Even to his detriment." Tears burned at the back of her eyes. "It cost him, Dad. It cost him his life."

Eustace looked sorry for his harshness. "He's dead?"

A tear escaped as Fate shook her head. "Worse." Her voice trembling as she described Finn's ultimate sacrifice to save her from the Green Man and his final internment within the giant oak.

Eustace was quiet a moment after he took it all in. "You're telling me this because you want to go back and free him." It was a statement more than a question.

"I do."

"When are you planning on going?"

"Right after we deal with the scavenger."

Eustace didn't move. Fate waited anxiously, watching the internal battle going on behind her father's carefully composed expression. "Have you figured out how you'll free Finn from the oak?" he asked at last.

Fate stared at him wordlessly. She'd been so focused on getting back to Oldwilde, she hadn't considered how she'd solve that particular part of the problem.

"I can help you with that," he offered. "I'll see what research I can dig up on the Green Man and elemental magic in general."

"You'd do that for me?"

Eustace reached over and placed his hand on her knee. "You have no idea to what lengths a father will go through to ensure his child's happiness, do you?"

The tears ran freely as Fate smiled at him. "I do, Dad. I really, really do."

38
WELCOME BACK

FINN KNEW HE WAS in trouble. Pain knifed through his core and a building nausea spiked into his brain, but the overwhelming glacial chill was the worst. The intense heat of the desert did nothing to cut through the bitter cold. He craved warmth in his bones. He felt empty, as if the very fire of life had left him.

Wracked with violent shudders, he fell onto his side and curled in on himself. "Do the summoning, Sithias. Let's get this done."

"Are you sure?"

"Aye, we need to get the Djinn here before I worsen."

"I don't know…I think I should figure out how to stop this above anything else," Sithias insisted.

"No!" Finn growled through chattering teeth. "The Lhiannan Shee is the only one who can fix this, and I won't call her back. I'm not putting everything else at risk. She did this. I know it. She must think I squelched on our deal. If I call her now, she'll have me selling my soul instead of a kiss."

"Did you say the Lhiannan Shee? And a kiss? Oh my, you might as well have made a deal with the devil. But you did the right thing, sssir. I once read a story about a young poet who captured the world's attention with his inspired poetry. He credited his works with a faery muse, who came to him each night to whisper lovely words into his ears. Her very presence filled him with the greatest joy. All she asked of him was his devotion and one kiss after he finished compiling enough poems to last a lifetime. When that day came, he kissed her with all his heart and soul. She left, quite satisfied, and never returned. He, on the other hand, grew terribly ill. The poor soul pined for her until he died. A young man, mind you."

Finn grabbed at the edge of the blanket he was lying on and wrapped the corner over his shoulder. "But I didn't kiss her. And she didn't have my devotion. I loathe her. Let's start!"

"She had to have inspired something in you or you wouldn't be suffering her absence."

Another wave of nausea had Finn grabbing his gut. "Why are you pressing me? Get on with the summoning."

"I suggest we clear this matter up first. What if the Djinn sense your affiliation with the Lhiannan Shee?"

Finn ground his teeth together, scrambling for a good argument. He had none.

"I'll take that as an approval to find a solution to this sticky situation." Sithias brought out his pencil and wrote in his notebook. He spoke the words aloud quietly and conjured a large, leather bound book.

Finn rocked back and forth, fighting against the temptation to call the Lhiannan Shee and end his misery. "During my darkest moments, she used to appear to me as Fate," he confessed. "It was so real. She moved like Fate. Smelled like her. I knew it wasn't really her, but seeing Fate in front of me that way…it meant everything to me. It gave me strength."

"Ah, I see." Sithias set the book down on the blanket.

"I'm so ashamed."

"Don't be. I was there. I understand what you two went through better than anyone. You fought long and hard to be with Fate, only to have her torn from you all over again."

Finn gave into the sorrow he'd suppressed. "I miss her, Sithias. I miss her so much it kills me."

"That's the part I hope to avoid." Sithias opened the book. "I have here a handbook called *The Discarded*. It outlines bindings, clearings and banishing spells for every type of harmful spirit, faery and demon." He flipped through the pages. "Here we go, *How to Banish Entities with Succubi Traits.*" He fell quiet as he read down through the page.

Finn waited in agony. Each minute felt like an hour.

"Hmm, it's a simple spell. Although I fear your part in this will be the most challenging." Sithias copied down a list of items, then muttered them aloud. A colorful pile of gemstones, a small silk pouch, candle and string appeared in front of him. He scooped up the stones and placed them in the pouch. "Here, hold onto this."

Finn squeezed the bag of stones in his hand. Some of the dizziness subsided. "What is it?"

"Oh some semi-precious stones like black tourmaline, bloodstone, black onyx and jade, to name a few. Can you feel the effects?"

"A wee bit."

"That's good. The stones are beginning to create an anchor for your spirit. Apparently, your spirit's left you to chase after the Lhiannan Shee. You're suffering from a soul sickness. The longer this goes on, the more your body will decline." Sithias lit the candle and handed Finn a piece of string. "Can you sit up enough to recite the banishment spell?"

Finn struggled to a sitting position.

"Hold the string above the flame and repeat after me."

Finn's hands shook uncontrollably as he gripped the string and held it taught above the candle.

Sithias read from the book. "*I hold this string, a symbol of my tie with you...*"

Finn gulped down the bile rising in his throat and repeated the words.

"*This tie of obsession, addiction, dependency, need, desire and lust, I hold to the cleansing fire to sever our agreement forever.*"

A wave of darkness filled with grief crashed over Finn. He did his best to repeat the line, but dizziness rushed back in and he couldn't remember what was said.

"Let's try that again." Sithias recited the line one word at a time, while Finn repeated after him.

"Good, now burn the middle part of the string," Sithias instructed.

Despair gripped hold as Finn swayed in place, trying desperately to target the flame. He missed and fell over. "I can't do it," he panted.

"You can," Sithias insisted. "This is the resistance the book mentions. Your dependency on the Lhiannan Shee for what little happiness she grants you is what's holding you back. Now sit up and burn the string."

Finn's yearning to have the Lhiannan Shee with him became unbearable. Chills raced over his skin and he couldn't move. The muscles in his body stiffened until he was bound with unbelievable pain.

He cried out for his muse.

Sithias clamped his hand over Finn's mouth, cutting off the words that would summon her back. "She's infected you, made you think you need her. Turn your thoughts to Fate. Remember the reason you allowed that vampire into your life. Free yourself. Think back to your most blissful time with Fate."

Finn squeezed his eyes shut. Little by little, a memory emerged, like a pinprick of light piercing the darkest night. An image came to him, of Fate standing in the doorway of her bedchamber. They'd been at odds with each other at the ball and he'd come to mend the divide between them.

She'd been a vision beyond imagining that night, with the moonlight sifting through her thin nightgown, casting her curves in soft silhouette. Her hair had been a perfect, tousled mess after she'd torn the flowers from her hair. When she'd opened the door, the look of surprise on her flushed face, still wet with tears, had nearly stopped his heart. In that moment, he'd lifted a silken lock to his nose and inhaled the heady scent of gardenias lingering in her hair. She had stepped close, touched her lips to his and melted all barriers between them.

A sudden fever rose beneath Finn's skin, spreading white-hot heat through him like a raging furnace, burning the chill from his bones. His mind cleared. He rose to a sitting position, his hands steady as he moved the string over the flame. Finn held it taut, welcoming the heat on both hands as the string caught fire. His only desire now was to be with Fate and cut his tie with the Lhiannan Shee once and for all.

The string broke and he let the burnt ends fall next to the candle.

"Welcome back," Sithias said.

Finn closed his eyes and inhaled deeply. "It's good to be whole again. I can't believe I never realized how broken I was."

"You were under her thrall."

Finn reached over the candle and held Sithias by the shoulder. "Thank you, my friend. You saved me yet again."

"Happy to be of service, sir." Sithias lifted the candle and blew it out. "Shall we move onto the next order of business?"

"Aye, I'm ready."

Sithias busied himself with the ceremonial items, carefully placing them in the cardinal directions, while reciting the incantation for summoning the *jann*.

Determination swelled in Finn's chest. Renewed strength flowed through his body. He hadn't felt this strong and vigorous since he'd last been with Fate. It bothered him to know he'd allowed the Lhiannan Shee to siphon off so much of his life force energy and will power. One moment of weakness had turned him into a complete and utter idiot.

"It's done," Sithias announced.

"Did it work? I don't see anything happening."

"There's no way to know for sure. All we can do now is wait."

And wait they did. The setting sun burnished the sky and endless sea of sand with tones of gold and scarlet shadows before they noticed a change within the seemingly changeless desert.

Sithias sat straight all of a sudden and pointed. "That's odd, I do believe we're in for a storm. I see thunderclouds brewing on the horizon. Does it rain in the desert?"

Finn stood. What looked to be clouds was actually the desert sand rising to swallow the sky. "That's no rain cloud. It's a sandstorm, and headed our way. Do you think it's the *jann* you summoned? You said they appear as whirlwinds or camels."

Sithias's eyes grew wide with panic. "I'd hardly call that tsunami of sssand a whirlwind." He pulled out his notebook with shaking hands. "I'll write up some shelter."

"Do it quick, it's moving fast." Finn grabbed one of the canteens, watered down some handkerchiefs and thrust one of them at Sithias. "Put this over your mouth. We need to protect against the dust. And conjure some goggles. I can already feel it in my eyes."

Sithias did as he was told and produced the goggles.

Finn tied the handkerchief over his nose and mouth. Just as he reached down for the goggles, a flurry of sand swept Sithias's notebook from his hands. With a squawk of fright, he scrambled after the book and vanished behind a dense veil of dust.

The sandstorm was upon them. The massive wave had blotted out the late evening sun, plummeting them into darkness.

39
THAT'S HOW WE DO IT

FATE AND JESSIE FLEW over a myriad of structures within Quadrant 537, searching for the hole the scavenger had made. They slowed when they spotted what was actually a crater. Shredded copper surrounded the opening of the pyramid the scavenger had chewed through.

They landed next to the gaping hole. Jessie leaned over the jagged edge, looking down into the deep black with a shake of her head. "I don't like it. How are we supposed to know where the scavenger's located from up here? We're going in totally blind."

Fate stepped in next to her and glanced down. Jessie wasn't exaggerating. Farouk's sensors had lost track of the scavenger after it dug below the subsurface. It could be hiding in the shadows and laying in wait at the very bottom. Hopefully it had tunneled its way in some other direction, which would give them the advantage of surprise. Either way, they were being forced to follow.

Jessie backed away from the hole. "Remind me why we're supposed to leave our aeronaut packs here instead of flying down."

"The scavenger can fly too."

"Right, but only a little better than us. Which is why I still don't see how us not being able to fly down there gives us any sort of advantage."

Fate set her pack down. "I don't like it anymore than you do, but Farouk said when Brune fought the scavenger, she was better off when her feet were on the ground than in the air."

"Whatever." Jessie shrugged her pack off.

"Just be ready for anything." Fate slung the backpack with the Gorgon's head over her shoulder. The horns dug against her back, hard and cold. She did her best not to shudder and cringe.

Jessie gave her a sour look. "That's your pep talk? Lame."

"Hey, it's all I've got."

Jessie spit down the hole and watched it disappear. "How about we yell at the top of our lungs and draw it out. I like our chances better up here, where we can blast it away from higher ground."

Fate considered the alternative, until her gaze landed on a nearby iron griffin and a centaur armed with a bow and arrow. Not to mention the gold Poseidon, the bronze Minotaur and silver Hydra a little further away–any of which the scavenger could animate and use against them. "Have a look around. I'd rather go one-on-one with the scavenger than have to take on all these potential army recruits."

Jessie glanced around. "Yeah, good point. Grapple guns out."

They each removed their guns from their utility belts, shot the grapple hooks onto the edge and lowered themselves down on steel cables. With the other hand, Fate dug for a sun disc and clicked it on. The disc shot from her hand and hovered in space with its light aimed down into the darkness. On guard for any type of movement, they slowly descended.

"Can I just say, I feel like Batman right now," Jessie whispered.

"Same here, except for the layer of terror smeared on top."

"Yeah, that part's a bit of a buzzkill, isn't it?"

"Understatement of the century."

They continued down, carefully avoiding being skewered on sharp edges of twisted metal, broken gears, steel rods and exposed cables. Every now and then they spotted spider bots in behind the shrapnel, their thin legs working on intricate circuit repairs or welding breaks.

Fate directed the sun disc with her remote control to aim its bright beam all along the bottom of the hole. "Looks like all's clear so far."

"Let's hope."

Fate planted her feet on moist concrete. The air was humid and the temperature had risen considerably. "Guess the scav couldn't dig any further once it hit concrete. Looks like it tunneled through that way." She pointed at a torn wall. "I say we Gorgon up from here. The scavenger could jump out at us at any minute, so goggles on."

Jessie carefully placed her goggles on over the Dragon Eye gear she was already wearing. As soon as she'd adjusted her headgear, she grabbed Fate by the arm. "Whoa, head rush."

"Yeah, the goggles take a little getting used to," Fate agreed as she waited for the dizziness to subside.

"Uncomfortable, too." Jessie tried to keep them from digging into her face.

"Don't bother. They weren't exactly ergonomically designed." Fate removed the Gorgon's head from the backpack.

Jessie grimaced. "Ew, warn a girl before you assault her senses with a face like that."

"You were expecting a beauty queen?"

"Well...no, but that's just fugly."

"Get used to looking at it, cuz you're carrying it next," Fate promised. "Come on, let's do this." Holding the gruesome head as far from her body as she could, Fate led the way, navigating through the debris littering the ground with the sun disc floating just above her on dim to avoid alerting the scavenger with a dayglow searchlight.

As they moved along the already huge tunnel, the radius grew larger. Fate swallowed down the fear building inside. The more iron the scavenger ate, the bigger it was getting. She tried to convince herself that size didn't matter. All she needed to do was get the scavenger to look at the Gorgon and the rest would be gravy.

If that was the case though, why did she have this awful nagging feeling that things were about to get a whole lot worse?

"I see something up ahead," Jessie whispered.

Resisting the urge to send the sun disc further ahead and shine it bright, Fate squinted into the dark. "All I can see is black."

"You don't see that blue glow?"

"I'm not special enough to have a Dragon Eye, remember?"

Jessie elbowed her playfully. "It's because you're too special."

"For someone who's about to be made special too, you're awfully calm about it all."

"That's the Dragon Eye. Feeling super human does wonders for your self-confidence."

"Since I'm still struggling with mine, maybe you should tell me what you're seeing exactly. Does it look like that blue mist we saw around the scavenger?"

"Nope, it's brighter and more greenish in color."

Fate slowed down. "Aquamarine?"

"Bull's-eye on the color."

Tension snaked through Fate's core. Why was that so bothering? Something played at the back of her brain. An elusive memory or detail she failed to mark as important. Her pulse raced out of control as it all came back: Her brief astral visit to the center of the Keep when she'd been wearing Hermes's helmet. The shrine and the blue-skinned Kaliena sitting on her throne. The formula the strange robot had fed Kaliena and the resulting glowing aquamarine liquid that had flowed from her six hands.

"This is bad," Fate whispered.

"Aquamarine's not exactly my favorite color either. A bit too beachy for my liking, but–" Jessie stopped and stared at Fate.

"What's the deal with that color? I know it's not some new pet peeve, so spill."

Fate didn't know where to begin. Kaliena's history wasn't exactly a short story, but it was one Jessie at least needed the cliff notes on. "Do you remember Farouk mentioned he was getting readings of lifeforms within the core when you first got here?"

"Not really. I was a little on the shocked side right after coming through that wormhole."

"Right, well when I went through my final initiation, I had to wear this helmet that showed me the history of the guardians and the Keep. While I was wearing it, I kind of veered off and did a little exploring."

"Of course you did."

Fate frowned at her. "Judgy much?"

"What? I'm just saying you've always been…curious."

"Anyway, I went down into the core, where I found this creepy science guy robot thingy. He had these spider robots mining the Keep for a bunch of blue gemstones. He had buckets of them, which he ground into fine powder. Then he ran the gemstone powder through his mad scientist lab and cooked them up into a sparkly blue-green liquid, which he took to a shrine."

"You do realize this sounds like you were tripping on something, don't you?"

"Like I'd ever do that." Fate rolled her eyes, though Jessie missed it because of the goggles. "I didn't even smoke those stupid clove cigarettes you experimented with."

"I know. You're so boring."

"I'll take boring over puking my guts out."

Jessie waved her off. "Continue explaining your trip."

"There was this woman sitting on a throne in the shrine, like she was some sort of deity. At first I thought she was a statue. Her eyes were closed and she was so still. Kind of frozen in time.

And she wasn't entirely human either. She had blue skin and six arms."

"See, you were high."

"Would you stop with that? This is serious. The sciency robot fed her that stuff he whipped up in the lab and her hands–all six of them–started glowing aquamarine. The energy in her hands turned to liquid and spilled down over her throne into these troughs that made this weird pattern in the floor light up all the way to the walls, which started moving these gigantic gears. It was obvious she's directly connected to the Keep. I'm not sure if she's running it, or if she's infecting it, but either way, I'm pretty sure it's not good for us."

"Why? You said she was asleep. She's probably just part of the Keep's ecosystem."

"No, she's not part of the Keep in that way. Farouk showed me who the builders were and she wasn't part of the original design. Wodrid had the shrine made for her and he helped integrate her deep inside the Keep's core, like life support, to keep her from dying."

"Whoa, hold on. Wodrid? How'd he enter the picture?"

"A few hundred years ago, he found the lock that opens the gateway to the Keep. She got cranky with him for trespassing and made him her prisoner. But after awhile they got all Stockholmy with each other and fell in love."

Jessie nodded. "Okay, that whole conversation you and Farouk had about Wodrid earlier is making a lot more sense now. So we're about to meet Wodrid's old lover?"

"Yup, and I'm dreading it. When I was wearing the helmet, she sensed my presence and woke. She was not happy with me being there and she let me know in no uncertain terms."

Jessie turned toward the long tunnel. "Is she a threat?"

Fate shifted the heavy Gorgon head to her other hand. Her cybernetically enhanced armor made it easier to hold her grip on the horn, but the lopsided weight was awkward. "I'm not sure. She's dependent on the magic being generated by the Keep to stay alive, so unless Wodrid shows up with the Rod and Orb to revive her, my guess is she can't do much to hurt us."

"If that's true, why does she make you so nervous?"

Fate bit down on her bottom lip as she thought about it. "I suppose because I saw how powerful she was when she first became a god. I watched her spread herself across the universe. She was like, "Hey, I'm totally omnipresent". My words, not hers, but you know what I mean. She was scary powerful. She could create and destroy with a thought. Anyway, Kaliena's been asleep this whole time, just waiting for Wodrid to deliver what she needs so she can return to her former god status." Fate shook her head with worry. "It's not just me who's scared. I saw real terror in Farouk when I told him she was awake."

"Why weren't the rest of us told? Does Brune know about this?"

"No, Farouk wanted to keep it between the two of us… I guess because we had so much to deal with already. He didn't want everyone distracted from what needed to be done first."

"I suppose that was best," Jessie agreed. She reached for the Gorgon's head. "Here, give me that. Not that I want to touch that thing, but the Dragon Eye gives me extra super strength."

Fate gladly handed it over.

"Hey, do I have to stop wearing the Dragon Eye after I'm made your proxy?"

"I don't see why you should have to. You've already proven immunity to any side effects."

"Good. I wasn't looking forward to being ordinary again."

"Yeah, don't remind me," Fate grumbled. She missed her super powers more every day.

"Maybe you should put the sun disc away since it looks like we might be closing in. I can get us through the dark without it,"

Jessie suggested.

Fate called back the sun disc, slotted it onto her utility belt while Jessie led the way, guiding them past fallen debris only she could see.

After moving quietly through the tunnel in utter darkness for at least ten minutes, Fate finally began to see the aquamarine glow Jessie had detected earlier on. They slowed and edged toward the opening, peering into the vast chamber. They didn't dare speak for fear of being discovered.

The entire space was lit from floor to ceiling. Kaliena sat on her shrine, still as stone, and by all appearances, asleep to the world as the luminous liquid poured from her many hands. Fate glanced around for Kaliena's robot and any sign of the scavenger, but the chamber looked empty.

They approached the shrine, careful not to step on the indentations holding the liquid flowing throughout the pattern covering the floor. There was no way to know what kind of effect the glowing fluid might have on them.

Jessie set the Gorgon head down and stepped close to the shrine. "You weren't tripping after all. She really does exist."

"Shhh! Keep your voice down," Fate whispered. "I don't want her waking up."

"She's so smurfy with that blue skin," Jessie mused.

"Trust me, she's nowhere near as harmless."

"And all those arms. Think how much more you could get done in the run of a day. Takes multitasking to a whole new level."

"I'm more concerned with what's pouring into the Keep. This is way more than I saw the other day."

"What should we do about it?"

Fate stared at the walls, where the giant gears rotated, moving the liquid to unseen parts of the Keep. Nothing amongst the wealth of information she'd been given about the Keep explained what this liquid was. She unsnapped the holster of her disintegrator gun. "I say we destroy the shrine. Dissolve it down to nothing so Kaliena has no more life support."

Jessie looked at Fate, surprise registering on her face, despite the goggles covering her eyes. "That's so cold. I never knew you could be such a hard ass."

Fate gulped. "You really think that's cold of me?"

"Well, she is dying and basically defenseless."

"Kaliena's a threat," Fate insisted. "She may not look it right now, but believe me, if she gets to feeling better, she won't be inviting us over for a nice cup of tea. She'll give us the evil eye and turn us inside out."

"Hmm, I guess when you put it that way." Jessie took her gun out. "I can get on board with this one."

Fate nodded, though she felt differently as she aimed her gun. Kaliena's smooth, peaceful expression wasn't exactly bringing out the killer in her.

A sudden squeal of grinding metal sounded throughout the chamber. Fate whirled round as huge chunks of the wall broke away and descended upon them. Jessie dove to the left, avoiding the thunderous crash of mangled steel between them as Fate lunged in the opposite direction.

Struggling to figure out what was happening, Fate looked up and up and up until she realized the walls hadn't actually caved in. The scavenger had reshaped itself, blending against the ceiling and walls of the chamber, fooling them into thinking the space was empty. The blue vapors emanating from the scavenger had mingled with the luminescent glow covering the walls, the color barely discernable, unless she'd been looking for it.

Fate shot the leg closest to her. An explosion of red gas engulfed a small part of the massive appendage, turning it to crumbling rust. Jessie aimed higher, shooting one cartridge into it after the next as she ran around the back. Within seconds, parts of the foot and shin disintegrated. The leg buckled, toppling the titan to its knees. The impact made Fate's teeth rattle in her skull.

Fate aimed for the hips, shooting again and again. Clouds of rust showered from the smoldering holes, collapsing the scavenger at the waist. The giant tumbled forward. Fate dodged to the right, avoiding the hammer of its jagged fist. She skidded to a stop. The scavenger fixed it gleaming eyes on her. She was directly in its line of sight. There was no better time to use the Gorgon's head. But she was too far away from it. "Jessie, get to the head!"

Jessie appeared on the other side. "Got it!"

The words were no sooner out, when the scavenger swiped at Jessie, knocking her through the air. She slammed against the floor, losing her goggles and headgear in the violent fall. Struggling to rise, Jessie scrambled to reach the Dragon Eye. Fate fired the last of her cartridges into the scavenger's supporting arm in the hopes of distracting it.

Hunks of the arm fell away. The scavenger's head ground against the floor. It floundered with its other arm and tried to rise. Fate reloaded and blasted another round of cartridges into the back of its head. The oxidation went to work, eating through layer upon layer of metal, leaving a massive hole in its cranium. Shrieks filled the cavernous chamber as the scavenger twitched and flailed.

Fate ran around the top of the scavenger, searching for where Jessie had dropped the Gorgon's head.

Jessie emerged from the cloud of gas, coughing and pointing. "Over there." She raced toward her Dragon Eye and plucked it from one of the troughs. She shook the blue-green liquid off the gear and placed it back on her head before Fate could warn against it.

Fate stuffed her concerns, grabbed the Gorgon by the horn

and turned. The scavenger's eerie ice blue stare tracked her movements. She held the Gorgon up to the nearest eye.

The second the scavenger looked at the Gorgon, the head came to life and shook in Fate's hand with a horrifying shriek. She looked at the head. An unholy light blazed from the Gorgon's glare.

The blue flame in the scavenger's eyes died. The sheen of metal turned to granite, spreading swiftly over the tangled heap until it became nothing more than a mountain of stone.

"Yes, and that's how we do it, people!" Jessie jumped around, doing a football player victory dance.

"Yeah," Fate agreed, though nervously. "So you're feeling okay? You're Dragon Eye's still working after being dunked in Kaliena's mystery juice?"

"Pfff, it's working fine. But I did breathe in about a gallon of rust back there. That can't be healthy."

Smiling with relief, Fate turned with Jessie to leave. Her smile froze on her face. Something was noticeably different with the shrine.

Kaliena was gone.

40
A MASTERFUL ILLUSION

FINN YANKED THE GOGGLES over his eyes and called out to Sithias but his voice was lost in the howling wind. Sheets of sand lashed against him, stinging his skin. Pulling his robe tightly around his body, he closed his eyes and turned his awareness inward to calm himself.

It was time to fight fire with fire. In this case, wind with wind.

Finn invoked Air in the Elder race language, engaging the energies of the runes embedded in his skin. The internal fire he needed to fuel his voice ignited. Heat erupted from deep inside, shooting through his chest and out his throat. Power flowed through him as he roared his command over Air.

The wind answered his call, so strong it knocked him off his feet. The furious hurricane rushed over him, crashing against the storm. Finn rolled onto his front, curling in on himself to protect his face as the opposing winds thrashed and fought to beat back the other.

Suddenly, all was calm, save for the sounds of the angry winds and swirling sands. He lifted his head and looked around. He was in the eye of the storm, enclosed by a circular wall of roiling sand that climbed to the heavens without end.

Finn stood, on guard and unsure of what was happening. The wind he'd summoned should've dissipated the storm. Had the winds merged? Had he created some sort of super storm?

The ground heaved beneath his feet. Finn took to the air and hovered above the bulging sand. His muscles coiled tight as he watched and waited.

The swelling earth exploded below him, blasting sand into

the air as an enormous monster formed of gnarled roots snaked from the depths.

Terror washed over Finn, flooding his heart until it slammed against his ribcage.

Mugloth had returned.

He shot straight up, higher and higher, his mind reeling with disbelief. How could this be? He'd killed Mugloth. This couldn't be happening.

Yet it was. A monstrous arm lashed out, snatching Finn from the sky, dragging him down, down, until he was face to face with the darkness he'd fought so hard to break free of.

A voice wormed its way into his mind, calling him by his Druidic name. *"Emrys, did you really think you could destroy me?"*

Mugloth's sinister voice shocked Finn to his very core. Fear paralyzed him.

"*When you merged with the oak, our souls united. I'm part of you now.*"

"No," Finn moaned.

"*It's time to shed this mortal coil and join me in the deep, dark earth. You will live in me, as immortal as the Earth, Sea, Sun and Air. We will be their champions. We will spread our roots throughout the world and devour all undeserving, weak mortals.*"

Finn struggled within Mugloth's grip. The roots coiled tight around him, squeezing until he could barely breathe.

"*Why fight the inevitable? You were born for this. It's in your nature to punish those with evil in their hearts.*"

Finn's thoughts went straight to the Lhiannan Shee and his resentment for the weakness she'd so easily unearthed within him.

"*There. You see it too.*"

Darkness swelled inside Finn. He'd forgotten the thrill of this wild, dark power merging with the energy of the Elder races runes inked in his skin.

"Yes, surrender to the power. Embrace your true nature. Forget about the girl. She should have died that day. The fact that she lives has made you small and weak."

The memory of Fate lying within the black sludge of the great oak's hollowed trunk flashed back, brilliant and painfully vivid. Mugloth had dragged her down into the earth, where he'd tortured and drained her of blood. Finn died inside all over again, unable to erase from his mind the crooked angles of her legs, the cruel puncture wounds and the deathly pallor of her face.

Allowing his hatred to overtake him, Finn stepped fully into the role of the punisher Mugloth wanted for him. The dark power inside hissed and sparked past his lips as he invoked the element of Earth. Rune energy crackled and surged inside his chest as the spell-rich words streamed from his mouth in waves of heat.

Pain fired through Finn's legs and torso as Mugloth coiled his grip tighter, cutting off his air. But the words had already been spoken. Finn waited, glaring at the twisted, tangled behemoth looming over him.

Mugloth's grip loosened as Earth locked onto him, hardening around the monster whose roots moved easily through sand, rock and shale. It was all Finn needed to twist free and fly out of reach.

Sucking in a deep breath, he called upon Air. The rune power burst free and poured from his mouth in a hot stream of red-gold sparks. His voice altered, booming with the deafening roar of the giants whose power he borrowed through the rune magic he was endowed with.

Finn rose even higher, climbing above the storm, where he could see the winds turning on Mugloth. Sand hammered the root monster from every direction, blasting chunks of wood from his tangled form. Mugloth's furious bellow joined with the sounds of the raging winds as he thrashed to free himself from the ground holding him captive.

Finn spoke to Earth once more and the desert rushed to answer his command. Massive dunes from all sides rolled in like gigantic waves to bury the abomination that was Mugloth under tons of sand.

Finn invoked Water, which responded from deep underground. Frothing spumes of milky water shot through the enormous mound, carrying the clay and rock needed to form the tomb that would hold Mugloth for an eternity.

As this took place, the winds died and the sky cleared of dust. The last of the setting sun shed its light and heat on the wet mound to dry the surface. Finn thanked the elements and slowly descended. As his feet touched down on the dunes, he held firmly to the dark, wild power Mugloth had reawakened in him.

He'd been consumed with unbearable guilt for the pleasure he'd taken in destroying those who'd harmed others. He was a Druid, sworn to protect life above all else. But he'd been changed. Turning his back on what he'd become, had weakened him. It was time he accepted his dark side. When faced with evil, he needed this part of himself to do what the Druid could not.

Finn turned when he heard a snuffling sound behind him. One of the camels walked toward him, carrying a limp form draped over the saddle.

Sithias lifted his head when the camel stopped in front of Finn. "Thank the gods, you survived. What a fright that storm was!"

The camel kneeled down and Sithias rolled off, falling like a lump in the sand. He rose to his feet, swaying like a drunk. "You won't believe what happened to me out there. After I caught up with my notebook, my pencil revolted against me. The wood split apart into hundreds of tiny stick men. They attacked and stabbed me with lead spears! They even tore my notebook apart and used it to give me paper cuts. Painful things, those. Can you imagine?"

"Not really," Finn said as Sithias stopped to draw breath after his lengthy description.

"I thought surely I wouldn't survive," Sithias continued. "But I was saved." He smiled at the camel. "She came for me. She honed in on my screams and fought her way through the stinging sand to find me. When she saw that terrible army and what they were doing to me, she trampled them. If not for her, I'd have bled to death from a thousand tiny cuts." He leaned over and patted the top of her head.

The camel nuzzled her nose under his hand and bleated.

"That's my Sasha," he crooned.

"You named her?"

"Oh yesss. Tell me she doesn't look like a Sasha." He tickled his fingers under the camel's bottom lip. "You like the name, don't you?"

The camel blinked and chewed its cud.

Finn wrinkled his nose in distaste. "I'm more interested in your nightmare sequence. I happened to have one of my own. Mugloth made a guest appearance in mine."

Sithias stood straight, his back rigid. "Mugloth is back?"

"As big as life, but now I'm not so sure. After your rather illogical experience, I'm thinking we've been the victims of a masterful illusion."

Sithias glanced over one shoulder and then the other. "Do you think this is the work of the *jann*?"

"Let's see…that sandstorm could be considered a whirlwind of major proportions, plus two simultaneous illusions, and a heroic camel rescue adds up to signs of the *jann* in my book."

"Are you saying Sasha isn't Sasha?" Sithias looked at the camel with a mixture of disappointment and distrust. "Sasha?"

The camel cocked its head and stared at Sithias blankly.

He sighed with relief. "Well, you're wrong there. See? She's just a–"

The air around the camel wavered like heat waves coming off the desert as the animal's form shrank and stretched upward to that of a robed figure. A young man close to Finn's age stared back at them with sky-blue eyes. His smooth skin was the color of mahogany, a dark contrast against his white robes.

"A man." Sithias finished his sentence with a horrified gasp and a look of pure humiliation.

"I am Aradif. I come to you because you passed the test."

"What test?" Sithias asked. "The directions for the summoning spell said nothing about a test."

"There was no need for any such spell," Aradif replied. "We were aware of you the moment you entered our desert. The storm we hurled at you brought forth the demons you harbor deep in your soul. Most others we have tested were defeated by the challenges their demons brought upon them, and perished because of this. You conquered your fears, which proves you worthy of our help. I am honored to be of service."

Sithias leaned close to Finn's ear. "I didn't conquer the stick men. Should I say something?" he whispered.

Finn was about to answer, when Aradif spoke. "This is my desert. There is nothing you can hide from me. The camel was your demon, Sithias."

"Oh dear, he knows I'm not Asclepius!" Sithias whispered again.

"By allowing the camel to save you and then opening your heart in gratitude to the beast you once loathed, you won our respect. As for this disguise, it is of no use to you here. We see through all illusions," Aradif explained.

His piercing blue gaze shifted to Finn. "It is good you conquered both of your demons."

Finn frowned with confusion. "Beg to differ with you on

that. There was only the one."

Aradif waved his finger at Finn in a scolding manner. "You tainted the sanctity of our desert by bringing that Fae abomination here. Your very life hung in the balance because of this. Had you not banished the creature and severed ties, your bones would now belong to the desert."

Finn gulped. He felt like a fool for underestimating this race of mysterious beings.

Aradif's expression softened. "I am pleased you escaped her clutches. Few ever do. It would have been a great loss for a champion of your caliber to fall prey to such a monster."

Shame flushed along Finn's neck and spread into his face. "You're being too generous. I'm no champion."

"Modesty is of no use here," Aradif corrected him. "You are the destroyer of destroyers, and the world is in great need of you."

He turned and waved a hand off to one side. The air shimmered as a tent of rich colors and luxurious fabrics appeared before them. "Come, let us share drink and food together while we speak of important matters."

They settled inside, where a banquet of fruit, breads and steaming rice dishes was spread over cloth gleaming with threads of gold. Veiled women with flashing dark eyes served them wine, while two sentinels equipped with long, curved scabbards flanked the entrance.

Aradif leaned back on a pile of silken pillows with a bowl of dates in front of him. "Our people are sensitive to all that is unseen within this world and beyond," he said. "Of late, we have sensed a disturbance rippling across the ocean of stars. This particular energy is one we have not felt in thousands of years. We fear the ancient seed of a great god has awoken. We sense anger and an unquenchable thirst for power radiating from her."

"From her?" Finn asked.

"Yes, she is the mother of the great goddess Kali. Her name is Kaliena, a high priestess who sacrificed herself to save her people by allowing a chaos entity to possess her. This merging created Kali, a divine force, which spread itself throughout the universe, creating and destroying worlds. After the goddess energy abandoned Kaliena, she returned to her mortal form. It was thought she died, but it appears she had been sleeping. Until now."

Finn reached for a grape. "She doesn't sound like a huge threat. Not if she's mortal."

"Yet we sense imminent danger emanating from her," Aradif insisted.

Finn stared at the grape, rolling it between his finger and thumb. "What does any of this have to with us?"

Aradif set the dates aside, sat up and leaned toward Finn. "The Oracle has Seen you fighting Kaliena here in the Marajaran Desert."

Finn tensed. Did Aradif mean to keep him here to defend his land? "Listen, I'm grateful for the hospitality, and as much as I'd like to help, I've got somewhere else I have to be."

"It is already prophesied. There will be a great war and you will face Kaliena to the death, here in this desert," Aradif pressed.

Dropping the grape, Finn pressed his fists into the softness of the sand beneath the carpet he sat on. "I can't stay. I won't." He found it impossible to keep the anger out of his voice.

Sithias shot him an anxious look. "Ah, what he means to say is–"

"I'm not asking you to stay," Aradif cut in. "Either of you. Your paths lead elsewhere, and so they must, lest we interfere with destiny. But I can assure you, we will meet again and under less agreeable circumstances."

"If that's true, then you'll respect our need to leave and lead us to the fiery divide so I can continue my journey." Finn stood.

He'd had enough of sitting around and waiting for the right moment to approach the subject.

Aradif rose to his feet as well. "Yes, of course."

He waved his arm again. A soft shimmer spread across the luxurious tent, the servants, food and flickering lanterns before fading away entirely. Night fell around them in a blanket of glittering stars. The half moon cast a milky glow over the dunes.

Finn felt a sudden intense heat at his back and he turned. A wall of fire, stretching endlessly in each direction, hissed with powerful magic. He knew without needing to test the flames that they were sentient, that they would reach out and turn him to ash if he stepped too close.

"I will take my leave before you summon the Feadh-Ree Triad to open the gate. Do not let them tarry," Aradif warned. "We will not tolerate their presence any longer than is necessary." A wind rushed in around him, whipping his robes into a white blur. He bowed and vanished within a whirlwind, before skimming out of sight across the sand.

Sithias wiped his brow. "Whew! Can you believe we made it out alive?"

"You needn't have worried. I'd never allow it to happen any other way." Finn stared at the only thing left that was standing between him and Fate. The fiery divide. Now that he'd come this far, he couldn't wait a second longer.

Closing his eyes, he recited the invocation he'd memorized from O'Deldar's grimoire. The spell-rich words sucked every bit of moisture from his mouth. His tongue grew thick, making speech difficult. Upon finishing the invocation, Finn opened his eyes. The same murky haze hovered in front of him and expanded into a circlet of gold with a blue-green center. As soon as he saw the disturbance of shapes gathering within the portal, he turned to Sithias. "Close your eyes and keep them shut. They'll be showing themselves in their true form. I have the

Elder race runes to protect me, but you have no defense against them."

Sithias clapped his hands over his eyes. "What happens if I can't keep myself from peeking? I do have a curious mind."

Finn watched the shadows grow dense. "Believe me, you don't want to know what'll happen, so keep yourself in check."

A cloven hoof broke through the portal's outer membrane. The rest of the creature's body emerged, bringing with it an icy chill that seeped in from the other world. The rough spiraled horns of a ram encircled a beastly face, which stirred fright on sight. Black, oily eyes devoid of humanity stared back at Finn. Creased lips curled into a snarl, displaying rows of needle-sharp fangs. Skin as gray as death clung like crepe to its sinewy torso. Thorns protruded from its alien skeletal structure, while shaggy, clumped hair covered its massive goat's legs. Finn had seen many whimsical illustrations of satyrs, but this was the scariest version by far.

The slitherer snaked in after the satyr. It was a horrifying creature to look at. Ill-formed wings jutted from the back of its tuberous body. Red eyes flamed from its black-scaled skull, the shape of a jaguar. The bottom jaw was a tangle of fangs that curled under its cheekbone and oozed drool. Finn could understand why the sight of such beasts might cause a person to go mad with terror.

Last, but not least, the Lhiannon Shee, stepped through the gateway. She fixed her dark gaze on Finn. Not a hint of emotion flickered over her hard, birdlike features. It was obvious to see the banishment spell had worked. Otherwise she'd be doing everything in her power to lure him back into her web.

"Open the gateway back to my homeland, to where I first entered this world," Finn commanded the Triad.

The satyr growled at him. "Admittance first requires the payment of unpaid debts."

Finn glanced at the Lhiannan Shee and gulped. "Really?" He edged close to Sithias. "Why's this coming up? I thought the banishment spell cleared everything back to zero."

Keeping his eyes clenched shut, Sithias shrugged. "I couldn't say." He yelped as the slitherer snaked against his leg. "What was that? Was that a snake? Get it away from me!"

"You of all people should be okay with snakes," Finn muttered. He turned his attention back to the satyr. "Has the form of payment changed?"

The satyr turned his horned head to the Lhiannon Shee. "Only your guide can answer that."

She closed the gap between them, her clawed feet digging into the sand with each step. "Close your eyes."

Every part of Finn resisted, but he closed his eyes all the same.

She leaned close to whisper in his ear, enclosing him within the dewy scent of the forest. "Think back to our time together." Her voice grew soft and silky. "I never abandoned you. I came to you in your greatest time of need. I was your constant companion, even when you couldn't see me. I watched over you. I guided you to this place, where we now stand. Look deep into your heart, Finn. Can you find even the smallest kernel of affection for me, and me alone?"

As much as Finn wanted to deny even the slightest hint of warmth in his heart for this insidious creature who had manipulated his every emotion, in truth, he could not. He was grateful to her for getting him this far. He honestly didn't know if he would've survived if she hadn't continued to keep his desire for a life with Fate front and center in his heart and mind.

"Yes," he whispered back, "I've grown fond of you. I'm thankful for all you've done for me."

"That's all I ever wanted from a soul as remarkable as you, Finn McKeen. You are the most human of beings I have ever encountered." Her breath feathered against his face. "Look at me."

Finn grew wary. Was she trying to entrap him again?

"Open your eyes."

He looked at her. She hadn't changed. She was still the predatory creature of nature she'd always been, but now her pale skin glowed with an inner radiance. The harsh planes of her face appeared softened and the black of her eyes glinted like a starry night. His breath caught in his throat, for the wild beauty standing before him.

The Lhiannan Shee stepped back with a smile that held a secret. "The debt is paid," she said to the others.

The Triad moved into a circle, speaking in an ancient language far beyond Finn's understanding. The spitting, seething fire of the divide parted. The Lhiannan Shee gestured for them to pass through.

Finn's eyes misted with gratitude as he nodded to her. Taking Sithias by the arm, he guided him past the Triad and they walked through the gateway. The flames raged around them but the scorching heat did not burn.

As Finn left Oldwilde and all its nightmares behind, fresh cool air touched his face. Relief washed over him as the world he came from opened onto a sunny spring day, where a field of yellow tulips spread out before him. Fables Bookstore stood in the distance. He was finally back where he'd first met Fate.

41
FATE HAS A PLAN

EVERYONE WAS WAITING IN the sanctuary for Fate and Jessie when they returned from the shrine deep inside the Keep's core. Fate had radioed in an emergency meeting on the flight back. It was time to fill everyone in on the threat Kaliena posed, not only to them, but to the universe at large.

Fate stood at the head of the table, her spirits strengthened by her father and Gerdie standing on one side, and Jessie on the other. Farouk, Steve and Darcy were there, but the absence of Brune, Lincoln and Mason was painfully noticeable.

"I have something you all need to see." Fate announced.

Darcy held up a hand to stop her. "Uh, hold on. So no thank you for making it easy to kill the scavenger?"

Fate frowned. "I would hardly have called it easy. But okay. Thank you."

"You're welcome." The disappointment Fate noted on Darcy's face had her wondering if she'd expected a big bouquet of flowers for figuring out how to defeat the scavenger.

Fate exchanged a befuddled look with Jessie as she removed the projector ring from her finger. When Farouk noticed what she was doing he jumped off his seat and grabbed the bars of his cage. "What are your doing with that? Those docuscripts are for guardian eyes only."

"Not anymore. Everyone needs to know what's coming." Fate grew quiet a moment. "She's fully awake and walking around."

Farouk's grip on the bars went slack. He dropped his arms and fell back into his chair. "No, no, no."

"Who's she? Are you referring to Brune?" Eustace asked.

“No I just came from the infirmary,” Gerdie said. “Brune’s still unconscious…and all green and veiny.” She fell quiet, her brown eyes filling with what looked like regret.

“Don’t worry, Gerdie. If there’s one thing I know about Brune, it’s that she’s a survivor,” Fate assured her.

“I’m confident we’ll find a cure for the infection,” Eustace added. “Steve and I have been looking into it since her arrival. For now though, I’d appreciate knowing what’s so urgent.”

“The best way to fill you in is to show you.” Fate walked over to Farouk’s cage. She held out the ring. “I presume you’ve got some sort of way to play a telepathicgram projector for everyone in the room.”

Narrowing his gleaming fox eyes, Farouk snatched the projector ring from her. “You guesstimate correctly.” He plugged the ring into a slot on his control panel.

A shower of fine mist formed over the center of their meeting table as the image of the three-eyed seer, Vasha, flickered into view. Her dry voice filled the sanctuary and everyone stood perfectly still, their minds held hostage to the unfolding story of the Keep’s origins.

When Vasha’s narration brought them to the birth of the chaos god, Fate edged away from the table, though this did nothing to block the intensity of the images gripping her mind. Once again, she witnessed the entity’s churning mass of darkness swarm over the Keep, breaking through the force field and merging with the High Priestess. She shivered as the dark power transformed the woman into the fierce, black-eyed Kaliena she’d come to fear.

The pounding of her heart increased when Wodrid invaded the scene. His trespass and the evolution of his warped relationship with the vicious woman, who was his jailor, made Fate nauseous. She feared Wodrid every bit as much as she feared Kaliena.

He too was closing in. Everything was converging. She could feel it.

As Vasha's voice faded with the last of her story, the words were nothing more than noise to Fate. She'd turned her attention to the others. The same terror she felt was written plainly on their faces.

Vasha's sad face flickered away as the misty screen evaporated. Silence descended upon the room, but only for a few precious seconds. Suddenly, everyone was talking at once, panic in their voices as the volume rose to shouts.

Jessie slammed her sword down onto the table with a loud crack. "Chill out, you guys, and listen up. Fate has a plan."

The others fell quiet, though stiff with tension and doomed expressions.

Fate looked at Jessie, speechless and petrified. What plan was she talking about? This was a meeting to figure out what to do next. "Uh…the way I see it, we're going to need a lot more help than what we've got here at this table."

Darcy snorted. "You think?"

Fate ignored her. "We need to find someone whose power is equal to Kaliena's and–"

Darcy laughed. The nervous laugh of someone about to lose it. "Good luck with that."

Jessie shook her sword at her. "Stop it, you're not helping."

"Oh really? And how do you propose to help? By getting yourself maimed or killed like Mason and Lincoln?" Darcy was shaking, her eyes wild with terror.

Eustace moved in next to Darcy. "I know you're afraid, but we have to remain calm and keep our–"

Darcy burst into tears, pounding her fists against his chest. Eustace took the beating until she collapsed against him. Placing his arms around her, he gave Fate an awkward nod to continue.

"As I was saying…" Feeling guilty, Fate trailed off. She was beginning to see why Brune had appeared so callous. As much as she hated it, the task had fallen to her to put the suffering of others aside in an effort to maintain some semblance of order. "We need help, and I know where to find it."

Farouk worriedly stroked the end of his tail. "This is the first I'm hearing of this. Why have you not conversilized with me about this before?"

"I'm doing it now."

Distrust glinted in Farouk's eyes. "Who is this omnivasive being you think will save us?"

"He's a druid who's been marked with the Elder race runes."

Farouk's eyes widened. "The runes of giants were gifted to a human?"

"Yes. I've seen him summon the ocean to drive a monster into the ground and drown it. He invoked a storm to contain a war goddess of wind and lightning, and embedded her into rock with a tornado. He called on fire to kill a sorceress and–"

Farouk dropped his tail and shook his hands to stop her. "I know how the Elder race runes work. How do you hypotheculate his powers over the elements will work here in space? The Keep is not a planet, it's a machine."

"There's air," Fate pointed out. "And some of the vaults are made of earth, trees and plants. Even water."

"That may be, but in relation to what a planet can furnishforth, there are few elements to work with here," Farouk argued.

Panic beat in Fate's chest. Why was he being so obstinate? Was he going to stop her from leaving? No, she refused to let anything get in the way of returning to Finn and freeing him. She'd fulfilled her duties as Keep Guardian and she'd chosen her proxy. Jessie was an excellent replacement. Besides, she had every intention of bringing Finn back to help. She'd never leave her loved ones to fend for themselves.

"What's this druid's name? How do we know we can trust

him?" Steve seemed every bit as intent as Farouk to meddle with her plans.

Fate looked at him with sudden anger. "Does it matter?"

Steve's dark brows formed a scowl. "As a matter of fact, it does. Not all druids are pure with The Order. Some lean toward the dark side."

"Who made you the druid expert?"

Steve squeezed his walking cane, twisting the glossy black wood until it squeaked against his leather gloves. Fate wondered why he was still wearing his meticulous warlock costume when everyone else had cast their costumes aside. Did he not have an identity of his own?

"I'm more of an expert on druids than you are." Steve's tone seemed carefully controlled. "While you've been out there, I've been in the library soaking in as much knowledge as I can. To be helpful, of course."

"Good on you," Fate conceded. "But you're going to have to trust me on this. I know this druid personally. We've been through a lot together and he laid down his life for me. More than once." She swallowed the hard lump forming in her throat and forced back the tears burning behind her eyes. "I trust him completely."

"I'm aware of the situation. Fate filled me in earlier," Eustace added, much to Farouk's obvious surprise and annoyance. "If my daughter trusts this man, who has proven himself time and again, then I trust her judgment, one hundred percent."

Fate swelled with renewed strength. She wanted to give her dad a huge hug, but Darcy was in the way. She looked at Steve. "I get where you're coming from, but you can put the books away on this one. You won't find this druid in any of them."

Steve opened his mouth to continue the argument, but Farouk cut in. "I cannot allow you to leave your post. You've sworn an oath to protect the Keep."

"Unless I appoint a proxy."

Farouk's ears stood straight. "You know about that?"

"Mhmm. It took a lot of digging through the archives, but Gerdie found it."

Gerdie lifted her chin and stood on her tiptoes in attempt to gain a few inches. "Yup, and it was almost like someone tried to bury the only copy of the original Guardian Handbook by filing it under Arcane Magic. Strangely enough, the stuff about appointing a proxy is gone from the…What was it, the 493rd edition of the handbook you gave Fate?"

Farouk stood still, his furry face stuck in a disgruntled expression. "Who did you appointinate? Brune is destructalized for the moment, so it isn't her."

Fate slung her arm over Jessie's shoulder. "Meet your new Keep Guardian in waiting."

"B-but, she's not from the Inkwell line." Farouk's mouth hung open.

Gerdie leaned on the table and kicked her feet behind her as she stared at Farouk. "She doesn't have to be. Another lie you handed down through the years."

Farouk stuck his tiny fists on his hips and frowned. "Excuse me? I was never the handbook's author. That credit goes to Elspeth Inkwell, the first Keep Guardian. She wrote the rules and stipulangments for her descendages. Every guardian since then has added her successes and failures to help guide and alertisize her successors. If something was elimified, it was by one of them along the way."

"Probably Brune," Gerdie muttered.

"Wouldn't put it past her," Fate agreed.

Farouk was quiet. His blank expression said it all. He didn't have one solid reason to keep Fate from leaving. She'd covered all her bases.

Fate grabbed her aeronaut pack and hoisted it over her

shoulders. "Now that everything's settled, I'll be off. The sooner I leave, the sooner I can get back."

Farouk tucked his nose against his shoulder and didn't look at her. His reaction surprised her. The sudden pang of guilt she felt surprised her even more. "Jessie's already taken the proxy oath, so you'll need to initiate her while I'm away." She watched him, hoping he'd stop avoiding her gaze. "She'll do a good job."

Jessie saluted Farouk. "You bet. I won't let you down."

Staring at the floor, Farouk gave them the slightest nod.

Feeling like a heel, Fate turned to tighten the straps of her aeronaut pack, telling herself she was doing the right thing. Her motives might feel selfish, but in the end, they would benefit everyone.

Eustace stepped in beside her and held out a folded piece of paper. "You'll be needing this. It's an invocation for summoning the Green Man. This will put the nature spirit under your command without any backlash. The invocation's safe and ironclad. I double-checked. Oh, and I researched the portal. It's a circle of standing stones. That's how the druids traveled between sacred places. You may have to go from one to another, but you'll eventually arrive within the circle of stones surrounding the giant oak."

Fate stood on tiptoe and gave him a hug. "Thanks, Dad."

Eustace lingered a moment, holding her tight before letting go, his eyes misty. "Anything for my Doodles."

Fate gulped back a surge of tears. She hated seeing so much worry in her father's eyes. Worse yet, she hated being the cause for that worry.

Gerdie marched over to Fate. "Don't stop until you get Finn out. Bring him back. We need him. We need you both."

"I will," Fate promised.

"And don't go getting distracted with a bunch of kissing and–"

"Jess!" Fate cut in, her face growing warm as she glanced

at Eustace.

He cleared his throat, grabbing at his tie as if he'd eaten something horrible. "Well, yes, that would be much appreciated."

Fate shot Jessie a heated look.

"Gerdie said it best." Jessie winked back at her. "Get yourselves back here before everything goes sideways."

"Roger that." Fate walked over to the breaching door and hit the button. As the door spiraled open, she started the motor of her aeronaut pack. The whir of the wings stirred the air as she turned to look at them one last time. If she stayed a second longer, she feared she'd never go. It hurt to leave them.

Fate forced a cavalier smile. "See you in a jiff." Waving goodbye, she jumped into space and flew in the direction her heart most yearned to go.

To Finn.

42
WHERE ARE YOU?

FINN BURST THROUGH THE front entrance of the bookstore and stopped just within the double doors. Much had changed since he'd last been there. Gone were the thick layers of dust and darkness. Lights illuminated the rustic interior, bathing the reading corners and bookshelves lining the brick walls with inviting warmth. The building emanated an underlying tone of strong magic that hadn't been present before.

He stepped over to the nearest bookcase, grabbed a book and cracked it open. The pages didn't crumble. The book was whole and intact. The last time he'd been there all the books had been moldering. He remembered burning some of them in a metal waste bin to keep warm.

"Fate?" His heart pounded in his ears as he waited for a response. Panic crept in. How much time had passed? Was he too late? Surely she was there. The place looked open for business. She'd said her grandmother had left it to her. "Hello?"

He walked through the center of the bookstore, heading toward the staircase, where the *Book of Fables* had rested against the wall. It was gone. Fate had told him the giant book was the bookstore's sign. Finn turned and ran back through the front doors, bumping into Sithias just as he was entering the building.

"Did you find her?" Sithias asked.

Finn brushed past him, checking the outside of the building again. He hadn't paid attention to the exterior on his way in. Sure enough, the carved, wooden book with its gold-leaf letters and tarnished lock was anchored to the brick on the topmost part of the wall. It even looked like someone had touched up the flourishes and letters spelling, *Bookstore*, with new paint. Confusion set in. What was going on?

"Is she in there?" Sithias pressed.

Finn ran back inside, this time calling for Fate as he ran up the stairs, banging the doors open to one empty room after the other. He leapt down the staircase, stormed over to the storage room in the back, didn't bother looking in the closet marked, *Janitor*, and pushed through the back door to have a look outside.

Nothing.

Disappointment caved in, knocking the energy out of him. Finn leaned against the wall for support, grabbing at the sharp ache in his chest. "Where are you?" he said to Fate, his voice hoarse with sorrow.

He staggered back inside, his feet dragging as he navigated the cluttered room. He slammed his knee against a box. Swearing under his breath, he pushed past the green velvet curtains. Sithias was behind the counter of the curved cashier's desk when he came out of the storage room. He'd discarded the elderly age, robes and staff of Asclepius for a tall lanky man in his early thirties. Looking rather bookish, he was wearing round spectacles and wearing an argyle sweater vest over a starched white shirt with a bow tie.

"How can I help you?" Sithias grinned. "What genre might you be in the mood for?" He waved his long arm at a section of books. "We have the classics over here. Possibly something light, like *A Midsummer's Night Dream*?" He paused to look at Finn's grim expression. "Ew, I see that one touched a nerve. How about a mystery, we have the entire canon of *Sherlock Holmes* over here."

"Why don't you be him and figure out why Fate's not here, and where she's gone to?"

"Hmm, tempting, but I rather prefer this persona. I confess,

I've been going through a bit of an identity crisis of late, and the role of a librarian fits me perfectly." Sithias sighed as he glanced around at all the books. "Lock me up in here and throw away the key. As long as I'm surrounded by all these stories, I could live in thisss bookstore forever."

"Are you listening to anything I've said? Fate's not here," Finn growled.

Sithias looked at him. "I heard you, sir. But you mustn't lose hope now. She's obviously been here."

"How can you tell?"

"Well, for starters, the *Book of Fables* is here. I was there when she left with it. If the book's here, she's here. Maybe not specifically here in the bookstore, but at least we know she's not somewhere across the universe. I mean, that would be ridiculous, now wouldn't it?" Sithias smiled and rolled his eyes. "Why don't you poke around with that keen sixth-sense of yours to locate her?"

Finn's agitation eased. Sithias was making sense. He'd panicked and lost all reason. "I'll go outside and take a knee. While I'm poking around, you see if you can dig up any clues as to where she might've gone, like maybe her home address."

"Will do," Sithias called after him as Finn headed for the door.

Finn stopped when he reached the edge of the tulip field. He looked out over the strips of yellow flowers stretching in rows before him. The image of a little girl with a wild mop of auburn curls picking bouquets too big to carry flashed in his mind. Smiling at the thought, he kneeled and placed his palm on the grass. If there was any one place to connect with Fate, it was here, where her fondest memories were the most alive.

The link to Fate was instant. Heat streamed along his arm like wildfire and exploded in his chest. Stronger than anytime before, she swirled inside him, triggering every sense with the crackle of fire, the scent of cinnamon and briskness of crisp autumn air. She soaked into him, straight to the marrow of his bones, touching his soul with her very essence. Her love and longing matched his own.

"You're here," he whispered, his eyes closed as he watched the dancing sparks of her spirit with his inner vision. "But where exactly?"

He probed further, skimming across highways, farms and cities, questing for the bright beacon of her presence within the house she lived in. Doing his best to push his frustration aside, he searched beyond the immediate area, crossing mountain ranges, oceans, deserts and forests.

He closed his hand over the grass, pulling at the roots and biting down until his jaw hurt. "Where are you?"

Unwilling to give up, Finn searched every corner of the world, but with each passing moment, his spirits dampened. What was going on? Fate was obviously in this dimension or he wouldn't be able to feel her. So where was she?

Was it possible she was somewhere other than Earth?

Finn pushed his senses beyond the planet, past the sun, the solar system and then the Milky Way, questing for the brilliant light of her spirit's red-gold flame. The stars became a blur of streaking light as he shot across the universe.

He felt her before he saw the massive structure with its revolving hoops. He sensed her desperate need for him. The magnitude of it mirrored his own. The strength of her emotions crushed him. He wanted to be there for her, to take away all the pain she was feeling, but they couldn't be further apart than at that very moment.

He also felt her determination to return to him. She was on a mission. But how would she know he'd returned? He wasn't in Oldwilde and trapped inside the oak anymore. He called out with every part of his being. *Wait for me, Fate. Stay where you are.*

I'll find you.

She suddenly radiated a mixture of fear and hopeful anticipation, as if she'd just parachuted from a plane. And then she was gone. The connection severed, like a door slamming in his face.

Finn's eyes flashed open. He yelled at the world, a growl of garbled pain he barely recognized. He tore clumps of grass from the ground, chucking them as far as he could. He knew without a doubt that she'd found another gateway into Oldwilde other than the *Book of Fables*. She'd accomplished what she'd set out to do.

Finn jumped to his feet and stormed back inside the bookstore.

Sithias waved a sheet of paper at him. "I found her address. This is a record of all the books Fate's grandmother ever mailed her," he announced proudly. "Who needs Sherlock Holmes when you've got me?"

"Nice work, but keep your sleuthing hat on. Her address is useless now."

Sithias dropped the paper and slumped against the countertop. "Really?"

"Fate's long gone. I tracked her to someplace in a galaxy far, far away." Finn felt ridiculous repeating the famous line, but it fit in this case. He smiled–more of a grimace–knowing Fate would've loved hearing him talk like the fantasy geek she was.

"What could she possibly be doing that far away?"

"I suppose it's wherever Gerdie said she could find a gateway back to Oldwilde. Except we don't know where that is." Finn gripped the edge of the counter and leaned toward Sithias. "You've got to think back to what Gerdie told you about this place. What did she call it? Did she say how they'd get there? I'm assuming it wasn't in a spaceship."

Sithias shrank from Finn's intensity. "I swear, sir. I don't remember much."

"I saw it." Finn stared into space. "It's some sort of manmade planet. The thing is enormous and it's surrounded by gigantic turning rings."

"Oh! That sounds familiar. I remember Gerdie saying something about a big city closed in by a cage of turning hoops." Sithias gave him a sheepish grin. "I thought it sounded absurd at the time."

"Did she say what it was?"

Sithias tapped his chin. "I can't recall exactly. She did say it was a big family secret. They've been guarding it because it's some sort of storage place for magical objects and whatnot."

"That's good. What else?"

Sithias strained as he tried to remember. His face lit up as if something had come to mind, but then he shook his head. "No. Nothing. That's about it."

Finn barely resisted the urge to grab Sithias by his bow tie and shake him into remembering. "Did she happen to say how her family got to the big city of hoops?"

"Hmm…nope, I don't think so."

The squeeze of Finn's hands on the counter made the wood squeak.

Sithias glanced down at Finn's coiled muscles and gulped. "Come to think of it, she may've mentioned something about a door. Here in the bookstore, if I'm not mistaken."

Finn let go of the counter and paced. "No, that can't be. I checked every room when I got here. None of them led anywhere but here."

"Are you sure? Were there any armoires upstairs? Fate gave me a wonderful book about a magical portal through a wardrobe. Maybe the bookstore has one too."

"No, I didn't see any, but there was one door I didn't bother looking inside." He raced across the room, brushed past the green velvet curtains of the storage room and stopped in front of the janitor closet.

Sithias hurried in after him.

"Flip the switch," Finn told him. When the lights came on, he noticed the lock on the door. There was nothing extraordinary about it, other than its obvious age and the starburst screws keeping it fastened to the wood, but he sensed an aura of magic around it. "This is it."

"But we don't have the key to unlock it."

Running his fingers along the edge of the doorframe, Finn kneeled down until he saw the matchbook at the very bottom keeping the door from fully closing. Relief washed away the tension bunching muscles into tight bands. "We don't need it." Smiling, he stood and opened the door wide. He gestured for Sithias to enter. "After you."

Sithias peered nervously into the long dark corridor and the strange light glowing off in the distance. "I don't think so. Definitely after you, sssir."

43
BAD TIMING

A FORCE UNLIKE ANYTHING Finn had ever experienced grabbed hold, hurtling him through a circular tunnel of churning energy. Jagged ribbons of lightning struck from every side, searing his skin. The G-forces increased, pulling his body through unbelievable pain. He was being stretched across space and time, growing thinner and thinner. Fear streaked through every nerve. He wasn't made for this. He was a construct of magic and Fate's imagination. If anything existed that could reduce him to nothing but stardust, surely this was it.

The jump ended as fast as it began. Finn catapulted through the air and slammed into stone. He curled into a ball, skidding on his side across a flat surface until he hit the sharp edge of something big and solid. He took a second to feel his arms and legs. His skin wasn't burned and he was still in one piece.

And sore. Very sore.

He raised his head to look around, seeing an enormous table hovering just a foot off the floor beside him when something crashed into him and flattened him. Whatever it was, coiled inward, slithering across his legs and back. Finn brought his arm around, jamming the thing between the point of his elbow and the table.

"Oomph, watch the wingsss!" Sithias hissed.

Finn scrambled back, eyeing the disturbingly large ivory snake with distaste. "What's with the snake outfit? You know I how I feel about that," he growled.

Sithias flapped his feathered wings and proceeded to coil

into an upright position. "I'm sssorry, sir. Whatever ability I had to shapeshift, appears to have been left behind on Earth. I'm back to being me." He swayed in place, turning his head this way and that as he took in the domed ceiling and circular walls lined with tall bookcases. "My, what wonderful sort of place is thisss?"

Finn stood, more interested in the shimmering light, which moved and made the bronze walls translucent. He walked over, staring in awe at the massive structure just outside the room and the enormous gears moving in slow rotation. The sweep of gigantic revolving hoops confirmed this was the same manmade planet he'd seen in his vision when he'd searched for Fate.

His pulse raced. He was in the right place, but was it the right time? He reached out with his senses, feeling for Fate's presence. His chest burned with disappointment. Fate was no longer there. He shoved the heartache aside. He wouldn't give up. Not when he was closer than ever to finding her. Nothing would stop him now.

"Don't move, hold it right there. Hands behind your head," a girl's voice said from behind him.

Finn moved to turn around.

"Down on your knees!" she yelled.

Finn charged the girl. Closing the gap faster than she could take the shot, Finn lunged and took her down. They tumbled to the floor, rolling over each other, each fighting to gain leverage. Her strength almost matched his and she was in full on armor, which made her harder to hurt. Finn twisted out from under her, grabbed her wrist and wrenched. Grunting with pain, she paused for one second too long. Finn slammed her to the floor and stood straight.

He checked to see what was happening with Sithias, when her boot shot into view and met with the side of his head. His skull filled with a bone-crunching sound. Sparks flashed across his vision, followed by a swarm of black.

Laughter roused Finn from a dreamless sleep. Struggling to wake, he touched the grating ache in his temple and winced. His brain was fogged, and when he tried opening his eyes, everything was blurry.

Carefully, he raised himself on one elbow and rubbed his eyes. The world tipped and spun around him, finally settling on the girl soldier he'd fought with. She had her back to him and had Sithias cornered.

"So, there I was, Dr. Benjamin Weathersby, to the rescue. Did I have to look into a few too many unsightly orifices to get the job done? Well, yesss, but I was willing to take half a dozen for the team."

When she laughed, Finn realized her stance was relaxed and her gun was holstered.

Thoroughly confused and wondering if he was hallucinating after being thumped on the head, Finn rose to his feet.

Sithias leaned around the girl and grinned. "Oh look who's awake."

The girl soldier turned to look at him. The dark-haired girl looked to be Fate's age. She was a fine-boned Asian beauty, and judging from her size, Finn couldn't see how she'd bested him the way she had. Normally, his extraordinary strength gave him an advantage over most others. But then on closer inspection, he noticed her armor had some sort of mechanical enhancements. No wonder she'd been so strong.

Sithias slithered over to him. "Finn, meet Jessie."

She nodded and smiled.

"Jessie here is Fate's bessst friend since kindergarten."

Jessie's wide hazel eyes roved over Finn's face. "Wow, you look exactly like she described you in all her stories."

Finn did his best to keep his expression neutral, but it was a struggle. He hated having the painful reminder of his origins open for discussion.

Her expression of awe turned to embarrassment. "Sorry, for staring…and for booting you in the melon. Fate's going to have my head for putting a bruise on that gorgeous face of yours, but I didn't know what to think when I found you here in the sanctuary."

Finn tried to smile but fell short. "I won't tell if you don't." He glanced around. "Where is she?"

"Gone to find you."

Finn looked at Sithias. "More bad timing. Has that become my specialty?"

"I think so, sir."

Finn turned back to Jessie. "Tell me where she went. I'll bring her back."

"No way, Jose." Her tone suddenly filled with surprising authority. "You're staying, even if I have to put you in lockup."

Finn tensed. "Listen, lass, you're off your nut if you think I'm going to sit around while Fate's out there looking for me."

"Always the hero." She wore a warning in her smile. "That's how Fate wrote you."

"Sir, I have to agree it's best you stay," Sithias cut in before Finn completely lost his temper. "The last thing Fate needs is you going off in what could possibly be the wrong direction."

"Listen to the snake, Finn. You've got no idea what Fate's gone through to be able to actually leave here and go after you. We've had one catastrophe after the other to deal with."

They were making sense, especially Sithias, but that didn't stop Finn from wanting to take action. He had to do something. "Just tell me where she went."

"She used the Druidic standing stones to access Oldwilde," a man's voice interjected.

Finn turned to see a distinguished, well-dressed man entering the room. A girl with jet-black hair, cut severely around her heavily made-up face, and a guy wearing a top hat with the same amount of eye-makeup strode in after him. If that wasn't enough, a small fox-faced creature in a bizarre moving cage clambered in behind them.

The older man strode over with his hand extended. "You must be Finn. I'm Fate's father, Eustace."

Finn recognized the family connection immediately. Fate had the same shaped eyes as her father, though hers were brown where his were gray. He shook the man's hand and gulped. "Good to meet you, sir."

Eustace held the shake a second longer as he studied Finn. The smallest hint of a shadow crossed his face before he let go. "This is incredible. Fate never expected you to come to her." Concern hardened his features as he shook his head. "I can't believe you missed her by a few hours."

Frustration and rage flared in Finn's chest. He wanted to destroy something. "Me either." He smiled but it felt stiff.

"Well, we have much to discuss concerning the matter of my daughter."

"Aye, I look forward to it, sir."

"I'll leave you two to get acquainted while I fetch Fate." Jessie hoisted some sort of pack with wiry wings the shape of dragonflies onto her back.

"How about I go with you?" Finn offered. "I can help."

Jessie buckled the straps and cinched them tight. "Sorry, only Keep Guardians can jump through the vault portals. Besides, there's plenty to keep you busy here." Giving him a wink, she walked over to the round hatch and slammed the button to open it.

"Be careful," Eustace said. "And hurry."

Jessie gave him the thumbs up. "Adios," she yelled, before

dropping backwards through the door.

Eustace shook his head. "If it's not Fate giving me concern, it's Jessie. I swear those girls will be the death of me someday."

"I know what you mean," Finn agreed.

They both smiled knowingly.

Sithias stuck his head between them. "Hi, Sithias at your service."

Eustace moved to shake his hand, then withdrew it upon realizing Sithias didn't have hands. "Nice to meet you." He gestured at the others. "This is Darcy, Steve and Farouk."

Sithias acknowledged them with a nod as he slithered over to Farouk. "And what would you be, little guy?"

Farouk's ears slanted back. "I could ask the same of you, big scaly thing."

Sithias weaved away from the cage. "Someone's testy. And rude," he muttered to Finn.

"What about Gerdie?" Finn asked. "She's here, isn't she?"

"Yes, of course." Eustace glanced at the others. "Come to think of it, I haven't seen her since Fate left a few hours ago. Has anyone else seen her?"

Darcy ran a black polished fingernail along the edge of her cropped bangs. "Nope. I think Steve was the last to see her."

Steve frowned at her. "What makes you think that?"

"I saw you talking in the residence quarters before we all went back to the library."

"Is she feeling ill?" Eustace asked. "Perhaps I should look in on her."

"No need, she was fine." Steve's jaw clenched and then eased when he caught Finn eyeing him.

Eustace turned to leave. "Nonetheless, I'll check on her. Come with me, Finn. I'm sure Gerdie will be quite pleased to see you."

"What about me?" Sithias asked. "I know Gerdie too."

Eustace tilted his head, surveying the snake over his scholarly glasses. "Come along then."

"What is this place?" Finn asked as he followed Eustace through several long corridors.

"We call it the Keep, though it was originally named the Obiectis by its builders," Eustace explained. "It's a rather long story, of which I'm happy to tell you another time. Suffice to say, this is a storehouse for magical objects."

Sithias hurried to keep up. "Sounds fascinating! The sanctuary had some interesting books. Might I look at them later?"

"Certainly, though that's a mere stack compared to what's in the main library."

Sithias shivered with excitement. "Ooh, can we go there?"

Eustace smiled. "Ah, I see you're a man…erh…snake after my own heart." He cleared his throat. "Uh, yes, we'll drop by the library next."

They stopped in front of one of the many doors lining the corridor. Strange symbols marked a panel off to one side, most likely some sort of identifying mark to tell one door from the other. Eustace placed his palm over the center of the panel, where it glowed with gold light. He leaned in and spoke into what appeared to be an alien version of an intercom. "Gerdie? It's Eustace here. I have some guests with me, whom I know you'll be pleased to see."

They waited for the door to open.

Eustace frowned at the door with concern. "Hmm, I wonder if we just missed her. Possibly she's gone to the library. That's where she spends the majority of her time, after all."

Sithias held his head high. "I'm the one who taught Gerdie to read."

Eustace raised his eyebrows. "Well done. She's got quite the curious mind and has become our best researcher."

"Now there's a job I could take to." Sithias fluttered his wings.

"We're always open to more help." Eustace gave a sigh of confusion. "Sorry I dragged you all the way here. I thought surely Gerdie would be in her room. Though I'm surprised her chamber robot didn't answer."

"This place has robots?" Finn asked.

Eustace nodded. "Everywhere, and thousands of them. Basically, there's some sort of maintenance robot for every part of the Keep, even ones to tend to room cleaning. It's rather nice, really." He paused for a moment. "Well, she's not here, so I suppose we'll shove off to the library now."

Sithias was the first to make a move back down the corridor. "You don't have to ask me twice."

Finn didn't move. "Wait. Was this scorch mark always here?"

Eustace bent to examine the dark flare burned into the wood around the door handle. "No, I don't think so." He tried turning the handle. "It's locked."

"Do you want me to unlock it?" Finn asked.

Eustace frowned at the door with concern. "By all means, if you have some sort of trick to–"

Finn kicked the door in.

"–unlock it. With your foot."

The room was dark when they entered.

"Lights on." Eustace stopped in his tracks as the room brightened. "Oh dear god."

Finn tensed as he took in the ruin around him. A scorched table and chairs were tipped on their sides and spinning in circles a few inches off the floor. The bed had been cut open. The soft, white down from the pillows covered everything like a light layer of snow. The chamber robot had been ripped in half, one piece near the door and the other flung to the opposite wall. Burn marks darkened the walls, as if someone with a flamethrower had been playing a game of cat and mouse with Gerdie.

44
ALLOW ME TO INTRODUCE MYSELF

FINN'S THROAT CONSTRICTED AS he moved through the debris, searching for Gerdie's tiny form and dreading what he might find. "She's not here." He breathed a sigh of relief, but it was a momentary respite. Whoever did this, must've taken her.

"Who would do thisss?" Sithias said from the doorway. "And why?"

"I have my suspicions." Eustace turned on his heel and stormed from the room.

Finn matched his stride. "Was it Brune? She's not to be trusted, you know. She left Gerdie all alone with a child-eating monster and she had her own grandmother burned at the stake."

"It wasn't Brune." Eustace was still walking fast. "She returned from her last mission with an infection. She's currently very ill and unconscious."

Finn jogged alongside. "Take me to her. I want to see for myself. That mingy woman's a snake–no offense, Sithias–and she's not to be trusted."

"None taken." Sithias flapped to catch up. "Though after everything I've heard of Brune, I'd prefer you call her something else, please."

Eustace slowed down. "Brune's in no condition–"

"Do you know about the Rod and Orb of Aeternitis, and how obsessed Brune was with them?" Finn said. "She spelled Fate into getting the Rod for her. Please tell me Fate didn't give it to her."

"No, Fate kept the Rod. She still has it, though I'd have

liked to have seen it go under lock and key, rather than keeping it on her person." Eustace stopped in his tracks.

Sithias bumped into him. "Oopsss."

Eustace barely noticed. "Come to think of it, Gerdie's been carrying the Orb around–also against my better judgment. She took it from Brune when she was....well, rotting." His eyes widened with concern. "You're right, if anyone's in need of the Orb, it's Brune. We need to get to the infirmary." He increased his pace to a full trot.

Eustace and Finn burst through the doors and entered the sterile room. Half a dozen beds lined one side. Only the first one was filled, and it wasn't Brune lying there. It was some doped up guy Finn had never seen before. He looked like an anime character by the way his black hair stood in straight spikes.

Two silver and white robots with medical apparatus built into their chest plates emerged from behind a white screen at the far end of the room.

"Where's Brune?" Eusatace asked.

Anime guy raised his head and pointed his thumb at the screen. "Behind there. Couldn't stand to look at her anymore. It was seriously freaking me out." He blinked groggily at Finn and Sithias. "Who are these dudes? One of them's a snake." He flopped back down. "I must be dreaming."

"You're not dreaming, Mason," Eustace reassured him. "This is Finn, and yes, Sithias is a snake."

Mason waved at them.

"Is Brune awake?" Eustace asked.

"No, she's more out of it than I am. But I gotta warn you, she's not Brune anymore."

Eustace looked at the divider screen, moved toward it and pulled the panel back.

"Oh my!" Sithias recoiled from the sight. "What is that? It's hideousss!"

Finn stood rigid, every muscle taut as revulsion churned in his gut. What lay on the bed was an abomination. The pale, blue-tinged face was still human, but the scaled, flesh-colored neck was splayed like a cobra. The skin around the shoulders and chest was a web of hardened, purple veins. Where hair used to be, a thick nest of tiny black snakes writhed drowsily around her head.

"Dear, lord," Eustace said under his breath. "She's turning into a Gorgon."

"A Gorgon?" Sithia shuddered and retreated to the other side of the room. "Why would you keep one of those around? They're dangerousss!"

"I'll say." Instinct pushed Finn to destroy the thing on sight. He reached for his flute, more than ready to transform the harmless item into a wind sword. The best thing he could do was cut the monster down before it woke. "What the hell are you thinking, keeping something like this around?"

Eustace recoiled. "I assure you, this is a new development." He raced over to the intercom by the door. "Farouk, get to the infirmary immediately. We have an emergency."

Finn walked over to Sithias. "At least we know Brune doesn't have the Orb and she obviously didn't take Gerdie. Which begs the question…who did?"

Eustace joined them at the opposite end of the room. "Before Fate left, she informed us of a new and imminent threat. Apparently, the builders, in all their wisdom, so many thousands of years ago, left us with a rather deadly legacy. She showed us a rather distressing recording of a priestess who merged with a chaos entity. She was transformed into a goddess of sorts, but this deity abandoned the priestess to spread itself across the universe. She was left mortal and has been in some kind of stasis ever since. But she's awoken, and she's after the Orb and Rod of Aeternitis so she can restore herself to the goddess Kaliena."

Sithias gasped. "This is exactly what Aradif predicted."

Shocked by the echo of the Djinn prophecy in such short time and with so much distance between the Keep and the Marajaran Desert, Finn froze with dread.

"What's this about?" Eustace asked.

When Finn remained quiet, Sithias explained for him.

"This is more than a little disturbing," Eustace agreed after Sithias finished. "The danger Kaliena poses must be unimaginably powerful for someone that far away to sense her awakening."

"I refuse to be thrown about on the winds of someone else's destiny," Finn seethed. He scowled at Brune–the one person responsible for everything that had happened thus far. "I'm the master of my fate, the captain of my soul."

Eustace and Sithias turned to him.

"Don't mind him," Sithias whispered to Eustace. "He's been abused and made–"

"Someone else's drudge," Finn growled.

Eustace nodded. "Fate told me."

"Well, I'm done being anyone's puppet." He paced back and forth. "I want to know everything you have on Kaliena. If there has to be a showdown, it's going to be here in the Keep. Not at some undisclosed date and time in the Marajaran Desert."

The clanking of Farouk's cage echoed down the hall. The three of them stepped aside to allow the wide apparatus through the entrance into the infirmary.

Farouk stopped his cage at the halfway point when he saw Brune, obviously too disturbed to move any closer. "She's a Gorgon." He pressed one of the buttons on his control panel, turned his cage around and frowned at Eustace. "How did this happen? I thought you were working on a restructifying cure."

Eustace frowned. "We were...are. It takes time to look through all the volumes we have on Gorgons. But this isn't the only reason I called you here. Gerdie's missing. Her room's been torn apart and I fear she's in terrible danger."

Farouk held onto his tail as he glanced over his shoulder at Brune. "Gerdie had the Orb."

Eustace pressed his finger against his temple like someone staving off a headache. "Yes, I know. We thought it might've been Brune at first, but she's obviously out of the running. Which leads me to believe Kaliena is the one who attacked Gerdie."

"This is not good. Not good at all." Farouk turned to one of the robots. "No more mediphoric potions for that one. Administreat a stimutonic. Mason, your recoverence is over. It's time to soldier up again."

Mason pushed himself off the pillow with a grumpy expression. "Hold on, I need those pain meds. I'm still healing."

Farouk turned away, even as he spoke to Mason. "Your bones set with the first round of curifications. The healing is completified. Any pain you think you feel is a result of hyponeurosis."

The medical robot trundled over and shot Mason in the arm with an air injection syringe full of neon-orange liquid. The tonic appeared to hit his system instantly by the way his eyes widened and his back straightened.

"What's in that stuff? I'm jacked!" Mason jumped out of bed and stood in pajama bottoms covered with pink hearts. "Where's my uniform?"

Farouk typed into his control panel. "On the way."

Mason glanced over at Brune and made a face. "So what is it you want me to do?"

"Put Brune in beltstraints," Farouk instructed. "I want her under guard at all times. And wear your goggles. We don't know how completified the monstramorphosis is yet."

A butler robot walked in with Mason's uniform and armor.

Mason jumped on one foot then the other as he slipped his pants over his pajamas. "What do I do if she wakes?"

"Do whatever is obligessary to keep her from leaving this room," Farouk ordered.

Mason buckled the last piece of his armor over his uniform then walked over to Brune. He gingerly took one of her wrists and tightened a strap around it. "Are you saying I should shoot her if she gets out of these?"

"If it comes to that, then yes, expirate her." Farouk shifted gears, jerking his cage into motion and marched out of the infirmary.

"Where're you going?" Eustace called after him.

"Back to the sanctuary for a predicamergency meeting."

"Shouldn't I be there too?" Mason called after him with a hopeful look.

Farouk ignored him.

"What about the library?" Sithias asked with a little too much disappointment. "Don't we need to explore every nook and cranny of that wealth of knowledge to confirm Gerdie's not there?"

Farouk continued down the hall without looking back. "I messaged Steve and Darcy to investispect the library. They confirmated Gerdie is not there."

Troubled and deep in thought, Finn fell in step with Eustace. He hadn't expected to be swept away by a series of urgent events the moment he arrived. He'd had a very different picture in mind–one of Fate running into his arms and him burying his face in the sweet softness of her neck. Had he been delusional to think he could reunite with her and enjoy at least a few hours of bliss? Why was he always coming up against obstacles when it came to being with her? Were they cursed to be apart forever?

Steve and Darcy were waiting in the sanctuary when they arrived.

"What's happening?" the Goth girl asked. "Is Mason alright?"

"He's out of bed and guarding Brune," Eustace told her. "It would seem she's turning into a Gorgon."

Her black-rimmed, red mouth dropped open. "You left my injured boyfriend behind to be turned to stone by a Gorgon?"

Eustace stared at her stiffly. "Uh, Mason's fine. He's completely healed."

"Since when?"

"Since his first treatment."

Finn could see she knew the truth, but she was being overprotective. Aha. That explained the pink heart pajamas.

"Mason needs time to recover. You can't go putting him in danger all over again!" Darcy yelled.

Eustace sighed. "He's currently in no danger. Brune's still unconscious."

"That's just great," Darcy grumbled.

"Is that what the meeting's about?" Steve asked.

Eustace walked over to the table. "Only part. We believe Gerdie's been taken by Kaliena."

Steve tilted his head to one side. "That's a leap. What makes you think it was Kaliena?"

"As you know, Gerdie had the Orb of Aeternitis, and Kaliena needs it to restore herself," Eustace explained.

Finn watched Steve's carefully poised expression. Something about the guy grated on him. He was hiding something behind that mask of carefully applied makeup. Finn sensed duplicity in him. The cracks in his façade, like small fissures, leaked the energy of lies into the air. "Weren't you the last to see Gerdie?" Finn kept his tone carefully neutral.

Steve fixed his gaze on Finn with one eyebrow raised. "Hmm, I suppose I was."

"Gerdie's room was torn to pieces. Scorch marks everywhere. The only time I've ever seen that was when I was dealing with a sorcerer who liked throwing fireballs. It's kind of a thing with them." Finn eyed him. "Isn't that what you're dressed as?"

"A warlock actually." Steve's grip tightened on his cane.

Finn shrugged. "Warlock, sorcerer. It's all the same really."

"Would you just spill already? What's all this about?"

Finn moved closer. "Well, Steve, I just met you, but I'm willing to bet you aren't who you say you are."

Finn pushed his senses outward, probing deeper. The muscles around Steve's eyes twitched. The cracks of his shield widened as Finn touched the darkness and power lurking inside. The energies recoiled in an attempt to stay hidden.

"Who are you?" Finn said under his breath.

Steve broke away from Finn's stare and laughed, more of a derisive snort, as he glanced around at the others. "Is this dude for real? What's he getting on with?"

Eustace stepped forward. "I'm not sure. Finn, please explain yourself."

Finn eased his flute from the side-pocket in the leg of his pants, ready to turn it into a wind sword if need be. "He's been lying to you about who he is. He's a sorcerer."

Steve laughed silently, his body shaking with amusement and only the briefest hint of a smile. "And here I thought I was the one with the wild imagination."

Finn blew two piercing notes into the flute. A sharp blade of air flared from one end. Moving toward Steve, he whipped the wind sword back and forth. "Show yourself."

A contemptuous spark lit Steve's eyes, before he shifted into feigned fear and cowered behind the table. "Why are you doing this?"

"Who are you?" Finn yelled.

"Nobody!" Steve cried. "Why won't you believe me?"

"Finn!" Eustace shouted. "Stop this at once. Steve has done nothing to deserve this. He's one of us."

Easing his wind sword down to one side, Finn turned to

Eustace. "You have no idea what's real here. He can't be trusted, he's–"

Red flames slammed into Finn, throwing him across the room. He smashed against the metal wall and dropped to the floor. Waves of pain crashed through his body as he struggled to breathe. Dazed, Finn rolled over and lifted his head.

Steve rounded the table with a fireball hovering over his open palm. He removed his top hat and gave Finn the slightest bow. "Allow me to introduce myself."

He let the hat fall to the floor and unleashed the power he'd been holding back. An aura of energy simmered against the rim of his body as his black overcoat transformed into a crimson robe with gold-plated armor covering his shoulders. The ebony color of his hair drained away into snow-white strands. His ears tapered to delicate points and jutted through his long silvery locks. At the same time, his cane elongated into a silver staff with a red jewel encrusted into the tip. He used the staff to steady himself and Finn quickly saw why. Cinched to his thigh, was a false leg cast in silver from the knee down. "I am Wodrid."

Gasps rose from Sithias, Eustace and Darcy. Farouk grabbed the bars of his cage, his slanted fox eyes wide with shock.

Fighting the sudden dizziness that flooded his skull, Finn's mind reeled around the name. Clenching his fist over his wind sword, he gripped the wall and moved to stand.

Wodrid tilted his head to one side. "I'd stay down if I were you."

Finn ignored him, though everyone else in the room scrambled toward the door.

Wodrid hurled the fireball at him.

Finn invoked Air, deflecting the fire with a rush of wind back at the sorcerer with even more force. Wodrid absorbed the deadly energy but he buckled at the waist, visibly weakened by the blow.

Taking advantage of the opening, Finn rushed at him with his wind sword, intent on cutting Wodrid's other leg out from under him. But the sorcerer saw him coming. Using his staff, he drew energy from the air in red, glowing waves and aimed the tip at Finn.

Finn launched himself off to one side, fully expecting to fly. He belly-flopped onto the floor. Shocked and gasping for air, Finn rolled behind a cabinet, narrowly missing another blast from Wodrid's staff.

"That was graceful," Wodrid remarked with a snicker. "Fate did the same thing. It was all I could do to keep from rolling on the floor laughing. I suppose you both assumed you'd keep all your powers after you left the *Book of Fables* and its field of influence behind." He laughed again. "Sorry, but that's not how I designed the curse, or the Words of Making."

Finn fumed silently. He'd forgotten Wodrid was the one who had cursed the *Book of Fables* by forcing unwary readers into changing the endings of each fairy tale into its mirror opposite. He hadn't realized the Words of Making had also been Wodrid's creation.

"Well, you didn't have anything to do with the Elder race runes I got while I was in there," Finn informed him. "That's all I need to end you."

Wodrid moved to the breaching door, the fall of each step interrupted by the drag of his silver leg. "Yes, you do still have that rather significant trick up your sleeve," he admitted. "In truth, we're well matched, you and I." He hit the button to open the hatch. "We could literally be at this all day. Which is why I'll take my leave."

Finn leaned forward, peering past the cabinet to see what Wodrid was doing. The sorcerer jumped through the hatch, dropped out of sight, then rose slowly, his red robe billowing around him.

"Unlike you, I *can* fly," Wodrid gloated.

Finn rose to his feet, calculating whether he could close the gap fast enough to leap through the hatch, grab hold of the arrogant jerk, and put his blade to Wodrid's throat.

"I can see the wheels turning in that undersized brain of yours," Wodrid warned. "I wouldn't risk it. After all, you do want to see Fate again, don't you?"

Finn gripped his wind sword so tight he shook. "What about Gerdie? Where is she?"

Wodrid's smile was smug. "You'll get Gerdie back, as long as Fate brings me the Rod. Beyond that, I cannot guarantee anything." He turned to leave.

Finn's insides filled with rage. Losing all reason, he lunged at Wodrid and launched himself through the hatch.

45
DON'T MESS WITH ME

THE AIR PRESSED AROUND Fate, thick and still as she passed through yet another portal. The second she stepped across the threshold, the air unleashed, blowing salt air against her face. Birdsong and the sounds of distant waves shattered the noiseless vacuum of space she'd left behind. She gazed out over the ocean from where she stood within the standing stones set high on a hill. The wind rustled the leaves of the enormous oak towering over her.

After traveling through fourteen portals, she was finally back on the island of Innith Tine.

Her pulse raced as she turned to face the massive tree trunk. Slowly, she moved toward the indentation of mossy roots at the base of the oak and gulped down the painful lump in her throat. How many months had she spent nestled against the tree, waiting for Finn to be released from his prison? Even now, it felt as if it had been an eternity.

The pain of that dark time resurfaced as fresh as if it was happening now. If Gerdie hadn't convinced her to leave, she'd still be here, curled against the oak's roots, wasting away from heartsickness.

She touched the trunk, remembering how the bark had been black and seeping with blood when she'd first seen the bloodthirsty oak. Chills rippled down her spine. She was grateful to see the tree was normal and the island was as she'd left it–lush and filled with life. Finn's sacrifice had not been wasted. The oak and the island remained free of Mugloth's malignant infection.

Fate leaned against the tree. "Finn?" she whispered. "I'm

here. I came back for you, just as I promised."

She waited for the signs he used to give her to let her know he was inside the tree–the change in the air, the sudden hush of leaves, birds and insects. The light breeze against her lips that felt like the softest ghost of a kiss.

The minutes ticked by without any halt to the normal sounds of the forest. Her heart shriveled. Had she been gone too long? Had Finn's connection with his humanity been severed? He used to speak of the Earthmind and how he often lost himself in his connection with it. Had he become one with the nature and forgotten who he was?

Fate blinked back the tears brimming in her eyes. "It doesn't matter." She dug into her pocket, retrieved the invocation Eustace had given her and shook the paper at the tree. "I'm getting you out, Finn! I got you into this and I'm getting you out. I've got the secret weapon in my hand. The Green Man can't do anything to stop me. He has to let you go."

"Who are you yelling at?"

Fate jumped, so startled, she tripped over a root and fell on her front. She turned over to see Jessie standing over her. She clutched at her thudding heart. "Jess, what're you doing here?"

Jessie held her hand out and pulled Fate to her feet. She glanced around before giving Fate a weird look. "I don't see anyone else, so what's with the insane babbling to yourself all about?"

Fate frowned. "I'm talking to Finn. He's still trapped in the tree. I'm worried though. I can't feel him anymore."

"Feel him? As in imaginary arms and lips?"

"His presence." Fate's face grew hot with embarrassment. "When he was first trapped, I could feel him here. But I don't know what's happened. I think he might be part of the earth now." She paused for a second then looked at Jessie with tears coming to her eyes. "I think Mother Nature took him for herself."

Jessie raised her eyebrows. "I don't know about all this nature talk, but you're right on one thing. Finn's not in there anymore."

Hearing her worst fears confirmed hollowed Fate out. She gasped as if Jessie had punched her in the stomach. Her chest tightened. She couldn't breathe. Her legs buckled and she fell to her knees. All the strength she'd been saving suddenly vanished. She was empty.

"Hey, what's wrong?" Jessie asked as she kneeled down. She put her hand on Fate's shoulder. "This is good news."

"How can you say that?" Fate yelled.

"Because Finn just turned up at the Keep. That's why I came to get you."

Fate stared at her in amazed silence.

"Did you hear me?" Jessie said, using fake sign language. "Finn's at the Keep and he's waiting for you."

Fate grabbed Jessie by the arms to stop her ludicrous hand motions. "Are you serious? Don't mess with me. My heart can't take it."

Jessie looked insulted as she stood and brushed leaves off her knees. "Come on. Not about this."

Fate's heart was racing at the thought of seeing Finn. She'd gone from barely breathing to breathless with anticipation. She rose to her feet, swaying with elated dizziness.

Jessie reached out to steady her. "Oh, and your snake friend's there too. Gotta say, he's not nearly as adorable as you made him out to be. He's anaconda-sized-big and scary."

Overwhelmed with happiness, Fate smiled. "Sithias came too? Wow!" She looked at Jessie's scrunched up face. "Don't worry, you'll get past the snake thing and grow to love him as much as I do."

"If you say so."

Fate walked over to one of the standing stones to activate the portal, then stopped when she remembered the beacon Farouk had given her.

"What's that?" Jessie asked as Fate drew out a small gadget from her pocket.

"It's a beacon." Fate placed it deep under one of the oak's thick roots. "Farouk's going to use it to connect to Oldwilde and make a portal to it. A permanent one."

"Why? Planning on buying property here?"

"Funny." Fate surveyed the pristine island. "At first I wanted Farouk to make it for insurance purposes. You know, in case I failed to get Finn out and needed to return to the Keep to find another solution, I wanted to make sure I could easily get back here at any time in the future."

"But the problem's solved. Why would you ever want to come back to this place again? From everything you've said, it's full of nothing but horrible memories."

Fate couldn't explain the pull she was feeling. Maybe it was because Oldwilde was where she'd shared her first kiss with Finn, where she'd discovered the true meaning of selfless love. She might feel differently once she was with Finn, but something told her she should keep the door open.

"I don't know why. I'm just not ready to let go of the place." Fate moved next to the standing stone.

"It's all the same to me." Jessie stepped in next to her and placed her hand on Fate's.

Taking in an excited shaky breath at the thrill of seeing Finn, Fate activated the portal, feeling the eerie tug of dimensions bending as her surroundings buckled and warped. Within seconds, the distorted blur of surrounding images reformed into a circle of standing stones with a backdrop of stars and giant hoops crackling against the Keep's protective shield.

Fate sighed with relief. "Nice! We didn't have to go through another half dozen portals to get back here."

"Copy that." Jessie lifted her aeronaut pack onto her shoulders.

Fate did the same, barely able to buckle the straps for the way her hands were trembling. Her entire body buzzed with eagerness. She was about to see Finn. Had he missed her as much as she'd been missing him? Would he still look at her the same way?

"How do I look?" Fate reached for her wild mane of long curls. "Am I a complete disaster?"

"Not unless you count that volcano on your forehead." Jessie smirked.

"What? No! No zits, not now." Fate worried her fingers over her forehead.

Jessie laughed. "Just kidding. I'm sure you'll look amazing to him. Only I can tell you've missed your beauty sleep."

Fate did her best to smooth her unruly curls with her hands. "Gee thanks, those back-handed compliments are always such self-esteem builders."

"Glad I could help." Jessie turned the ignition, revving the pack's dragonfly shaped wings into motion. "Shall we?"

Nodding, Fate gulped, started her aeronaut pack and launched skyward. As they neared the breaching door, her heart hammered violently against her ribcage and her pulse pounded in her ears. Jessie hit the button to open the hatch. As it spiraled open, Fate peered in, hoping to catch a glimpse of Finn before she went inside.

Jessie looked at her. "You first."

Fate nodded stiffly as she closed in, navigating her way through the hatch, suddenly awkward, as if she'd just learned how to fly the machine. "Some entrance," she grumbled to herself as her feet touched down on the sanctuary floor.

Eustace, Farouk and Darcy were gathered round the big table, studying the 3D projection of the Keep. Finn was nowhere in sight. And where was Sithias? Her heart sank into the pit of her stomach. Had she been tricked into coming back?

She turned on Jessie as she came in for a landing. "What's going on? Where's Finn? Was it all a lie to get me back here?"

Jessie stood speechless, her mouth open.

Eustace rushed over. Fate knew something was terribly wrong the moment they locked eyes. "What is it? What happened?"

"Wodrid's here. He's taken Gerdie. And the Orb. We'll get her back in exchange for the Rod."

Icy fear trickled down Fate's spine. "It'll be game over if we let him have both the Rod and Orb."

Farouk looked up from the table, his fox eyes stern. "Which is why you'll have to figure a way out of that occuralizing."

Fate was flummoxed. "How did he find a way into the Keep? You said he couldn't get inside. You should've listened to me, I told you he'd find a way!"

"He came here with you." Eustace placed a hand on her shoulder. "Wodrid disquised himself as Steve."

His meaning took several seconds to sink in before nauseating fear set in. Steve was Wodrid? No, that was impossible. Steve had helped them rid the Keep of every threat they'd faced together. A chill spread through Fate. How many times had she turned her back to him? Trusting he was a harmless guy who liked dressing as a warlock even after the party was over. If she was honest with herself, she'd sensed something was off about him. But she'd ignored the signs. It was her fault Gerdie's life hung in the balance.

Fate hung her head. "I should've known."

"None of us knew." Eustace gave her shoulder a gentle squeeze. "We were all taken in by his deception. Except for Finn. He seemed to know right–"

"So Finn *is* here?" She turned to Jessie. "I was beginning to think you only said that to make sure I'd come back with you."

"Apology accepted."

Fate looked around again, turning from side to side. "So where is he?"

Eustace took a deep breath and closed his eyes. He only did that when he had bad news to deliver. When her father finally looked at her, his eyes held such deep regret and sadness, she had to look away.

Darcy edged around the table. Grief had softened her usually grim expression. Fate's body turned heavy and she could hardly move. The worst had happened if Darcy was showing sympathy.

Fate's gaze landed on the scorch marks on the walls, the tipped over furniture, the books strewn over the floor. A battle had taken place within the sanctuary. A battle between Finn and Wodrid. Sorrow seized her heart like a cold fist. "I have to see him. I can't accept what you're telling me. I have to see his body for myself." She choked out the last few words.

Eustace, Darcy and Farouk exchanged an uncomfortable look and the room filled with an awful silence. Her father finally spoke. "That may prove difficult. Finn tried to go after Wodrid. Without any means of flight."

"He…he fell?" The words cut Fate's throat like broken glass.

Eustace shifted in place, his expression pained. "Well, yes, he–"

"Oh my, I could spend the rest of my life in that library. But not until we've–" Sithias stopped within the doorway. "Miss, is that you?" He swept all the way into the sanctuary with a librarian robot carrying a stack of books for him.

"Sithias!" Fate cried. She ran across the room, wrapping her arms round the snake as sobs wracked her body.

"There, there, misss." Sithias enclosed her within the downy softness of his feathered wings and patted her back with his tail. "Don't lose heart. I haven't. We both know how strong Finn is. He's alive. You can be sure of that."

Fate glanced at her friend, barely able to see him clearly for the tears swimming in her eyes. "Do you really believe that?"

"A hundred percent," Sithias assured her.

"It's cruel to give her false hope," Eustace said, his voice sharp and protective.

Sithias looked at him. "With all due respect, sssir, you haven't witnessed what I have when it comes to what Finn can do."

Fate sniffed back her tears and moved one of Sithias's wings aside so she could see her father. "Dad, he's right. Finn has amazing powers. He's done incredible things."

"That may be," Farouk interrupted, before Eustace could respond, "but I have not been able to detectify any signs of life on the surface."

Doubt slammed back in and Fate gulped down the tears.

Sithias drew her back into the shelter of his wings. "Don't listen to them." He gave her a scolding look but there was warmth in his amber eyes. "Are you ready to proceed with the assumption Finn isss alive?"

"I wasn't finished," Farouk informed them. Fate roughly wiped the tears from her eyes and edged over to the table as he used the pointer to indicate a red spot on the 3D projection of the Keep. "I have however been getting readings of bioillogical activity deep beneath Quadrant 86, directly below this tower."

Fate turned to him with hope swelling in her heart. "Is that your way of saying there are live bodies down there?"

Farouk's ears slanted with annoyance. "Plaindubitably. Disfortunately, they're far enough below the surface to bloterate my readings, which means I'm unable to tell how many lifeforms are down there. I can tell they have not dug below the subsurface, because they're moving with the vault. Docuscripts show a hidden section beneath the structure and eludevade to a secret entrance inside the tower."

"Is this your one and only lead?" Fate had hoped for more.

"Yes."

"Then I guess we start there. It's got to be where Wodrid stashed Gerdie. More than likely, Kaliena's there too." Fate marched over to the weapons rack, grabbed a laser gun, sword and several daggers. She reached for the crossbow, but realized she couldn't carry it with her rifle and aeronaut pack taking up the room on her back.

Jessie stepped in beside her to replenish the ammunition for her gun.

"We need to go in with the expectation that Wodrid's there and he's found some way to subdue Finn." Fate holstered her gun and sheathed her sword. She felt good saying that. It sounded believable, which is what she needed to avoid falling apart completely.

"It's too bad Mason's still out of commission," Jessie said. "We could really use the extra back-up."

"Oh, he's back on his feet, thanks to the rat," Darcy said, her black-rimmed eyes leveled on Farouk. "But his orders are to guard the Gorgon *you* brought back." Her heated gaze shifted to Fate. "Why is it you don't even have to be around to put my boyfriend's life at risk?"

"Is this about the Gorgon's head?" Fate asked, astonished by Darcy's short-lived moment of compassion. She looked at Farouk. "What happened? Did it slither out of the box you locked it in?"

"No, Brune's been infected," Eustace explained. "She's turning into a Gorgon."

"Ew." Fate suddenly understood why Brune hadn't wanted to return to the Keep. She must've known she'd become a threat. But Fate had insisted on bringing her back, when in fact, she should've left her behind in that cave. She had allowed sympathy to cloud her judgment. If Brune hurt anyone, Fate would have to shoulder the blame for that as well. "Is she dangerous?"

"Of course," Darcy argued. "She's a Gorgon!"

Ignoring Darcy's barbs, Fate turned to her father for answers.

"She's still unconscious. We won't know how badly she's been affected until she wakes," Eustace told her.

Fate gave Darcy a sheepish look. "You're right, Gorgon's are deadly. But we need Mason to stand guard to make sure she stays put." She walked over to the breeching door and lifted her aeronaut pack, hooking the straps over her shoulders. "Jessie and I'll handle the rest on our own."

Eustace stood stiff and nervous. "You must be extremely careful. Wodrid's power is formidable."

Fate could tell he was more fearful than ever and wanted to say something to put him at ease. "Dad, don't worry. I survived my last encounter with him. He's the one who lost a leg and I'm the one who walked away." She said it with more confidence than she was letting on.

Eustace didn't look convinced. "That's what worries me. He'll go after you with a vengeance. You mustn't give him the slightest opening."

Sithias weaved across the room and stopped next to Eustace. "Trust in your daughter." He gave her a wink. "She's stronger and more capable than you can imagine. I should know. I've witnessed amazing feats of courage from thisss girl."

"You should come with us," Fate suggested. "We can use all the help we can get."

Sithias drew back in horror. "And how would I help? Kill Wodrid with a litany of insults?" He shook his scaled head. "Unfortunately, I'm not the shape shifter you left behind, and I've lost my ability to use the Words of Making. I'm sorry to say I'm nothing more than the amazing artist and playwright you first met. Besides, someone has to record this hissstoric event with the panache your grand story deserves."

Fate smiled and shook her head. "Same old Sithias. It's okay. We'll have the upper hand as soon as we find Finn." She turned and hit the button to the breeching door before any of them could see the doubt creeping back in.

But Jessie caught it. Her friend didn't say a word, she simply signaled it was time to leave and jumped through the hatch. Forcing a brave smile for her father and Sithias, Fate leapt into space, terrified of what awaited them down below.

46
THE WHITETHORN TREE

AFTER FOLLOWING FAROUK'SCOORDINATES, Fate and Jessie landed. They killed the engines of their aeronaut packs, drew their laser guns and scanned their surroundings. After deducing all was clear, they relaxed somewhat.

"Looks like the right place." Jessie craned her neck to look at the top of the tower. "I don't know how we're supposed to get down below this thing. From everything I know about towers, they only go up."

Fate stared at the ornate tower with its smooth, needle-sharp point. "Don't assume anything, just quiet your mind and wait for what comes."

Jessie gave her a questioning stare. "Since when did you turn into a Zen monk?"

"I'm nowhere near Zen. In fact, I'm barely holding it together at the moment. I have no idea if Finn's dead or alive." Fate fought to hold back the tears that so readily sprang to her eyes everytime she let her thoughts touch on her worst fears.

"Sorry," Jessie muttered.

Fate drew in a shaky breath and clutched at the tight, painful ache in her chest. "No, I'm sorry. You're the last person I should be snapping at." She tapped her temple with her finger. "Remember the guardian initiation and the download you received?"

"How could I forget? It felt like someone hammered a nine-inch nail through my skull."

"That's because you had the combined experience and

knowledge of hundreds of guardians crammed into your brain all at once. Which means you can access whatever you need to know about the Keep and everything in it."

"Oh right. I remember Farouk saying something about that, but I was kind of out of it at the time. So how do I get it to work?"

Fate struggled to hold her impatience at bay. "That's the quiet your mind part. How about we both take a second and try it now."

"Someone's getting snappy again."

Fate flashed an exaggerated smile. "No. I'm not." She turned her attention back to the tower. "Okay, closing my eyes now. You too," she said, using the happiest tone of voice she could muster.

The information flooded Fate's mind immediately. Visions of blossoms and thorns, and wise men in flaxen robes stood in a circle with a tree in the center. A name emerged and she began to say it when Jessie interrupted.

"The Tower of the Whitethorn Tree. How awesome is that? It just came to me!"

Fate nodded. "Yup, that's how it works."

"Come on, let's go in."

They slowly entered the arched entrance with laser guns aimed and ready. The dim interior was lit with tiny luminescent particles floating in the air like snowflakes. As Fate and Jessie edged forward the lights scattered in all directions.

The round chamber was empty, save for the colossal statues lining the circular walls. There were nine of them, each as tall as the tower, their heads bending where the ceiling curved into a point. Each statue was a hooded figure with arms crossed and stern bearded face frowning down at them. They were the wise men Fate had seen in her mind's eye, and by their fierce expressions, they seemed to be standing guard over…nothing.

Fate walked into the center. "Where's the tree? It should be here."

Jessie peered at the statues. "Maybe that's why all those Gandalf look-a-likes seem kinda grumpy. Do you think Wodrid stole it?"

"I don't know, something tells me there's more to this picture." Holstering her gun, Fate switched on her aeronaut pack and lifted off.

"You think the tree's up there?" Jessie called after her.

Fate didn't answer and continued to climb until she was level with the faces of the statues. She glanced down at Jessie, noticing for the first time, the maze-like design of the tiles on the floor. "Jessie, stand on that round tile in the center," she yelled down.

Jessie did as Fate instructed. When nothing happened, she looked up and held her hands out in frustration. "That's your brilliant solution?"

Fate hovered in place, studying the pattern from the same vantage point as the guardians in the room. Then she saw the break in the outer ring of the tiles. "Stand over there." She waved her arms in the direction she wanted Jessie to go.

Jessie followed her directions, though rather begrudgingly.

"Good, now follow the path."

Jessie looked at her. "What path?"

"The beige tiles."

"It's all beige."

"The lighter beige tiles."

Jessie shot Fate an irritated look before taking her first steps along the zig zagging path.

"No, that's the wrong way," Fate said when Jessie came to a dead end. "Turn around and turn left at the next bend."

"This is a waste of time."

Rather than lose her temper, Fate bit her tongue and

patiently steered her reluctant friend along the maze until she finally reached the center.

Jessie glanced at her with an expression of being thoroughly unimpressed. "Now what?"

Fate gulped. She'd thought surely, she'd cracked the code to gaining access to the secret entrance. What else could the statues be staring at? "Jump up and down." Fate slowly descended.

Jessie crossed her arms. "Seriously? I think I'd be better off saying 'open sesame' or–"

The round tile beneath Jessie suddenly jerked beneath her. The sound of grating stone echoed throughout the voluminous chamber as the large tile sank below the floor line.

Fate swooped down to land on the tile next to Jessie and turned off her aeronaut pack. "You were saying?"

Jessie smirked. "It was the 'open sesame' that did it."

"Uh huh." Fate squinted into the dark as they descended a good fifteen feet below the floor of the chamber. As they neared the bottom, a cloud of light particles like those above but thicker, illuminated the stone walls.

Fate stepped off the tile, watching the tiny lights as they floated toward the opening. "We're on the right track. The faery lights are coming from down here. Just a guess, but I'm pretty sure that means Wodrid used this entrance."

"If that's true, he could be anywhere." Jessie kept her voice low as she looked around. "Jinkies, don't you feel like we're in the Scooby gang, what with finding out Steve is Wodrid? How creepy is that? The enemy, right under our noses."

Fate shuddered. "I'm trying not to think about it too much." She glanced at the low ceiling and started unbuckling her aeronaut pack. "Doesn't look like we'll be doing any flying down here."

"Agreed." Jessie removed her pack and set it down next to Fate's.

Fate gestured for Jessie to follow as she made her way over to the only opening leading out of the small chamber. They entered a curved closed-in corridor, which took a sharp turn into another curved corridor. Each turn they took, seemed to take them in the opposite direction they were heading. The zig-zagging course seemed all too familiar.

When they came to their second dead end, Fate stopped. "We're inside a maze."

"That's what I was afraid was happening." Jessie wiped the sweat from her brow. She looked close to panicking. "These walls are suffocating. Do you realize we might never find our way out? I've heard of people getting lost in corn mazes. It's awful. Dehydration sets in, then there's headaches and heatstroke. People die of that, you know."

"Since there's no sun beating down on us, I think we can strike death by heatstroke off the list," Fate assured her. "Wodrid's what we need to be worried about. He could be waiting around the next corner for all we know."

Jessie's eyes grew wide with fright. "We should probably whisper."

"Exactly," Fate whispered back. "Just stay calm and follow me. I'm ninety-nine percent sure this is the exact same maze pattern as the one upstairs."

"Do you remember it well enough to get us out of here?"

"Sheesh, what do you think?" Fate gave her a dismissive wave.

Jessie latched onto the vague answer like she'd been thrown a life raft, when in fact Fate had no clue whether to turn left or right at the end of the corridor. It was a complete toss of the coin. She decided to take a quick left so Jessie wouldn't notice any hesitation.

After a good while of weaving through the maze aimlessly, Fate slowed down when she thought she heard a distant high-pitched scream from Gerdie. Signaling to Jessie for complete silence, Fate edged along the wall to the very end and peered around the corner.

They'd finally come to the end of the maze, which opened into a domed room. Countless ancient scrolls filled the shelves lining the curved walls. In the very center, growing out of the cracked stone floor was a tree, beautiful and gleaming with a bluish, white light. Each branch was covered in long, hooked thorns and heavily laden with glowing white blossoms. An invisible breeze tossed the limbs, scattering luminous clouds of pollen and petals into the air.

"That must be the Whitethorn Tree," Jessie whispered in awe.

Fate started to nod, but froze in place when her gaze landed on a limp form at the base of the tree. It was Finn. His arms were extended over his head, his wrists bound by a rope and bloody from being tied to the thorny branches. His head hung to one side. He wasn't moving.

Love surged through her, clouding all reason.

Fate lunged forward, but Jessie grabbed her by the arm and yanked her back behind the wall. "You can't go charging in there. It's not safe. We need to go in slow and strategic."

Nerves and icy fear collided as Fate fought the urge to run to Finn. This was the first time she'd seen him since they'd been torn apart. The memories of him and his astonishing strength hammered through her body. She couldn't begin to imagine the fight Finn must have given Wodrid to bring him to this broken and bloody state. Her heart withered to see him this way. Pressing her hand to her chest, she tried to force the unbearable ache away.

Jessie stopped when she saw Fate's tears. "Get a grip. You'll be useless to him if you lose it now."

Drawing in a shaky breath, Fate rubbed at her tears and nodded.

Jessie edged toward the opening and peeked around the corner. She inched back and turned to Fate. "I don't see any sign of Wodrid or his girlfriend, but I saw Gerdie. She's on the opposite end of the room, tied and gagged. She saw me and shook her head. You know what that means, right?"

Fate stared at her, unable to think past Finn's distressing condition.

"It's a trap," Jessie hissed. "We've seen it a thousand different times–the classic scene from every movie, where the kidnapped victim is trying to warn the rescuer with a shake of the head. I say we leave and bring back reinforcements."

"Leave them behind?" Fate whispered. How could she do that when she was this close to Finn? She had to go to him. She literally ached with the need. Every part of her being reached out to him. Nothing in this universe could make her leave him now. Anger cut through the fog, clearing her head like nothing else could. "No way. We're not leaving here without them. We all go, or none of us go."

Jessie nodded. "That's what I like to hear. Welcome back. So what's the plan?"

Fate examined her laser gun and checked the fuel gauge. "We go in and empty everything we've got into Wodrid before he can say, 'What the...?'"

"Not exactly a plan, but I'm all there for improvising." Jessie clicked the Dragon Eye gear down over her eye. "I'm ready when you are."

Taking the lead, Fate turned the corner, willing herself to breathe steadily and take control of her racing heartbeat. Setting all fear aside, she focused her energy on the task at hand, the way she'd been trained by the most skilled knights of Beldereth. It was time to reclaim her knighthood and be the warrior she once was. So what if she didn't have wind and lightning coursing through her veins anymore and could no longer break bones with a war cry. She was strong in other ways, and this was a battle she had to win, even if she had to fight to the death.

47
VERMIS PHOBIA

FATE DIDN'T DARE LOOK at Finn as she stole past the tree and fixed her gaze on the other side of the room. Her heart screamed at her to stop and go to him. The memory of everything they'd shared flowed through her veins like an intoxicating drug. In the same way an addict craves the next high, she fought the weakness with everything she had and used it to embolden her movements forward. She needed to believe destiny was at work here. It didn't matter that forces had thrown every obstacle in the universe at them. She and Finn were meant to be together.

Just not this very second.

A few more steps, and she locked eyes with Gerdie, where she sat with her back to the wall, her wrists and ankles bound. She looked tiny and vulnerable. Gerdie's eyes widened when she saw her, then looked the other way, letting Fate know the direction of her captors.

Signaling to Jessie, Fate directed her to go around the other side of the tree. She slowed down when she saw the alcove Gerdie was staring at, every muscle coiled as she aimed her gun into its shadowy center.

Wodrid suddenly burst forth. An aura of electricity crackled around him. Crimson bolts lashed from his upturned palms as he stormed toward her.

Fate squeezed the trigger, blasting a lethal beam into Wodrid's center. The ray's crimson light scattered into harmless particles across his protective shield of energy. She didn't let that stop her. She charged forward, closing the distance, strengthening the beam's intensity until the laser pierced his shield and scorched his shoulder.

Wodrid staggered, glancing down at his wound. With an angry snarl, he shot her a scowl and hurled a fireball, knocking the laser gun from her gloved hand.

Without skipping a beat, Fate drew her sword and stormed toward him. She sliced through the next fireball, feeling the heat against her face as flames glanced off the blade.

Catching the briefest flicker of fear on Wodrid's face, Fate fell into a run with her sword held high.

Raising his staff horizontal to the floor, Wodrid conjured a thick green fog, which gathered and fell down around him. Forms congealed within the swirling mist, shapes that slithered behind the hazy veil. He gave her a smile that made her slow down. "*Vermis phobia.*" His shoulders shook with laughter and she wondered what was so funny.

A slimy feeler poked through the mist, and then another and another. The dark fleshy color of them stopped Fate in her tracks as her spine tingled with a deep-seated fear. Her knees went weak with terror as the creatures spilled from the fog and she recognized what they were.

Giant earthworms as big as pythons, but so much more repulsive.

Snakes, she could handle. This was a whole new level of horror. She'd never recovered from her fear of worms, not since a terrifying encounter in the third grade.

Fate dropped her sword arm, unable to move.

Wodrid stopped laughing. "Oh, Fate, I must admit it's been entertaining watching you all these years. Life in that pitiful world you were born in was becoming a real bore, until I finally tracked down you–the last living descendent of the Inkwell line. You're a magnet for extraordinary events! And here I thought magic was weak in a society obsessed with money, celebrities and looks."

Fate took her eyes off the worms for a split second to glance at him in shock.

Wodrid smiled at her reaction. "For a while there, I was afraid I'd become irreversibly infected by your sickening pop culture. But it turns out such inculcations can come in quite handy. All the nauseating vocabulary and backwards thinking I aborbed made it easy for me to meld into shadowing you while I waited for you to find your way into the Keep."

Fate's mind raced as she tried to remember a feeling of being stalked. But nothing stood out.

Tilting his head, Wodrid studied her with mock sad lines creasing his brow. "Don't strain yourself, Fate. You never knew I was in the background watching and listening…learning everything I could about you, because you never noticed me. I always appeared as someone far too ordinary for your taste. That is until I stepped forward as Steve. I suppose that's because I was playing one of your adoring fans and–"

Jessie drew in behind Wodrid and shot him.

He'd let his guard down too long. The blow knocked him to the floor, but he rolled over, blasting Jessie with a fireball. She dodged the flames, recovering swiftly with a kill shot to the chest. Wodrid slumped onto his back.

Jessie raced over, slammed her boot over his throat and aimed her laser gun at his head in case he could still move. She looked at Fate. "Don't just stand there. Untie Gerdie!"

Shock and terror locked Fate in place. Forcing her gaze from Wodrid's still form, she looked down. The worms squirmed toward her, lifting their pointed snouts, pushing the sphincter of their soft, moist mouths up through the tips. Sweat slicked down her back. Her stomach lurched with bouts of nausea. Bile rose in her throat.

"Fate, they're just worms–humongous ones–but they can't

hurt you. They don't even have teeth!"

All Fate could do was shake her head. Jessie didn't understand. The hugeness of the worms only magnified what hideous, gelatinous tubes of gore they were. Jessie also didn't know that when she'd been inside the *Book of Fables*, Mugloth had trapped her deep inside the earth, where thousands of worms had squirmed all over her. Chills prickled over her skin as she relived the experience.

"Use your sword, cut them into pieces!"

Fate tried to tighten her grip, but the hilt of the sword slid against her sweaty palm. "I can't do it!" Her whole body shuddered. "The thought of slicing through their gummy skin and seeing all that goop spill out makes me want to hurl!"

Jessie checked Wodrid for any signs of life. Satisfied he wasn't a threat anymore, she holstered her gun, drew her sword and slashed the head off the nearest worm. The worm vanished in a puff of green mist. "See? No goop."

Fate shook with unbridled relief. "I'm on it." She sliced through a worm wriggling next to her ankle. When it dissolved into harmless, green vapor, she went berserk on the remaining worms. Panting, she wiped the sweat from her brow when she was done and grinned. "Well *that*was therapeutic."

Jessie smiled back as she cut Gerdie's bonds. "Glad to see you're over that silly phobia." She rolled her eyes. "Of all the things to be afraid of."

Fate frowned at her. "You were there, and you know what happened with the worms. I was traumatized for life. And don't tell me you wouldn't have reacted the same–"

Gerdie removed the gag from her mouth. "Kaliena. She's here too!"

Fate glanced over her shoulder. "Where?"

Gerdie's brown eyes grew wide with fear. "There! Behind you."

Fate turned as the clatter of metal against stone echoed

throughout the chamber. A mechanical aberration shaped like a long beetle or centipede, with too many legs to count, scrabbled from the alcove. The thing stopped abruptly when it came to Wodrid's limp form. It reared upright, revealing Kaliena's torso, which crowned the top portion of the freakish contraption. Her six arms swayed in a hypnotic rhythm as she peered down at Wodrid.

Fate's breath came in ragged starts as she scrambled to make sense of what she was seeing. Countless metal tubes from the lower mechanics were plugged into Kaliena's back and into an ornate but functional helmet formed in the shape of outspread wings. Her complexion was paler than Fate remembered, waxen and tinged with a web of fine blue veins, which glowed beneath her translucent skin.

Fate stepped next to Jessie, her sword in one hand as she reached with the other for her laser gun.

"That's not the Kaliena I remember seeing. What's with the creepy, crawly bug thingy she's attached to?" Jessie said, voicing Fate's thoughts out loud.

Fate stared at the monstrosity. "Looks like she had to move from the shrine's life support to something more mobile."

Gerdie edged in between them. "She may be weak, but she's got the Orb, and now she wants the Rod," she warned. "*Please*tell me you didn't bring it."

Fate gulped as her hand reached automatically for the chain holding the Rod beneath her armor.

"Terrific," Gerdie muttered.

Seeing Kaliena was still distracted with Wodrid, Fate chanced a glance at Finn.

Gerdie patted her arm. "He's just knocked out."

Fate swallowed down the painful lump in her throat. "Go check on him while we keep Kaliena busy." She scooped her laser gun off the floor.

Gerdie nodded and slipped over to Finn.

Fate and Jessie advanced on Kaliena with laser guns blazing. The killing beams drilled into her pallid skin, but not with the desired effect. She was lighting up and appeared to be absorbing the energy.

Kaliena reared her head, glaring at them with eyes as empty and black as space.

"Scrap that." Fate holstered her gun. "Switch to blades."

They split up, circling round Kaliena from opposite ends. Kaliena leveled her steely gaze on Fate. Her vulnerable form was too high for Fate to reach with her sword. She wished she'd brought the crossbow after all.

Jessie jumped onto the back of the mechanical centipede, climbed the rise and swiped her sword at Kaliena from behind. It was a good move, but not quick enough. Kaliena twisted round, jerking Jessie's lower half out from under her before the blade could meet its mark. Jessie hit the floor hard with an impact that left her gasping. Kaliena climbed over Jessie, pinning her under the carriage of machinery before she could get away.

Kaliena turned her attention to Wodrid. Using her lower centipede limbs, she lifted Wodrid off the floor, raising him along each set of legs until she held him cradled at her waist. Her smooth, expressionless face twisted with rage as she looked up from Wodrid and glared at Fate. "You know better than most, there's no destroying true love." Her voice roared with power and sheer volume.

This sudden woman-to-woman chat startled Fate. Her gaze darted to Finn, and in that instant, she knew exactly what Kaliena meant. She was a woman in love, and she would do whatever it took to keep her man safe.

Fear flooded through Fate as she watched Kaliena swing the Orb over Wodrid. She was using it to bring him back to life. Only he wouldn't actually be alive. He'd be a zombie the same way Brune had been.

As the Orb's golden light fell over Wodrid's body, he convulsed and came to life in her mechanical embrace. Kaliena took the chain holding the Orb and clasped it around his neck. "This will keep you here with me, my love," she said to him before lifting her black gaze to look at Fate. "But now we must have the Rod for the everlasting life we both deserve."

"Over my dead body," Fate seethed.

"This can be arranged." Kaliena gently set Wodrid on his feet.

"How? By sicking your zombie boyfriend on me?" Fate glared at Wodrid.

He frowned with confusion, obviously still dazed. He started to speak, when Kaliena cut him off.

"He's sacrificed enough. I'll deal with you myself." She reached at her sides and drew six sabers from the scabbards built into her machinery. Rearing back and raising the front legs of the machine, she whipped the blades in the air expertly.

Fate edged backward as Kaliena crabbed sideways and stepped off Jessie. "Jess, get out of there!" she yelled.

Jessie stood, but stayed next to Kaliena. She wore a blank look on her face and her Dragon Eye headgear was haloed in blue-green light.

A chill ran through Fate as she remembered how Jessie had tripped near Kaliena's shrine when they'd fought the scavenger. Jessie's headgear had fallen into the luminescent liquid filling the runnels of the shrine floor. Neither of them had given it any concern beyond that moment. But they should have. This was the liquid that had poured from Kaliena's hands and it must have contaminated the headgear. "Jess?" she cried out. "Are you still with me?"

Jessie didn't answer.

Kaliena smiled coldly at Jessie. "She's under my control. Mine to command as I please." Her black gaze shifted to Fate.

"Hmm, you two have a long history with each other. I sense a deep bond. Give me the Rod, and I'll let you have her back."

Indecision locked Fate in place. If she gave the Rod to Kaliena, the entire universe would suffer. But how could she sacrifice Jessie? They weren't just friends. They were sisters. No one should ever have to make such a horrible choice.

Turmoil turned to outrage and exploded into a fit of blind hatred. Cutting tight lines in the air with her sword, Fate charged at Kaliena.

Three blades deflected the blow, while another set of blades swiped down. Fate arched backward, barely escaping the slice of three razor-sharp tips at her neck.

Kaliena screamed in defiance and frustration. "Try what you will. I'll have your head and take the Rod from your severed neck!"

Terror surged through Fate as she parried Kaliena's swift, precise attacks. The force behind each strike jarred Fate to the bone, despite the strength gained from her cybernetic armor. The effort of blocking three blades at a time weakened her with every blow. There was no way she was going to win this sword fight. Not when it was six swords to her one.

She needed something else to win the battle. But what could she use? Kaliena fed on the energy from the laser gun. All she had was her rifle and deducting fluid cartridges.

Fate ducked low, feeling the wind of the blades slicing the air just above her head. A lock of hair fell to the ground. She glared at the unwelcome haircut she'd been given. Anger cut through some of the fear as she dropped and rolled to avoid the next strike.

When Fate righted herself, her glance landed on the machinery Kaliena was plugged into. Most of it was made of iron. Why hadn't she seen it earlier? Reaching over her shoulder, she drew the rifle and targeted the under carriage supporting

Kaliena's mechanical legs. The gun kicked hard against her shoulder and an explosion of red gas engulfed Kaliena.

With the rifle aimed, Fate stood, ready to fire again.

Kaliena screamed and teetered, her swords flailing as the cloud thinned. The front bottom part of the machine and legs crumbled into rust and fell away. Kaliena's swords clamored to the ground as she gaped at the damage Fate had caused.

Fate took a step forward. "What was that you were saying? You'll take my head off? Kind of hard when you're falling to pieces."

Wodrid raced to stand in front of Kaliena as she struggled to remain upright. He was swinging the Orb and muttering some sort of incantation. Golden light poured from the Orb, pooled at his feet and flooded toward Fate.

Fate had seen Brune do the same with the Orb and she didn't care for a repeat performance.

In a rush of fear, Fate targeted what was left of Kaliena's machine and pulled the trigger. Another red gaseous cloud swallowed both Kaliena and Wodrid. Kaliena's shriek of fury reverberated from behind the misty curtain, while Wodrid's conjurations seemed to have stopped.

Fate picked up her discarded sword, intending to run into the cloud and start slashing wildly, but a storm of blue fire dispersed the red gas. Wodrid was thrown aside in a heap, whereas, Kaliena floated in the air above her disintegrated machine. Her cyanotic skin gleamed with the fire raging from her six hands. Malignant wrappings of dark power radiated from her as she turned her vicious gaze on Fate.

Caught off guard by Kaliena's swift and powerful recovery, Fate scrambled for answers, hoping against hope that a helpful piece of Keep knowledge would kick in and offer a solution. But her mind remained blank. She had nothing to fight with.

48
FOREVER CURSED

FINN WOKE TO A sharp sting on his cheek. Memory nagged him as he tried to orient himself. Opening his eyes, he glimpsed the blur of a small hand whipping through the air. Jerking his arm to block the blow, he discovered his wrists tied above his head and instead angled his elbow before he received another slap to the face. "Gerdie? Whoa, stop. I'm awake."

"Finally." Gerdie's shoulders hunched with tension. "I've been tryin' to wake you for the last ten minutes. Fate's in trouble."

Finn swallowed hard as he stared past Gerdie. He first spotted Wodrid. Something was different about the sorcerer, but the clash of swords drew Finn's attention to Kaliena, who was heavily armed with six swords. She was fighting a highly skilled fighter in enhanced armor. His heart nearly stopped beating when he recognized Fate.

In that instant, everything else fell away. The sight of her filled all the empty spaces of his heart. For seconds, he remained paralyzed by a battling mixture of joy and disbelief. The only movement was the rise and fall of his chest as he drank her in with thirsty eyes.

His mouth went dry as his mind fogged with desire. She was breathtaking, her movements mesmerizing–a perfect blend of grace and efficiency. His bonnie warrior lass. She wore her strength majestically, stunning in her power.

Gerdie tugged on his shirt. "Snap out of it. Can't you see Fate's going to lose? She's fighting Kaliena."

Adrenaline blasted through him, clearing his head. He forced his gaze from Fate. "Where's Jessie? Why isn't she helping?"

"Kaliena's using that headgear Jessie's got strapped round her noggin to control her."

Finn strained against the ropes, but they were bound too tight. "Reach into my left pocket. Get my buck knife and cut me loose."

Gerdie retrieved his knife and went to work cutting the bonds. Finn strained forward, anxious to leap into the fray. Terror stretched through him when Kaliena came frighteningly close to slicing Fate's neck. He watched her recover and block the next strike, but he could see her arms shaking against Kaliena's tremendous strength.

"Hurry up," he growled.

"I'm doin' my best."

Fate dodged another close call. Finn caught the fear in her eyes. His stomach wound into a tight coil as she drew her rifle and shot at Kaliena's machine. "That's my lass," he whispered.

Kaliena's shriek filled the underground chamber as he watched the gas particles quickly oxidize her machine and crumble out from under her. "Blast her again," Finn hissed under his breath. But Fate was waiting for the cloud to dissipate. Then Wodrid raced in, swinging the Orb.

Finn wrenched against the slack in his weakened bond. His left hand fell free. Gerdie moved to his other arm and started sawing at the rope. Relief filled him when Fate shot another round at Kaliena, interrupting Wodrid's incantation. "Get yourself to the exit as soon you cut me free. You don't want to be here once I get going."

Gerdie bent her head to look at him. "You don't have to tell me. I've seen what you can do."

Finn went rigid with fear when Kaliena dispursed the gas with a blast of enscorcelled flames. The explosion threw Wodrid and he fell a few yards away from Finn. The sorcerer lifted his head and locked eyes with Finn.

Finn yanked at the rope, breaking through what remained of the half cut tether. He looked for Fate, but the gas had drifted and blocked his view. Bolting to his feet, he faced Wodrid as Gerdie ran in the opposite direction.

"Looks like a lot happened while I was resting my eyes. Thanks for that. I needed a wee kip. I feel mighty refreshed." Finn studied Wodrid, while expanding his senses. The air around him looked gray and felt void of life. "Unlike you. I see you've gone and gotten yourself undead. Is that my girl's work?"

Wodrid stopped a good twelve feet away and sneered at him. "Death won't stop me. The Orb's keeping me alive, and once your girlfriend's dead, I'll have the Rod and become a god."

"I thought that was Kaliena's goal."

"Enough talk." Glaring with contempt, Wodrid held his palm out to conjure another fireball.

"Having some trouble there?" Finn glanced past the sorcerer to check on Fate. He still couldn't see her and that made him all the more nervous. "I imagine it's tough calling on the elements of fire to move through those shriveling veins."

Wodrid scowled at his hand. "I still know how to use magic." He lifted his staff while murmuring an incantation. The jewel at the top of his silver staff lit with gray-green ethereal flames, which ghosted down around him in swirling waves.

"Impressive light show, but what does it do?"

Wodrid gave him a crafty smile. He thrust his staff, unleashing the ghostly fire at Finn. The power hit like an arctic wind, sending him sprawling against the tree roots burrowed into the floor. A barrier of flame rose around Finn, making a noise like scalding steam, only without the heat. Instead, an icy chill pressed in.

A violent shudder as forceful as an earthquake passed

through Finn. Frigid air lashed against his skin, bringing with it the smell of death, endings and horrific change. Doom hung over him like a shadow. Fear tormented him as he fought against thinking the things he dreaded most–that Fate would die because he'd underestimated his enemy. That he would die only a few yards away without holding her in his arms ever again.

Wracked with chills and fits of despair, Finn curled into a ball. When he most needed to move, fear seemed to have robbed him of every drop of courage he possessed. He lifted his head, squinting past the crackling wall of flames, straining to catch a glimpse of Fate. The red gaseous cloud had cleared. Kaliena was illuminated with power and hovering above Fate, who for the first time looked helpless. Fate took her eyes off Kaliena and turned to look at him. Their eyes met and held across the span of space stretching between them.

"Finn!" she cried out.

The sound of her voice sent a surge of strength through his limbs. But it was short-lived. He inhaled terror when Kaliena unleashed spears of blue fire at Fate. Her body went rigid as the barrage of malevolent energy struck her. Time stopped for a heartbeat as the girl he loved dropped to the floor like a fallen bird.

Cold sweat iced Finn's back as a sickening wave of grief came over him. This couldn't be happening. Not now. Not when they were this close to reuniting.

Pain and fury lashed through Finn, summoning something deep inside. Something that fed on hatred and retribution. A dark power swelled, pressing in all sides, begging to be set loose. Gripping hold of the roots beneath him, Finn connected with the spirit of the Whitethorn Tree, and he spoke in the clipped language of the Elder race to ask for its help.

The tree's energy flowed into him, open and welcoming.

He invoked the rune power of Wood. An inner fire blazed at

his core, burning off the paralyzing chill and malaise Wodrid's spell generated. Crimson sparks laced with gold poured from Finn's mouth, altering the volume of his voice into the roar of giants. Magic flowed through him. As he rose to his feet, he gloried in the expansion of power.

The sorcerer staggered back in fear as the ghost fire dwindled to nothing around Finn.

Unconcerned with Wodrid, Finn fixed his gaze on Kaliena as she continued her fiery attack. With a deafening shout, he commanded the tree to attack.

The floor quaked and cracked open as the tree tunneled through stone. A tangle of roots burst free in an explosion of rubble and dust beneath Kaliena and coiled around her. Finn raised his hand, squeezing as if he held her in his grip and watched the roots tighten. Kaliena's many arms flailed as she struggled to breathe.

Gerdie shoved him from behind. "Finn, that's enough! You need to get Fate out of here."

Finn turned on her. "I told you to leave."

Gerdie shrank from him. "I've seen that black look before, but I hoped I'd never see it again."

Shame flooded through Finn. "Please, go tend to Fate," he muttered.

With a frightened nod, Gerdie picked her way past the roots and broken stone to Fate where she lay on the floor. An agonizing mixture of rage and sorrow thrashed in his chest at the sight of her motionless form.

Painful memories rushed in to torment him: Fate lying in the mud, broken and wounded, after Mugloth had dragged her underground. She'd been so close to death then. All because he'd failed to see that he was the reason she'd put herself in danger. Was he forever cursed to keep repeating the same mistake and reliving the same agonizing punishment?

His answer came in a torrent of fiery spears. Finn dove to one side as the bolts struck where he'd been standing. Azure foxfire laced the trunk of the tree. Feeling the tree's pain as if it were his own, he buckled at the waist and groaned. He lifted himself to check on Kaliena. She'd escaped the tree's grip and was closing in.

Finn invoked Air and commanded the Whitethorn Tree to release its barbs. Within seconds, countless thorns streaked through the chamber, hailing untold poison down upon Kaliena.

Kaliena screamed and shielded her face. Dark blood stained her pale blue skin as the wall of thorns stabbed her. Weakened by the massive assault, she fell onto the rubble and Wodrid shuffled to her side.

Finn wanted to finish the job, but his concern for Fate was too great. He rushed over and knelt next to her. Her armor was scorched, but there were no visible burns or wounds. She had suffered some kind of energetic injury, of which he had no idea how to heal. He smoothed his hand over her soft hair and swallowed. The deathly pallor of her face tore at him as he checked her pulse.

Gerdie looked at him and shook her head. "She's hurt bad. But I don't see any wounds. I've ever seen anything like this before."

"Her pulse is weak, but she's still with us. She'll be fine," he insisted.

The doubt in Gerdie's eyes stretched him thin with terror. "We gotta get her back to the sanctuary. Hopefully Farouk will know what to do."

Finn gathered Fate in his arms and kissed her forehead. "I'm with you, love. You hold on. Hear me?" He stood and looked for Kaliena and Wodrid. They were gone, as well as Jessie.

Gerdie stood and brushed the dust off her knees. She

caught the vengeful look in his eyes. "There's nothing more we can do here."

Finn nodded and carried Fate as fast as he could toward the exit. They entered the curved, narrow corridor. "You'll have to lead the way, Gerdie. I wasn't exactly awake when Wodrid brought me here."

"I'll try but I'm not sure I remember the route."

Finn followed her through the narrow passageway. "Is this a maze?"

"A complicated one." Gerdie stopped and turned. "Dead end. We have to go back the other way."

Finn's heart thudded with panic as he turned around. "We don't have time for all this backtracking." He had to get Fate topside. Now.

He traced the path back to the two-way split, taking a right this time. Something wasn't right about this. When he'd connected with the Whitethorn Tree, he'd sensed the tree's sacred connection with the Druidic Order. He remembered something his grandfather had taught him in his many lessons to become a druid. *You enter a maze to lose yourself and a labyrinth to find yourself.* If druids had built this place, this would not be a maze. It would be a labyrinth.

He took a deep breath to control his mounting fear and pushed his senses outward. With each step, he followed the natural flow of energy, feeling for where the energy was stopped by walls and avoiding them. His movements became more fluid as he followed the energy to the center.

He stepped onto the center tile in the small chamber he found himself in. He knew he was in the right place when he saw the two flight packs Fate and Jessie had left behind.

Gerdie stepped in beside him. "How did you know the way?"

The sound of stone grinding against stone, echoed as the tile rose slowly toward the opening in the ceiling. Finn gave her a grim smile. "I looked for my center and found it."

They were halfway up when something sliced into Finn's shoulder. He reeled with pain–almost losing his balance and dropping Fate. Regaining his footing, Finn checked his shoulder and saw a smoking gash.

A red beam streaked past his head before he realized where the shots came from.

Jessie stormed forward, unemotional as she fired her laser gun at them. Gerdie hugged herself and cringed as Finn turned away from Jessie to shelter Fate. Another shot hit the heel of his boot, hot as it melted the sole.

The tile leveled out with the floor of the vault, cutting Jessie off. Finn glanced at the giant druid statues staring down at him. He carried Fate to the entrance of the vault. The only way he was going to get her out of there was to fly. He set her down gently and went back for the flight pack and started strapping it on.

"Do you even know how to fly an aeronaut pack?" Gerdie asked.

"Not at all, but what choice do I have?"

"None, I guess."

When he finally had the pack fully secured, he tested the gear on the handlebars and shot straight up, letting off the speed before he bashed into the ceiling. He hovered for a few seconds, steering sideways then up and down. When he was satisfied he'd mastered the controls enough to fly Fate to safety, he descended.

"I'm sorry, Gerdie, but I'm going to have to leave you here. I'll send someone back as soon as I get Fate to the sanctuary."

"I know. Just go. And be careful."

Finn nodded as he lifted Fate, adjusting her limp weight with his free arm until he had a firm grip around her waist. "Gerdie, take my belt and run it through her utility belt."

Gerdie worked as fast as she could, then stepped back and

gave him the thumbs up. "Go."

Giving her a nod, Finn lifted off the floor and floated slowly past the entrance, looking around to see which direction he needed to go.

All of a sudden, the terrible rending of stone filled the vault. He turned with a start. The center tile had been blown open. A cloud of sparkling pollen and pulverized stone filled the chamber as Jessie climbed out of the hole.

"Gerdie, run!" he shouted.

Gerdie raced from the vault as Finn rose higher. Through the billowing dust he could see Jessie strapping on the other aeronaut pack. He wouldn't stand a chance once she was in the air. His only option was to get as big a head start as he could.

"Move another inch, and I'll blow you out of the sky."

Finn turned. It was Brune and she had a laser gun aimed straight at him.

49
SOMETHING'S FLAWMAGED

"LAND AND LET HER GO!" Brune shouted as she flew in close to Finn. She hadn't changed since he'd last seen her in the infirmary, except she and her head full of snakes were awake, and she was dressed in the same enhanced armor Fate and Jessie wore. Thankfully, she was wearing goggles with thick red lenses, which he guessed were protecting him from her Gorgon gaze.

"Brune," Gerdie yelled from where she was hiding down below, "that's Finn! Let him go so he can take Fate to the sanctuary."

Brune stared at Finn, her head cocked to one side and forked tongue flicking from her mouth. "Hmm, you must be the boy I conjured when I summoned Fate. Guess your face went the way of my brain cells when I was inconveniently undead. Sorry about the gun." She nudged her head at Fate. "I thought you were the reason for her being unconscious."

Finn swallowed back his guilt. Brune was closer to the truth than she realized. Fate was in trouble because he'd been stupid enough to get himself caught and she'd had to come rescue him.

A laser beam burned into Brune's thigh. With an angry hiss, she turned as Jessie hurled through the air, shooting at them both.

A deadly beam arced past the wing of Finn's aeronaut pack.

"Go. I'll take care of this." Brune turned in Jessie's direction.

"Don't kill her," Finn said. "It's not her fault. She's under Kaliena's control."

Brune dodged a beam aimed at her head and shot back. "Are

you kidding me?"

"No, I'm not. Knock her out if you have to. Just don't kill her."

"I'll try, but no promises. Now go!"

Finn climbed high as fast as he could, searching for the breaching door to the sanctuary, which he knew was located within the nexus point of the colossal hoops. Only, he couldn't spot the hatch he'd so rashly jumped from. The hoops swept overhead, crackling against the atmosphere's firmament without yielding the location he so desperately needed to find.

Panic almost took over before he caught movement from the corner of his eye–two specks flying through the air toward him. Finn sped toward them, relieved when he recognized Sithias and Mason. A few minutes later, they met in the middle and Sithias slowed down, flapping in place, his amber eyes round with worry when he saw Fate.

"Is she…?" He trailed off and gulped.

"No, but she's in trouble," Finn told him.

Mason stopped and hovered. "Where's Gerdie and Brune?" His expression filled with concern as he regarded Fate.

Finn nudged his chin. "Down at the tower. Brune's fighting Jessie."

Mason screwed up his face. "What? Why? Has Brune gone dark already?"

"No, Jessie's under Kaliena's control. You'd better get down there and make sure Brune doesn't kill her."

Giving Finn a nod, Mason sped toward the tower.

Sithias watched him leave then turned his anxious gaze to Fate. "I came to see how I could help down there, but I think its best if I lead you back to the sanctuary."

"Agreed."

With a vigorous nod, Sithias flapped furiously, weaving through the air until they reached the hatch what felt like hours later, even though it was only minutes. He pressed the button, pushing it over and over again, even while the iris of the hatch was sliding open. Finn passed through the opening, landing slowly and gently.

Eustace was next to them in an instant, his face chalk-white as he checked Fate's pulse. Relief softened his expression when he confirmed she was alive, but his gaze transformed to stone when he looked at Finn. "What happened? Where are Jessie and Gerdie?" He kept his voice carefully low but it was edged with fury as he took Fate from Finn.

Finn unbuckled the last strap and set the aeronaut pack down. He did his best to explain the sequence of events, but he grew more and more ashamed with every word. The entire situation was his fault. He'd failed to protect any of them, and he could see that Eustace felt the same.

Eustace eased Fate onto the table and looked at Farouk. "Can you help her here or should I take her to the infirmary?"

Farouk set a box down on the table and unlatched the lid. Several tiered drawers sprang up to offer their belongings in an orderly fashion. He reached for an instrument with lots of buttons. Turning it on, the contraption beeped as he held it over Fate's head before moving it down over her chest. When it reached her heart, the small panel lit up and the beeps became one long alarm. Farouk set the instrument down and turned it off with a grim expression. "My diagnostifications show gimmensive cellular destructalization."

Finn's hopes sank into despair.

"Which is easy enough to repair." Farouk reached for another gadget.

Finn, Eustace and Sithias all sighed with relief at the same time.

Farouk activated the device. A spray of golden green light shot from the end and he proceeded to run the beam along the length of Fate's body. "Who did this to her?"

"Kaliena blasted her with some powerful energy. I've never seen its like before." Finn looked at Eustace. "I'm sorry. There was nothing I could do at the time."

Looking sick with grief, Eustace wavered in place. "This is your doing."

Finn nodded. "I know."

"You never should've gone after Wodrid the way you did. You didn't give us the chance to come up with a strategy. Is this how you do everything? Is this what my daughter has to look forward to?"

"No, sir. I've learned my lesson. I'll never–"

"It's too late for that. The damage is done."

The tension grew thick in the room. Sithias fluttered his wings nervously as he watched the heated exchange. "Uh, how long will it take before Fate wakes?"

Both Finn and Eustace turned their attention to Farouk, who looked up from his examination with a puzzled expression. "The restructification is completified. She should be waking by now." His ears sagged as he shook his head. "Her vitals are slowing. Something's flawmaged. Hurry, we must get her to the infirmary and on life support."

Eustace gripped the edge of the table and slumped in desperation.

"I'll take her." Finn scooped her up in his arms and headed for the door. His heart hammered as he rushed down the hall. His worst nightmare was coming true and none of it made sense. Why was this happening?

As he raced forward, he dove deep, questing for the red-gold flame of Fate's spirit essence. It wasn't there. She was a shell. Her spirit had abandoned her. If he didn't chase after her spark and anchor it to the living, Fate was going to die.

50
ENOUGH CHEERING UP FOR ONE DAY

THE WORLD LOOKED STRANGE to Fate. Everything had taken on a silvery smudge, as if her surroundings had turned into an old black and white movie. The details of objects around her blurred whenever she tried to focus on them, just as her memory blurred when she tried to remember where she was or what she was supposed to do.

The muffled sounds of voices, like people speaking in the next room crept into her awareness. They were familiar. Though when she tried to identify who was speaking, the name eluded her. The only thing she could be certain of was the tension in their voices, two of which stirred a storm of emotions.

But exhaustion had settled in and she didn't have the strength to face the distress the voices were causing her. She turned away, allowing herself to recede into the nothingness, where the slowing beat of her heart drowned out the voices. The rhythmic noise came in the form of a thin whooshing sound, much like distant waves ebbing and flowing against a sandy shore.

A thread of fear unwound at the back of her mind. Why did her heartbeat sound so weak?

A heartbeat should be strong. Like when she was a knight and her heart had beat so boldly it glowed bright through bone, muscle and armor. She'd been invincible then. Not just in body but in mind as well. Living fire had surged through her veins and had burned away all memories of her former existence. She'd been unencumbered by debilitating emotions. Unlike this agonizing sense of loss that had her locked in endless sorrow.

A yearning for indomitable strength and emotional freedom pushed to the surface. With the wishing, she suddenly found herself clothed in silver armor. She lifted her gauntleted arm, smiling at how easily it bent, like a malleable second skin. The booming roar of her heart filled her ears and had her glancing down at the luminous red glow emanating from her chest.

A dead calm came over her, washing away the unnamable grief that had been torturing her. She had her armor back on, nothing could ever hurt her again.

Something disturbed the silvery shadows swirling around her. A figure emerged. He stood tall, muscular and unmoving as she stared at him. Was he friend or foe? She couldn't tell. His features were smudged within the shifting gray shadows.

"Fate?" His voice rang throughout the void, an echo from the past that brought the heartache back.

Widening her stance in preparation for a fight, she drew her sword. "Stay back."

"It's me, love. It's Finn. I'm here."

Her heart thudded and skipped. Love and loss clashed inside her chest. Thin lines cracked over the breastplate of her armor, and it hurt. Unable to bear the anguish, Fate resisted with a howling shriek that sent the intruder hurtling through the air.

He vanished within the twisting, churning shadows. Shaking from head to toe, she turned and walked in the other direction.

He stepped from the thrashing darkness. "You can do your worst to me, but it won't make me leave you. I love you. So much that I'd rather cross over death's door with you, than go back to the land of the living alone."

The memory of Finn encased in sickly green flames, dying before her very eyes, stopped Fate in her tracks. Losing him all over again had ended her.

It was all too much. She didn't want to remember. Remembering meant pain. An incredible amount of agony she could no longer endure. Fate squeezed the hilt of her sword and turned to look at him. "You're a ghost. You don't exist anymore. You're just a cruel trick of my mind."

"No, love. I swear I'm here with you."

She wanted to believe him with all her heart, but another let down would shatter her into a billion pieces. As much as it killed her to do it, she needed to rid her heart of this tempting trickster.

He moved toward her.

The second he was within striking distance, she targeted his chest and plunged her sword. As the blade drove deep, Fate let out a strangled cry and the air locked in her lungs. Never again, would she feel the warm touch of his lips against hers. Not even in a dream. Finn was gone. Forever.

The shifting surroundings came to a standstill. His blurred features became crystal clear, bright with silvery hues glancing off the peaceful planes of his face. She'd never seen anything more beautiful. His luminous green eyes gazed straight back, piercing her heart with immeasurable guilt.

"I'm sorry." Her voice was so thick with tears she could barely speak.

"For what? You didn't hurt me. See? I'm still here."

Fate dropped her sword. Nothing could make her do again what she'd just done. It had taken everything out of her. She dropped her face in her hands and cried. Her throat burned with each sob. "Stop torturing me. You're not real. Wodrid killed you. I watched you die."

"Oh please. That zombie deadbeat didn't get the best of me. Sure, he got in a few good punches, but I got back up."

Fate lifted her gaze. "Really?"

"Aye, I'm right here next to you, love. In the flesh. All you have to do is stay here and wake up."

She frowned. "I'm awake."

"No, you're not. You're dying in my arms at this very minute."

The overwhelming sadness in his eyes made her turn away.

"No I'm not. Look at me. I'm stronger than ever. There's no more pain. I'm free."

"Is that why you're leaving us?"

"Us?"

"Me, your father, Gerdie, Sithias… and Jessie."

Fate's heart plummeted into the pit of her stomach. "She's gone. My best friend's gone."

"We'll get her back. I promise."

Pain and distrust rushed in. "Nobody can keep that kind of promise. Not even you."

"So that's it? You're giving up?"

"I don't want to, but I'm tired of hurting all the time. I need to stop feeling."

Finn took her hands in his and held them close to his chest. "Even love?"

"Love hurts the most."

"But it heals too.

"You really believe that?"

"Abso-bloody-lutely. No matter how bad it gets, love is what sees me through."

Fate smiled, but it was short-lived. Finn let go of her and receded into the shadows. "Don't go," she pleaded.

He vanished and all that was left was his voice. "You need to come to me, Fate. I'm waiting. All you have to do is wake, my sleeping beauty."

Panic flooded through her veins the moment he left her sight. The thin whooshing of her heartbeat became a stubborn, hammering drumbeat. Blood pulsed hot and fast, warming her, pushing her to move, to fight against the weight of her heavy lids.

Fate opened her eyes to a ceiling filled with diffused light. Pain bit at the back of her eyes. She squeezed them shut and groaned.

"Hello, sleepy head."

Her breath caught in her throat and she let out a half sob, half laugh. Cracking her lids open, she squinted at Finn.

He smiled down at her, his eyes shining bright with love and relief as his gaze traced over the curves of her face. "There you are. Back to the land of the living." His voice cracked with emotion.

She was suddenly aware of his body lying next to hers. His weight shifted infinitesimally, as if he feared hurting her with even the slightest movement.

"You're here," she croaked, her throat too dry to swallow. She touched his chest, pressing her palm to a wall of muscle. His heartbeat thudded fast against her hand.

"Always," he whispered as he carefully leaned to kiss her forehead.

Fate closed her eyes, savoring the soft graze of his lips against her skin. Nuzzling against his neck, she inhaled the woodsy scent of sandalwood soap lingering on his skin. Her lungs filled with bliss as the gaping hole that had been in her chest since the day they were torn apart healed. She was whole again, as if the wound had never existed.

"Finn, I missed you so much. You have no idea what it was like."

"Oh I think I do, love. Every minute we were apart was pure torture." He stroked his thumb along her jaw and then across her lips.

Shivers of delight passed through Fate's body. She wriggled onto her side, pressing herself against his body. A storm of heat and desire churned inside, bursting to be free. Hungry for more, her mouth found his. Her heart pounded out a chaotic rhythm as she coiled her fingers into his hair and pulled him close.

The sound of someone clearing his throat rang through the quiet room.

Alarmed by the familiar noise, Fate drew back, staring at

Finn while struggling to steady her breathing.

"You guessed it, we're not alone. You're dad's here," Finn whispered as he slid off the bed to stand next to her.

Cold air rushed in to replace the warmth of his body, leaving her with the sharp pang of separation. Now that she had Finn there, any distance at all caused untold pain. She reached for his hand, holding tight as she rolled onto her back and turned to look behind her.

Eustace was sitting on the next hospital bed. He did his best to smile, but the tightness of his mouth betrayed his discomfort. "Hey, Doodles. It's good to see you've…woken."

Fate's face flushed with the heat of embarrassment. "Dad, I didn't know you were here just now."

Eustace's smile remained wooden. "Mmhmm, I picked up on that. Hence, the need to be noticed."

Sithias burst into the infirmary carrying a book. "It took awhile, but I finally found a wonderful book of fairy tales I think she'll like." He stopped when he saw Fate. "Misss, you're awake! Oh, thank the gods. Well then, I'm happy to say we won't be needing this." He set the book on a nearby table, before slithering to her bedside, his wings fluttering with excitement. "I was preparing to read to you. To give you something to anchor to in case Finn failed to pull you from the Reaper's grip."

Fate smiled wearily. "That's thoughtful, but don't you think you're over exaggerating a bit? I wasn't that far gone."

His amber eyes turned alarmingly sober.

She glanced at her father and Finn. "Was I?"

"We were all scared, miss. But all is well now. You're back where you belong."

Fate gazed at Finn. "Yes I am."

Picking up a glass of water with his tail, Sithias handed it to her. "Thirsty?"

A mischievous smile tugged at the corners of Fate's mouth as she squeezed Finn's hand. "Very." She sipped the water.

Finn squeezed back, rubbing his hand over her forearm. Tingles raced over her skin, making her hungry for more. They desperately needed some alone time.

An angry voice from the hall carried into the room seconds before Darcy stormed in. "That's it, Mason. We're done!"

Mason followed her into the infirmary, battle armor still on, and with scorch marks. "You're breaking up with me? Why? I thought you were happy to see me."

"Happy to see you alive, but that's all. Why do you keep volunteering for these missions, even when I ask you not to? Do you have any idea what it's like staying behind and worrying about whether I'll ever see you again? It's torture. I can't take it anymore!"

"So you're going to fix it by breaking up? That's insane!"

"Would you two shut up?" Brune called from the hallway at the same time Gerdie entered the infirmary.

Fate held out her hand. "Gerdie! You're safe."

Gerdie marched across the room and gave Fate's hand a squeeze. "Thanks to Finn." She smiled at him then climbed onto the bed to sit next to Eustace.

Mason skirted past Darcy, who'd fallen into a silent pout. "Fate, you need to prepare yourself." He kept his voice low as he began removing his scorched armor.

"For what?"

"You haven't seen Brune yet."

"She's out of the coma and up and around?"

"Oh, yeah, and it's not pretty. She's–"

Brune walked in before he could say another word.

Fate drew back in horror when she saw the Gorgon.

"Don't fret, love. She's on our side. At least for now." Finn muttered the last part.

"Good to see you didn't croak." Brune made her way over to Fate's bed. She leaned against the wall, tilting her snaky head as she gave Finn a sidelong glance from behind her goggles. "And the lovebirds are back together." Her forked tongue flicked between her lips as she smiled at them both.

"Uh...so how's it going, Brune?" Fate finally managed to say.

Brune rubbed her gloved hands together. "Well, other than having to wear these goggles all the time, so I keep from turning you guys into stone, it's not as bad as it looks. I'm strangely calm about the whole thing, probably because this beats being a zombie any day. Once you've been undead, you find a whole new appreciation for being alive, regardless of what that looks like."

Fate nodded in surprise, but she was still nervous. "Good attitude. So...there's no chance you'll get all Gorgony on us?"

"Can you promise you won't get that monthly bad mood?" Brune asked.

"Well, no."

Brune lifted her hands and shrugged. "There's your answer."

"That won't do, Brune," Farouk said from the far end of the room, where he was busy instructing the medical robots. He turned his cage and trundled forward. "We can't be trepidanxious about a loose cannon in our midst. You'll need to submit to lock-up until I can investispect the full effects of your monstramorphosis."

Brune pushed away from the wall with fists clenched, her stance plainly displaying the obstinance that drove her every decision, whether for good or bad. Fate imagined if they could see Brune's glare from behind her goggles, the entire room would become filled with stone figures.

Several tense seconds of silence ticked by. "Sure, do what you have to." Brune sighed.

Relief filled the room.

Fate frowned at Farouk. "Seems a bit harsh to keep her behind bars, Farouk."

"Soft, weak thinking like that's what gets people killed," Brune snapped. "You know you never should've brought me back after I was infected. I'm a threat, and I'll always be a threat. The same goes for your friend Jessie. She's the enemy now."

"She's being mind-controlled." Fate struggled to sit up in bed, but an overwhelming fatigue had her slumping back onto the pillow.

Finn stroked his hand over Fate's arm to calm her. "Speaking of which. How did things play out down there?"

"Jessie got away from her," Mason offered. "Wounded, but alive."

Fate's stomach clenched with fear. "Whose fault was that?"

Brune shifted uncomfortably. "Hey, I was going easy on her. She's lucky she left with a hole in her hand and not in her head.

Fear streaked along Fate's nerves as she stared at Mason. "If Jessie was hurt, why didn't you go after her?"

"And do what?" Mason asked. "Hand her a bandaid before she said thank you and killed me?"

"Jessie doesn't know what she's doing right now," Fate argued.

Brune surrendered her weapons to Mason and offered her hands behind her back to be cuffed. "Doesn't matter, you can't focus on why she's the enemy. You just have to accept that she is and stop thinking of her as your friend."

Tears stung Fate's eyes as she looked at her father. "I won't give up on her."

Eustace gazed back with an equal measure of sadness, but there was also a hint of defeat in his eyes. Did he think she was fighting a lost cause?

"I suppose not," Brune continued. "Now that you've lost your proxy and I'm out of the running again, you must be dreading your life sentence as Keep Guardian."

Fate scowled at her. "That's not all there is to life. You should think about getting one."

"At least I'm free to pursue one. Unlike you."

"What's she talking about?" Finn asked.

Fate looked at Finn, but she couldn't find the words to begin to explain. The last thing she wanted to do was ruin their reunion with bad news.

"She's chained to this place until she dies," Brune explained. "Which could be sooner than later. Kaliena's down, but she not out. From what I can tell, she's just getting started."

Mason tugged on Brune's arm. "Come on, snake girl, let's get you in lock-up. I think Fate's had enough cheering up for one day."

Farouk shifted gears, navigating his cage to lead the way. "Follow me. I'm the only one with keys to high security."

Darcy stomped her foot. "That's right, Mason. Go do your job. I know that's all that counts."

Mason stopped and pointed at her. "This isn't over. Go to my room and wait for me. You and I need to have a talk."

His commanding tone took Fate by surprise. Darcy looked shocked as well, but it was nice to see Mason finally standing his ground. It appeared as though Darcy's henpecking days were about to come to an end.

"Now." Mason stared Darcy down until she headed for the door.

Gerdie stretched and yawned. "Romance. If you ask me, it's for the birds."

"After my time with Elsina, I mussst agree," Sithias added.

"I'll bet." Gerdie jumped down off the bed. "I'm tuckered from that nasty ordeal. I'll see you all tomorrow after I've had a good long sleep."

"We should all get some sleep." Eustace pointed a stern gaze at Finn. "In our respective beds."

Finn leaned down and kissed Fate lightly on the lips. "Aye, he's right. You need your rest. We'll have plenty of time to catch up afterwards."

Fate grabbed his arm in a panic. She didn't want him out of her sight now that he was finally with her. "No, please stay."

Finn took her hands and positioned them gently at her sides.

"Sleep. I'm not going anywhere. I'll be here when you wake. I promise."

Her chest constricted as she watched Finn cross the room. He turned and gave her one last glance before leaving. The familiar ache bloomed in her heart. She shot her father an angry look and caught the instant hurt in his eyes. He suddenly looked tired and aged, more than she'd ever seen him.

Eustace stood and put his hand on her shoulder. "I'll check in on you a little later after you've slept a bit."

Fate remained silent. Her anger was too fresh to do anything about his hurt feelings.

He lingered for a brief moment then left the room.

Feeling guilty and miserable about her father, Fate turned on her side and curled into a ball. Eustace had always encouraged her to get out into the world and socialize. Even meet boys. He used to say she was missing out on life. But that was before all this, when she'd preferred staying in the comfort of home to write. At that time her stories had always been far more interesting than anything ordinary life could offer.

So why had he turned into the typical, protective father, giving her boyfriend a hard time? He should be happy for her. Her heart sank. Why was it that every time she had a modicum of happiness with Finn, it was overshadowed by turmoil? Was it too much to ask that she be allowed to enjoy her reunion? She let out a shaky sigh as the truth sank in.

Even if Eustace had welcomed Finn with a big handshake and an invitation to smoke cigars together, she wouldn't have been completely happy anyway. Not after she'd lost Jessie. Darcy was right. Fate was to blame for losing Lincoln and putting everyone else in continual danger. She needed to fix that, especially for her father's sake. If anything ever happened to him, it would absolutely destroy her.

Sithias poked his head down in front of her. "I'll stay and read until you fall asleep, misss. The way we used to on those long wintry nights by the fire in the cabin when we were stuck in the Twisted Bone Forest. Remember?" He flashed her a fanged smile. "Big points for guessing what story this is before I'm done with the first paragraph."

"Oh joy," Fate muttered.

Sithias slid onto the empty bed next to Fate's and coiled himself neatly over the mattress before opening the pages. "*Once upon a time a woodcutter lived at the edge of a great forest with his wife and their two children. They had a boy called Hansl and a girl called Gretl. The family's house was very small–*"

Fate lifted her head off the pillow. "Really?"

Sithias drooped. "I wasn't expecting the clue would come that soon." He rifled through the pages. "I'll find another story that doesn't have the title in the first few sentences."

Fate's turmoil lifted slightly as she smiled drowsily at her friend and took comfort in his presence. Sithias was a gentle reminder that no matter how bad things got, they always found a way through the trouble, somehow, some way. She wanted to believe the same would hold true for the future. Was it too much to hope they would find a way to get Jessie back safely before Kaliena and Wodrid mounted an attack?

Before the answer came to mind, Fate slipped helplessly into a deep, dreamless sleep–her only rest from a long and perilous journey, which as far as she could see, had no end in sight.

51
TOGETHER

"ARE WE THERE YET?" Fate asked. "Can I take off the blindfold?"

Finn chuckled as he pulled her along by the hand. "Just a few more steps."

The dusky odor of damp earth and sweet scent of honeysuckle, peaches and jasmine suddenly enveloped her. She inhaled the perfumed air and moaned. "What is that heavenly smell?"

"You'll see." Finn stopped and she felt him turn toward her. His fingers were warm as they caressed her cheek then cupped her face gently. Barely able to contain her excitement, she stood still, listening to the sound of his step drawing close. The heat of his body radiated warmth as his breath brushed her face lightly. Then his lips pressed against hers, soft yet insistent. Her body shivered with need. She leaned into the kiss, only to fall against air when he withdrew.

Laughing softly, Finn caught her in his arms and lifted the blindfold. She gazed at her surroundings and gasped. Shafts of golden light streamed through a dome of lead glass windows, cut into diamond shaped patterns. A distant moon shone bright amongst the stars, and down below, a view of the Keep glimmered beyond the wall of glass. Refracted light cast bright spots of color over a lush garden filled with exotic flowers, giant mushrooms and mounds of blooming moss.

"I had no idea this was here. Where are we exactly?"

"We're on the other side of the sanctuary. The garden is positioned further outside the axis, so as the hoops revolve, our view of the Keep and sky will change."

"How'd you find it?"

"I had lots of time to explore while you were recovering."

"You should've brought me here sooner. The infirmary's boring."

Smiling, Finn shook his head. "You have the patience of a five-year-old. Meaning zero."

"You have no idea how patient I've actually been."

The laughter left his eyes and he nodded. "I think I do." Overcome by emotion, he pulled her into a firm embrace, his mouth hot against her skin as he buried his face near the nape of her neck. "I've missed this more than you could ever know."

Her heart hammered and she could hardly breathe. She ran her hands over his broad shoulders, down the sculpted flesh of his arms. Her knees weakened with a rush of blind passion and she melted against him.

"Whoa, lass. Slow down." He cleared his throat and stepped back with a nervous smile.

Alarmed by his sudden hesitation, Fate stared at his eyes to see if the light in them was being swallowed by the darkness he'd been possessed with.

He recognized the fear on her face. "Don't worry. It's not what you're thinking. That's all behind me. I promise."

"Why are you holding back then?" She stepped close, slipping her arms around his waist. "We can be together now. All the way this time."

"And I want that. God only knows how much." He squeezed her waist, his fingers digging into her back, sweet and painful. "We can't go any further than this. Not yet."

Her throat constricted and humiliation roiled in her chest. She tore her gaze away to stare out over the Keep. "Why not?" She blinked through hot tears.

Finn hung his head. "Because I promised your father I'd be a perfect gentleman."

Shock held Fate speechless. She didn't know what to think. Eustace had never actually had "the talk" with her. Probably because her interest in other boys had been non-existent up until...well...now. She'd had no idea her father was so old fashioned.

She searched his face. "That's the only reason?"

He gazed back openly. "Of course."

The sharp stab of anger came without warning. Fate was furious. She wasn't about to let her father's Puritanical rules get in the way. She would just have to work around him. "Okay...so we don't tell Eustace what we do when we're alone. It's none of his business."

Finn smiled and shook his head. "Weren't you supposed to go through this rebellious stage about four or five years ago?"

"I was too busy being reasonable back then. I made the mistake of spoiling my dad. Now he thinks he can get away with anything."

Finn took her hand in his. "Listen, before you go getting angry with your father, you need to know that I agree with him."

Fate stared back mutely.

Finn chuckled as he nudged her open mouth closed. "While you were sleeping off your near death experience, he had a sit down with me. He asked me what my intentions were concerning you, and when I told him, he was crystal clear about how he felt on the matter."

Her heart plummeted. "Are you saying my dad doesn't want us to be together?"

"No, nothing like that. He just doesn't want to see his daughter deflowered before she's...ready."

"I'm ready."

"Not according to your father. He doesn't think you're old enough and–"

"I'm eighteen in a few months. Technically, I'm older than that after being stuck in the *Book of Fables* for six months."

"He doesn't see it that way. You're his wee lass."

"Meaning if he could keep me ten-years-old forever, he would."

"True enough. But that's only part of it. He feels you've been running on adrenaline for so long, you're in constant reaction mode. He doesn't want to see you rushing into things you might regret."

Fate pressed against Finn and smiled. "How can you call this rushing after how long we've been waiting to be together?"

His body trembled beneath her touch. "You're a vixen."

Taking that as an open invitation, Fate kissed the edge of his lips, teasing him until his mouth captured hers. The air grew hot between them, buzzing with energy. His mouth descended to her neck, the wet touch of his tongue lanced sparks of heat over her skin. Tracing his hands over the outside curves of her body, he scooped her off her feet and laid her down on the soft moss. The commanding move took hold of Fate's senses and her body responded of its own accord. She floated outside herself, giddy, as if in a hypnotic state.

A voice shattered her blissful trance. "My, what a lovely place for a stroll. Don't you agree, Gerdie?"

Fate opened her eyes, struggling to rise from the thick haze of desire as she focused on the surrounding foliage.

Sithias and Gerdie emerged into the clearing. The snake stopped, feigning surprise. "Misss? Fancy meeting you here."

"Yeah, fancy that." Gerdie's mouth turned up in a small, sarcastic smile.

Finn let go of Fate and sat up. "Hey, what brings you two here?"

Sithias flew over before plunking down beside them. "Merely taking in the scenery." He winked at Finn.

Irritation scratched at Fate, like carnivorous pixies gnawing on her nerves. Gerdie settled in next to her, wearing an apologetic expression. "Just so you know, this wasn't my idea," she muttered.

Fate fumed as she watched the transparent attempt at secrecy pass between Finn and Sithias. "Whose idea was this exactly?"

"Mine, all mine," Sithias said, all too quickly.

A faint flush stained Finn's cheeks. "No, don't listen to him. It was me. I asked him to be here. I knew I'd be too weak to be left alone with you for too long."

Fate crossed her arms. "Since when is my virtue everybody else's business?"

"Since I made a promise to your father."

"I don't care about that!"

"Well I do. I respect the man, and I want him to respect me. I'm already on thin ice with him after allowing you to come so close to dying."

"That wasn't your fault."

"That's not how your father sees it. He needs to know that I'll protect you at any cost."

"You have, and you've proven that more than once. I told Eustace about everything you did for me and everything you gave up."

Finn sighed and let his head sag a little to one side. "It doesn't matter. I have to prove I'm worthy of his daughter, which ultimately means keeping my word to him."

A dull ache spread through Fate's chest. She'd been looking forward to stealing a few hours of joy so she could forget her problems. Ever since she'd regained her strength, she'd been filled with impending dread. She was plagued with worry over Jessie. She had no idea if she was still alive and under Kaliena's control.

Not to mention, Kaliena and Wodrid were planning

something horrible. Farouk had already confirmed he'd lost contact with large sections of the Keep. It was torture knowing they would pull the trigger on their plans at any time and most likely involve Jessie. It killed Fate to think about fighting her best friend to the death.

But even if the world was perfect, and Jessie was safe, and there was no imminent threat looming in the near future, Fate was cursed by an oath she never should've taken. Brune had said it best. She was a prisoner of the Keep.

Fate laid her hand on Finn's to quiet him. "Don't you get it? You can't get my father's permission to court me, because it's not his to give. You might as well consider me married to the Keep. Ever since I got here, it's been one emergency after the other and it's never going to stop. There'll always be monsters to fight and someone or something to protect. And the worst thing is, I chose this. Albeit, ignorantly."

Fate pulled her hand away and stared at the guardian seal glimmering under the skin of her palm. "If I'd known how lonely and scary this would be, I never would've taken the oath. You have no idea how much I've been wishing for a do-over. But life doesn't work that way. I'm cursed and I have to focus on saving the universe instead of being with the love of my life. So with that in mind, I think that gives me the right to do what I want, when I want for a few measly hours once in a while."

Compassion moved in Finn's eyes before his gaze flicked to Gerdie. "Tell her."

Gerdie wriggled in place as she tucked her dress over her crossed legs. "I may've found a loophole around the oath."

Hope instantly wedged its way through Fate's growing despair, but she was too afraid that soul-crushing disappointment might be the end result. "We thought we figured it out last time, and look what happened then."

A soft breeze ruffled Gerdie's frizzy hair. "It's good you're bein' cautious, cuz I can't promise anything yet."

Despondency settled back in and sat like ice in the pit of Fate's stomach. "Then why even talk about it?"

"Because we have to." Finn's eyes burned with feeling. "You're not alone in this. Wherever you are, I am there. Do you hear me?"

Fate gulped dryly. "Finn–"

"You're not alone in this place or in the fight against Kaliena and Wodrid," he pressed. "We'll figure this out, love. All of us, together."

"Yesss indeed." Sithias started to smile, when a butterfly-winged green caterpillar the size of a mouse fluttered in front of his face. He ducked with a frightened squeak.

Sithias's presence was, as always, entertaining and Fate couldn't help but smile. "But shouldn't you get back to Elsina?"

Sithias shook his head vehemently. "And risk the shrieking that's sure to ensue? I'd rather die in battle than deal with that, and you know how I feel about fighting."

"I do." Fate's smile faded as optimism gave way to concern. "Which is why I can't let any of you stay. Kaliena's cooking up some major league damage, and I've already lost Jessie." She choked down a sob. "I couldn't bear to lose–"

"It's not up to you, misss. I'm staying." Sithias gave her a serious stare. "See this face? This is determined, obstinate, inflexible, stubborn–"

"Thanks, I…I get the point." Fate gulped and glanced at Gerdie.

Her doll-like face gazed back with the soft, measured weight of the adult inside. "Where would I go? You're stuck with me, whether you like it or not."

Fate turned to Finn. Light and shadow reflected in the luminous green of his eyes. The mere sight of him soothed her troubles like nothing else could.

"See? You're just going to have to accept it. We're here for as long as you are." He rose to his feet and held out his hand. "Now that we've got that settled, how about we see if the food simulator can whip up a half decent pizza? Heavy on the Parmesan, of course."

Smiling through tears of gratitude, Fate took his hand and stood. "You know the way to my heart."

He leaned in and kissed her cheek. "Aye, I do, and I always will, love."

EPILOGUE

BRUNE PACED THE TWENTY square feet of her cell, furious she'd agreed to be locked up.

If she wasn't suffering mind-numbing boredom, she was enduring hours of examination by Farouk's robots. Surely by now he had everything he needed to run the tests on her mutation. Either way, she'd made a stupid mistake. She should've insisted on being shackled and allowed to roam. At least then she could go about her business and look into a cure on her own end. She couldn't trust that anyone else would care enough to keep digging until a solution was found.

And then there was Fate. Who was going to ensure she was staying on top of her duties? It drove her mad to leave the Keep's safety in the hands of a greenhorn who had her head in the clouds one minute, and in the depths of depression the next. Especially with Kaliena taking over the Keep one section at a time.

Brune stopped and kicked the wall. The abrupt motion set the snakes around her head to hissing. "Shhh, shhh," she whispered to them. They slithered down around her face, caressing her cheek and neck with their cool scales as they calmed down. She couldn't help smiling at them.

But then she caught herself. She should be repulsed. It bothered her she wasn't. This mutation was not a condition she *ever* wanted to get used to, despite the increased strength and endurance she'd been enjoying.

Brune leaned against the wall and hung her head. Was she destined to become a vicious reptile? Maybe Farouk was right to worry she might lose herself completely and become the Gorgon she'd fought in those caves.

The clamber of Farouk's cage sounded from down the hall. Pushing away from the wall, Brune rushed to the edge of cell, careful to stop several feet from the force field keeping her locked in. Her heart beat fast. Maybe he had good news.

Farouk ambled over to the shimmering force field and parked his cage. Wearing goggles to protect against her lethal Gorgon gaze, he scrambled out of his chair and held a bottle of what looked like swamp water swirling with tiny beads of light. "I have your curification," he announced proudly. "And just in time. The lab tests show your monstramorphosis is doublefying."

Brune's throat went dry. "The mutation hasn't stopped?"

"I'm sorry to say it has not." He said the words, but he didn't look sorry. His slanted eyes gleamed with excitement.

Brune waited for him to let her out. When he made no move to do so, she edged closer to the force field. "What are you waiting for? Hand it over."

Farouk sat back down in his chair. "Not until we've had a confabulation."

"About what?"

"As you know Kaliena is shutting down my connectifications with vast portionages of the Keep. This can only mean she's prepurating an attack."

"Yes, I know, but what does that have to do with me getting my cure?"

Farouk settled in his chair, reached for a small brush and smoothed the soft bristles over the white downy fur of his chest. Apparently he wished to torture her by dragging the conversation out.

She slowly sucked the air in between her clenched teeth in an attempt to control her impatience. "Stop dangling the carrot and tell me what you want."

Farouk's ears twitched with eagerness as he lifted his gaze. "You know what I want."

Brune's mind was a blank, but only for a moment. Red fire flickered in the pupils of his eyes. Something Farouk kept hidden, unless he was feeling especially enterprising. It was all she needed to see to know what he was thinking. "No. Absolutely not."

He dropped his brush and stood without releasing her from his keen gaze. "It's time."

Dread iced through Brune's chest. "You're jumping the gun. Kaliena hasn't shown her hand yet. There's always the possibility she isn't the threat we've been building her up to be."

Farouk's steady gaze burned into her. "She governated Jessie by using the Dragon Eye, which means she can also governate the Keep."

"What you're suggesting is a last resort."

"It is the only resort."

"How exactly?" Brune's breathing grew ragged with tension, which set the snakes to hissing again. "By unleashing yet *another* monster into the Keep? No way. Just because you erased yourself from the records, does not mean I've forgotten what you really are under all that neatly manicured fur."

Farouk wagged a finger at her. "But you're the only one who knows about me, and you're in no positionality to tell anyone. I diagnostificate you have between ten and twenty hours before the reptilian genes destructalize your human cells beyond restorstruction. Nothing will curify you after that happens."

Brune's snakes lashed out and struck the air "You're actually holding my cure for ransom?"

"I like to think I'm using it as a motivcentive. Think of the gambletunities a cure will give you. Once you're restructified, you can be Fate's proxy. After she leaves and takes the others with her, it'll be just the two of us again. The way it should be."His eyes blazed a deep red as he leaned forward. "You know as well as I do that Fate isn't preperated to handle this forthproaching war. I'm the only one who can stop Kaliena. And you're the only one who knows how to find the key to open my cage."

Brune glared at him in horror. While it was true they needed a force powerful enough to lay waste to Kaliena, how could she unleash an evil whose appetite for mischief, madness and carnage could destroy everything she held dear? Farouk had been caged for thousands of years for good reason. He may be wise and helpful, but only because the magically infused technology wired into his cage forced him to be. If she unlocked the door to his cage, she would be releasing a nightmare.

She wished she'd never stumbled upon the truth all those years ago. At least then, she wouldn't be faced with such a terrible choice. How could she in good conscience, possibly agree to his demand?

Yet her eyes fell to the bottle sitting at Farouk's feet and her longing to be normal and take back her position as Keep Guardian stretched her sense of right and wrong to the breaking point.

Farouk's gaze slid to the potion. Using his tail to lift it, he dangled the glass bottle beyond the bars of his cage. "Decide now, or I drop it." He let his grip slip along the neck of the bottle.

"Stop," she gasped. "I'll do it."

READ THE FIRST CHAPTER OF

Book 3 of Her Dark Destiny

FATE'S WAR

T. RAE MITCHELL

I
DOOMSDAY

FATE PULLED BACK THE arrow, straining the bow, directing the sum of all her failures through the muscles of her arms and down the steel shaft. She held the full draw until her bow arm trembled. Inhaling deeply, she relaxed her shoulder and released the arrow.

The shot cut the air, slicing through the holographic Chimera's leathery wing.

"Damn," she muttered. Another soft shot. Thirty arrows in, and she still hadn't hit the creature's vulnerable underbelly. She couldn't seem to relax her fingers on the release and kept dropping her shoulder too much.

She could easily make herself feel better about her rusty archery skills by choosing an easier target, but this was one mark she needed to conquer. When she'd faced the real Chimera a few weeks earlier, she'd had to be rescued by her best friend who'd had far less experience with monsters than Fate.

Fate's heart grew heavy, as it always did, at the thought of Jessie and what she must be suffering as a prisoner of the power-hungry sorceress, Kaliena. Was she being tortured? Or was she still the unfeeling automaton Kaliena had turned her into? The last time she'd seen Jessie, there'd been nothing left of her childhood friend. Kaliena had taken control of the Dragon Eye Jessie had been wearing. She shuddered at the memory of Jessie's vacant stare as her friend had idly watched Kaliena unleash a fiery storm onto Fate that had nearly killed her.

Was Jessie even alive? She hated to think it, but it probably didn't matter if she was. Either way, her best friend was gone.

The tightness in her chest increased. "When reality sucks, the tough get fighting," she muttered under her breath. Fate nocked another arrow and let it fly. The dying roar of the holographic Chimera as it thrashed at the arrow stuck in its belly gave her little satisfaction.

Working herself into the ground to sharpen her combat skills would only get her so far. At this point, all she had to show for it was increased fatigue and aching muscles. Dropping the bow at her side, Fate sighed tiredly as she tilted her head to stare at the electric daylight shining from the training arena's arched ceiling. She was up against too much. Kaliena's reach was growing. She'd taken over three-quarters of the Keep already. It wouldn't be long before she controlled every inch of the arcane storehouse of magical objects.

The dread Fate woke with intensified each morning, wondering whether that would be the day Kaliena finally mounted her attack upon them. She knew deep down inside she would lose if it happened now. The only way she could protect her loved ones was if she possessed powers equal to Kaliena's.

The shadow of her failures inevitably darkened Fate's thoughts to desperate levels. They haunted her daily. If she hadn't lost the extraordinary powers she'd gained from a war goddess during her time in the *Book of Fables*–as well as the courage those powers had given her–she would've saved herself from that Chimera. Had she been as swift as before, she could've rescued Lincoln from being devoured by a dragon. If she'd been stronger, she could've prevented Jessie from falling under Kaliena's control.

Everything would be different…better, if Fate hadn't been reduced to her normal human frailty. She clenched the bow with all her strength. She didn't know how she would do it, or when, but she was determined to get a major upgrade in the very near future.

"Nice shot, love."

Startled by Finn's voice, Fate glanced over her shoulder. He crossed the expanse of the training court in long easy strides. His cotton shirt breezed loosely against his tapered waist as her gaze trailed over him. His hair had grown while they'd been apart. The burnished gold of his wavy hair now grazed his broad shoulders. Her heart raced as the sight of him chased back the darkness like nothing else could. Dropping the bow, she shrugged off the quiver with a clatter of arrows falling over the stone floor and went to him.

Finn smiled, his eyes glittering like emeralds as he took her in his arms. She sank against him, breathing in the woodsy scent of sandalwood soap lingering on his skin and tightened her hold on him. She didn't think she'd ever get used to the thrill his presence incited after suffering his absence for so long. Their relationship had been riddled with hardships from the moment they'd first met, and even though Finn assured her they would always be together, she couldn't shake the feeling he would be taken from her again.

He nuzzled his face against her neck. Waves of excitement rippled along the length of her spine. "You missed breakfast with everyone." His voice grew husky with desire. "I missed you. How long have you been down here?" The heat of his breath on her skin made her knees go weak. Dizzy with longing, she swayed backwards. He held her closer to keep her from falling. "If you're feeling light-headed, you should eat," he warned.

Fate leaned her head back and looked at him with a drowsy smile. "I'm only hungry for one thing."

Finn tried to hide his amusement behind a scolding look. The effort was entirely ineffective. "Stop trying to coax the devil out of me." His eyes gleamed an even brighter green as his gaze traveled over her face. The Elder race runes inked on his skin had blessed him with power over the elements, as well as superhuman strength and speed, which he used only when needed. But there was another side effect that was always evident. The runes had turned his irises into mood rings. The more excited he was, the more luminous his eyes became. Something she loved seeing. "You're making it impossible for me to keep my promise to your father."

The mention of her father was every bit as unwelcome as a pail of cold water splashed in her face. "You never should've made that promise in the first place. It's not up to either of you to protect my virtue. The decision as to when I give my virginity away is up to me." She broke free of Finn's embrace and bent to pick up the mess of arrows she'd left on the floor. "I can't believe you two. You're both being completely...antediluvian."

"Which means?"

"Outrageously old-fashioned."

Finn shifted his weight from one foot to the other as he tried to form a defense.

"Oh, don't bother. I can't bear to hear the whole spiel on earning his respect all over again." Having gathered up the bow and arrows, Fate stormed across the court to put them away.

Finn jogged to catch up with her. "Don't be mad, fireball."

Fate stopped and glared at him. He shut his eyes and raked his hand through his thick locks. She crumbled inside knowing her anger hurt him. Finn was simply caught in the middle and doing what he thought was best for everyone concerned. She really needed to stop taking her anger out on him. It wasn't his fault her father had so thoroughly convinced him she was still a fragile little girl in need of protection.

Frustration boiled in her chest. It was time she and her father had a talk. Ever since Eustace had extracted his ridiculous promise of honor and respect from Finn, she had directed no more than a few curt words at her father over the last few weeks.

Dropping her scowl, she stood on tiptoe and gave Finn a

light peck on the cheek. "Sorry for being such a bear."

Before she could take another step, he pulled her close. His heart thudded hard beneath the palm of her hand. "Whoa, lass. You can't leave me with a granny kiss."

Fate laughed, a harsh sound betraying her irritation. "Hey, I'm not the one who made this bed. You did, so you're just going to have to lie in it." She headed for the exit before glancing back to flash him a bitter smile. "Alone."

Fate entered the library, her gaze sweeping over the six story high ceiling and full surround of terraces filled with collections of scrolls, tablets, grimoires and vast accumulation of texts. She spotted Sithias on the top level. The unusually large ivory-colored snake slithered by the shelves, his head bobbing up and down as he read the spines of each book. She sensed his excitement with whatever he was reading by the way his golden-brown wings fluttered and twitched. A ghost of a smile formed on her lips. Was Sithias narrowing in on the solution she'd asked him to find for her?

Resisting the urge to call out to him, she dropped her gaze to the main floor, which was as large as an Olympic-sized skating rink, interrupted only by islands of huge tables and chairs. Her smile faded when she saw Eustace sitting at one of the tables near the far end of the library. He hadn't noticed her presence. He was engrossed in reading and the stacks of leatherbound books on the table blocked his line of vision.

Finn stole silently in beside her. The walk between the training court and library had been tense and quiet between them. "How about we head to the galley so you can get something to eat before we spend the rest of our day in here researching how we're going to defeat Kaliena. If you take care of the basics, you can handle any–"

Fate silenced him with a look. "Who's being the granny now?"

At the sound of voices, Eustace rose from his seat. He was a tall man, and always meticulously groomed, but from this distance he looked smaller somehow and unkempt in the way his silver-dusted hair hung over his glasses. Fate caught the hopefulness in his eyes as he stared at her.

Two parts of her battled with one another. The little girl who wanted to run into her father's arms and have everything be what it used to be–unconditional love and acceptance–but the woman she was becoming could not forgive the boundary he'd crossed.

She tore her gaze away, but not before she saw the light go out of Eustace's eyes. Her throat constricted and she lost the courage to speak her mind to him altogether. The subject matter was simply too uncomfortable. She'd thought she was ready to confront him, but in truth, she wasn't.

She looked at Finn. "Can you see if Eustace needs any help with his research? I'm going to see what Sithias has found."

"Fate, you can't keep freezing him out. He's your father."

She shook her head at Finn's pleading gaze. "Stop pushing me. I need more time."

The corners of Finn's mouth turned downward before he nodded and walked away. Fate willed herself to keep from stopping him. Any amount of sadness she caused him cut like a knife, but on the same note, she needed him to understand the effect his promise to Eustace was having on them.

Forcing down the pain of hurting the two people she loved most in the world, Fate scaled the terraces to the top level. She used to complain about the library's lack of stairs or ladders. The architects of the Keep had provided two librarian automatons–robots designed to climb the walls and retrieve all requests. But Fate had developed excellent wall climbing skills ever since she'd been forced to spend an exorbitant amount of time in the library. Most of all, she enjoyed increasing her speed to beat her last climb.

She jumped over the balcony rail, startling Sithias when her boots hit the floor behind him. "Sweet! Thirty seconds faster than last time."

"How wonderful for you, though not for my rampaging heart." Sithias waved his tail in front of his face while trying to steady his breathing. "You really must stop sneaking up on me, misss."

Fate shook her head and smiled. While Sithias had somehow managed to lose most of the hiss in his speech since they'd last been together, he hadn't stopped exaggerating his so-called fragility. He liked to think of himself as a lover, not a fighter, but he was much tougher than he let on. "You can take it." She glanced at the two stacks of books sitting next to him. "Anything in there for me?"

Sithias grinned wide, baring his fangs as his amber eyes twinkled with inspiration. "Ah yesss, I believe there is." He pointed at the first stack with his tail. "After much laborious cross-checking, between what's stored here in the Keep, against all historical texts documenting war goddesses, I've narrowed your options down to two deities."

Fate leaned against the railing. "I'm listening."

Sithias lifted a book from one stack and opened it to an etching of a dark-haired woman whose hooded cloak swirled into a murder of crows. "This is the Morrígan, once revered as the goddess of battle and later known as the phantom queen. She is listed among the Tuatha Dé Danann as the granddaughter of King Nuada. You'll be interested to know, the Morrígan was instrumental in defeating the Fomorians."

Fate stiffened at the thought of the Fomorians. She'd experienced the repulsive, reality warping creatures first hand. The memory, though blurred and distorted, was unpleasant to say the least. "The phantom queen's got my vote so far. What are her powers? Did she blast the Fomorians away with some sort of reality rejection mojo?"

"Well, I don't think so. I do know she's associated with fate in the way she foretold doom and death in battle by taking the shape of a crow and flying over the battlefield…" Sithias turned the page and skimmed the text.

Fate fidgetted while she waited. "If there's one thing I can relate to, it's the fate thing. Having the name's been more of a curse than anything else. Did I ever tell you about the time a meteor landed on the car my dad gave me for my birthday? I never even got to drive it." She waited for his reaction but he was too intent on reading.

"Ah, I found it." Sithias looked up from the book. "It appears the Morrígan used her feminine wilesss to great advantage to win the war against the Fomorians."

Fate wrinkled her nose. "Really? That's it? She batted her eyelashes at the right person? Not impressed."

"Well, she did a little more than that, misss."

When she realized what he was alluding to, heat rushed to her face. "Oh, she…"

"Kept a tryst with the powerful druid, Dagda."

Fate's thoughts rushed to Finn. Her longing to share more than a kiss with him flowed through her veins like quicksilver. She gulped dryly. "What's the other option?"

"You don't like the Morrígan?"

"Not if I have to tryst with some stranger to get the results I want."

"Don't underestimate the power of female sexuality, misss. Many a war has been lost and won because of a woman who was able to harness that wild force of nature."

"Nope. Next."

Closing the book, Sithias set it down and took a tome from the other stack. "All right then, you might like this goddess better, though I haven't completed my research." He showed her an illustration of a fierce looking woman holding a spear and shield. She wore a breastplate over a long dress. Thick golden locks flowed to her waist from beneath a winged helmet.

Fate liked the balance of strength and feminity in the portrait. "Tell me more."

"This is, Freya, the Norse goddess of war and death, and leader of the Valkyries."

Fate leaned forward with interest. "I've heard of the Valkyries–expert battle maidens with kickass supernatural abilities."

Sithias nodded. "Yes, and like the Morrígan, they too determine the fates of fallen soldiers in war, as well as escort their spirits to the afterlife. While Freya possesses these same abilities, as well as the usual superhuman strength, speed and invulnerability, she is sssupremely powerful in warfare and makes the Valkryies seem like playful puppies on the battlefield."

"Now that's what I'm looking for. How do I get me some of that?"

"One of the vaults is holding Freya's armament, one of which is the legendary Brisingamen–a magical necklace made of gold filigree, ambers and rubies."

"Hmm, sounds like it'll match my eyes."

"Uh, before you get excited about the necklace, you should know it was crafted by four dwarves." Sithias squirmed with discomfort.

"So? What's wrong with that?"

"Freya trysted with them in exchange for the necklace. She was famous for trysting rather freely."

"Ew! Is that all those goddesses did back then?" Fate chewed on her bottom lip. The Morrigan was sounding better by the minute. At least she was sacrificing herself for the benefit of others, while Freya sounded like a party girl. Albeit, a powerful one. "What does the necklace do?" she asked with reluctance.

Sithias glanced down at the book. "It says here the Brisingamen gave her the power to create treasures. When her tears fell on the earth, they turned to gold, and when she wept at sea, they turned to amber." He lifted his gaze. "Apparently she cried a lot, especially when she was searching for her missing husband."

Fate understood that kind of sadness. The memories of her desperation to get back to Finn and free him from the *Book of Fables* were still fresh. She let out a heavy sigh. "I don't know. The necklace sounds lame. What else is in the vault?"

Sithias closed the book he was holding and referenced a new volume, which looked like a log of records. "Well, there's her sword and shield, but you'd need superhuman strength to wield them since all goddesses were giantesses…" He scanned further down the list. "Ah, there are three other items. A crown, a guantlet and a girdle."

"A girdle? Sounds uncomfortable. Who wears a girdle anymore? What does the gauntlet do?"

"It grants the wearer the strength to wield weapons of colossal size."

"I suppose that solves the problem of being able to use her sword and shield, but I don't exactly see myself hauling around a shield the size of a dining room table and a sword that's taller than me. What about the crown?"

"Hmmm," Sithias mused as he read the description. "The crown appears to amplify the magical powers of the wearer."

"Which is useless to me, since I'm magicless." Fate huffed. "I guess we're back to the girdle."

Sithias nodded as he searched for the item's attributes. "Oh my, I think you're going to like this. The girdle imbues the wearer with Amazonian powers."

"Ooh, me likey. Wonder Woman's an Amazon and she *never* has to give herself away to get business done."

Sithias shook his head at the page. "Thisss doesn't make any sense. Why would a Norse goddess have a girdle of Hellenic origin?"

Fate shrugged. "The lady got around. She probably laid it down to get her hands on that one too."

"Possibly." A shadow of concern crossed Sithias's face.

Fate frowned. "What?"

"You're being rather blasé about assuming the powers a goddess once wielded. Are you certain you want to risk being changed into something else entirely? Remember Bremusa's plight from the *Book of Fables'* story of *The Lightning Sword*? The gods and goddesses of old were famous for leaving behind fragments of their power in which to slip back to this world for a chance to unleash their might."

How could Fate forget? She'd lived through that fable. But what Sithias was overlooking was how Fate had been embued with a war goddess's powers, which was exactly why she'd survived that particular story.

Sithias set the book down. "Pleassse, give it more thought before you go through with this."

The metallic clicking of a librarian robot sounded from below. Fate leaned over the railing to see Gerdie riding piggyback on one of the robots as it traversed the wall of shelves with its six arms, moving as easily as a spider. Catching sight of Fate, Gerdie waved before directing the robot to climb over to her.

The wispy, twelve-foot librarian made of blinking gold lights, brass coils and porcelain face, stepped over the railing and placed the little girl gently on the floor. Gerdie's frizzy, fawn-colored hair fluttered around her impish features with the delicacy of a dried dandelion. Her brown eyes moved from Fate to Sithias, and to the stacks of books sitting next to them. "Whatcha doin'?"

Fate shrugged. "The usual. Searching for something to help us kick Kaliena's royal blue butt."

Despite her six-year-old appearance, Gerdie had spent untold centuries evading the clutches of a child-eating monster and now was forty-five pounds of pure stubbornness. The wise old soul stared, unconvinced. "Mmhmm. If that were true, you'd be down there with Eustace. He's collected all the books we need."

Sithias squirmed under Gerdie's stare. "We're exploring other avenues of thought."

Gerdie bent to read the spine of one of the books. "What does *Lebor Gabála Êrenn* have to do with the Sanskrit Vedic texts we've been siftin' through everyday for the last month? Celtic myths won't give us the answers we need." She glanced at the book Fate was holding. "The same goes for Norse legends."

Sithias huffed. "Why did I ever teach you to read?"

"Too late to take it back now."

He tsk, tsked. "I've created a monssster."

Gerdie crossed her small arms and looked at Fate. "Spit it out. What're you up to?"

Fate gulped. Just as she hadn't told Finn of her intentions to power up, she couldn't tell Gerdie either. Especially Gerdie. Her great-aunt had witnessed how power had corrupted her older sister, Brune, when she'd become obsessed with the Orb of Aeternitis. Gerdie's grandmother had died because of Brune's use of the magical object, and Brune's obsession was the reason Gerdie had been suspended in time and trapped inside the *Book of Fables*.

But what choice did Fate have? Gerdie wouldn't let this go. She could only hope she didn't tell the others. Fate looked at Gerdie. "Well, we were–"

"What're those books you're lookin' at?" Gerdie stooped and read the spines. "Celtic and Norse myths? What's that got to do with the Sanskrit Vedic texts we've been siftin' through everyday for the last month?"

Fate and Sithias exchanged a baffled look. Then she remembered Gerdie had been researching forgetting spells. "Gerdie, did you happen to try one of those forgetting spells you've been digging into?"

Gerdie's expression went blank. "I think so…"

An alarm blared throughout the expanse of the library, making all three of them jump.

Sithias looked at them round-eyed with fear. "Oh dear. Do you think this is the day?"

Fate's heart hammered as she threw her leg over the railing. "I don't know."

Gerdie climbed onto the back of the robot. "Fate..."

The tone in her voice held Fate in place. "Yeah, Gerdie?"

Gerdie stared then shook her head. "I…I forgot what I was gonna say."

Fate nodded. "It's okay. You'll remember if it's important." But she hoped the forgetting spell wouldn't fade too terribly soon. She couldn't let anything get in the way of taking action on what she'd learned from Sithias. Not with the alarms ringing out what may be the doomsday she'd been dreading all along.

This concludes the
first chapter preview of

Fate's War

Read more by T. Rae Mitchell for FREE!

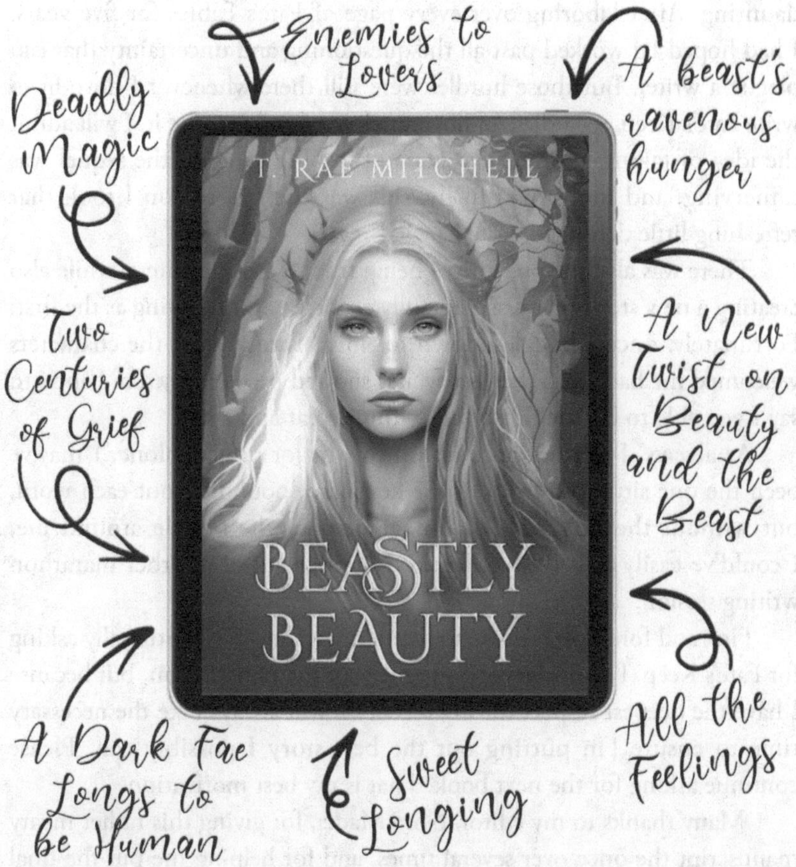

An urban fantasy retelling from the previously published bestselling anthology, *Once Upon a Happy Ending*. This gorgeously written novelette weaves together the echo of the classic fairy tale with deadly magic, a dark heroine, and a romance sure to sweep you away.

Visit www.traemitchell.com/signup

Acknowledgements

I had no idea writing the second book in a series would feel so daunting. After laboring over every page of Fate's Fables for five years, I had hoped I'd worked past all the questioning and uncertainty that can plague a writer. But those hurdles were still there whenever I dove in to write Fate's Keep, regardless of how much I wanted to write it. I will admit the idea of taking another five years of my life to write the sequel was unnerving, and more than likely, this was the real reason I took that refreshing little detour to write Magic Brew.

There was also the pressure of being true to the characters, while also creating a new story that was hopefully every bit as interesting as the first. Fortunately, once I buckled down to finish Fate's Keep, the characters welcomed me back into their story and showed me the way. I'm happy to say I was able to hit the finish line within a year and a half.

As always, I did not accomplish this major project alone. I may've been the one sitting in front of the keyboard, pounding out each word, but without the help and encouragement of the people around me, I could've easily talked myself into dropping out of another marathon writing session.

First and foremost, I'd like to thank my readers for continually asking for Fate's Keep. I know it was quite the wait for some of you, but because I have the deepest respect for my readers, I will always take the necessary time to ensure I'm putting out the best story I possibly can. Please continue asking for the next book. That is my best motivation.

Many thanks to my editor, Nora Mader, for giving this rather meaty manuscript the once over several times, and for helping me put the final polish on the story.

I am eternally grateful to my son for pulling me out of my own head and making me laugh daily. Your insights and feedback on my writing are always valuable. I'm a blessed mom.

Thank you to my husband, my best friend, soul mate, mentor and greatest supporter. Without your constant belief in me, this writing journey I've chosen to embark upon would be much more challenging, if not impossible.

Bestselling author T. Rae Mitchell is an incurable fantasy junkie who spent much of her youth dreaming up worlds and bringing characters to life. While most kids outgrow such things, T. Rae didn't and sometimes took playing make-believe a bit far. Like the time a wizard hid a bottle of dragon beans in the back yard and left her son convinced he could grow his own dragons. Needless to say, the beans failed to produce and disappointments were had. That's when T. Rae decided to funnel her crazy imagination into writing young and new adult fantasy.

Sign-up for T. Rae Mitchell's
Exclusive VIP List
for upcoming notifications:
www.traemitchell.com/sign-up

You can also find T. Rae Mitchell on...

Instagram: www.instagram.com/t.raemitchell

Facebook: www.facebook.com/mitchelltrae

Bookbub: www.bookbub.com/authors/t-rae-mitchell

Goodreads: www.goodreads.com/author/show/6926344.T_Rae_Mitchell

Twitter: www.twitter.com/TRaeMitchell

Pinterest: www.pinterest.com/TRaeMitchell

Bestselling author L. Rae Mitchell is an incredible fantasy junkie who spent much of her youth dreaming up worlds and bringing characters to life. While other kids outgrew such things, L. Rae didn't and sometimes took playing make-believe a bit far. Like the time a wizard hid a horde of dragon beans in the backyard and left her son convinced he could grow his own dragons. Needless to say, the beans failed to produce and disappointments were had all around when L. Rae decided to funnel her crazy imagination into writing young and new adult fantasy.

Sign up for L. Rae Mitchell's
Exclusive VIP List
for upcoming notifications:
www.raemitchell.com/signup

You can also find L. Rae Mitchell on...

Instagram: www.instagram.com/LRaeMitchell

Facebook: www.facebook.com/mitchellrae

Bookbub: www.bookbub.com/authors/l-rae-mitchell

Goodreads: www.goodreads.com/author/show/[illegible].L_Rae_Mitchell

Twitter: www.twitter.com/LRaeMitchell

Pinterest: www.pinterest.com/LRaeMitchell

www.ingramcontent.com/pod-product-compliance
Lightning Source LLC
Chambersburg PA
CBHW010142030826
48979CB00032B/2831/J

* 9 7 8 1 7 7 7 1 4 7 2 0 4 *